*Detective Strongoak and the
King of Elfland's Little Sister*

Terry Newman was a research lecturer, working on heart and lung function, who one day happened to find himself in the BBC's Broadcasting House writing comedy. He is still rather vague about how this happened, but after he decided that writing was more fun than sitting at an electron microscope in the dark, he has gone on to write comedy and drama, with some success, for TV, film, radio, Internet, games and the stage.

His first novel *Detective Strongoak and the Case of the Dead Elf* which introduced the well-dressed, axe-wielding, Master Detective Nicely Strongoak was a #1 Kindle Epic Fantasy Bestseller. This new adventure takes us back to those 'mean cobbled streets where a dwarf has to walk tall'.

Terry now works in a nice bright room with a view of the Sussex Weald, but he does sometimes still miss his microscope.

Other books by this author

Detective Strongoak and the Case of the Dead Elf

The Resurrection Show
(with David Alter, as Dalter T Newman)

For children

The Duke of Delhi

Tarquin and his Troop
(with Tarquin Taylor)

The King of Elfland's Little Sister

TERRY NEWMAN

MB

MONKEY BUSINESS

MONKEY BUSINESS
An imprint of Grey House in the Woods

www.greyhouseinthewoods.org

This paperback original 2018

A catalogue record for this book
is available from the British Library

Paperback ISBN: 978-1-909295-11-7
ebook ISBN: 978-1-909295-12-4

This novel is entirely a work of fiction.
The names, characters and incidents portrayed in it are
the work of the author's imagination. Any resemblance to
actual persons, living or dead, events or localities is
entirely coincidental.

Set in Adobe Garamond Pro

CONTENTS

Book One – ELFLAND

Prologue: Sleeping Dogs Lie   3

1 Tall Trees   10

2 Missing   22

3 Rudebeard the Relaxed   33

4 A Really Swell Party   43

5 Milkwood   53

6 The New Tree Renewal Parlour   64

7 Olobato the Wise   78

8 The Citadel Guard   91

9 Bron's Place   108

10 Bigelow Pictures   119

11 The White Council   129

12 The Golden Ring   139

Book Two – THE MINES OF ORIA

13 The Arrival   157

14 An Old Career in a New Town   172

15 Interrogation Time   178

16 Nightlight   191

17 Escape from Oria   201

18 Last Train to Coal Town   212

19 A Night Out   227

20 Old Friends   239

21 Back Home   263

22 Solutions   274

23 Payback   285

Epilogue   299

Glossary   305

BOOK ONE

ELFLAND

PROLOGUE

SLEEPING DOGS LIE

The big goblin has a shooter. He also has poor dentition, stripes far too broad for his suit, and a very long reach. I, however, have the muscles that Mother Nature, who now goes by the name of Eve O'Lution, has bred into me and others of the dwarf race. Oh yes, fine muscles … and an even finer axe. Hardly more than a sharp's comforter, but none the worse for it.

I took his arm off just below the elbow; blood escaping in a manner that almost awoke some latent poetic impulse in me. It is a good axe, not much bigger than the comforter I first clutched as a child back in New Iron Town. I keep it a lot sharper, though. Unfortunately, some random goblin nerve twitch sent a bullet ricocheting around the scullery, as I hastily measured my length, four foot eleven and one-half inches, on the floor. The bullet aerated my third-best hat in a manner that reminded me that I had been pushing the survival odds for some time now. It goes with the job, and if I'd wanted tedium I would have taken up a different branch of the 'customer care' industry.

The shooter's barking and the goblin's scream woke up the dog. That started barking as well, at a volume guaranteed to wake the half of the Citadel that was safely sleeping the sleep of the just and night-tan avoiding. I hoped the dog was chained – I had enough on my plate without having to avoid ending up on his.

The goblin was now fully occupied stopping the blood flow to his severed stump. Clever boy, he might live. My chances of getting through the night therefore depended on the location of the large goblin's runty colleague.

'Don't move, dwarf! I'm packing ironmongery that would drop a dragon at ten paces and I'm right behind you.'

Oh well! Location confirmed. I put my axe down and my hands up, that being what you do under such circumstances.

'Now turn around slowly,' the runt spat.

I did as requested and was treated to the sight of the runt, now revealed in all his skinny goblin splendour, resplendent in an ill-fitting double-breasted jacket and a tie/shirt combination that, in a more enlightened community, would have been a criminal offence. Also, not the best choice of suit tailoring when you lack anything that might be described as a breast.

'Let me rip his head off!' gasped his larger fellow, pulling tightly on the ripped towel that now bound what remained of his arm.

'I'd keep the pressure on that knot, handsome,' I reminded him, 'otherwise the healers won't be able to get you fitted for a nice hook to scratch your arse with.'

Chummy, with the projectile ironware, slapped me one with a kiss from the shooter barrel that I never saw coming. He was fast for a lean, mean, streak of mid-flow. I fell back, very involuntarily.

'Watch your mouth while you can, goose guard. That's a friend of mine you've just lightened.'

'Sorry,' I said, picking myself up slowly. 'In your position, I appreciate that friends must be hard to find.'

The runt grinned, showing ruined teeth that made his friend's look like a string of shiny pearls. 'Keep it up, doorstop! It's only going to make wraithing you even sweeter.'

My hands had now reached behind my hat and were pulling out the flexible shiv that lived in the hatband. I just needed to get close enough now to use it. And live that long to get that close.

Fortunately, the runt liked the sound of his own voice. 'What gave us away?' he asked.

'The dog,' I replied promptly.

'No way!' he said. 'You know how long it took us to find a spotty dog like Old Woman Pumfrey's?'

'And paint on any missing spots?'

'Yeah, that too.'

'Well, you missed one.'

'No!'

The plan was ingenious; I'll give them that.

Old Woman Pumfrey was a rich old bird who lived on the second level of the city. Real Old Gold, loaded so high that if she ever went boating she'd sink without a trace. One day, though, she became a witness to a particularly brutal slaying – showing that fate doesn't really care how wealthy you may be, violence is democratised now and no longer just the occupation of the young and male.

Old Woman Pumfrey was actually privy to a takeover bid by one Citadel goblin gang, the Nightfangs, for the territory of a rival company, the Crossbites. She even saw the heads roll down the street. Her personal guard was thankfully well armed and scared off the other gang members, although he took some structural damage and was still not capable of testifying. Cue Master Detective Nicely Strongoak, in his capacity as Shield-for-Hire.

Now that Old Woman Pumfrey was the main witness in the trial of the year, it wasn't looking good for the chances of Old Woman Pumfrey becoming Very Old Woman Pumfrey, which was why the Council Court had appointed me as her Shield. Not that she really needed one. She had Spot the Dog, after all.

Spot was a dog from some place where they think it's cute if you can play join-the-dots on a small mountain of mutt fur.

Dwarfs, as a rule, aren't big on pets – no point when you live on and in the Northern Mountains, where routinely they under-went periods of great plenty and periods of terrible starvation. Hence our ability to quickly slap on the pounds and yet survive for weeks on less food than you'd normally find in a pixie's snap tin. For a dwarf, a dog would not be a loving companion; it would be a food reserve. One should not get attached to a food reserve. You do not get chummy with dinner.

Spot and I soon reached an understanding. I understood that he would bite me if I ever turned my back. He understood that I would boot him up the rear if he came closer than I could throw a spotty dog. To leave him in no doubt as to how far that was, I threw him just the once. He, in return, cornered me in the kitchen for a whole afternoon while his mistress had her after-lunch nap. When Old Woman Pumfrey awoke and came downstairs, he was innocence incarnate, of course.

Spot was a deceptive pooch, you see. He looked like butter wouldn't melt in his mouth – which it wouldn't. It would be swallowed whole before it had a chance. Dwarf might need a bit more chewing; I didn't plan to find out.

We had one thing in common, Spot and I: neither of us was too fond of Old Woman Pumfrey's niece, Verland. Verland was as gorgeous as a vision conjured up by one of the Old Age master painters and as cute as cut glass in your intimate lubricant. She hovered over her aunt with all the attention of a starving vulture. Spot the Dog doted on Old Woman Pumfrey in a completely un-food related manner and didn't trust the niece. I was also fond of the old girl and didn't trust Verland, as she was what we detectives technically call 'a nasty piece of work'.

I was rather peeved, then, when, a week before the trial, I was told my services would no longer be required. Verland and husband Crimley Coddlestone, a two-handkerchief type with less backbone than a jellyfish, were moving in – that, and the large devoted spotty dog sleeping outside her door, were consider deterrent enough, by the niece at least.

I was considerably more peeved when, two days later, Old Woman Pumfrey died in her sleep of 'natural causes'. The trial was postponed indefinitely and Verland was rich. Nobody considered foul play – after all, everybody knew that Pumfrey's mean-tempered mutton-head dog wouldn't allow anybody through that door, certainly not to administer any 'natural causes'. He hadn't so much as budged the whole night. And, after all, sleeping dogs don't lie.

So, I did some investigating. Investigation of this sort can look very like breaking-and-entering, I must admit, but I needed to see inside the Pumfrey Mansion. I went at night, because I'm a traditionalist about such matters. It didn't occur to me that, given Verland and Spot's mutual loathing, the mutt would still be in residence. However, as soon as I was through the rather rudimentary security system and inferior locks (why will these people never learn? Only buy locks from dwarfs!), I heard the padding of paws on marble. I was greeted with a friendly tongue lick that could have stripped wallpaper. Then I knew something was really wrong.

After that encounter, I went through lists of recent spotty dog purchasers and found a familiar name, the name of somebody likely to take two handkerchiefs with him on an adventure.

'You really knew how many spots that mutton-head had, dwarf?' The goblin runt was genuinely taken aback and quite chatty, considering his friend, now passed out, was still bleeding slowly to death.

'You should try spending an afternoon with a spotted nadge-chewer growling at you. It's surprising what you can find to occupy your mind. You should never have replaced him with a friendly version so that you could get in and put something nasty in the Old Woman's nightcap.'

'Sickleweed,' he said, with pleasure. 'A handy cure for sleeplessness in the young and fit and a one-way ticket to the West for the old.'

'Very convenient for Verland and you Nightfangs, eh?'

'Sorted it all out, have you?'

'I'm not sure how you managed to dognap Spot in the first place. Sickleweed again?'

'One smart detective!'

'Smarter than a goblin that leaves his home address at a pet shop.'

'Yes, my friend Lefty here, he was never the quickest rat up the drainpipe. He also ain't Lefty any more, on account of you having chopped that particular paw off!' This the goblin runt found particularly amusing.

'Well, I guess it doesn't matter now.'

'I wouldn't say that,' I told him, as straight-faced as was possible, given that the dognapped mutton-head in question, having escaped his bonds, was at that moment only a short leap behind the runt.

It could have worked out better, but a goblin finger, as mentioned, is quick to twitch – even with a spotty dog gnawing at your neck. The third-best hat was a write-off and this time even my thick dwarf skull knew it. I span, falling badly, and felt my arm bend in a way that arms are not supposed to bend and make a noise they're not designed to make either.

By the time the Cits arrived, kicked into action by a helpful neighbour with good hearing, I was sitting dazed and bloody on the floor with my new spotty best friend chewing happily on goblin arm – him, not me – and two goblin henchmen in various stages of incapacitation about us. I managed to put together a reasonable story of how I figured out Verland's plan to use the dog substitution as the perfect cover for removing the rich old aunt and how I tracked down the missing Spot the Dog. At least, I assume I did, as I walked free –as far as the nearest healer's.

It might have been my close encounter with goblin artillery, but I never thought anybody did fully appreciate my 'let sleeping dogs lie' line. Shame, it was a good one too. One thing did stick in my mind as they wheeled me into the accident ward for my appointment with Physic Tollingburn: without a shadow of a doubt, I needed some leave – somewhere warm and sunny would do the trick. I promised myself a break, as soon as Physic Tollingburn, a deceptively adroit healer built like a stone outhouse, put me back together again.

1

TALL TREES

Some way from the Citadel, on the south side of the Bay, lies the residential area that the administrators call Tall Trees. The criminal element has another name for it: Grabda. It's an old goblin word for a large fat bird with a mean disposition. In this context, it means 'look, but don't touch'. As to what the locals call Tall Trees, well, that's their own business, thank you very much. However, to the majority of the population of the Citadel, it's known simply as Elfland.

Whereas the peak on which the Citadel is built is a geological anomaly – a granite outcrop punctuating the far end of the High Havona Range – Elfland, as befits its station, does things properly. It rises steadily from the Havona Plain, eventually forming a series of gently sloping hills, wooded with groves of the huge redwoods so fancied by the elves. There are babbling brooks, there are enchanted glades, and there are probably whole herds of unicorns, if you know where to find them. If you are looking for a nice place to live within easy reach of all the amenities of a major Widergard metropolis, then don't bother looking in Elfland; homes aren't bought and sold in Elfland – the original owners have never moved out.

It was a warm day in the Citadel that morning I drove out to Elfland for the first time. The roads were packed with traffic, but the air was at least still pollution-free. Spring was picking up speed and looking like it was about to sprint into the sort of summer liable to smash all the records and send the water authority bosses straight out for extra-strong soporifics. By the time I arrived in Elfland, my shirt and the bucket seat of my cherished, racing green, '57 Dragonette convertible had become more than just good friends: they were inseparable.

I drove along the Great Wizard Roadway that winds up to the top of Elfland, one hundred goblin drummers still pounding in my head from my recent misadventures. I caught occasional glimpses of the Citadel in the rear-view mirror. From this distance, it looked like a huge discarded ice cream cone that had landed, splat, in the middle of the Havona Plain, with a puddle of melting suburbs running all the way west until they dripped exhausted into the Bay. I knew just how the Citadel felt today.

My beloved wagon was feeling the heat too, and it struggled up the hill like a greybeard who's sucked on too much pipeweed. Just as we were both about to give up, a cooling breeze sprang up, as if by magic – but we're all too grown up to believe in magic, aren't we?

The road followed a tortuous course, bereft of road signs or street names. If you did not know where you were, you had no business being there. Fortunately, the letter requesting my services had also contained a detailed map, as well it might, considering I was on my way to see the duly elected leader of the Elfin Enclave – their chief executive on the High Council – Evermore Solitude Truelight. Better known to the general population as the King of Elfland.

It would not do to call him any such thing, of course. Since the elves returned to Widergard, bringing with them the democratic process, state legislature and the trappings of power politics, all folk were declared equal. Go tell it to the Gnomes, I say.

I drove down a long, tree-lined avenue – there is no other sort here – and pulled up on a gravel forecourt, leaving my wagon with a flunky. At least, I'm guessing he was a flunky – all elves look like they just climbed out of the same enchanted pool of unicorn widdle to me. He took my Dragonette somewhere more discreet, in case even a certified classic steam wagon lowered the tone of the neighbourhood, and I took the elevator up the tree. Way up the tree.

I found a steward waiting for me in the entrance hall. 'Is Master Dwarf the detective?' he asked.

Was this guy tugging my topknot? I mean, at four eleven and one-half inches, and two eighty pounds, and with the build of a small gorilla, did he maybe think I was selling cleaners door-to-door in Elfland? One look at his baby blues told me that humour was not this elf's strong suit. In fact, I doubted that humour was even in his pack at all. Maybe it was my grey moleskin suit with matching snap-brim shovel hat that was confusing him – a lot of folk still expect us dwarfs to be wearing chain mail and pit helmets. My tailor would have a fit.

However, Gaspar Halftoken would also have a seizure if my account wasn't cleared soon, and the treasure chest was currently looking a lot more chest than treasure. In the end, I simply handed over my business card to the steward and gave him my speech.

'Nicely Strongoak, Master Detective and Shield-for-Hire.'

He took the card and examined it with the gravity I would give to the roster at a really good inn.

'Ah yes, the Councillor is expecting you. Please, walk this way.'

I resisted the temptation to crack-sharp and followed him across the hall to a large spiral staircase that wound elegantly around the tree and led to a low storey between the first and second floors. This entresol was obviously used as a reception area, as there were a number of comfortable couches and some exquisite examples of elfin artwork on display, plus a business-like desk. The steward left me and soon a woman appeared who might well have been bought along with the desk. She introduced herself as Mistress Ensanders, the Councillor's private secretary. She was a short, stout, severe-looking middle-aged lady with an obvious dye job and a rather incongruous permanent wave, impeccably turned out in tailored tweeds. I recognised the type. She had probably been with the family for years, fiercely loyal and dedicated. She had a professional manner and a grip that suggested she could drop-kick an ogre.

We made our way up a smaller flight of stairs and down a tapestry-lined corridor that ended at a solid oak door.

'If you would care to wait in the library, Master Strongoak, I will inform the Councillor that you have arrived.'

She ushered me into a volume-lined chamber – not large enough to host a political rally, but you could have lost a good-sized party in there.

'Please take a seat, Master Strongoak. I am sure the Councillor will not be long – he is just upstairs on the tennis court.'

I tried to look as if I was at home with the type of company that built sporting facilities in trees. I do not think I was too convincing. Well, always look at the burnished bit, I say. At least I didn't have to fetch the balls.

Mistress Ensanders left and I paced a bit. Even though the room had some fine pieces of furniture, there was still plenty of pacing room, so I did a bit more. To one side of the library there was a small conservatory, heated even in this weather. I walked round a desk the size of a refectory dinner table and investigated the plant life. That's my job and it's in the contract. If you don't like, don't hire me – it's a free country; the elves say so.

Water running down the glass and steam in the air both sought to obscure the view, but I could easily make out the exotic shapes of orchids – looking like waxy ingrates in a floral cell. The putty leaked a pungent smell. I had a sudden vision of shrunken old men of power, kings and councillors with poor circulation, sitting in there on winter mornings; trying to get some warmth in their old, old bones. My reverie was interrupted by an energetic exclamation from behind me.

'There's nothing I enjoy more than a good workout on the hard court!' I turned to face the owner of the voice: all blond hair and sport-whites that would shame your own mother's wash day. 'Do you play tennis at all, Master Strongoak? I can't recommend it enough!'

For a moment there I had been forgetting the type of individual I was dealing with. This was, of course, the perpetually youthful King of Elfland.

I took a moment to examine the uncrowned monarch. Although elves can have a certain sameness, at least to the untrained eye (dazzling blond good looks, unblemished complexions and a bearing that even in the humblest woodland folk can only be described as regal), this one had something else entirely. A certain boyish charm, which, considering what his age must be, was good going, and a wistfulness that shouted sensitivity. He had youth appeal, he had grandmother appeal, and he had one-eyed, half-stoned troll appeal. I could see how he'd achieved his position – axes and blood, he had my vote already and I don't even have pointy ears.

'No,' I said, finally answering his question on sporting preferences, 'never had the opportunity. I must admit golf's more my game.'

'Yes. I always found that strange. How a folk that spend so much of their lives underground could have taken up golf with such enthusiasm.'

'Well, I was never going to be competitive on the ball and basket court,' I replied.

'No, I suppose not. Oh well, anyway: I am Councillor Truelight, and you are?'

'Nicely Strongoak. Same as on the card you're holding.'

Councillor Truelight looked down, as if seeing my embossed token for the first time.

'An interesting name. I cannot quite place it.'

He mused in the manner of an actor on the stage. It was probably the first time that I had ever seen anyone truly 'muse' to such effect. I knew a tree-friend once that could ponder like you'd never seen, and of course us we dwarfs are famous for our brooding, but this guy could muse like he invented it. I did nothing to help him in his cogitation, so he mused some more. Finally, I gave in, and informed him that: yes, it was a given name, and therefore elvish in origin. This, I'm sure, could have come as no surprise to him, but I had decided that no muse is good muse as far as I am concerned.

'Ah yes, a given name, of course that's it!' He was all arched eyebrows and feigned enlightenment now. I wondered who the act was for. Maybe he had spent too long in politics and considered the rest of Widergard to just be an extension of the debating chamber of the High Council and every conversation was therefore a chance to get his face in the scrolls.

'A given name,' he continued, in the same vein. 'Yes, it just slipped my mind for a moment there.'

I wasn't too sure about the point he was making. If he was trying to convince me of his great age and authority, then he was on the wrong track. My respect can be earned, but not bought. However, my time is certainly for sale, and currently he was putting in a bid, so I was all smiles and best behaviour. I changed the subject though:

'I was just admiring your orchids.'

He put his racquet down on the large desk and reached for a small bell that he shook before motioning me to a seat. He perched himself on the end of the desk, looking as composed as a model in a male order catalogue, the sort they produce for lonely widows in need of attentive company.

'You are familiar with the flower then?'

'Just nodding acquaintances.'

'A hobby of mine.'

'An interesting one.'

'How so?'

'Orchids up a tree. So many of them being parasitic on trees.'

'What better place to find them then?'

Mistress Ensanders entering the room interrupted this marginally witty exchange. He addressed his secretary: 'Ah, Ensy, would you mind organising some drinks for Master Strongoak and myself? Something long and cold would be just the job, I think.' He raised an eyebrow in my direction and I signalled my approval with the same.

'You've met Ensy, I take it?' he continued, after the woman had left the room again.

'Mistress Ensanders?' I queried.

Truelight looked genuinely nonplussed for a moment. 'Oh yes, Mistress Ensanders, we haven't called her that for a while. She's been here for years, practically one of the family. Marvellous woman. I don't know what I would do without her. My sisters use to call her Ensy when younger. It rather stuck.'

He did another of what I now recognised were trademark stares into the wild blue yonder, perhaps still auditioning for 'Young Romantic of the Year', not a role I'd ever considered for myself due to an allergy problem – that sort of body makes me want to throw up.

'Actually, it was concerning one of my sisters that I asked you here today,' he said, finally delving into a desk drawer and pulling out a manila envelope that he carried over to where I sat. 'These arrived yesterday,' he said, by way of explanation. 'I take it you are not unduly sensitive.'

I am, of course, remarkably sensitive. I take economy-sized paper hankies to soppy picture shows and I spend long hours reading soul-searching poetry by young men who shave alternate weekends. Plus, I mooch around expensive galleries where the inner workings of the liberated mind are expressed in squiggly lines – I just look like I chew kitty litter and spit hoggart bones, honest.

The envelope contained a number of large, glossy black-and-whites in a painted pastoral setting. They were group shots, but hardly formal. The boys were an interesting mixture, a goblin, a couple of gnomes, and even a troll. One of the women was young, on the short side and dark-haired, the other, slap-bang in the middle of every shot, was blonde and elvish. They were all dressed in air, as naked as the day they were born.

The elf lady looked kind-of familiar, but seen one elf, seen 'em all, I say. As for the smutties themselves, I'd seen worse, or better, depending on your preferences.

I put the pictures carefully down on the desk and shrugged before speaking:

'I understand that this mixed-race material is very popular now in certain sections of the Citadel. However, I take it you did not request these and so I must hazard a guess that you are acquainted with the lady taking pride of place in each shot?'

The Councillor walked over to the conservatory and peered at the orchids before answering. 'My younger sister, Vericeema.'

'I see. Well, she does not seem to have been coerced, which is reassuring. Have you talked to her about this?'

'No, she is away at the moment, visiting relatives apparently.'

'Your parents?'

'Our parents grew tired of Widergard and went west many years ago.'

'Then who?'

'Master Strongoak, I do not want to have to disturb them or her. I would like this cleared up, if possible, before she returns.'

'I see, and the White Finger.'

'White Finger?'

'Yes. The White Finger!' I repeated then, seeing his lack of comprehension, explained further. 'The White Finger, Councillor – it's Citadel gutterspeak for extortion. I take it someone is demanding corn for these smutties? I don't imagine they intended them for the family album or the celebrity glossies.'

'No – nothing, yet,' the King of Elfland said, with a sigh. 'No White Finger, no letter, no demands for "corn". Just the prints of my sister.'

'Doing her naked best to improve race relations with a goblin, a couple of gnomes and a troll?'

'Not an initiative that the High Council has been actively encouraging,' he added drily.

'Any reason for why she might have gotten herself involved in this form of recreational activity?'

Evermore Truelight shook his noble head.

I considered all of this. 'I am afraid this probably just means that they are leaving you to sweat for a bit. I think that it's reasonable to assume that at some point the White Finger will point.'

The Councillor turned around. 'I don't know, Master Strongoak. I just want this matter stopped before it goes any further. Do you understand, I don't mind what it takes, what it costs? I want it stopped and I want my sister protected. Is that clear?'

Another steward knocked and entered with a silver tray holding a cut-glass flask and two tumblers. He very prettily placed the glasses before us and poured as well. I remembered my 'thank yous' and sipped at the pleasant mixture of pulped woodland fruits over chipped ice with a snort of wormback.

I waited until the steward had left before continuing. 'In matters of this sort, Councillor, I must advise you to talk with the Citadel Guard. I think you might be surprised at how discreet they can be.'

'Even if, as you pointed out, Master Strongoak, there has been no threat? No – what was that phrase – no White Finger? And as you also remarked, as there also appears to be no coercion involved?'

I rubbed the stubble on my chin that had sprung up since I'd shaved earlier that morning. 'You have a point, Councillor. I'm sure the White Finger won't be far behind, but I could certainly begin enquiries, so that you are prepared for whatever eventually might come up. Perhaps trace where these were taken? I'll need to take them with me, if that's permitted.'

Councillor Truelight nodded and added: 'Of course, it goes without saying that I rely on your absolute discretion, to ensure that the minimum number of folk are involved. I have been assured that you are most discreet.'

I nodded. 'All my operatives are as tight-lipped as a troll in a sunbathing booth as well, Councillor.' I got up and pocketed the envelope. 'Just one more point, if this doesn't sound too stupid. The young lady in question, you are sure it is your sister? She is rather obstructed and what with the hair over her face, there isn't really that good a shot of her.'

He smiled ruefully:

'Yes, I'm sure, Master Detective. It's Vericeema. I would not fail to recognise my sister, and you can make out the ring I presented to her for her Coming of Age birthday. She'd never remove it.'

'It looks suitably impressive. Magic?'

'No, just very expensive.'

'Still, rings can be faked.'

'Perhaps, but if you look carefully, you can also make out a rather distinctive birthmark on her inner thigh.'

I flipped through until I found the image, a small round blemish shaped nothing like a strawberry, raspberry, crown or star, or much like anything in particular. I said as much.

'I only said it was distinctive, Master Strongoak. I didn't say it was artwork,' he added.

I asked for a more conventionally posed picture and he walked round to the front of his desk.

'Here.' He opened a drawer and took out another picture that he passed over to me. 'You can take this one. I have others.'

It was a studied portrait of a young elfess; she was all summer sunshine and forget-me-nots. It was difficult to equate her with the star of the previous shots. I did not mention this; it wasn't my place to point out that there was a dragon on his lawn if he wasn't worried about the greenery. I placed Lady Sunshine carefully in my inside jacket pocket. Naughty Miss Midnight I tucked tightly under my arm.

'All right, Councillor, I will do what I can. I've brought a standard contract with me, just to make it legal for now. We can discuss final payment when we have a clearer idea what is in store. It just needs a seal. Will Mistress Ensanders deal with it?'

'I think not. I trust Ensy implicitly. She has always been incredibly fond of the girls, but I think it better if she does not know for now.' He took out a candle and a jack from the same desk drawer, and melted a small pool of wax onto the contract using a spirit lamp. Evermore Truelove put his seal to it, the Tree in Flower, which was also the seal of the whole of the Elfin Council in Widergard. Democracy indeed. Don't you love it?

I left the Councillor, who said Mistress Ensanders would see me out. I didn't want to get lost while up a tree. How embarrassing would that be?

Mistress Ensanders, however, was not at her desk on the entresol, so I made my own way down the main staircase to the entrance hall. I had a bit more time to take in my surroundings and the incredibly tasteful artwork: as superb examples of craft with wood as you are ever likely to come across. The way that the living tree was worked in with carved and inlaid surfaces was quite remarkable. The smell, a mixture of polish and fresh flowers, just shouted springtime and, indeed, I felt an extra bounce in my step as I made my way to the hall.

As I walked, I felt a touch of the neck hair action that usually tells me when I am getting a surreptitious once-over. I turned and there on the entresol, looking down at me, was the lady whose glossy was currently settled in my breast pocket. She was clothed in an elfin robe, with her hair put up in a towel, as if she had come straight out of the shower. I tipped my cap politely, but a statue poured from brass might have shown more of a reaction.

Mistress Ensanders entering the Hall distracted me, and when I looked back the elfin vision was gone. Mistress Ensanders apologised for her enforced absence. She did not clarify what the problem was, and I found it very difficult to imagine what exactly it would take to enforce Mistress Ensanders to do anything. A dragon maybe, but I wouldn't give good odds on the dragon. I took the lift down the tree, wondering why the King of Elfland should lie about the presence of his little sister.

2

MISSING

The journey back to the Citadel felt like a trip into a sorcerer's steam room – a descent into something hot and wet with a suspicious background sub-stench of foetid odours that you really didn't want to know anything more about. I made good time, though, and with an hour or two on my hands before my next appointment, I decided to mix a little business with pleasure, and headed to a small store I knew on the lower fifth level.

My years in the Citadel Intelligence Agency had left me with knowledge of many of the more colourful inhabitants of this never drab metropolis. Candy Lief ranked among the eccentric of the good guys. Along with his goodwife Cassada, a beautiful but rather dour lady that I had never really struck it off with, he ran one of the finest sweetmeat stores in the Citadel, probably the whole of Widergard.

Candy's store was an unprepossessing place some way round clockwise on the fifth. Unprepossessing if you were already used to walls made of gingerbread, tiles of red mint and windows of clear sugar. They weren't real, of course, but the effect was so convincing you couldn't help but want to break a bit off and have a nibble just to see.

I found myself a free parking bay nearby for the Dragonette; maybe some of that magic had travelled back with me from Elfland. So, whistling a merry tune, hat pushed back, and as chipper as a knocker in a tin mine, I went to visit Candy Lief the sweetmeat maker.

Candy was a fine advertisement for his trade. Round as a jawbreaker, with a bald pate as shiny as butter toffee, he dressed in the same pastel shades that filled his jars of fizzballs, rocettes and magic mushrooms. When not bustling around his store, he could be found in the little manufactory behind, making magic with sugar, fruit syrup and dreams. They say that every child in the Citadel has, at some stage, been through the door of Candy Lief's Sweetmeat Store and it sometimes seems like he can remember every one. In a different age, he might have wandered, singing, down sun-dappled forest paths, collecting berries, or danced by moonlight while mushrooming – in modern Widergard he made sweetmeats. I was hoping his unique knowledge could help me out with a tricky missing person's case

I was currently contracted by a genuine major Citadel dwarf personality, one Getgold Grounding. For many folk, Getgold was the face of Citadel dwarfdom: embroidered weskit, luxuriant beard, magnificent gold watch chain and all. Not just wealthy but a representative on the 'White Council' that oversaw government business in the Citadel: hence, a fully paid-up member of the 'White and Wise'. He was always good for a quote, was Getgold, or a picture at an opening, or an extravagant purchase, but amongst the Citadel Brotherhood he was generally considered to be something of a cut-glass dwarf: not quite the real thing. I am not somebody who insists that a dwarf needs to have worked a full apprenticeship down the mines to qualify for their topknot. And it isn't his fault that the Groundings have lived in the Citadel for generations, but perhaps Getgold could behave a little less like he'd just left his pick and shovel in the front porch. Embroidered weskits? Gaspar would weep.

However, the Groundings were also renowned for always paying their bills and I had no objections to them paying mine for a while. Never count your treasure 'til it is sitting in your chest, as my Uncle Wipehatchet used to say – when sober.

The doorbell hadn't even stopped jingling and Candy was at my shoulder. 'Master Strongoak! A delight, oh yes, my deario! I'm so sorry I missed you previously! So sorry, indeedio!'

And I do mean literally at my shoulder. Mr Lief was not a tall man, some two heads shorter than his elegant, statuesque wife who nodded as I entered, but didn't smile. It was a shame, with her chestnut hair and dark brown eyes, smiling might have suited her. But, as a result of Candy's diminutive stature, the two of us saw eye-to-eye on almost everything else.

I looked quickly around. The store was quiet at that hour, the children still at their studies, checking the clock, small coins clinking in their pockets waiting to be converted into treats and sweetmeats.

'Can you spare me five minutes of your time please, Candy?'

He nodded, his head dabbling like porcelain duck at a fair, and then signalled to a white-coated assistant who was talking with his wife Cassada. The helper looked like a younger, hairier version of his boss. I knew the Liefs had no children – a nephew maybe?

We retired to Candy's manufactory of delights. The smells and colours hit my nose and eyes and they had a little fight about who was having the best time and then called it a draw as they were both having far too much fun for their own good anyway. I walked past a bench of goodies and tried not to nibble. I have a rule about that. As dwarfs are rather renowned for rampant girth growth in their later years, I never nibble at anything between meals that doesn't come in a glass or have a lady attached.

'So, any luck with my missing person, Candy?' I said, getting my mind on business and off temptation.

'Sadly not, Master Strongoak,' he replied, his head now shaking like a children's toy doll. 'Oh deario, no, I really have no recollection, alas and alack, of ever seeing the child in question. I showed the picture to the goodwife and around to my guild fellows, but again with no success. I am so sorry, oh yes, my deario, so sorry indeed.' Candy was indeed the very picture of sorrow.

'Don't worry, Candy,' I sighed. 'It was a long shot.'

'What was the child's name again, please, my deario?'

'Daisy.'

'Of course, how could I forget?' Candy sat down with a sigh at his workbench. 'Is it just my weariness, Master Strongoak, or has the Citadel becoming a harsher, more wicked place? Once upon a time, surely, a missing child would have had every able-bodied man out searching night and day until they were found? Now, we shrug and say it's a terrible shame and then the next day we can't even remember the poor child's name. Not a good place to be these difficult days, the Citadel, oh deario, no!'

It was hard to disagree with Candy. A missing child is indeed a terrible thing and the stuff of my worst nightmares. Consequently, I had explored every passage and looked down every well shaft with this one, but I was not coming up with even a hint of high-grade information. This failure was not improving my disposition at this particular moment in time.

'It makes it so hard to maintain any optimism, Nicely, my friend. My goodwife and I both give our time to help where we can, my Cassada especially! She is on all sorts of boards and councils to assist those less fortunate, especially children. I think it helps her cope, with our not having our own little darlings.'

My old friend was certainly downcast. I pulled up another stool and sat next to the confectioner, took off my snap-brim, and had a good scratch before answering. 'I think, my friend, that there have always been children who have wanted to be someplace else, even if they are loved by their parents where they are, and evil doesn't always come swathed in dark robes and carry eldritch weapons. The only solution I can conjure up, is to ensure that evil is kept as far away from these children as possible, while they sort out where they need to be. I'm just hoping that's the case here, anyway.'

Candy sighed before replying, 'I only ever want to see the poor mites happy. Oh yes, my deario. Children should be happy.' He rubbed his bald head like it might be a good-luck charm.

'Oh well,' I said, getting up, 'if anybody has done their best to achieve that, then you have, Candy. It's just that there are some things that can't be cured with fizzles or taffy.'

'Surely not, Nicely?' he smiled.

'I'm afraid so – always remember Strongoak's Second Law.'

'And what would that be again, my deario?'

'It takes very few folk to ruin things very badly for an awful lot more other folk.'

'Yes, indeed, I remember it now and the rest of it, too: it also takes an awful lot of folk to sort matters out again!'

'Well done, Candy!' I grinned, trying to raise his spirits. 'That is now officially the "Candy Lief Corollary to Strongoak's Second Law"! We'll make the pointy-head fraternity yet!'

Candy reached into one of his waistcoat pockets. 'Would you like young Daisy's picture back?'

'No, hang on to it, Candy. You never know, and I am picking up some more prints later anyway.'

'I would suspect, or guess, from the girl's attire and ribbons, this would not be that new an image of Daisy?'

'The most recent my client has!' I said, with some frustration. 'It seems the little girl was rather sensitive about having her picture taken. Something about her teeth and nose – self-conscious as they can be at that age.'

'Then, Master Detective,' he said, with only the smallest trace of side to his speech, 'do the Guards not employ artists for the express purposes of ageing folk by use of pen and ink?'

I could have kicked myself. Of course they did! I'd used their talents many times myself, once famously to put twenty years on the image of an errant husband. An advocate who needed to tell him his rich old uncle had died was seeking him. Such things really do happen. In this particular case, the long-neglected spouse would be the default beneficiary, but in the sketcher's picture it looked as if the missing husband had not only aged twenty years but had also swapped species and turned into a goblin. I found the errant ex without any additional help from the sketcher and then found the vengeful wife in bed with the police artist. His pencil looked rather over-worked and I think he was quite glad to be arrested for 'perverting the course of justice' and to get some peace.

I had just never thought to consider the same 'artist' option when it came to children.

'Candy, you're a genius!' My friend blushed right to the top of his smooth round head. 'Hang that, you're two geniuses, as your skill in the kitchen already qualified you for the first accolade years ago.'

'Which reminds me, Master Strongoak.' He grabbed something from his workbench. 'Try this – try two! Oh yes, my deario! Take the lot!' He offered me a small bowl containing small round sweets, a rather innocent-looking lemon-coloured fruit confection. I took a couple and had a suck. All very nice. So I bit down on one and something exploded in my mouth, snapping and a-cracking. And it kept on going. Then it went on some more! I was so surprised that I nearly spat it out. This had Candy laughing, just in time for the second ball to explode in another amazing mouth-rush of flavours and textures.

'What have you put in them, Candy? Firework powder?' I finally spluttered.

'I call them Wizard's Balls. Do you think they'll catch on?'

I had to laugh. 'Oh yes, they're going to be a hit all right, but I wouldn't hang around with any sorcerous folk for a while if they become a big seller.'

Candy poured the rest of the sweets into a paper bag and tucked the bag into my jacket pocket. 'I would never hang around with wizards! Oh no, my deario – too unpredictable!'

Candy was certainly right there; the unpredictability of wizards was, if anything, highly predictable. And I was on my way to meet one.

First, I needed to get those extra prints I had mentioned. So I swung by the Citadel Guard's Central Watchtower to see Josh Corncrack. My somewhat ambiguous role as an occasional consultant to the Guards gave me a tin badge that I could motion at the desk sergeant. Depending on who was on duty, the phase of the moon and whether he was getting enough of what a middle-aged man needs to stay happy, I either passed after a cursory inspection or was made to wait. It must have been Sergeant Moon's birthday and I could guess what his goodwife had given him, because I was waved straight through.

Josh Corncrack was a pale, thin creature with bulging eyes who spent his life in a small dark cave built into the hillside. That's because he was the police photographer. I knocked and waited outside the door to his gloomy domain, lit only by a single unflattering red light. From inside, I could hear the familiar swallowing noise always associated with Josh: his automatic picture processor as it circulated revealer and fastener. I knocked again and was greeted by a shout: 'Talk to me or bite a troll, either way you'll likely lose your teeth.' Josh Corncrack was good folk.

'It's Nicely Strongoak, Josh! Put some clothes on,' I shouted back.

'Nicely! Hang your helm on the hat stand and I'll be with you before you can say, "Elberbry did it for free".'

Josh's little red light went out and I went in.

I perched up on his workbench next to the chugging machine and watched it churn out multiple close-ups of a particularly gruesome corpse missing something to keep his hat on.

'Your glossies are on the side,' Josh said, adjusting the focus of the image thrown from the glass plate in his enlarger. I picked up the stack of 4 by 4s and looked again at the young girl looking back at me. Even in the dim darkroom light the image was unforgettable.

Daisy had a slightly crooked nose and a gap-toothed smile that was as cute as forget-me-nots on a bride's bonnet. Her eyes were bigger than cartwheels and looked forward to a future that was brimming with more happiness than a trug full of kittens. An ornate hair grip fought a losing battle with the unruly mop of brown hair perched above the startlingly pretty freckled face.

I felt Josh's hand on my shoulder. 'No joy then, Nicely?' he said, serious for once.

'Not so much as a pixie's sniff. It's proving hard to pick up a trail this cold.'

'Any theories?'

'None that don't wake me nights in a cold sweat.'

'It doesn't get any easier, does it?'

'What does in life?'

'Oh – defaulting on your taxes, finding more reasons for not stopping smoking and jumping to the wrong conclusions about women.'

'But never anything to do with children,' I added unnecessarily.

'No – even goblin mothers love their little baby goblins, bless their pointy heads and teeth.'

'Was ever the way.'

'But, you do not want to know how many young children we've had missing the last few years, Nicely.'

'It was bad enough when I was in the Guards. You mean it's worse now?' I was genuinely surprised.

'They don't exactly advertise the fact, my friend, but yes. Go ask Wrafe! It's over the city like a rash. A nasty itchy blotchy rash.' Josh was obviously upset by this, which wasn't like him at all. He was usually much more self-possessed.

'I had no idea, Josh – finding missing children is not my normal beat.'

'I don't blame you, Nicely. So how come this trail was allowed to cool?'

'The first my client heard about it was from an advocate. It was a last gasp wish from the girl's mother, Mistress Cartersong, a former employee of my client. She was taken by the Wilting Hurt, but had never given up hope of finding her missing daughter. Her dying wish was for my client to pick up the ball and now I'm running with it. I've got precious little on the girl, not even her DOB or father, although a showman is rumoured.'

'That original wasn't too new a picture, you know?'

'So I've been reminded. The only one available, though, which reminds me, Josh, any sketchers in the department who might want to earn themselves a drink?'

Josh laughed before he replied, 'Show me one that doesn't and I'll show you my pet elephant in his tinder box!'

'I'm wondering if maybe he could add some years to Daisy.' I looked down at the pile 'of originals. 'I'm guessing she was maybe five or six in the original and that now we should maybe add five to that. Anybody good at that sort of thing?'

'I'll ask around.'

'Quietly.'

'No, I was thinking of lighting one of the Seven Beacons and then shouting the news from the top of Snow Dol!'

'Calm down, Josh! You'll get your girdle in a twist.' I jumped down from the workbench and opened the envelope I had been given by the Elf King earlier.

'And if that had to be quieter than an Elf Queen's curse, then this must remain between you and me and the Baldy Man.' I gave Josh the smutties and like, the true professional he is, he didn't flinch. Switching on an adjustable lamp, he took out an augmentation glass and gave them the once over.

Finally, he spoke. 'Well, as regards the content, these are tamer than a kobold's knitting these days. The lighting is top of the tree, though, better than any backdoor mole peddler's I've come across – the sort of thing a major picture house might run to. You know, proper lamps and reflectors, and that would go along with the backgrounds, which look like picture house stage sets.' He touched the paper between thumb and finger. 'Interesting, this isn't your normal trade grade stock either.' He held it up close to his lamp. 'These must be raising some proper corn.'

'And the mixed-race angle?'

'The filth-fellowship boys say it's all the rage these days. Seems the average Citadel smut body is falling over themselves to take integration one step further, or at least look at smutties of it.'

'Where might I find the snapper then, Josh?'

He scratched his chin. 'I'm thinking maybe not in the normal swamps. Like I say, there's plenty of picture houses out in Milkwood that have invested the mine in a lot of equipment, hoping to make a killing. They are not averse to loaning lamps and such out to anybody well minted enough, even if they put flesh before artfulness.'

'I don't know what this place is coming too, Josh.'

'Same old Hill, Nicely. You've just seen closer than most folk.' He picked up the smutties and gave them back to me. I made a contribution to the Police Photographer's Benevolent Fund and arranged to catch up properly with Josh over a crock of the dark stuff.

'Just one more thing, Nicely,' he mentioned as I pocketed my glossies. 'Seen Wrafe recently?' I admitted I hadn't. 'We've got a new captain, name of Shephall, you see,' he continued. 'He's making life difficult for your old partner. He might also make life difficult for you too, so keep your nose clean and give me a toot on the horn before coming in and I can tell you which way the wind is blowing.'

I thanked Josh again and hurried out. Not that I wanted to linger. It doesn't pay to keep a wizard waiting: they're liable to charge you double.

3

RUDEBEARD THE RELAXED

When I arrived at my next port of call, the abode of Rudebeard the Relaxed in the Wizards' Quarter, he was pulling a hat out of a rabbit. It's a good trick, but first you have to get your rabbit to eat the hat. Rudebeard's answer was to make the hat out of pressed lettuce. The rabbit was not having any of it, literally not having any of it. Not until the wizard spiked it up with something a little special from a phial he kept on a shelf with numerous other phials – all unmarked – designed for every purpose you can think of, and presumably many that defied the imagination. Now the coney was not going to give the headgear up for anybody, especially not a snot-covered hedge charmer with delusions of adequacy. That being the description of him given to me by Tollingstaff the Expedient, the same mage who had recommended him.

'And the point of this is what exactly?' I finally had to ask Rudebeard.

'It was a bet, Detective,' he muttered through a beard that looked like it should have its own planning policy.

'Ah, a bet!' Well, that explained everything – explained, even if it did not quite rationalise it in a way that would make sense to most folk.

'I bet Tollingstaff the Charlatan that I could perfect this little trick in time for the Wizard Guild's Annual Dinner and I am not going to be defeated by this cursed coney's reluctance to do as required.'

The attitude of wizards towards games of chance is very hard to fathom. Surely if there was ever a single set of folk in the whole of Widergard who should appreciate the capricious nature of fortune it should be wizards, those best in tune with the music. But if you ever see two beetles climbing a dung heap, you can bet your last leaf of pipeweed that there'll be two wizards standing nearby willing to risk their staffs over which beetle gets to the top first. In case of any confusion, the beetles will be the two better-dressed individuals present.

Probably the most famous bet between wizards is judged to be that between Vlanmire the Red, Barantrust the Blue and Grunweald the Green, back in the days when wizards still came handily colour-coded.

At that time, in the long ago, there was a large she-dragon called Smeleck, alive in the Perilous Wastes, who had in her possession the largest moonstone that had ever been found. So large was it that it was known as the Dragon's Egg. This was a thing of great beauty, full of a pale translucent milky glow that seemed to shift in flux to reveal hidden sparks of magnificent colour.

The three wizards fell to arguing about who could best recover the gem from the dragon. Vlanmire said, 'I, Vlanmire the Red, with my great command of fire, will recover the Dragon's Egg. For fight fire with fire, as the old proverb tells us.'

Barantrust laughed at Vlanmire and said, 'Even the mightiest fire can be put out by a rainstorm. I, Barantrust the Blue, with my command of water, will recover the Dragon's Egg.'

Vlanmire laughed at Barantrust's watery boast.

'No,' said Grunweald, 'neither water nor fire shall recover the Dragon's Egg. I, Grunweald the Green, will foil the dragon Smeleck with my command of… plants.'

Now, both Barantrust and Vlanmire fell about with laughter at this, because as everybody knows, plant wizardry is just a bit, weedy.

And so the three wizards had a bet as to who could get their hands on the moonstone known as the Dragon's Egg.

The three wizards travelled together to the Perilous Wastes, the domain of the great dragon Smeleck, and mighty indeed was she because at that time men had not yet invented the high-grade steel with improved grain distribution necessary for easily piercing a dragon's hide. The journey of the three wizards was full of incident and adventure because at that time the Perilous Wastes were indeed Perilous and it wasn't just a handy strapline to bring in the sight-seekers. However, as none of these incidents or adventurers has a convenient take-home moral conclusion, they shall be ignored.

Eventually, though, the three wizards arrived at the dragon's mountain. The mountain does not get a name in this story, which just shows that dwarfs had no hand in the writing of it. A dwarf scribe would have spent a couple of days thinking upon the name of the mountain and then probably just called it the Lonely Peak.

Inside her mountain, Smeleck slumbered curled around her egg. She knew it wasn't really a dragon's egg, and would never hatch, but hey, a girl can hope, can't she?

Vlanmire the Red went first to the dragon's door and, having set a spell within so that flames engulfed the mountainside, shouted: 'Fire, fire! Flee, flee, flee for your lives, lest you should burn.'

'Fire?' said Smeleck, opening one enormous eye. 'Why should I fear fire?' And with one huge gape of her mighty jaws she swallowed the fire whole.

Vlanmire went off, his face as red as the red on his robes.

Next came Barantrust the Blue to the dragon's door. He had set a spell to divert the waters of the mountain river so that they ran through Smeleck's sleeping chamber, and then he shouted: 'Flood, flood! Flee, flee, flee for your lives, lest you should drown!'

'Flood?' said Smeleck, opening one enormous eye. 'Why should I fear water?' And with one huge gape of her mighty jaws she sent out a plume of fire so large that it turned all the water into steam.

Barantrust skulked off, his robes as wet with steam as they could possibly be.

Next came Grunweald the Green to the dragon's door. 'Delivery for Smeleck, delivery for Smeleck!' he shouted. 'Delivery?' said Smeleck, opening both her enormous eyes. 'I wonder what that could be?'

'A beautiful bouquet, two dozen red roses, princess peonies, all sorts of irises and some of that baby's breath they always put in. But you'll have to come and sign for it.'

'Oh very well,' said Smeleck, getting unsteadily to her feet and making for her door, because, after all, all women love flowers.

Meanwhile, Grunweald had sneaked round to the back door and, while Smeleck was admiring her bouquet, was busy helping himself to the Dragon's Egg.

'Ha, ha, ha!' How Grunweald laughed. 'I've put one over on that Vlanmire the Red and Barantrust the Blue. Now for a quick get-away.' Except Grunweald had forgotten exactly how much a moonstone the size of a dragon's egg would weigh and could barely lift the gemstone off the floor.

So it was that when Smeleck came back from admiring and then eating her bouquet – hey, flowers are pretty, but roughage is roughage and Smeleck had a very high-protein diet – she easily pounced on Grunweald.

Smeleck grasped the wizard in her huge claws, but was surprised to see him laughing like a goblin on gas. 'Why are you laughing, wizard?' she said. 'I am about to eat you.'

'Oh yes,' said Grunweald, 'but I won the bet! I won the bet!'

Wizards, go figure.

It is harder to judge a wizard's speciality these days, but with Rudebeard the jackdaw on his shoulder was a clue, as was the family of wrens nestling in his cowl and what I sincerely hoped was a ferret rummaging in his trouser pocket. However, like everybody else, a wizard has to adapt to the modern world and, instead of becoming animal physics, the erstwhile browns have become the best trackers and tailors in modern Widergard. That is why my wizard contact Tolly (also most definitely not known as Tollingstaff the Charlatan) had recommended Rudebeard to me.

'Hat retrieval aside, any other progress here – on my MP for example?'

Rudebeard looked up at me and blinked a couple of times. 'Well, these things can't be rushed, you know,' he said finally.

'You forgot.'

'I forgot.'

'But, it's no problem,' he said, hurrying me towards a small room in the back of his quarters. 'Time will only improve this spell.' He paused, his hands on the door handle. 'Well, up to a point.' He opened the door and the noise level went up a good three notches.

A large antique steam engine, and a small glass dome on a desk, dominated the room. A reinforced flexible tube connected the happily chugging engine to the dome, and, hanging from thin twine, in the centre of the dome, was the missing girl's hair grip that I had received from Grounding and passed along to Rudebeard.

'This,' said the wizard with a flourish, 'is a vacuum!'

'What is?' I asked.

'This is!' He pointed to the centre of the dome.

'It looks like a hair grip to me.'

'No, no, no – all round the hair grip!'

I looked closer at the dome. 'I don't see anything around the hair grip,' I had to admit.

'Exactly! Because there's nothing there!'

I was being to wonder if Tolly had sold me a prance-less pony when he recommended this hedge-botherer, but Rudebeard continued his explanation, undaunted. 'The steam engine here is acting as a pump, you see, but instead of pumping anything into the dome, it's pumping everything out – to form what we call a vacuum.'

'Why?'

The wizard looked at me as if I had just insulted his mother's chances of making it to the final of the Wizard's Mum's Best Homemade Hooch contest. 'Why what?'

'Why call it a vacuum, which has got to be just about as unpleasant and unwieldy a noise as you can hear this side of a goblin's nose-clearance?'

'Well, because we had to call it something, and "no-air" just sounds faintly ridiculous.' The wizard played with his tubing and the dome began to emit a loud whistling akin to the noise you get when you ask your grease goblin mechanic for an estimate on how long, and how much, it will take to get your wagon back on the road.

'The thing is, Master Detective, a tracking spell relies on a sympathetic resonance set up between an individual and an object that they carry with them over a long period of time. In this case, the young girl's hair grip. The problem is that the object also picks up "interference" from the world outside. By placing the object, the hair grip, here, in a vacuum, we remove these extraneous influences, leaving the core resonance, and making the tracking signal manifestly clearer.'

I looked quizzically into the dome again, to where the hair grip had indeed now aligned itself like the needle of a compass.

'You have absolutely no idea how this works, do you?'

'Not a clue,' said Rudebeard, 'but I get paid for results. Come on, we'll take your wagon.'

Rudebeard's rooms are in the Wizards' Quarter and the Wizards' Quarter is a throwback to an earlier age, all tiny alleyways and lighting discreet enough to be nearly invisible. In fact, in some places, I swear that when the lights go on the streets get darker. Some streets are also not built for the modern steam wagon, which makes driving very difficult. The one good thing is that the average wizard earns so little that nobody can afford to drive, and so the roads are remarkably clear. Well, apart from the cats – black cats, of course. More cats than you could shake a broomstick at.

I asked Rudebeard if having a cat familiar really does help with the conveyance of magic.

'Not at all,' he replied, 'we just like cats. And it does keep the mice out of the magical supply cupboard, which is always a good idea, because who wants to be plagued by invisible mice?'

Rudebeard sat in the passenger's bucket, hand held out straight, eyes fixed on the turning hair grip. I took his point and gave my concentration back to the road, cats and all.

Getgold Grounding had himself a cat apparently. Enough said.

I followed Rudebeard's directions as best I could, given that a tracking spell works in straight lines and the Citadel is sorely lacking in that commodity. We were certainly going by the scenic route and it was getting to rush time, with traffic building up. Round and around we went, but where we were heading no one could know.

'I fear, Master Detective, that the efficacy of this particular spell is not being assisted by our circumlocutions,' he added, eyes following the hair grip.

'And in common speech?'

'We are running out of supernatural steam.'

There was, however, very little I could do about that. I cast my eyes across to the dangling hair grip and made a decision. 'Look, we're heading in a general Bay-wards direction. I never thought we'd find the girl in the Citadel itself, so let's take a chance and hope we can pick up the trail out of town.'

Rudebeard nodded his agreement and I looked for the speediest escape route.

It wasn't easy, but I finally got us to Scrab Way and lost some of the Citadel commuter traffic. Big shouty hoardings lined the route: 'Renewed Shall Be the Blade that was Blunt – with Branding's Disposable Blades', 'Take the Easy Way with Cirrif's Secret Staircase Lifts', and 'Step Lively with Vainfoot Corn Plasters'. Eventually we found ourselves passing through a light industrial zone I wasn't familiar with. In amongst the anonymous prefabricated units already closing down for the night there was an interesting mix of small businesses designed for other purposes: physics, wagon repairs and a lot of folk trying to sell you more floor coverings than you could ever conceivably need. Everybody has something to sell you: their time, talent or, indeed, their corn plasters.

One signpost for 'The New Tree Renewal Parlour' caught my eye for reasons I couldn't fully explain: it seemed a strange area to be running what I took to be some sort of beauty parlour. I pointed it out to Rudebeard.

'Does that seem to be in our direction?'

He had a little spin of the hair grip and watched it settle again. 'From what I can see, it most certainly is.'

'Let's go have a little look-see then.'

I followed the signs and we ended up outside a well-shuttered building that didn't seem to want to shout too loudly about anything in particular. The New Tree Renewal Parlour was as discreet as the markings on a magic ring. It wasn't either old or new, in good taste or none – it just occupied space like a eunuch at a camp follower's hen night. The board outside, carefully positioned on the immaculate lawns, said 'By Appointment Only' and gave a number.

'Looks like I'm going to need an appointment.'

'Surely seems that way, Master Detective. You really are sharp today!'

We did a leisurely circuit of the building on the service roads and the hair grip turned as we turned. Whatever was going on was all happening in that building and that's where it remained. We had found Daisy, at least as far as the hairgrip was concerned.

'So, Master Wizard, what exactly does this mean?' I asked, when we were far enough away from the building not to look suspicious.

'I'm not sure,' Rudebeard replied. Well, this was a first. One thing you can never accuse a wizard of is a lack of certainty. They are sure of most things, except where the next meal is coming from and who is going to get the next round in – the wizarding trade not being quite as well respected as it once was.

'To have such a focused loci is highly unusual when tracking. For it to complete such a full stop is doubly unusual. A resonance will fade with time, of course, or if the individual being tracked was to undergo... a major change,' he continued carefully.

I didn't like the sound of this. 'A change like from being animate and vital to being inanimate and becoming best chums with a necromancer?'

'That is what one might consider to be a worst case possible outcome.'

I felt a shiver in places I don't like shivers, unless somebody with nice legs and more curves than a wrought iron gate is causing them. There was something about The New Tree Renewal Parlour I didn't like and my concern for the missing Daisy had just been ramped up a notch.

'That's the worst possible outcome then,' I said. 'How about we try the other options?'

'Something of similar import, a major change – but not quite so final.'

'Such as?'

'Well, when a boy becomes a man…' he gave a small cough, 'or a girl becomes a woman. That could cause such a discontinuity.'

'Oh, right.'

I put my foot down and sent the Dragonette speeding back towards the Citadel proper. This was a child we were talking about. I wasn't too happy with any of these 'discontinuity' options at all.

4

A REALLY SWELL PARTY

I dropped Rudebeard off in the Wizards' Quarter and wished him luck with his rabbit. He wished me luck with the case. I had a feeling we were both going to need it. Probably the rabbit needed it most of all.

I made it back to my rooms at the Armoury in record time and left my wagon in its space in the converted powder cellar. I ran up the steps to where Old Peat, the doorman, had his desk.

'You back for the evening, Master Nicely?'

'Just time for a shave and shower, Peat.'

'Ah, the busy lives you young folk lead!' said Peat with a sigh, rolling up his evening scroll. 'I'm glad I have a nice quiet time of it.'

I know for a fact that Old Peat led a troop in the last Great Goblin War, has had three wives and three mistresses, and still keeps a little seamstress, somewhere near the White Horse Hostel, who has a mean way with a thimble. If he leads a quiet life now, it's because he's keeping his tinder dry.

I had me the shave and the shower and felt like a thousand crowns. I chose a lightweight cream shirt with a little axe design and slipped into it with a small thrill of pleasure. The feeling of putting on a cool, freshly laundered linen top on a warm spring evening is one of the great joys in life, like a well-balanced axe, a moonlit mountain stream and a woman with bad intentions. A powder blue spider-silk suit and I was ready to go. I added Lief's paper bag to a pocket as an afterthought.

The Party Hut was one of those temporary structures that achieve permanence in the Citadel simply through no one ever having had the wherewithal to get round to taking it down. Over the years, various other temporary additions, outhouses, lean-tos and such like have been added, until the original prefabrication is hard to find until you are in it.

A street-train took me all the way there. The Hill, as us long-time inhabitants like to call the Citadel, was looking pretty fine. The air had cleared with the evening breeze off the ocean and everyone was hoping we had really seen the last of winter.

Window boxes full of 'spring soldiers', at attention in their yellow finery, were dotted everywhere and the scent of nimlo blossom sailed down from the first level gardens of the White and Wise. A few maidens were shaking out their summer outfits and the sight of many a well-turned ankle made me glad I had left the wagon at home and could concentrate on the scenery.

I'd missed the great rush home to the New Little Hundred and all the gnome girls were back making dinner for their gnome husbands, except for those lucky enough to have an invite to Vrelo Vornetelo's '123'. A '123' is no longer an official birthday party – sadly few gnomes make it to that fine age in the modern era. Now a '123' is considered part retirement party and part an opportunity for a prominent member of the gnome community to swank around a bit and say, 'Hey, they may despise us and put us down, but I ain't done so bad and maybe you won't do so bad either!' And Vrelo Vornetelo hadn't done too bad at all. Starting out as just another street-food vendor, his patty buns soon became insanely popular with all levels of Citadel folk. He progressed to small carry-outs and now there was barely a street, passage or path without its own 'Vrelo's'. A certain amount of vendor envy occasionally got some of our more excitable friends and neighbours a little, well, excited and I had been called in to help calm things down on more than one occasion. It's not that dwarfs are renowned for their diplomacy, but we are recognised as not playing favourites – often even when other dwarfs are concerned. This is partly down to an innate sense of fair play and partly because we are just bloody-minded. Carrying an axe helps, too.

One time proprietary matters did get a little more serious. A nasty clan of goblins from Off-the-Hill, the Scrabs, had moved in and tried to convince Vrelo that his business needed 'safe-keeping'. Vrelo thought otherwise. Not wanting to kick off another round of goblin–gnome hostilities, the guards were playing it very cautious – far too cautious. There had been one or two minor skirmishes – drive-by shootings and a bombing that killed one of Vrelo's many nephews. It looked like we could see something as bad as the Breakbread War of '82. At Vrelo's bidding I took it upon myself to point this out to the leaders of the Citadel's traditional goblin clans and explain how all the nice new and legitimate enterprises, as well as some of their greyer areas of commerce, would be affected by this. Old Bogwart Blagger himself, despite his six decades in charge of the Combined Clan Board, explained this to the leader of the Scrabs and his crew. They never found the bodies but it is no coincidence that the new throughway, 'Valley Pass', built at that time to give faster access to the coast from the Citadel, is known colloquially as 'Scrab Way'.

I let Vrelo take the credit for getting everything sorted with the Scrabs, paid some bills, bought myself a new suit and got a wax for the Dragonette. From that time on, Vrelo was referred to in the gnome community by the respectful, but strictly non-administrative, title of 'The Mayor'. And today was 'The Mayor's 123'.

I got to The Party Hut just in time for the big speech. I made my way forward through the tables of guests to where Vrelo, flushed and resplendent in a purple velvet three-piece, was standing talking on a small stage. He was thoroughly enjoying himself.

'My dear gnomes,' he boomed out, 'I don't know many here as well as I should, but as for the rest of you – just remember, I still have the negatives!'

This got huge cheers and the traditional shout of, 'Why don't you just disappear?'

Vrelo sailed on, oblivious. The gnomes love a speech and above all love a short speech.

'Today is my 123!' Another big cheer from those gnomes that like nothing better than a statement of the obvious, which is most of them.

'I have something to do. I have put this off for far, far too long.'

Now the cheering stopped and a hush spread over the guests. As is also traditional, a speech at a '123' usually has a surprise at the end, and the guests didn't want to miss it.

'I have to announce now, I have to announce that I am going … going to be a father!'

Now this got a really enormous cheer that swamped all the previous cheers. It had indeed taken everyone well and truly by surprise. Vrelo certainly was full of spit and spirit and if his virility had ever been in doubt, well it wasn't any longer!

Vrelo was carried off the stage and taken for a circuit round the hut. A gnome band started off with some of those syncopated rhythms that the gnomes do so well and everybody got to dancing. I found a passing steward and relieved him of the burden of two glasses of beezer teaser. One for me and one for the friend I was hoping to meet – Vrelo's parties always attracted a good mixture of folk and I was a dwarf just overflowing with the joys of spring.

I mingled and caught up with a few of the Citadel faces that a well-connected dwarf like myself has in his address roster – mostly the catering staff – before Vrelo came round again.

'Well, Vrelo, you certainly have a way with a punchline!' I said, catching Vrelo as a half-dozen high-spirited gnomes decided that they had done enough carrying for one day and needed to get on with the important drinking part of the evening.

'Nicely! Nicely, old chap! How very, very splendid to see you! So glad you made it! Are you having a wonderful time? Do say you are!'

'I'm sure he'll have an even better time not carrying you around, Vrelo. Hello, Nicely.' I turned around and passed Vrelo carefully on to his wife Carnation. She looked wonderfully healthy and wholesome in her ruffled party dress. You would never guess that Vrelo had met her when he volunteered during her knife-throwing act. As he later insisted, 'I knew she was the girl for me, the first time she missed. The other two times were less fun.'

'I am having a particularly wonderful time, Vrelo. And hearty congratulations both on the news. If I'd known, I would have crocheted booties.'

'Thank you, very gallant, Master Strongoak,' said Carnation. 'There is still time if you're quick with your pins. Vrelo's hoping for twins as the businessman in him always likes to get two-for-the-price-of-one.'

Vrelo blushed vividly, which, considering his already florid features, was quite some trick. 'Well, not getting any younger you know and with a new young wife, now seems as good a time as any.' Carnation gave this the 'huff' it probably deserved. Vrelo leaned forward and winked conspiratorially. 'The family line to consider as well.'

'Got to consider the family line, of course.' I raised an eyebrow dramatically. 'You must only have, what? Fifty nephews that I've met?' I looked at Carnation for confirmation but only got the shrug of someone struggling to keep up with an effervescent, over-active husband, let alone his relatives as well.

'Ah yes, Nicely, but it's the family name too, isn't it? No more Vornetelos, you see. I have only sisters.'

'Well, here's to many more little Vornetelos. All sons!' I grabbed two more glasses of beezer teaser and handed them to the prospective parents. We toasted and Vrelo downed the glass in one.

'Now, my fellow – my good lady and I must press the flesh with her family too.' He leaned up towards me and spoke quietly: 'We hadn't told her side and they're probably going to roast my toes now!'

'I'm sure they can find something more imaginative than that, being circus folk,' Carnation said, tousling her husband's curly hair like he was the one only barely out of their twenties.

'Sure, Carnation, just one thing before you go, please, Vrelo. Do you have any guests from the picture business here tonight?'

Vrelo thought for an instant or two before clicking his fingers and replying: 'Of course, Elsera! Lovely lady, did all our TV advertising work; beautiful eyes, beautiful hair, beautiful skin …' He leant forward again and spoke in another exaggerated whisper. 'But don't tell my wife I said that!'

Carnation tutted and took her husband's arm, before turning to me. 'I just saw her by the finger bar, Nicely – you won't miss her, I'm sure,' she added with a wink.

'Indeed,' said Vrelo, 'by the finger bar!' He pointed in completely the wrong direction, and embracing guests along the way, headed off in what was probably the wrong direction too, Carnation trying to steer him from behind.

I took my bearings and followed my nose. I found the finger bar in a smaller tented annexe and found Elsera surrounded by men. Yes, definitely hard to miss: hair darker than midnight, skin whiter than moonlight and lips redder than sin – she was dressed in the faux scullery maid look that was very much the thing that year. All black hair, pale skin and ruby red lips.

'Snow White,' I said, when I finally found a break in her crowd.

'Coal black,' she replied.

Wow, weren't we both just so cute?

'Vrelo said you're in the picture business.' I eased her away from the pack by applying scowl number sixteen, the one that can wither saplings at sixty feet.

'Why, are you looking for a break?' she asked.

'Maybe.'

She shook her head. 'No maybes about it. If you want to make it in the rolling pictures, you have to want it heart and soul to succeed.'

'Lots of maybe then.'

'Ah, but what does your heart say?'

'That I smoke too much leaf and eat too many fatty foods.'

This raised a smile. 'Anything else?'

'Yes, dwarfs are underused, stereotyped "beards" in much so-called popular entertainment, exploited for their comic potential and never allowed to carry the main narrative arc.'

'Not bad. Impress me some more.'

I put my hand in my pocket and pulled out the bag from Candy. I offered it to Elsera and she hesitated for a moment before reaching in. Her face became a picture of concentration, then mild disappointment, before she bit down and the explosion hit.

I had a handkerchief ready and some more wine at hand too.

'Alright, alright!' She gave in, spluttering and laughing. 'I'm impressed.' She took the offered wine and tried to regain some self-control; she failed. More coughing and spluttering followed, all mixed with a large amount of laughter and frankly childish giggling. 'That was incredible! Where are they from?'

'Sorry, I can't reveal my sources. I'd have to put a spell on you to make you eternally subservient to my will. We wouldn't want that, would we?'

She looked at me with the attention dial turned to eleven. 'So, what's your name, soldier?'

'Nicely, Nicely Strongoak.'

'Great name. Who thought it up?'

'Mummy Strongoak and Daddy Strongoak. I didn't even get a look-in, which I always thought was a bit rich, considering I'm the one that has to parade it around town.'

'Most bodies in the business give themselves a title they think will look better in the fancy scripts.'

'Maybe I'd better work on something then. How about Angst Kingsaver?'

'Too prescriptive.'

'Candlecoot Collop?'

'Too restrictive – unless you want to stay with comedy.'

I pushed back the helm and scratched my head before replying, 'There's more to this acting business than meets the eye, isn't there?'

'Oh yes, it's not just remembering the lines. You have to try to be pretentious at all times as well. Remember that!'

'So, "Elsera", one you pinned on yourself?'

'No, very old family name.'

'And there was me thinking you were probably more of an Elsie.'

'Oh thanks!'

'Elsera what exactly?'

She sighed. 'Elsera Undimming. I'm glad my fame precedes me.'

'Apologies, but dwarfdom was something of a niche market for most rolling pictures when I grew up, and since I've been in the Citadel I've not had that much time for entertainment.'

'Really?' she pouted, with a little lick of those oh-so-red lips: 'You look like someone who has had their fair share of entertainment to me.'

The Party Hut suddenly got a whole lot warmer and Elsera, sensing my discomfort, awarded herself a nice plump chuckle and a 'Gotcha!'

'I'm got,' I had to admit.

'Well, sorry to be the party killer but I have an early shoot tomorrow at Meridian Pictures, I'm afraid. However, I can leave your name at the gate with the guard Ropey if you're really serious. He'll pass you in.'

'That's very kind of you.'

'No promises, I'm not like a major name, as you so artfully managed to point out – but I did happen to overhear that they were having trouble casting a dwarf, so who knows?'

A clock struck the hour as if by order.

'And there's my exit cue, I had better head off. The camera shows every line, you know!'

'Then you are in the clear,' I observed.

'Very gallant, Nicely. You've done this before.' She smiled at me with those big dark eyes and the smallest of smiles playing about the pout pillows.

'I have, but there's not been much time to practise recently,' I found myself saying.

'I find that hard to believe – maybe we should see about some lessons?'

'You know, I was thinking exactly the same thing.'

'Nicely,' she sighed. 'I wish could do this all evening, but really I had better scoot. Not that it's not been nice to meet you.'

'Made my evening,' I admitted.

She went to pick up her wrap and waved a goodbye over her shoulder as she left. She looked back – always a good sign that, when they look back.

So scoot she had done, and I was left wondering how it is that truly beautiful ladies of every race can even manage to half-choke to death with style and elegance.

The rest of the evening was fine. I met the mother-in-law, who was finding the prospect of incipient grandmother status, much earlier than anticipated, somewhat of a challenge. I even moved a bit on the dance floor to those crazy gnome rhythms, but it sort of felt like the main event was over and so I said my goodbyes and easily made the last street-train back up the Citadel.

I watched the late-night folk enjoying the warm evening and chasing their dreams round and round the Hill as the street-train struggled to keep up. And here I was about to chase the biggest dream of them all. Tomorrow I was going to Milkwood.

5

MILKWOOD

Legend has it that after the elves left, Milkwood gained another, far nastier name – a name that became a byword for all sorts of dark magic and unpleasantness. Not just any old dark magic and unpleasantness either, but the full screaming, spirit-destroying, horror bag. Even after the scary stuff was cleaned up and kicked out, it didn't rank as 'most desirable residence' material and the area stayed pretty undeveloped.

When the elves returned, they didn't show much interest in their former residences and Milkwood, along with many other locales, was neglected in favour of untouched areas like High Trees that represented the new, forward-looking, involved face of elfdom. 'New Elves for a New Era', as the slogan went.

So when a new industry burst upon the scene, one that needed plenty of cheap space to build and expand, Milkwood proved ideal. Now it's a land of different magic and of different dreams, where fame is the currency and wonderful deeds are portrayed but not actually done. Some folk say that all that horror and unpleasantness in Milkwood never went completely away and now it has simply found a new home. But that's the usual junk folk of every race come out with when they've found that the merry-go-round has started and they don't have a horse.

Say what you like; Milkwood is without a doubt the major entertainment hub of Widergard. As a young dwarf growing up in New Iron Town, it managed to conjure up for me visions of glamour and excitement as potent as the greatest dwarf saga. Although we dwarfs eventually got round to making our own 'rolling pictures', there was no doubt that sneaking out to catch a Milkwood picture also had an extra layer of excitement; not that I'd ever tell Elsie that, of course.

I'd be lying if I didn't admit to shaving a little closer that morning, tying the family knots in my hair just that bit neater and putting on that lightweight linen suit with that little trace of dwarf silver in the detail. Sink my boats and blunt my axe – this was Milkwood I was going to … and … what a dump it was.

There were still some trees in Milkwood: the big picture houses guard their privacy and they like to keep some space between themselves and the neighbours, who are, after all, the competition. The bottom line, though, is that making pictures is a business, and business, whether it's a dwarf smithy, Candy Lief's manufactory or an elf lord's foundry, is a messy affair. Yes, even the elf aesthetic gets compromised when it comes to finding places to do the messy stuff and hide away the messy stuff that does the other messy stuff as well.

Not that I'm saying Milkwood is exactly the Blasted Wastes of Asingard, but although they may make magic there, it all goes into the canister and there is precious left over to sprinkle on the buildings and scenery. Still, there was a nice buzz of industry about the place, and I got a thrill – that thrill you get watching a whole lot of folk being busy at things you have absolutely no idea about.

Meridian Pictures was, I estimated, a small to middling concern. No pretence to anything other than entertainment in their pictures, and what's wrong with that? We can't all be artists; some of us have to work for a living.

Old Ropey turned out to be quite a character and then some. He had been up the hill some and down the other side as well. He was 'Ropey' because he looked like he had been put together from a selection of old knotted ropes with various frayed bits sticking out – the sort of guy who knows what really goes on in a place and where they've hidden the bodies. He had my name on a list in his guardroom and he issued me a pass with no problems. I kept his hand warm with some insulation that I passed through the small open window of his hut and said I'd see him later. I most certainly would do that.

The shoot was taking place in a big old barn of a place that had probably been converted from a big old barn. It's hard to get one past me. They were currently making a little something called 'The Elf Queen of Fire Mountain'. I hadn't seen the script of course, but I'm guessing it probably involved a noble elf queen and an evil wizard with maybe one or two equally evil dwarf sidekicks. There would also be a ranger type with a hidden pedigree who turned out to be the rightful king. An army of goblins would get slaughtered along the way, courtesy of the ranger's semi-magic sword, and some more noble elves would be at hand to help him out. If the ranger was lucky, he would have an outrageously clumsy comedy dwarf sidekick who sacrificed himself by the end of reel three. The ranger would, of course, marry the Elf Queen and then be elected King. That last little innovation being a sop to the fact that the Citadel was supposed to have functional democracy now.

'The Elf Queen of Fire Mountain' would not be playing in New Iron Town.

I crept into the barn, through some heavy doors, hat in hand, and up close to where the magic was happening. The noble ranger type, all high cheek bones and windswept hair, was banging on to his men about how it was a particularly fine day to get slaughtered and better this than living under the tyranny of an evil wizard who was about to convert the scenery into ashery. This analysis completely neglected to address the fact that an evil wizard's goblin army needs to eat too. And wasn't it the goblins who first invented husbandry anyway when they domesticated the horse – admittedly for eating purposes, but it all counts? Give credit where it's due, even to goblins.

So, let's just all agree that it's a good day to slaughter and be slaughtered and get on with it and if anybody happens to mention that I have a magic sword, which rather edges me towards the not-being-slaughtered camp, I shall be very cross.

The actor, name of Blaze Rampant (where do they find them?) was really getting fired up. I think he honestly expected his crew of extras to fling themselves bodily at the goblin army, who were mostly sitting around the stage looking bored and playing cards. The goblin army was not actually goblin, on account of the fact that nobody in their right mind now arms up a large number of goblins, even with pretend weapons, not unless they want an actual riot of the proportions that happened during the making of the ill-fated 'Revenge of the Goblin King' – which is what I believe they call irony. The upshot was what you get now: small groups of very ugly men sitting around, cards in hands, all with a false set of goblin gnashers on the tables in front of them, next to their coin stacks.

I had just about had enough of this toshery, and was wondering how I was ever going to find Elsera, when they called a halt and I turned around and found myself face to face with a flame-haired Elf Queen. The full fairy ring: bejewelled tiara, dwarf-silver girdle and a dress made from spider's silk and dreams. She seemed to float about a foot off the ground and if I hadn't been so busy dropping my jaw I would have checked for hidden strings.

'Master Dwarf,' she said, 'first my brother's house and now here. Are you by any chance following me?'

I did a double flip and then began to put the pieces together. Of course, this was who I had seen looking down at me from the entresol at Councillor Truelight's. With a towel round her red hair, I had mistaken her for her sister. Why shouldn't old pointy ears have more than one sister? Just strange that he hadn't mentioned it, but then again, I hadn't asked.

I bowed deeply as this always goes down well with elves. 'Not at all, M'Lady.'

'Nice manners. I'm Selicia Truelight – I'd offer my hand, but the blood's still wet.' She presented the aforementioned hands by way of evidence. The ruby red did indeed glisten as if freshly spilt.

I was nonplussed for a heartbeat before I realised: 'Ah, the old magic of make-believe, eh?'

'No – simply an understudy who was getting above herself. Now, I'd better find the half-wit who calls himself a picture maker. Good day, Master Dwarf.'

She walked off in a cloud of something remarkably close to magic fairy dust.

I noticed a few interested faces now turned in my direction; one was Blaze's and another of them was Elsera's. It was not a smiley face. It was as far from a smiley face as you can get and still actually be a face. She completely froze me and took her non-smiley face outside for some air. I followed her out of an emergency door to the less than salubrious surroundings of a number of large waste bins and immediately found myself on the defensive.

'I'm surprised you needed me for an introduction when you are obviously so well acquainted with the star of this picture,' said Elsera, in a dudgeon so high she'd need a ladder to get down again.

'Steady on, Princess! What makes you think I know her from the tooth fairy?'

'Master Strongoak, the rest of us have been on this film for two weeks now and we've hardly warranted a curt dismissal. You wander onto the scene and you get the full five stars from the Elf Queen! And don't call me Princess!'

'I'm sorry if I walked into your spotlight, but the dainty delight did speak to me, not the other way around.'

Elsera looked at me as if I was rubbing her wand. 'You do know who that was, don't you?'

'Sure, Selicia Truelight – the Councillor's little sister. Big-shot political family. No idea what she's doing here. Is she involved too?'

'Selicia Brightfire Truelight is one of the biggest names in the picture business! And dainty she is not – harder than diamonds is Lady Brightfire.' She almost spat the name out like it was poison.

Brightfire, of course! It all fell into place. Even I had heard of Brightfire – her face was only in every news scroll and on half the hoardings in the Citadel. The official actor in the family, as opposed to her brother's more informal position. No wonder Vericeema had looked familiar too. Brightfire! I really needed to bone up for my popular culture audit. I was failing dramatically on the facial recognition section.

'And she's only his half-sister!' Elsera added venomously.

'Hey, don't get elfish!'

'I'm half elf as well. I'm allowed to be!'

I raised an eyebrow in surprise.

'Yes,' she said, in a voice that suggested she had been asked this more times than she would like to recall, 'just on my mother's side. We don't like to make such a fuss about it and we don't get the perks either!' She went into something like a sulk, pursing those lips in a dramatic fashion.

I find it hard to equate the ladies up there on the screen with the ones walking around on the same streets as you and me. Not that I put them on a pedestal, rather the opposite – they are just creatures of light and fancy and quickly forgotten. Me? I like my women in three dimensions, especially if those dimensions fit a bodice as well as Elsera's currently did. And, even more so, if they also came with flashing dark eyes and lips more inviting than red velvet cushions. So I just reached up and planted my lips on the cushions – it seemed the only thing to do at the time.

It didn't get any complaints, so I did it again. It was rather nice. I think I could be doing it still, if some technical body with a spanner in his hand hadn't stepped out for a quick pipe and disturbed us. They muttered an apology, awkwardly hefted the spanner, and stepped back in again.

'You are certainly full of surprises, Master Strongoak,' said Elsera, straightening the coal-black hair that didn't really need straightening.

'I am that – I can juggle baby dragons, and my needlepoint is admired all the way up to the Lonesome Mountain.'

'Spend a lot of time at your needlepoint, do you, Master Detective?'

'I like the fact that you are effectively making a new fabric via a grid rather than just embellishing a pre-existing one.'

She giggled at my seemingly inappropriate knowledge – hey, I'm a well-rounded sort of dwarf!

'So why don't you introduce me to your boss here and I can let you get back to work – then we can discuss the merits of grid stitching later over dinner.'

'I'm rehearsing a play at the moment. Last night was my only time off for a while. We open at the end of the week, if you're interested?'

Was I interested? Oh yes, I was interested! 'That would be swell,' I said.

'It's serious,' she said, giving me another of those looks with the dial turned up to eleven. 'The play, that is.'

'So am I,' I replied. 'The happy smiling face I show the world is just a mask to hide the pain that the weariness and discontent of everyday existence impart.'

She added to my everyday pain with a swift pat to the noggin and then I followed her indoors.

I got the promised introduction to Elsera's boss and we spoke briefly while she went away to prepare for her next scene as 'encouraging handmaiden 3'. The boss said that my 'battle scars' might be a bit too much 'character' for a comedy sidekick and he would 'let me know soonest', which I'm guessing is rolling picture business talk for 'go pick a fight with a troll'.

I tried not to let my bitter disappointment show too much and made my way back to the Dragonette and the emergency bottle I kept there in the glove box. I wasn't about to drink it alone and instead took it for a walk over to Old Ropey's guardhouse.

'I'm guessing a man could get thirsty stuck out here,' I said.

'I'm guessing a dwarf could too,' he replied.

I waggled the soldier in its brown paper sentry box. 'Wouldn't know of a place where a dwarf could find a couple of cannikins? Just might make killing the soldier look a bit more respectable. There's only one thing worse than a dwarf sucking on a full brown paper bag, and that's a dwarf sucking on an empty brown paper bag.'

Ropey hung up the 'ring bell' sign and motioned me with a well-practised thumb: 'Door's round the back.'

'And so is the dwarf.'

Ropey's guardhouse wasn't much bigger than a gnome's privy, but it was decorated in a style that almost defied description.

'I get my choice from all the company bits and bobs that they are a-throwing out,' he said, by way of an explanation, after noting my very raised eyebrows.

So I sat myself down in a remarkably comfortable iron torture chair, thankfully de-spiked, surrounded by axes, shields, spears, goblin sticks and a far-too convincing yarg skin, as we toasted our wellbeing out of two, thankfully artificial, goblin skulls.

'What do you make of this picture business then, Ropey? You must have seen some things.'

'Ahem.' He cleared his throat. 'A lot of time, talent and trouble goes into making them, of that there is no doubt. Makes you wonder why they don't do something useful with all that energy and endeavour, like maybe building a bridge, discovering something important, or finding a cure for something that needs a-curing.'

'Have to agree with you there. I've always thought there were a lot more interesting things for folk to get up to in the dark.'

'So what brings you up here then, if you're not a-after fame and fortune?'

'The fortune bit sounds fine. I'm just particular about how I earn it.' I decided to level with him and handed over a business card. 'Just between you and me and the Baldy Man for the moment, if that's agreeable?'

He read the legend carefully, 'Well, well, and another well, a Master Detective, eh?'

'I've got me a hand-engraved certificate on the wall that says as much. Plus some honest scars by way of testimonials.'

'I hope you're not looking for anything honest around here. That investigation could stump even a master detective!' Ropey had a good chuckle over that one and then took a good long swig from his skull.

'What I'm looking for, Ropey, is a picture house that might not be averse to having a sideline in the sort of material that's not going to be suitable for the children's early picture show.'

'Ahem, I take it you a-mean the smut circuit?'

'Got it in one.' I brightened his drink as he scratched his ropey chin.

'There's a new outfit, name of Bigelow Pictures. Out to the north, barely in Milkwood proper. Don't seem to have much in the way of any productions out as yet, or so the story goes.' He sipped more slowly at his drink now. 'But, they certainly seem to be busy, oh yes – especially at night!'

'Is that the approved time for such activity?'

'Can be, especially if the owner's trying to rent out to more legit concerns during the day and some of the "talent" have proper day jobs too – or don't want word to get round concerning what they're a-doing.'

'Would this be for the rollies or for glossies too?'

'Probably a-both at the same time. Not an expert meself – like you said, there's better things to be a-doing in the dark!' He chuckled some more and we kicked the soldier about some more too.

I made a mental note of the name and location Ropey had given, and then, insulating his hand some more, headed out in the direction he'd just given. There wasn't much to see, on account of the trees still growing pretty densely in this part of Milkwood. I finally found it. The name 'Bigelow Pictures' promised 'Tomorrow's Entertainment Today'. A long fence, two large gates, and a guardhouse more worthy of the name than Ropey's hut did not look too promising for a look-see, as far as I was concerned.

I parked the wagon some distance from the entrance and slipped quietly through the undergrowth for my look-see. It was dark and surprisingly chilly under the close-growing pines. I felt a shiver that wasn't all down to stories told to dwarf children to stop them sleeping at night and growing too tall. There was an atmosphere in the wood that was far less than pleasant.

The trees were all evergreens; there were none of the broad-leaves more usual for this area. Not the majestic redwoods of Tall Trees, though. These were skinny, sunlight-excluders that huddled together to prevent any other plant life getting a look-in. The shed needles seemed to swallow the sounds of my footsteps, like an impet nipping at my ankles. The local bird-life had voted with their wings and flown off to some warmer, cheerier habitat where the chance of a nice fat grub or two seemed more promising. Something dropped onto the back of my neck and the big tough detective jumped halfway out of his well-buffed skin. The anticipated spider turned out to be all the size of a thumbnail and about as lethal-looking as a hair snarl. Mind you, they do say the smaller ones are the more dangerous. However, you can't stamp on something four feet long, so I'll take the tiny ones any day.

'Come on, Nicely,' I muttered. 'Get a grip! You've been in scarier-looking places trying to find a parking space on a public holiday.' I trudged on, not feeling at one with the world. The ground was getting wetter too and I was about to give this all up as a bad job, and save the tailoring from a trip to the cleaners, when I saw a break in the trees ahead of me.

There was indeed a breach, but a lot of good it did me. Behind it, the fence was just as high and off-putting as it was near the gates. The large buildings within the fenced perimeter looked closed up and were not advertising their function. Somebody had gone to a lot of trouble to make sure Bigelow Pictures was not amenable to casual passers-by. 'Tomorrow's Entertainment' must certainly be something that needs to be kept under close wraps.

$$6$$

THE NEW TREE RENEWAL PARLOUR

I was glad to get the Dragonette back on the road and some fresh air in my lungs. The day was still fine, the ragtop was down and Milkwood was fading behind me. Spiders, who's scared of spiders? Not this dwarf, not driving along in racing green '57 Dragonette anyway.

My meeting with Elsera's boss and the off-hand comment about my 'battle scars' had given me another idea. It has to happen occasionally. I didn't actually question whether it was a good idea or a bad one; sometimes I just go with the flow.

I drove west and south until I hit Scrab Way and from there it was pretty easy to find The New Tree Renewal Parlour again. Even the Greater Citadel traffic system can't outwit a folk bred to find their way around underground in the dark – well, not most of the time, not unless they introduce a one-way system, and then even Rudebeard gets stuck.

I pulled up on the opposite side of the road to the Parlour, under a large low blossoming cherry tree that still provided plenty of peeping space. The Parlour looked as unchanged as a marble monument. Not so much as a shutter had moved. The immaculate lawns might have been painted, for all the movement in the grass. I sat for a short while, eyes open for passing trade. There was none, so I sat for a long while waiting for anything. Around

Midwatch, a delivery wagon of some description drove down the short entrance path and round the back where, presumably, it delivered. If business was any brisker, it would be stagnant.

I thought about a pipe, but knew I was only putting off the inevitable. So I stowed the axe safely away and walked across the road to the path laid through the immaculate lawns, and up to the unprepossessing front door.

I had expected the door to be locked, but it opened easily. On the other side was a quite elegant waiting room, with comfortable-looking recliners and a reception desk, currently unoccupied. There were two white doors leading off the reception area, one on either side of the desk. Which one contained the gold, though, and which one contained the gubbins? That was the thousand-crown question.

I tried one of the seats and they were as comfortable as they had promised to be. In front was a low table that contained artfully arranged promotional material printed on good quality paper with all the right lettering. At The New Tree Renewal Parlour apparently 'it was never too late to feel young again' because 'rejuvenation is only a heartbeat away', and The New Tree Renewal Parlour takes my health very seriously. Well, that was a relief. I didn't want the joker injecting me with monkey glands to have a smile on his face.

Another scroll with a rather fetching image of the New Tree in full flower promised to 'help rectify those minor track marks that injury and the passage of time leave on all of us'. This was more my style, especially if it also included those minor track marks that goblins and the passage of a needle blade leave on us.

The left-hand door opened and out walked a woman only marginally neater than a snowflake and about twice as cold-looking. Her two-piece suit looked like it had been cut in one piece from a rolled plate of silvered steel – not so much business apparel, more occupational armour.

'I'm very sorry to have kept you. Does the Master Dwarf have an appointment?' I had to inform her that the Master Dwarf did not, unfortunately, have an appointment.

'In which case, I'm afraid that Physic Argebester can't see you. He's very busy, which is why we have to insist on a strict appointment system.'

I had seen exactly how busy Physic Argebester was, but I didn't intend to let her know that.

'Look, Dollface,' I said, 'I have fifty gold crowns in my purse and every one of them is shouting at me that maybe Physic Argebester just might find room for me in his busy day.'

Dollface blinked a few times, just for practice, gave me the smile she's been keeping all these long years for this very occasion and then sat down behind her desk to check the diary. 'I can check and see. You might be lucky. Oh yes, we had a cancellation! I had clean forgotten.'

'Well, if you had a cancellation already I guess maybe it's only worth a couple of buckskins,' I quipped, sitting one butt cheek on her desk.

'I don't know what sort of place you think this is!' she huffed.

'We've established that, Dollface, now we're just haggling about the price.'

Sadly, Dollface did not appreciate the niceties of classic gag-making, but we were saved the embarrassment of an explanation by the appearance of what could only be Physic Argebester himself, walking in through the right-hand door.

In The Young Dwarf's Guide to Widergard, wizards are shown as hirsute individuals wearing cheap-cut suits, in a variety of hard-wearing materials, but leaning heavily towards twill. They wear a variety of loud ties, with nasty stripes, that signify that they belong to something that everybody – wizards included – has forgotten. This most worthy of compendiums describes in detail the wizards' habits (lax), origins (unclear) and the likelihood of them wielding any real magic (slim). At the bottom of the wizards' entry, there is a line that says: 'see also sorcerers'. If you do 'see also sorcerers', the first thing in that entry that you will notice is a single phrase, in big, red, unmissable letters: 'WARNING, YOUNG DWARF! DO NOT APPROACH! NOT IF YOU EVER WISH TO BECOME AN OLD DWARF.'

The sorcerer therein depicted is not only hairless, he leaves you with the distinct impression that nothing as trivial as hair growth would ever, under any circumstance, be tolerated – not while there are still virgins to be sacrificed, natural laws to be violated and dreadful dark deeds to be done. The sorcerer's hands are large with long fingers that end in talon-like nails, because nothing else can rip through a young dwarf's flesh with the same ease. Sorcerers generally dress very well with properly tailored suits, although certain aspects of their attire, like wearing spotted ties with striped shirts, do point to the underlying evil of their nature. Extra warning: 'SORCERERS ARE SOMETIMES KNOWN TO WEAR CRAVATS.'

A warning in The Young Dwarf's Guide to Widergard is not to be taken lightly, a double warning more so, and if Physic Argebester was not the very model for the sorcerer entry then he was so close as made no difference. Especially as, around his neck, horror of horrors, there was a cravat.

'Is there any problem here, Nurse Calders?' Physic Argebester enquired.

'None at all,' I shot back before Dollface could pipe up. 'We have just established that I do indeed have an appointment to see you.'

'Then you had better come through.' He gestured towards the still open door.

I smiled at Dollface and gave her a wink for good measure. Her sort always loves a cheery wink. It makes them seethe on long winter nights while they polish their blade collections.

I walked past Argebester's still extended hand (such sharp nails). 'Nice cravat,' I said. 'Such pretty spots, same colour as the shirt stripe.'

We walked down a short picture-less corridor to a picture-less office whose walls were instead broken by a number of very fancy parchments, which all told me just what a smart chap Physic Argebester is. And they told me as much in more languages than I would have thought were strictly necessary to get by anywhere in Widergard.

'We have not had the pleasure of a visit from a dwarf to our little parlour before,' said Argebester, sitting at his desk and offering me, with another gesture of those oh-so-long fingers, the seat opposite. He smiled a smile that was as close as you can get to nails down a blackboard without making any noise.

'Yes, I had a recommendation from somebody in the business.'

'And what business would that be, Master Dwarf?'

'Why, lights and sounds, Argebester! Rolling magic!'

'Oh, yes – entertainment, I see. And you… perform?'

'That's the idea, only this is rather holding me back.' I brushed back the hair that falls over my left eye to reveal the finger-long gash that an inebriated goblin had left as a calling card when I ducked a little too slowly during my first year in the Citadel. Argebester got genuinely excited for the first time and leapt up, rather too quickly for my taste, to get a closer look.

'My, my, Master Dwarf, that is a rather magnificent reminder you have been left with there,' said Argebester. He touched the scar with one of those very long talons and I felt a cold sweat creep up my back and try to escape to some place where a cold sweat can live in peace.

So, I had that much right. Physic Argebester was a skin-changer. Got a problem with your skin? He can change it. Not necessarily a crooked profession, but certainly open to abuse. And Daisy's trail had grown cold here: at the parlour of a skin-changer, and what else might he be?

'So what do you reckon, Physic? Will I ever make the ladies swoon in the front row?'

'I can't promise you that, Master Dwarf, but we could certainly make the scar less noticeable. It would not, alas, be cheap.'

'Let's not mess around, Physic – hit me with the full shovel.'

Argebester picked up a quill and paper and scratched a few notes and then double-underlined what I took to be a total. He then folded the paper neatly in half and handed it to me. I opened it and was instantly reminded that my tax restitution was overdue and this was probably quite close to the last year's earnings.

I scratched my chin and pretended to give it some thought: 'Maybe I'd better see if I can get the job first?'

'Admirable idea… Master…' He paused, waiting for a name. 'Just in case I see it in lights?'

'Bedwell, Bunny Bedwell,' I replied, adding quietly, 'It's my stage name, on account of the fact that Rasillansk Roughneck-Fellingaxe is rather too long for the credits.'

'Excellent then, Master Bedwell. I will wish you a pleasant rest of the day.'

I was fresh out of quips, so I just pocketed the quote and headed to the door, only to find it opened for me by a white-coated, albino assistant, previously unseen. He only bore a passing resemblance to a major snowdrift, snowdrifts not normally coming this big in this part of Widergard. If he wasn't pumping some troll blood then I was a pixie's blind date.

'And Master Bedwell,' said Argebester, from behind me, 'please do make an appointment next time.'

I glanced back over my shoulder at Physic Argebester, but he was already busy at work with the quill, so I had to content myself with laying another cheery wink on Dollface as the albino walked me out. I hoped she appreciated all the effort I was going to, but I had a feeling she had just declared herself a wink-free zone.

I got back to my wagon and made myself comfortable: I had some waiting to do. I got out my pipe.

Business at The New Tree Renewal Parlour continued at its non-existent pace. All those appointments, I hoped Dollface was keeping on top of everything. I finished my pipe and wished I'd thought to bring another bottle for company. However, I did not want this drinking business to become a habit, otherwise I'd need to find another vice. So, I stayed completely professional instead, and if I did happen to nap, I did it on my own time and would in no way bill the client. However, whatever the cause – before I knew it – dusk was upon us and I woke with a start. And as the sun said its goodbyes in the west, The New Tree Renewal Parlour proper opened for business.

Every thirty minutes, sedate headlamps would announce the arrival of a tinted-windowed wagon only slightly smaller than a steamship. A uniformed driver would step out from the front and open a back door for a stooped grey figure who was helped into the parlour by the aforementioned steward. A short while later, the now erect figure would come skipping out of The New Tree Renewal Parlour and have a little dance round the wagon before heading out again.

And this was kept up all through the evening. They were certainly getting through those monkey glands – I hope the monkeys weren't missing them.

Finally, the last set of headlamps disappeared back towards the Citadel. A white delivery wagon I recognised turned up a short while later and stopped in the parking circle round the back. The albino came out and had a sniff, then opened the back doors. After another of those short whiles, Dollface came out, followed by Physic Argebester, and they both got in front. It must have been nice and warm and cosy up there, except

Dollface Calders would drop the temperature down close to freezing the minute she stepped in. The Albino got in the back of the wagon and closed the doors behind him. The wagon pumped some steam and reversed out of the circle, and then fairly rocketed off, heading east. Presumably Physic Argebester had virgins to find, never easy in the Citadel in the spring, and even harder in the summer.

An invisibility cowl or a major magic ring is recommended for serious burglary attempts, but they are rarer than legs on a selkie. So, dressed in my best black breaking and entering two-piece, with matching full-head hood, I snuck across the parking circle like a shadow in a coal mine. The back doors to The New Tree Renewal Parlour had some of the best locks made by man, but then again, I am a dwarf. It took me about five minutes to break in – I'm out of practice with that too.

There is an argument in some quarters about who first invented the lock, dwarfs, elves or men, or whether, perhaps, it was invented independently more than once. Dwarfs don't get involved in this debate because they are convinced of their primacy, but they're also slightly ashamed to admit that they invented the lock before the wheel or fire, in case it reinforces stereotypes.

I didn't want to turn on any lights that might announce my presence to a passing security sentry, but then again, I didn't have to. If you're looking for night vision, go find yourself a dwarf, and we don't even need to eat carrots.

Just to make life even easier, I'd brought a dwarf-light. This handy device throws out light especially suited for those races, that is dwarfs, who come equipped with vision that operates a good bit better at the far end of the spectrum. For me, The New Tree Renewal Parlour was awash with light; for any passing man, goblin, or even elf, it would appear as dark as an ogre's out-hole.

It's great being a dwarf and I wouldn't change a thing for all the magic rings in Widergard, thank you very much.

I made my way carefully from the parking circle entrance to the offices proper. I was interested in Argebester's treatment room, but I was willing to take a sniff at whatever my nose could find. The corridor offered a choice of doors. I picked the most likely one – it led to the cleaner's room. Score 'no points' for the great detective. The second room was more interesting. From the various objects and items of female apparel, I guessed that this was where Dollface hung out when she wasn't on desk duty.

And what a naughty girl Dollface turned out to be! I'd say that she was due a spanking, but from what I found in Calder's cubbyhole, I was pretty sure that she would enjoy it. The number of articles designed specifically for the purposes of restraining and control pointed to a seriously spicy love life or a less than enthusiastic customer list. There was nothing of any use to me, though, my tastes not running in that direction.

I had better luck in the next room. This was some sort of surgery. It was all very clean and the equipment seemed up-to-date and expensive. Maybe Argebester really did warrant the prices he charged. He certainly spent enough on hygiene.

There was a large icebox in the corner. It was locked. Then it wasn't. The various potions inside looked even more convincingly expensive; all those glands can't come cheap. I sniffed a few of the easier to access bottles and came up with a few items that might interest the boys down at Guard Central and a whole rack of plungers lined up ready to go. I guess you don't want to keep the old folks waiting when they've got a party to get to.

I thought I'd hit the dragon's load with my next choice of room. This was obviously Argebester's private office. If I was expecting to find pictures of the goodwife and children, I would have been disappointed. I hadn't and I wasn't. The room had as much character as chewed gum. It was even more sterile than the treatment room. Who cares about a room's character though when it's got filing trunks?

The lock was even more laughable than those on the doors and I was soon engrossed in a little alphabetical investigation. There was nothing under 'D for Daisy' or 'C for Cartersong', but I didn't think there would be. In fact, everything looked depressingly above board. Too well presented, in fact. I had a feeling I was viewing the official version. I looked around the room again. The proportions were wrong. We dwarfs are big on that sort of thing, proportions. It was long and thin when there was no cause for it to be. I went banging on some walls.

The hidden door was behind a bookcase; good to see some people still respecting tradition. It opened onto a short corridor with yet another locked door – when will they ever learn? The lock yielded eagerly and the door opened with a blast of chilled air. I swung my lamp around another smaller treatment room, suppressing an involuntary, very un-Master Detective-like yelp as two eyes stared back at me. It was the million-mile look, the one that sees everything and nothing. The gaze of those who have no interest in whatever may be taking place because they no longer have any contribution to make.

This was obviously not a room meant for public viewing. It was all very clean to be sure, with a ferociously efficient cooling system. The equipment looked as modern as the other room's. However, I couldn't help but think that the severed head of the dead man on the marble slab would have put the paying customers off.

As dead bodies go, this one was deader than most. I've seen statues carved of granite that had more life in them. Then again you can always find marble busts of the old time 'White and Wise' sitting on the shelves in galleries; bodiless real heads are a lot less common. His black hair and handsome face looked familiar, like I'd seen it at the pictures, but we're all family as far as death is concerned. If Argebester was going to manage a renewal job on this squire, he would have earned his gold. I know that popular wisdom has it that a lot of physics must have a sideline in grave-robbing in order to learn their grisly trade, but I've never bought into that. The alternative prospected here was quite chilling. It was where my money was going though, and I did not like that. This was a discontinuity all right.

Trying hard to ignore my severely truncated companion, I quickly explored the rest of the room. I safely concluded that our Physic Argebester was up to something which we detective types refer to as 'no good', but I didn't fancy walking out of The New Tree Renewal Parlour with a head tucked under my arm, even at this time of night. I wanted something equally incriminating, but a little more pocket-sized. I hoped the large filing trunk would provide what I required.

Night lamp clamped between my teeth, I looked to the lock and swore quietly. It was dwarf-made. I could open it, but it would take time – time I now realised I did not have, as voices, one male, one female, leaked through the thin partition wall of the secret room.

'See, I told you there was no one here!'

'That Hidden Watcher is the best on the market.'

The unmistakable tones of Dollface and what had to be the albino assistant; I did not want to be tackling him armed only with a handful of lock picks.

'Then Argebester was fleeced, Calders – they're not going to be stumbling round in the dark.'

'That's Physic Argebester to you, Whitestuff! And it's Nurse Calders. Just remember your place!'

I cursed my over-confidence. No wonder the locks were only rudimentary. A Hidden Watcher could detect a pixie fart and respond with anything from an alarm call to an arrow in the back. I had been lucky.

'We need to check the treatment rooms.'

Thanks for the warning, Dollface. I was out of the room and back in Argebester's office, with the bookcase in place, faster than a pixie's blink.

Here, though, I was stuck. The corridor would lead me into an unwanted confrontation with Dollface and the charmingly named Whitestuff. I looked around the sparsely furnished room. Lacking an invisibility cloak, my onion was surely pickled. I returned to the treatment room, shutting everything behind me. Back in the treatment room, I checked out the grill leading to the cooling system, tough dwarf fingers and nails making short work of the bolts holding it in place. There was just enough room for a small dwarf in the ventilation passage. Unfortunately I am a large dwarf. I am still a very supple one, though, and sympathising empathetically with tinned pilchards everywhere, I quickly crawled out of sight.

A large groan of disbelief marked Dollface's entrance. I gathered she was cross about her boss littering the room with body parts.

'Fetch me a box, Whitestuff – we can't leave this sitting there like so much eel bait!'

'But the doctor…'

'Just do what I say, ice pole! Sometimes Physic Argebester's enthusiasm for his vocation means he leaves his common sense where the ghouls can get at it.'

I'd never considered murder a vocation, but Dollface had just confirmed my fears that this was not a one-off slip with a bunion knife gone horribly wrong.

'You're right though,' Dollface admitted, 'looks like the Hidden Watcher was wrong this time.'

'You want I should phone the company tomorrow?'

'No, the less poking around the better, Whitestuff. Maybe I was being over anxious, but there was something about that gurning dwarf I didn't like.'

Gurning! I can't say my feelings weren't hurt, but as my dear departed grand-da used to say to me, 'It's better to be rich than popular. You can always buy friends.' Sometimes I think I might have inherited a bit too much cynicism from grand-da's side of the family.

The chilled air was getting to me and I had a terrible urge to sneeze. The instant I judged the two were out of the room, I shouldered my way along the passage. Dwarfs are particularly good at this sort of thing, moving in tight spaces. I come from a long line of dwarfs who were good at this sort of thing, which is why there is a long line to begin with. If you're not good then you never make it out of the mine after a cave-in and you don't get to make more little dwarfs. This is what I believe they now call natural selection.

Following the mini-maze of passages was easy for a well-trained surveillance dwarf; circumventing the large fan and cooler was harder, but eventually I reached a vent heading straight to the roof. I chimneyed up this. This involves 'walking up' a narrow opening with your back against one wall and your feet pushing against the other. It's a recreational sport in New Iron Town and a lot of money gets bet on the races, to see who will make it to the top fastest and who will get to the bottom messiest.

It was very pleasant to be out in the warm summer air, not so much fun to be stuck on the roof. It did mean that I got a good view of Dollface and the albino as they carried a box to the waiting white wagon.

BUZZZ for a hundred crowns, Nicely Strongoak – can you guess what is in the box? Yes, I could guess what was in the box. Unfortunately, I had a feeling that if I was to call the Cits to come take The New Tree Renewal Parlour to small pieces, we were both going to end up looking more foolish than those types who wear three-quarter length trousers with pockets at the knees. Of the bodiless squire, I judged there would now not be a trace.

I crouched down and watched the ill-matched pair drive off. There was little chance of me getting to my wagon in time to follow them, as I was stuck on a roof. It was a very nice roof as roofs go. I was particularly pleased to see that the builders had not skimped on the drainage pipes. It does make climbing down so much easier, but the parlour employees were long gone.

My Dragonette was waiting for Daddy and I threw my now dusty burglary-wear into the trunk and made my way carefully home in a strange, grim mood somewhere between thoughtful and spitting-blood. I did not believe the upper body part I had seen had been a voluntary donation.

There was a scroll from my message service waiting for me when I finally made it back home to the Armoury. Getgold Grounding was looking for me, not for information on the missing Daisy as I'd expected, but because a friend of his needed a favour – if I wasn't too busy. The sort of request that did not improve my disposition – favours being very hard to eat, drink or romance on a moonlit summer evening.

I went to my bed still worrying about Daisy and thinking about how exactly I was going to make sure that Physic Argebester found himself inconvenienced in the liberty stakes. I woke up shouting some time before dawn in a terrible sweat with a multicolour dream still running in the picture house of my mind. In the distance, a severed head was trying desperately to tell me something. I got closer, but with no air to draw on, his wordless message was impossible to hear. I felt sure I should know who this head belonged to. On closer inspection, I realised it was mine.

Getting back to sleep after that was not easy, and I kept waking with a start, grabbing at my legs and torso, as if to make sure they were still there. I was glad to greet the sunrise with everything still in place.

7

OLOBATO THE WISE

The next day I spoke on the horn with Getgold's mealy-mouthed assistant, who put me in the picture. It turned out the celebrated Getgold's friend was the reasonably famous dwarf, Lobsk Wideswing, and the favour concerned the marginally only less well-known gnome Olobato the Wise. I was familiar with both the names, Lobsk Wideswing and Olobato the Wise being two of the sort of characters for which the Fourth Level is renowned.

The Fourth Level is a strange place, although strange is a very relative term in a Citadel where a transvestite troll will hardly turn a head, but spitting without a licence can get you three years in Dun Thievin. In the whole of Widergard and in the whole of the Hill, there is probably no place like it, except for the Fifth Level, and the Third, and most of the Second. The Fourth, though, is the Citadel in a microcosm, infuriating, uplifting, fascinating, and if you could bottle it, you could at least throw it into the ocean.

I'd first heard about Olobato Bolobo some years ago, when I thought I could help folk more and hit folk less. The gnome, known to all as Olobato the Wise, was revered amongst all the folks in his neighbourhood, and half the Fourth Level, for being the person you went to when you had a problem.

Should my father plant barley next year, Olobato?

Should I let my daughter marry the stranger from Lower Hungerstone, Olobato?

Should we devalue the gold half-sovereign, Olobato?

All right, the last one wasn't true, but essentially problems remain pretty much the same, whoever you are and whatever the year: food, love and money. And so folk were always coming to Olobato with their worries, gripes and fears, because he was very wise and excellent on matters of the stomach, heart and purse. However, as we all know, virtue is its own reward, and so Olobato the Wise, for most of his life, was also Olobato the Broke. He did not have two blods to rub together. And you never got many blods to the half-crown, not even in those happier, sunnier days when you could go out for a night on the tiles and still come back with two kidneys and a fair collection of tiles.

Because he was always swimming in Prince Penury's moat, one day, or so I was told by Getgold's assistant, Olobato the Wise had gone to his neighbour, Lobsk Wideswing, hat in hand, to ask a favour. The favour was granted, and another favour was then granted, and one thing led to another, until now, Getgold Grounding was asking me to do Lobsk a favour – that's how things tend to work in the Citadel. Here, favours breed favours at a rate even conies would envy.

Lobsk was Old Mine: mean and belligerent, and if he had a good word for anybody, he never used it. He wouldn't want it to wear out, as he might never find another. He was the sort of dwarf who reminded me why I had moved out of New Iron Town in the first place. Unfortunately, he also arrived in the Citadel long before I did and was now a prominent member of the Citadel's dwarf community too, which was not large, but was influential, which is how he knew Getgold. It was said that Lobsk had the ears of several elvish aldermen, and I believe this to be true, but I don't think he kept them in a small box under his bed as is also rumoured. If you did not want to get on the wrong side of the Citadel Brothers, when Lobsk Wideswing sneezed, you offered him your sleeve.

This was a distraction I could have done without at the moment. I needed to get onto Physic Argebester's trail straight away, but had better tread carefully. His client list looked like it could generate a lot of trouble for a small businessman like myself. Wrafe was out on a case when I called, so I left a message advising him to check out the good physic, as he might have the answers for some of the Guard's 'health' problems. I also contacted Doroty, at Criminal Records, to start the search for the body without the body. I gave her a very full description of his looks, but when I explained why I couldn't even guess at his height she went very quiet. Doroty has an innate sense of justice; Argebester now had a plaid-wearing bespectacled bloodhound on his trail. I wouldn't be sleeping nights if I were him. I also mentioned Dollface, as I didn't think her past was milky white. Then I sat and worked out the connection to Daisy and how I could bring maximum pain down onto The New Tree Renewal Parlour and all who worked there.

However, I also still have to pay the bills. So in the afternoon I went to meet Lobsk Wideswing on the Fourth Level, sleeve at the ready, and found Lobsk had a whole pot of pepper up his nose. Once there, I let him embroider the rest of the tapestry for me. It made for a rather bizarre picture.

'Let me get this straight, brother Wideswing, in a pure un-adorned, ungilded nutshell, you want me to go to this Olobato the Wise … and ask him for your pot back?'

'That, Master Detective, is indeed what I want you to do. If it is not beyond the abilities that your previous years in the Citadel Guards may have eroded away.'

I took another sip from the glass of Dragon's Breath that had been placed into my hand as soon I passed through the threshold of his Fourth Level retreat. Although it was early, I didn't fight too much, as Dragon's Breath is harder to find in the Citadel than an elf's modesty. Also, the bottle was in the charge of a young woman that I took to be Lobsk Wideswing's housekeep, and she could have stolen the breath from a midden-wight. I tried not to stare at her, but you had more chance of getting an ogre to use a deodorant – it just wasn't going to happen. She had more curves than the River Everflow and legs that were wasted on locomotion. A tilt of her head was a treatise in philosophy and her hair was a purer gold than any metal a smith could ever hope to make. It was the eyes that really made you stop in your tracks though: a honey colour that was every summer day you ever wanted to waste away with your feet dipped in a cool stream as you listened to the bees go about their business in the mountain meadows. To see her was to be reminded that elves do not have a monopoly on blonde gorgeousness – especially if your taste runs more to the animal than the ethereal. 'Woof,' I say.

What she was doing waiting house for Lobsk Wideswing was anybody's guess.

I was very sorry to see her dismissed with no introduction and a casual wave of one of Lobsk's heavily ring-decked hands. I turned my attention back to my drink, which was also worth the effort. Lobsk Wideswing may have had a reputation for being tighter than a water sprite's out-hole, but he was old-fashioned enough, and indeed old enough, to understand the obligations of a host.

Dragon's Breath this good rarely made it as far south as the Citadel and there were probably several laws that tried to enforce the situation. My wage in the Citadel Guards had certainly never allowed the purchase of even the smallest bottle –

colourfully known as a Pixie's Spit. On the table next to Lobsk Wideswing, the unnamed housekeep had left a whole Necromancer – a bottle so large it is said the contents were enough to raise the dead or promote you to that very state of being. For it is universally known that when you pour Dragon's Breath, you measure the quantity in drops, or you measure your hangover in days.

'Wouldn't it be easier, not to say quicker, to go ask this Olobato for the pot yourself?' I felt obliged to ask finally.

Lobsk shifted his not inconsiderable frame uncomfortably. He filled his seat like wine fills a barrel. I am tall for a dwarf, the size of many a short man, and Lobsk was short by dwarf standards – hardly taller than a gnome; not that anybody with more than a passing attachment to their head would ever have mentioned this of course. His hand axe, sitting on its rest, was beautifully crafted and you could hear drafts get cut in two – sisssh – whenever the housekeep opened the door.

What Lobsk lacked in the vertical, he more than made up for in the horizontal. Lobsk Wideswing was, without a doubt, wide. He did not concern himself overmuch about personal grooming; his hair and beard were unknotted and unkempt and a valuable food supply in times of famine. He did not seem a likely compatriot of the urbane Getgold Wideswing, but you never can tell.

Lobsk's glass of Dragon's Breath disappeared one more time into the bushy undergrowth covering his face before he finally replied to my question. 'I have spoken with him. The answer did not satisfy me.'

I could tell that Lobsk was not to be drawn further and so I took his case, if case it might be called, and made my way round the Hill to where Olobato had his home.

The Citadel is a defence commander's dream and a town planner's nightmare. The five large gates, in the five large walls that subdivide the original monumental municipality, are offset to make any invading horde have to maraud just that bit further. Then maybe, just maybe, they might decide they've had enough of all the pillaging, and the sea looks very inviting today, so let's all go for a dip down on the Gnada peninsula. The Gates provide the only way up and down between levels and life tends to get rather lively around them, although property prices never seem to mind. Olobato's home was as far away from the Fourth Level gate, The Tree Friend's Gate, as you could be without getting closer to it again. It was also north-facing, which is not a major selling point in the Citadel either. These two factors combined to make the area as quiet as almost anywhere in the Citadel can be – slightly eerie when you are used to the shouts, grunts and whistling steam trains that form the normal soundtrack to Citadel life. If you couldn't exactly hear a pixie sneeze, then you could at least hear yourself think. This makes for a pleasant change, but as lifestyle choices go, I'll take the bells and whistles.

I knocked on Olobato's door, but all inside seemed even quieter than without. I found a business card and left a short note saying I would return the next day after Midwatch. I had enough chores to keep me busy. Getgold's missing youngster and the King of Elfland's White Finger were both going to need serious attention.

I felt the need for a drink with more head, volume and body than a Dragon's Breath and I followed my hanging tongue to a small inn not too far away.

The Hand and Hart was busy for a work night, heavy with the smell of gnome weed and none the worse for it. Thankfully they had not neglected the quality of the ale and it positively flung itself from the barrel into the pot, demanding immediate consumption. Who was I to argue?

I noticed an interesting mix of folk heading into a back room and, being the sort of dwarf who is up for anything after a couple of shots of Dragon's Breath, I followed them. The room was larger than I expected, actually hewn into the very hill itself, all pleasantly homely with a small stage at the far end and the tables arranged to help the view. There was already a considerable buzz of excitement, especially from the large gnome contingent. I planted myself on one of the few available seats with some curiosity, just as the lanterns dimmed.

I never noticed when the singing started; it was like trying to catch the sound of a far-away waterfall while standing in a summer forest glade, impossibly sweet and full of longing. But soon it grew, became a bubbling brook coursing over bright pebbles in the sunlight and I was carried back to a time when the only voice that could be heard in the land was the song of water as it made its journey to the sea. The brook became a river and the singer took the stage. I had met her hours and an age ago in the house of Lobsk Wideswing, but here she was the Mistress. Clad in lily-white, she carried me, carried all of us, coursing across the land as she sang her river song; now wild white water cutting deep chasms and reshaping the earth, then swollen with winter storms to flood meadows and grasslands. Finally, mighty now, deep and invincible, she gave herself to the wide sea. Then she was gone. I leapt to my feet, applauding madly along with everybody else in the room. We wanted more, but knew we had to be content – I mean, you don't ask for a repeat performance from a sunset either, do you?

I went to refill my pot, having no recollection of emptying it the first time. I had just paid when a now familiar voice spoke to me from behind.

'Did Lobsk send you?'

I turned to greet the warbler. She was wrapped in a long green robe and looked anxious.

'Now why would you think that?' I asked.

'You are kin.' I wasn't sure if this was a statement or a question.

'We only share a Citadel address and a taste for good spirits.'

'Do you share his other tastes?'

I managed to look deep into her honey eyes, unsure what she was saying, and she looked right back like she'd done it before. 'You were at Lobsk's and now you're here.' She shrugged and pulled her robe tighter, looking away before adding, 'He doesn't like me singing.' As if that explained everything – well, not to me it didn't.

'My Lady, it is a free country – slavery is hardly ever fashionable and even the goblins get a vote.'

'So, a coincidence then?'

'Lady, I was only in need of a drink.'

This seemed to satisfy her and she nodded once and then walked away. I still hadn't picked up a name, but then again, she hadn't dropped one. At least the barkeep was impressed. 'She doesn't normally talk to the paying custom,' he let me know, as soon as I could tear my eyes away from the departing figure. 'That makes you a special friend, I'm supposing.'

'In which case I suppose I won't need to pay in future?'

'A man, or dwarf, could get thirsty that way.'

'But would I even notice with singing like that?'

'You would with your tongue hanging out like it is – it would shrivel up eventually.'

Once we had convinced ourselves of just exactly how cute we both were, we got to some proper conversation while the barkeep cleaned some pots.

'The warbler – I don't see no playbills up – not even a name?'

'Professionally, they call her "The River Woman".'

'And unprofessionally?'

'The River Woman.'

'Guess, I'll call her The River Woman then.'

'And we don't need to put up playbills. Whenever she sings, the place is full.' The barkeep put some life back into my pot and waved away the change.

'You won't get rich that way.'

'Hey, any friend of The River Woman is a friend of mine, remember!' He shook a tray of pots straight from the washer and began shaking them. 'But just so you know, she has a lot of friends.'

He carried the pots away to the drying cupboard, leaving me unsure as to whether I had just received a warning or been welcomed into the club.

The next day, as the last Citadel bell rang midwatch, I knocked on Olobato's door. A distinguished, familiar-looking gnome with a broad smile opened up. I asked if he was Olobato. He said 'yes' and asked me my business. I gave Olobato another card. He asked me in. I like it when matters proceed like that. I am just a sucker for the old-fashioned approach to life.

Olobato's home was cosy enough in the gnome style, all round windows and doors. Everything was old and slightly foxed, which spoke of a family that has seen better days. At least they hadn't been turfed out to the Bayside slum that became the Little Hundred.

We settled in his snug study and he offered me a pipe. It was a little early for me, but sociable is my middle name: 'Nicely Sociable-liable-to-die-of-overdoing-it Strongoak' to be exact. He passed me a pipe and a flap-match with a nice promotional image on it.

Olobato's version of the story was somewhat more involved than Lobsk's, but between the two tales I pieced together a reasonable version of events. Olobato had indeed gone to Lobsk, hat very much in hand, and from there I judged the tale to have unfolded something like this.

'Neighbour,' said Olobato to Lobsk, 'I am in distress. I have many relatives coming for the celebration of my boy's kelefko and I cannot buy a pot that is large enough to cook for all of them, could you lend me one?'

Lobsk was obviously not happy with this. He was not happy like a constipated troll who has just been diagnosed with porcelain piles, but Lobsk wasn't able to think of a reasonable excuse for not lending the pot to his neighbour. As mentioned, dwarfs are big on manners, if not on generosity, and so Lobsk lent Olobato the pot. It was indeed a fine large pot and Lobsk Wideswing did not use it much, because he really wasn't that well liked. It suited Olobato down to the ground, which admittedly wasn't very far.

The day after the kelefko, Lobsk was pacing, anxiously waiting for the pot's return. Truth be told, he probably hadn't slept well ever since the pot had left his sight. Some dwarfs give the rest of us a really bad name, but never ask to borrow my razor.

Olobato promptly returned the pot and on looking inside (most likely to see if it had been cleaned properly), Lobsk saw another, much smaller, pot.

'Neighbour Olobato,' said Lobsk, 'there is another pot in here.'

'A miracle, neighbour,' said Olobato, with a smile and a wink. 'The pot has had a child.'

Much pleased, Lobsk took his pots into the kitchen and admired his new acquisition. There is nothing a dwarf likes better than what is technically referred to in Old High Dwarfish as a 'damn good deal'.

If only events had stopped there, I would probably have never heard any more of Olobato the Wise and certainly had no occasion to visit him, despite his wisdom. On matters of the purse, I have long ago accepted that I won't ever purchase a detached property in the rarefied air of High Trees. On matters of the heart, I believe that true love is rarer than a goblin's breath mint, and on matters of the stomach: I've got a cookbook. Olobato the Wise, unlike Lobsk Wideswing, may not have had much to shout about in the crockery department, but he did however, have a large family and many friends.

So, some weeks later, Olobato returned to his neighbour Lobsk and said, 'Neighbour, it is time for my daughter's birthday and many relatives will be with us once again. May I use your fine large pot again?' Lobsk was actually secretly delighted, hoping to increase his pot collection further. He hurried to fetch his large pot and the day after the birthday, when Olobato returned, Lobsk was very pleased to find that there were two small pots inside.

'Neighbour Olobato,' said Lobsk, 'there are two pots in here.'

'Another miracle,' said Olobato, with a merry wink. 'The pot has given birth to twins!' Lobsk took his new pots and put them on the fine new pot shelf he had especially constructed. The cost for the wood and the labour for its erection were more than any reasonable number of small pots would have cost, but that wasn't the point. And if you don't see the point, then you are not a dwarf and I do not recommend that you pursue a career in the understanding of dwarf psychology; actually, I don't recommend that under any circumstances.

Now, after the third time that Olobato borrowed the pot (for his brother's anniversary – they do have a lot celebrations, those gnomes), Lobsk could hardly wait for Olobato to return. He looked at his fine new pot shelf and the space that just cried out for further pots and told himself to be patient – a trick akin to getting a dragon to gargle.

The day of the anniversary came and went, and the day after that, and the day after that, and still no Olobato. On the fourth day, Lobsk could not bear it any longer and he called upon Olobato.

'Neighbour Olobato,' said Lobsk, his hand only lightly resting on his fine sharp hand axe. 'I have just come to enquire about my pot.'

Olobato cast his eyes down, shook his head sadly, and took a breath before replying, 'Dear neighbour, please prepare yourself. I have been trying to find the right words to break the news. Your pot, your poor pot… has died.'

Lobsk went immediately home and told Getgold, and Getgold tooted on the speech horn to me. Now here I was, sitting in Olobato's comfortable home, with the well-polished wood and the well-worn rugs and scratching the stubble that had grown since my morning shave. Finally, I spoke: 'Good Olobato, I think perhaps it's a little too much to expect Lobsk Wideswing to believe his pot has died.'

'Oh yes?' said Olobato, fixing me with the very stare that might well have earned him the designation 'wise'. 'However, he did manage to believe it had given birth – twice!'

I had to admit the gnome had a point. I made my way slowly back to Lobsk, my dawdling not totally down to the gnome weed.

On the Fourth Level, there is a rather splendid viewpoint. Locally it is called, with typical Hill economy, 'the viewpoint' – in case you ever need to ask for directions. I stood there and leaned on the balustrade to clear my head, looking over the famous Lion Rampart, the lower levels and the suburbs, all the way to Bayside and the distant delights of the Gnada Peninsula. All very – and deceptively – pretty. Because out there was a mix of folk that might well use a common language, and breathe the same air, but otherwise had less in common than the small dog and cat, some way below me, currently disputing ownership of the remains of what I sincerely hoped was a rabbit. I heard a true tale on the squeak box the other night about how we all actually share a common ancestor, dwarfs, elves, men, goblins – even the tree friends, apparently. Enough to make a few of my departed ancestors start gnawing coal in their graves, and I don't know if the idea holds water. What I do know is that if we don't want this overheating cauldron of a Citadel to blow up in faces, somebody has to keep one hand on the pressure release valve. As if on cue, the whistle of a street-train woke me from my reverie and I caught a whiff of that oh-so-familiar mix of steam, coal and oil. An unlikely combination in many ways, as is the Citadel.

I stepped back lively now to Lobsk's to acquaint him with Olobato's explanation. The honey-eyed housekeep let me in without meeting my eye, or mentioning our conversation, and led me through to where Lobsk sat at his desk. She left quietly, closed the door behind her and then, I am willing to wager, pressed one perfect ear softly up against it.

I retold Olobato's tale. Lobsk chewed his beard and hummed and harred and even produced what I can only describe as a 'harrumph'. Finally, he settled into a state of what I sincerely hoped was enlightened acceptance. I even waved my normal fee – well, apart from expenses, of course. The housekeep let me out again with a barely audible 'thank you'. I wasn't sure what for. I went home and poured myself a drink in a tall glass that I didn't really want or need. I proceeded to then pour it down the sink. I said, 'Thank you.' I wasn't sure what for either.

8

THE CITADEL GUARD

The next day I got to the office, picked up the post and transferred most to the bin, working on the assumption that I hadn't already 'won a thousand gold crowns' and had probably read as many scrolls as I was ever likely to – condensed or not. My rooms in the Two Fingers are not extensive or expensive, because if I am busy enjoying the office I am not busy paying the rent on it. There is a room for waiting that I generally refer to as the waiting room, and the main office, which sometimes I crazily call the main office. The two are connected by a door as I am also something of a traditionalist too.

My main office has the expected selection of chairs, files and trunks and a rather nice desk that has admittedly seen better days. Pride of place goes to my dartboard. The purpose of the dartboard is to keep my eye–hand co-ordination in tip-top condition and to allow me to vent my spleen by using pictures of prominent Citadel personalities for target practice. The fact that the dartboard only currently featured the regular arrange-ment of rings just shows what an even-tempered, mild-mannered and amiable dwarf I am and that the last picture of Verland Coddlestone had been shredded to pieces.

The waiting room has a sofa and dust.

I kicked the bin about a bit before sitting down to plan the day. I needed to see Wrafe of the Citadel Guards about the White Finger, but the Citadel Guards needed to see me more. They were in the waiting room before I'd even dented the office seat and they weren't keen on doing any waiting. Sometimes it's just a complete waste of a room.

The new Captain himself turned up, as bright and cheerful as guards always are, with two very self-consciously serious Rangers who looked like they were only just familiarising themselves with razor use and hadn't found time to even consider detective work. Captain Shephall was one of the new breed of guards – the sort who values procedure more than instincts. So instead of a nice friendly chat in my office, we went round and down the Hill to the Citadel Guards' Central Watchtower and did it all officially.

Shephall sat me in a small room, with only a single table, a flickering lamp and a large glass ashcup for company. He gave me some time by myself just to feel at home. Whether he considered that the appalling lighting alone would be enough to have me break down sobbing and admit to whatever it was I was down there to admit to, I don't know. I just wished I'd had time to make myself some coffee. The coffee in this place was terrible.

A little while later, a big old unicorn bug joined me, all shiny armour and a horn that would have made a Witch Queen blush. He trundled across the table top towards me with all the confidence of a goblin army about to pillage a children's nursery; until he hit the ashcup. The ashcup didn't move. So he reversed and went at it again. Still the ashcup wouldn't budge. He kept on hitting his head all the time I was sitting there, but the ashcup didn't and couldn't move. I think that big old unicorn bug was trying to tell me something, but I've always been hopeless with portents.

This break in my routine actually provided some very useful thinking time and allowed me to begin to shift a few pieces around in my mind. I could have done with the same time again, but the guard only had to go and spoil it by interrupting. Shephall came in and gave me the silent treatment while a rather over-excited mouthpiece I didn't know asked a lot of questions about Lobsk Wideswing. I answered them, giving it back as straight as they needed. How well did I know him? When had I seen him last? How had he seemed and what was the nature of our business? The last question got particularly short shrift, as if I was really going to hand them that sort of information with a paper. They then went away again, before coming back some time later with the same questions in a different order. I complied, but the third time they tried this game I got kind of bored and said as much, adding that if they wanted to detain me, I needed to see the charge-sheet, otherwise I had a heavy date later and needed to go have my top knot waxed.

'Got something to hide, dwarf?' said Shephall, finally wading in, practising his hard man act.

'Only my genius and my modesty,' I replied. I had my smart dwarf act perfected and didn't need to practise.

'Oh, we like 'em modest, don't we?' Shephall looked at his mouthpiece for confirmation of his toughness, which was immediately corroborated.

'Look, Captain – I know you're only fishing. You know I know you're only fishing, and while fishing is a swell thing to do on a sunny afternoon while the ale is cooling in the river, wouldn't we all be better off doing some real detective work or maybe taking up a proper occupation like bee-keeping? I hear they are in danger, all those poor bees; got to feel for them, haven't you?'

They both went away again. Then someone in a small office somewhere wrote up all my answers using one of those new machines that have put a whole bunch of scribes out of work and given a whole lot more jobs to the happy goblins brought in to fix the machines when they break down. I then was given a quill to sign the printed paper – got to love progress!

I left the little room to the unicorn bug and the ashcup. I knew he was never going to move a thing that size, but I wished him luck anyway.

I still had no idea what had happened to Lobsk Wideswing, but I was guessing it wasn't anything that came under the heading of 'good'. Leaving the watchtower, I 'bumped' into Wrafe and he offered to give me the heads up after he had walked me out. We found a quiet spot to share some smoke behind the lifted wagon pound. We filled our pipes, I gave him a flap-match, and we sat down for a minute or ten while he told me the full story.

The word was that after I had left him yesterday, Lobsk sat in his room for the rest of the afternoon watch, the contents of the Necromancer by his side steadily diminishing. According to a statement given to the Citadel Guard by his housekeep, one M. Almondspring, and later released to the news scrolls, he ate a light supper and said he would be taking some documents with him early to his bed. The documents were found in his room and several were signed with that same date. However, it appears that Lobsk later, after dark, slipped some clothes on and went out and torched Olobato's house and all the inhabitants and all the goods therein.

Lamp fuel, tinder and flint were found the next morning stacked neatly in Lobsk's front porch.

'Looking pretty cut and dried, Nicely – a silly argument over a pot that got completely out of control. Would you credit it? Unless there is something you can add that maybe didn't make your statement to the Captain?'

I turned to Wrafe and shook my head slowly. 'Like you said, a quarrel over crockery – go figure!'

Wrafe looked out over the lower levels. 'Maybe I'm getting old, Nicely – but what happened to the days when saying "sorry" did the job after an argument?'

'Ever heard of an iron apology, Wrafe?' He shook his head. 'It's dwarf slang for an axing. My kin do not always work by what other races might consider the normal rules.'

'So I've heard. Present company included.' Wrafe threw me back my flap-matches. 'Just remember, I'm not the only one who knows that.'

I pocketed my matches.

'Just one other thing, Wrafe. I was talking to Josh, he was saying how missing children numbers are increasing. Is that news from the Old Thrush?'

Wrafe pulled on his pipe before he spoke. 'It is against official Guard policy to comment on such unsubstantiated rumours. I'm sure you appreciate that.'

'That bad, eh?'

'That bad.'

And on that sour note, we said our goodbyes. The only thing I had not mentioned to Wrafe was the reason that Olobato had seemed familiar to me at that first meeting. It had nothing to do with his famed wisdom or possible previous encounters. I realised just this morning that he had been one of the gnomes I'd seen watching The River Woman sing. How can I be sure? Well, the next day Olobato lit my pipe with a flap-match emblazoned with an image of a white hand and a running deer. I'd seen a bowl of them on the bar at the Hand and Hart. I'd got one in my pocket now. Wrafe had just given it back to me. I'd picked it up last night when I went back to speak with The River Woman again, except she was long gone.

I left the watchtower and walked back to the office via the Hand and Hart; she wasn't there today either. I had a feeling she never would be there again, not now. Speaking to the barkeep, it appeared that she had given her statement to the guards at Citadel Central, come round early to collect her pay, and then high-tailed it, leaving nothing personal at the inn.

I'd wanted to ask her about something that she had mentioned after her set. A question about 'tastes' – it was bothering me, like a rusty ring in your chainmail, but I'd left it too late now. I had a drink with the barkeep, just to be sociable. We talked about Lobsk and the unfortunate Olobato, and what this particular hard luck story from the Naked Citadel told us. That we should be more tolerant of each other's failings and foibles perhaps? After our third or maybe fourth flagon we agreed that most of all what this tells us is this: in the Citadel, it is good to know a smart trick, and good to know a clever story too, but it is even wiser to know your neighbours.

It's good to know your clients as well, as I was about to learn. When I got back to the office, there was a note from the message service saying Getgold Grounding wanted to see me. Even as dwarfs go, Getgold Grounding was not a happy, small hairy individual. Now, many might say that dwarfs are not by nature designed for the cheerier emotions, prone as they are to fits of melancholia and rage. It is true that rampaging blood lust is more usually associated with my kin than a snappy way with an amusing aphorism or punchline, but to consider us lacking in humour and happiness in general would be a totally wrong conclusion to jump to. The comedian or joker has always had an important role in dwarf communities. He is, after all, the person who, by tradition, everybody throws the dung at. Now, you might think that this is to belittle the position of joker – not at all. I mean, as we were all aware, while the joker was getting the dung thrown at him, they weren't throwing it at you. There was therefore a lot of good will extended to the joker in a dwarf community and he could always be guaranteed extra helpings in the refectory, even if nobody wanted to sit next to him.

Why a comedian should get dung thrown at him is central to the very concept of dwarf humour, which, admittedly, does tend towards the scatological, amongst many other bodily functions. Add to this a fondness for both observational and physical comedy, resulting in side-splitting quips like, 'Oh look, Sobright's cut his foot off with his own axe – ha, ha, ha!' and you can begin to see why throwing dung at somebody might be considered such a belly laugh.

Fortunately, dwarf humour has become somewhat more sophisticated in modern times, thanks to the introduction of enormous pulped paper heads. This most fertile of additions to the comedic arts has taken off big time in the dwarf world, and why not? Is there actually anything funnier than a drunk dwarf lurching round wearing an oversized head, made of paper, usually featuring the features of a prominent personality, preferably an elf? No, I thought not.

One unexpected consequence of the original role of the joker in dwarfdom was that the colloquial shorthand for 'comedian' and 'latrine' became the same. This has caught out many an old-mine dwarf visitor flicking through their phrase scrolls on a visit to the Citadel. However, having seen some of the stand-ups in the local bars here, maybe it is more appropriate than you would think.

Are constant laughter and jollity actually a good indication of happiness, anyway? In New Iron Town, they would probably get you locked up. But then again there is an old dwarf saying that goes something like 'gold does not give you happiness – gold is happiness', which explains a lot more about dwarfs than I should probably let on.

Whatever, Getgold was certainly not a happy dwarf by anybody's criteria, and like many a red-blooded dwarf, when not happy, he liked to hit things and hit them hard. At the moment, the thing he was hitting was a small, white, dimpled ball made from dried tree sap. He could hit it a long way, that was for sure.

'Six hundred yards if I'm not mistaken,' said Getgold, looking through the range spyglass to find his distant ball.

'Give or take a pixie's spit,' I replied.

Getgold looked for further confirmation down the body of the tube. I whistled a happy tune, very quietly. Anybody else might have thought my lips were pressed tighter than an elf's purse, but inside I was whistling a happy tune.

The shooting range at the Very Royal and Very Ancient Golf Ground was a relatively new addition and I hadn't been there before. Not that I'd exactly had to fight off that many invitations to play the normal nine holes either. To say the VR&VA was exclusive was like accusing a dragon of kleptomania. For many of the White and Wise, getting their son's name down at the VR&VA came before the announcement of the birth or figuring out anything as trivial as schooling. It had taken me an hour to find the range, on account of the fact that, for many folk, exclusivity equals inaccessibility. The range could be accessed quite easily from the golf ground by foot, but driving there directly was like trying to follow a grey host through a fog bank.

The shooting range was certainly a great place to get some driving practice in, or to work off your frustrations by pretending the golf ball was your least-favoured private detective.

'Yes, six hundred yards, Sir! Excellent shot!' Getgold's rather wan-looking mouthpiece confirmed his drive distance. A man with some pedigree apparently, but all the personality of wet parchment; he had a name, but it was one of those names that you'd forget almost before you'd heard it. His only function in life was to make sure everything was rosy in Grounding's garden – whatever he got paid, it wasn't enough.

'Have you ever struck a ball that distance, Master Detective?'

'I can't say I have,' I admitted. But I didn't mention that I'd never used a box to stand on either, or worn trousers of the length he was sporting – fine on the long legs of an elf lord like Truelight, not exactly dwarf apparel. And life is far too short to wear pastels anyway.

The use of the box is somewhat controversial in dwarf golfing circles. There is no doubt that dwarfs can hit things hard – no race can hit harder: these shoulders aren't just for filling jackets. However, golf is all about levers too. Tall races get a wider arc with their longer clubs but they can easily lose control. I played a round with one junior scout while I was in the Guards, who was definitely packing troll blood. He earned himself the nickname 'Slice', so wayward was his aim. Those longer clubs get heavier too, which makes the swing harder to control again. You need to stand comfortably over the ball, not crouch or stretch back, and the normal, shorter, dwarf club then loses something in zip. So it's all about compromise, or standing on a box and using a longer club.

I wouldn't use a box and neither would I wear the ridiculous trousers Getgold had on either.

He sent another ball flying. I was now sure that they each had 'Nicely' written on them. The mouthpiece broke into another well-practised spontaneous round of applause: 'Oh, well hit, Sir!'

'Yes, looks like another six hundred yards,' Getgold said, looking down the spyglass provided for this purpose.

'At least, Master Grounding!' Fawn, fawn, fawn, give the boy a raise.

'I find,' continued Getgold, 'that golf can provide us with many useful lessons for life.' He picked another ball out of his bucket and examined it before commencing. 'You may make your finest, longest shot but find yourself with a terrible position, whereas a poor shot might get rewarded with an excellent lie.' He set his ball on the pin and addressed it carefully. 'Either way, you have no choice but to play the ball where it sits. And then at the next hole you do it all over again.'

Getgold struck the ball with considerable force, only to see it squirt off to his right. 'See, now I've sliced it.'

I'd had enough. 'Master Grounding, as much as I'd like to stand here and discuss the finer points of golf with you, I've got a business to run. So, if you want to chew me out about your chum, Lobsk, go ahead. I was doing you a favour and did as he asked me to as well. If he then decides to fade and torch some poor gnome's home over something as trivial as a cooking pot then he's a big boy and now he has to take his medicine.'

Getgold gripped his club even tighter. 'I am not accustomed to being spoken to like that, not by my employees.' Indeed, it looked like the mouthpiece was about to pass out with the sheer shock of the language being thrown around.

'Look, Getgold, you bought my time, not my papers, and that makes me a contractor, not a servant. So, if you want an update on young Daisy, you are owed that. I think it's a conversation to be had, as I am currently very worried about the disposition of the missing girl.' I chose a spare club and picked up a ball. The mouthpiece flinched as I put the ball on a spare pin and gave the club a swing.

'If, on the other hand, you want me to bleat on about how sorry I am that Lobsk Wideswing is currently sitting in a hole awaiting the word from the High Council, then you won't get to hear that. I'm saving my sympathy for the family of Olobato, who seemed perfectly good folk.'

'I don't like your manner at all, detective' said Getgold, the club now getting twitchy in his hands as I bent to place the ball.

'Yes, funny that. I do seem to be getting a lot of complaints about it these days. I put it down to my diet – not enough red meat.'

I addressed the ball on the pin and with one THWACK sent it flying. After what seemed an age it finally found the turf. I looked on carefully.

'That looks like six fifty yards to me. You're dropping your left shoulder too far as you swing, Getgold.' I handed the club to the dumbstruck mouthpiece and left the range.

Dwarfs! Sometimes I despair for my kin.

Being a little preoccupied with seething, I didn't keep my eye on the road heading home and quickly found myself lost. This did not improve my mood. I passed a genuine country inn, so genuine it didn't have to describe itself as such. It was still a beautiful day so I thought I would treat myself to a little mental health break while getting some directions.

Inside the inn was everything the outside promised and then some. An old man with enviable side whiskers was polishing glasses that didn't need it, simply because when you are at work that's what you do. The place was picture card perfect and waxed to within a bee's nipple.

'What'll it be?' he asked, after I had got myself seated.

'Cherry and white?'

'Cherry and white it is,' he passed back. 'Haven't been asked for a cherry and white in many a year! Lovely drink, the cherry and white! Cherry and white coming straight up, oh yes.' He got busy with the making.

'Quiet,' I said looking around.

'Sure is. We mostly do summer trade – little early yet. Got a pixie's kiss of a view from the garden. Clear over the Bay. Lots of Citadel folk come for a look-see.'

'I'll have a look-see too then.'

'You won't be disappointed.'

'I'll sure try not to be.'

'Out for a drive?' he asked sociably as he mixed.

'Lost my way. I'll be needing some directions too.'

'No problem. Looking for Harrowfeld Hall by any chance?'

'No, heading back to the Hill.'

'Only we get the occasional lost body looking for the Harrowfeld, dwarf personages too.'

'What would the Harrowfeld be?'

'Don't know exactly.' He got busy with the shaker. 'Something for young folk who have lost their parents, or their way, or both. Very private, built more like a stronghold than a retreat, in my opinion anyway. Here we go.' He filled a high glass one-third with ice, added the drink and grated just the right amount of nutmeg on top.

I took a bite. The clear cherry spirit cut the nutty creaminess to leave just the right, slightly bitter aftertaste that comes from leaving the cherrystones in the fermentate.

'Perfect,' I said.

'Real pleasure. I like a man, or dwarf, that knows his drinking.'

I thanked him again and took my cherry and white out to admire the view and share a pipe with it. The afternoon had turned into a blazing advertisement for freelance working. Who would want to be doing an afternoon watch indoors on a day like this? The idle rich and the idle poor have one thing in common, apart from the idleness. They both can swing with the weather; of course, the rich get to play more golf. As for poor over-worked private detectives, they just have to grab a little happiness when they can. I sat myself down on some of that furniture they seem to make from pipe cleaners and grabbed some happiness.

The barkeep was sure right about the view. The Bay down below sparkled like a whole sea of sapphires laid before the emerald-topped hills of Elfland. The wharves and manufactories were lost some way below me and it might have been a different age. There was even a sailing ship making its slow way out to sea. I would have painted a picture if I had any paints and any talent for it.

I had been a bit foolish to let Golding get under my skin and I might have to knit myself a pair of meek mittens before I saw him next. I was never fond of being playing 'throw and fetch' with clients and something about this whole case was making me itchy and I had nothing to scratch with as yet. Plus, I hadn't heard from the King of Elfland either. That was off. If this was a White-Finger job picking up on Vericeema's deviant behaviour, it should have pointed by now. Maybe my message service would have a catch-up for me at the office.

After a while, the barkeep brought me out a handy little map back to the Citadel he had drawn on a napkin and I thanked him and paid the necessary, leaving some extra corn by way of appreciation.

The route back took me past the Harrowfeld Hall Home for Troubled Children. It wasn't built any more securely than a small fortress and didn't have higher walls than the Citadel itself. I wondered just how troubled these children could be. I pulled up for a closer look, because that's the sort of thing we detectives do. It's in the contract, and apparently I hadn't been the only dwarf interested.

There was an impressive long driveway leading to the impressive entrance to the impressive Harrowfeld Hall. Unfortunately, there was an equally impressive set of gates to the driveway and they were closed with an impressive lock. Of course, this was no barrier, but in broad daylight and with no good cause? I got out of my wagon to read the details on the signboard. The head of the Harrowfeld Hall Home for Troubled Children was apparently one 'Phy. Deselia Stormcock', who had more initials after her name than I had letters in mine. I didn't have a clue as to what any of them meant, but I hoped they kept her warm at night. There was a contact number, which I took a note of – because that's in the contract too – and next to that, in block capitals, was the legend 'BY APPOINTMENT ONLY'.

What was happening to the world? Folk just seemed to be so anxious to rob it of any spontaneity. I'm more of a spur of the moment sort of dwarf, and as if to prove it, when I saw the bell pull, I pulled it. It was a very old looking bell pull, but it was attached to a very new piece of kit. There was a buzz, and a female voice from a hidden speech horn said: 'Harrowfeld Hall, how may I help you?'

'Can I speak to Deselia Stormcock, please?'

'Do you have an appointment?'

'No, I was just passing by and I'd be interested in talking to the Head in connection with a private matter.'

'I'm sorry, but we don't see anybody without an appointment.'

'I may not be coming this way again for some while.'

'I'm sorry, Master Dwarf. We don't make exceptions. Good day.'

There was a 'click' and that was that. I got back into the Dragonette and set off back to the Citadel, wondering how they had known I was a dwarf.

Gaspar Halftoken is, in my humble opinion, the best tailor in the Citadel. He knows cloth. He knows how to cut it and he knows how to hang it. His eye for colour is extraordinary and no detail is too small or beneath his attention. He is also one of the most well-connected bodies in the Citadel and a remarkable source of gossip of the inconsequential kind that does no harm but makes you feel as if you are right at the centre of this fabulous hive of activity we call the Hill.

I wanted some background on Selicia Brightfire and he was the gnome to provide it.

'Innate sense of what to wear and when to where it, but just as likely to turn up in something nobody has ever seen before and start a whole new fashion trend,' was his succinct opinion.

'I was asking about her acting, Gaspar!' I said, flopping onto one of the daybeds he kept for special clients. His store was that sort of place, a temple to the garment-maker's arts – it also functioned as a halfway house for his longest, loyal and most devoted customers. I'd caught his star act early and I'd stayed loyal.

'Acting! Acting! Who knows? Who cares? That elf is about to go star queen on us, and you worry about her acting! Ouch!' An overwrought Gaspar stuck himself with a pin from the arm's eye he was sewing in.

'Sorry, Gaspar – really didn't mean to offend your sensibilities. Just trying to get a handle on the woman.'

'Elf, dear boy! Elf and don't you forget it!' He took a breath, before continuing at a much-reduced volume: 'Or rather half-elf, if the stories are to be believed.'

I sat up now. 'Yes, I'd heard that she was only the Elf King's half-sister, but I'd assumed she was still a full-blood.'

Gaspar took the pins out of his mouth and looked around as if he might be overheard before speaking. 'The word is that Papa Truelight Senior tumbled more than one mortal princess of noble birth and his wife simply looked the other way. Especially if the other way happened to be in the direction of some dark-haired mortal warrior type.'

'What's the story on the other sister, Vericeema?'

Gaspar had to really think hard. 'Very conventional – long trailing frocks and diaphanous gowns. If she was any more worthy they'd have to build her a shrine.'

I had to laugh at Gaspar's description, but it did provide fodder for some full-on contemplation later.

'Who does Brightfire run with?'

'The crowd at Bron's mostly. You have heard of Bron's Place, haven't you dear boy?'

I hadn't heard of Bron's Place, but after Gaspar's description I felt the need to know more.

'Quite an exclusive crowd then?' I asked.

'Oh yes! They all think they're "it" but they can't be because I am!'

I had to laugh at Gaspar's indefatigable self-belief, but if I could cut cloth like he could I guess I'd be as confident too. I mentioned I'd maybe have to test Bron's guest policy.

'Well, dear boy,' said Gaspar, 'we cannot have you going somewhere as high up the tree as Bron's wearing last year's headgear. Here, I was saving this.' He disappeared out to his stockroom and came back with a hat.

Now there are some folk who might say that a hat is just a hat. It offers protection and keeps your head warm in the winter and the rain off in the summer. It can be tipped at attractive ladies and pushed back when you're feeling like heading out and swinging the axe a bit. A very useful thing is a hat.

And then there are Hats. These are objects of desire designed to encapsulate dreams and become as intrinsic a part of your being as your thumb font and your whistle. These Hats transcend art and laugh at shoes and gloves and other such items of everyday apparel. And this was the King of Hats. So dark you assumed it was black at first sight, until you saw the warm tones of a wine hue that was richer than bruised markberries. The Hat did not suffer a dent or crease; the brim was round and flat, as was the crown. The hat-band looked to be of the softest leather and the proportions alluded to something that transcended design and approached perfection.

'Like it?' said Gaspar.

'It's all right,' I replied. 'What do you want, the keys to my rooms, the wagon or simply my first-born?'

Gaspar laughed: 'Do try it on! We haven't had a fitting for a while and you know this is just a sideline for me.'

And what a sideline.

I found a mirror. I took off my everyday hat that had gone into a terminal sulk and was threatening hat self-immolation. I lifted the new hat. The fabric felt wonderful and it was somehow light, yet solid, and when I put it on it seemed to fit perfectly, dipped at an angle towards one eye. This wasn't just a hat; it was a Hat. I looked in the mirror and dwarf royalty looked back.

'What have you made here, Gaspar? Have you struck a deal with some dark sorcerer?'

He clapped his hands with delight as he spoke. 'So pleased you like it, Nicely!'

'Like it? It's love and everything that goes with it.' I took the hat off simply for the pleasure of putting it back on again.

'But what is it made from?' I just had to ask. 'It feels really quite tough, yet it's so light.'

Gaspar reached up, took the hat and banged it against a daybed arm. 'Don't worry!' he laughed, seeing the look of horror sweep over my face. He gave the hat a brush and said, 'Look!'

I looked and there wasn't a mark.

'Dragon's hide!' I murmured, incredulous.

'Brushed dragon's hide!' said the delighted Gaspar.

'But that's rarer than …' I was lost for words, which doesn't happen often.

'Rarer than live dragons!' confirmed Gaspar. 'And it's on a fell-beast frame, dent-proof; so even you should not get into serious trouble with that on!'

Trouble, what me? He was forgetting that I have a talent for trouble.

9

BRON'S PLACE

Unlike many other nightspots, Bron's Place didn't advertise; it wasn't signposted and it didn't have flashing lights outside. If you didn't know where it was, and what it was, you didn't have any right to be there. Thankfully Gaspar knew, but then again he knew everything there was to know about such things – couldn't spot a dragon if it was widdling on his lawn, mind.

There weren't any stewards around to park your wagon at Bron's as that would have been considered just a little bit too highborn. Bron's patrons could park their own wagons, thank you very much. Bron's patrons could do a lot of things, like park their own wagons, and buy up most of the rest of the Citadel if they had a mind to do so.

So there was nothing ostentatious at all about Bron's. Apart from, maybe, the flight of thirty marble steps that led up to a portico the size of a nursing home, sheltering a door that had probably been borrowed from a decommissioned fortress when they decided it was now too large for their needs.

There was an elf standing outside the entrance to Bron's, at the top of the stairs, hands clasped in front of him, as relaxed as a five-pipe gnome.

'A very good evening to you, Master Dwarf,' he said pleasantly, as I walked up.

'And the same to you, Master Elf.' I stopped a step or two from the top and weighed him up. The long straight blond locks were pulled back tight with a pin-stick slide-clip that flashed a sapphire or two as he turned his head to survey the night-time Citadel. A two-button suit in midnight blue was expertly cut in a style that did not impede movement. Lean and nicely balanced and probably fast with it, this was one elf that would need careful watching. 'Taking the air?' I asked casually.

'Alas no. Door Guard duties.'

'Oh well, no shame in honest labour.'

'Indeed,' he said, 'especially when you enjoy your work.'

'Can't ask for much more from life.'

'Certainly not.'

We nodded and I went on my way past him saying, 'Nice suit.'

'Nice hat,' he replied.

A nightspot with an elf bouncing the rowdies, this was about as exclusive as you could get.

The stockade grade doors opened with one finger, leading to a vestibule you could lose a horde of ravening goblins in. A charming woman greeter with all the right parts in all the right places, in the right amounts, came up close to greet me, just like it says in her contract. She introduced herself as 'Sassire' and asked if I would like a table. It wasn't the piece of common household furniture that sprung to mind looking at her, but I was on my best behaviour and didn't mention it. I just politely declined the offer and she escorted me through to the main room anyway. It wasn't as large as I expected; I could almost see the far walls. A large number of booths with comfy seats and looped-back midnight blue curtains were available for those averse to open spaces and this, along with impeccable lighting, helped prevent Bron's from appearing too imposing.

The place was pleasantly busy, but not heaving. A few well-dressed couples fooled around on the dance floor, more interested in each other than the music, which was a little too cultured for my taste. The bar itself was just slightly shorter than a redwood was tall. I parked myself at one end and waved to somebody at the other, but without the signal flags he didn't notice me at all. There was no roster, the implication clearly being that if you can drink it, then we can make it, and will make it for you even if it does involve ritual sacrifice. I was just considering whether to test them on this when a male voice, marinated in charm and sex-appeal, spoke from behind: 'Please allow me – I always like to buy the first drink for all my new guests.'

I swivelled on the barstool to find myself facing what had to be the proprietor, Bron. He was an older man than I expected, greying at the temples in that way so many women like. His smile was convivial and at home in a face that generated geniality and good cheer. His fabulously cut formal suit did nothing to disguise a physique that owed more to the great outdoors than smoky nightspots. You had to look twice to notice that he only had the one arm in the immaculate jacket.

'Well, that is very kind,' I replied, 'but what if I was the reviewer for the Citadel Press? I might just be failing in my duty and might even be accused of taking a tribute.'

Bron smiled wider: 'I guess that's a chance I'll have to take.' He turned to the waiting barkeep and ordered, 'Could we have a Dragon's Tooth here for my guest, please, Tenser?' before addressing me again.

'I wouldn't normally presume to choose another body's drink, but this is something special we have had especially devised for us. I'd value your opinion, especially if you were the reviewer from the Citadel Press.'

'Always glad to be of service.' The barkeep was making very busy with his back to us and I was intrigued as to what the result might be like.

Bron smiled again before asking: 'And how is Gaspar?'

'Flourishing,' I replied.

Well, the man knew his tailoring and his lighting – I just hoped he knew his drinks.

The Dragon's Tooth arrived in a glass that didn't shout too loud, a lump of rock sugar dissolving gently in the pale red, slightly viscous, liquid, like the dragon's tooth of the name. I took a bite and it bit back.

'Any thoughts?' Bron asked.

'Good, very good. Real fire.' I had another taste and rolled the liquid around my mouth. 'You could maybe consider rubbing salt around the glass lip and having a lemon fruit-lick with it.'

'Yes, yes! I can see that,' said Bron, genuinely pleased. 'Excellent, we'll call this after you if we may?'

'Nicely Strongoak,' I said, offering my hand to his good right arm. His grip was strong but showed he had nothing to prove.

'Dragon's Tooth, the Strongoak Variation, excellent! Well, do enjoy your evening, Master Strongoak. We have gaming tables next door, including pinpig, and a fine restaurant with one or two dwarf specialities. We look forward to your custom. If you would care to leave an address card with Sassire.' Bron smiled that genuine smile and went off to work the room.

I took another instalment of the drink and thought about looking for Selicia, but she'd already got her dwarf detector activated. She came from the dance floor in shifts: first the body, then the motion and then the eyes. The body got you all warmed up, the motion made you feel mean, but it was the eyes that stayed with you.

'My Master Dwarf, but you are full of surprises. Three for the elves it is then?'

'Hi Twinkle, how's the make-believe business?'

She took the stool next to me with only the slightest of wobbles to betray that she'd had an early start. 'Twinkle?' she tried the word, rolling it around in her mouth for consideration. 'I have a number of names, in low and high elvish, and most of the common tongues, but I can't recall Twinkle being one of them.'

'What?' I said, with feigned surprise. 'That must mean we've moved on to pet names already?' I leaned forward. 'You can call me "Bunny", on account of me being so cute and cuddly.'

She smiled and gave me that look elves do so well before replying: 'Yes, you are rather cute – handsome even, but handsome is as handsome does as they say. What exactly do you do, Master Dwarf?'

'Twinkle, it's not what I do, it's the way that I do it.'

She leaned forward as well. 'Now that's got me wondering.'

'Wondering what, Twinkle?'

'Wondering whether to let you kiss me.'

'Ah Twinkle! Such a shame!' I leant back before continuing: 'There's a window for that sort of thinking and DING, it just closed – never mind, got to be faster than that next time.' I toasted her with my glass.

She leaned back as well, laughed and took a bite from the drink that had almost magically appeared at her side. 'I had decided against it.'

'Then we'll both just have to consider what might have been,' I said, with a shrug.

'To what might have been,' she toasted me. 'And out of interest, Bunny, can I ask what your business was with my brother?'

'Ask away, Twinkle.'

'I know he has very little time for anything as ephemeral as rolling pictures.'

'Ain't that the truth.'

'I wondered if it could have anything to do with my older sister.' She'd tried to drop it in as casually as possible, but nobody was fooled. There were little signs of tension all over that perfectly put-together body – if you knew where to look. That sort of skill didn't come without practice; the things I do for my profession.

'Now, why should he want to talk to me about Vericeema?' I asked softly.

Brightfire laughed unconvincingly. 'I happen to know she has a fondness for dwarfs. I was only asking, anyway.' Her feigned indifference did not augur well for her ability as an actor.

'Oh, dear,' she said, with a sigh, changing the subject ineptly and looking across at the dance floor.

Selicia's dancing partner had finally realised he was now one person short of a couple and was coming over to demonstrate his undeniable right to make a complete little puck of himself. It was Blaze Rampant himself, and even out of his picture outfit he still looked like he was about to make a speech designed to inspire somebody to do something they really should think twice about. I soon realised that Blaze was one of those folk permanently on the cusp of speech-making and that most of the words when he got there weren't worth the wait or the effort of listening.

'Well, well, well,' started Blaze, because he was also one of those folk who think 'hearty' is a suitable way of talking instead of just being reserved to describe stew. 'A dwarf in Bron's, how very egalitarian.'

'Egalitarian? Well, that's a word for a rainy day and no doubt about it – something to do with riding horses, isn't it?' I asked.

Selicia Brightfire stepped in quickly to say, 'Bunny is trying to make it in the business. Though I have a feeling he may already have something to do with pictures.'

Blaze gave me a highly dismissive once-over look before commenting: 'I suppose there is always room for one more comedy sidekick.'

'No, sidekick's not really my kick,' I answered. 'I'm more interested in leading man status.'

This gave Lord Blaze of Rampant a good laugh. 'Oh really?'

'I hear there are plenty of opportunities now, if your face fits.'

'Well, you must have a better ear to the ground than the rest of us. Work is never plentiful and competition is always fierce.'

'Bigelow Films have been hiring. You should try them.'

I could see the name meant nothing to Blaze but something like recognition passed across Brightfire's perfect features, before she corrected her demeanour and said, 'Bigelove?'

'Bigelow,' I corrected.

Blaze shrugged and said, 'Must be a new company. The name means nothing to me.'

'I'm sure they could use a man of your talents. If you can deliver.' When that crack didn't earn me a cuff I felt he was giving it to me unmolested.

Blaze wasn't satisfied yet, though. 'And what makes you think the merry folk of Widergard are going to be willing to invest their gold to see a dwarf?'

'Mostly on account of how the current batch of heroes seem so unconvincing and old hat.'

'Talking of old hat, I really must try that one on.' Blaze reached out to me and I was just considering whether to bend a finger or thumb when – the elf was fast!

I hadn't seen him enter, but before I even knew it, there was the friendly elf door guard, his hand grasping Blaze's arm with a grip that the surprised man could not even begin to break.

'Nobody touches the Hat,' said the elf quietly.

The scene entered a tableau moment, like a painting by one of those old guys who really knew how to daub oil on a canvas. 'The Reaching for the Hat' it would probably have been called and you'd be able to see the tension in every face and trace the tautness in every muscle and sinew. I'd like to think there would be something a little more impressive than an 'O' of surprise on my features, but chances are not.

'Any problem here, good folk?' said Bron, reappearing from the gaming tables.

'None at all, Bron,' said the elf, casually releasing Blaze's arm. 'Just a reminder about the clothing formality code.'

'Excellent!' beamed Bron. 'Then let's all have another drink, shall we?' He snapped the fingers of his one hand and they popped like a wizard's cracker. 'Another round, please,' he said to the smiling attendant. 'Now, Selicia Brightfire, do you think you are up to giving us a song this evening?'

The elfess jumped nimbly to her feet, all traces of over-indulgence now gone. 'I might be persuaded later, Bron, but for now I feel like dancing. See if you can stir some life into the band will you, or I'll go find us a bunch of gnomes that can really swing.'

Bron made a short bow and headed off towards the stand. Selicia walked off as well, showing how to really swing the parts that are designed for this very purpose. 'Come on, Blaze,' she added, almost as an afterthought. A still-seething Blaze followed Selicia to the dance floor.

'Now there's a lady who's used to getting her own way,' I commented to nobody in particular.

The elf looked on dispassionately before answering: 'So it would appear.'

'Anywhere round here where a dwarf can smoke a pipe in peace?' I asked, getting off my stool.

'The roof garden is very agreeable at this time of year,' he replied and pointed me at a sign with this very legend engraved. I followed the arrows.

The roof garden was indeed very agreeable at this time of year and deliberately so. Just about every blossom-bearing tree and plant in Widergard must have been potted up here for a full nasal onslaught that left you reeling slightly. The seats were beautifully crafted for every size of person and allowed you to relax and enjoy the lights of the Citadel spread before you.

I sat and enjoyed.

There was a particularly good view of the Council Hall in the dizzy heights of the First Level, Oloin's Glass glimmering brightly in the steeple as it had for more years than anybody really knew. It reminded me that I needed to be seeing Councillor Truelight – still no word about the White Finger, and this worried me. I wondered if it was worrying him too.

The band had finally kicked themselves into something like life, but the noise was pleasantly muted up here on the roof. A momentary increase in volume told me I was not alone.

'One Dragon's Tooth, Strongoak Variation,' said the elf, placing the drink on the table at my side. 'Lemon fruit and salt as suggested.'

'Bron won't get rich this way,' I said, picking up the drink and trying the salt and citron combination, which worked as well as I'd hoped.

'Bron is already rich,' the elf replied.

'Very kind of you to take the trouble then.'

'No trouble at all. I am about to go on my break.'

'Then join me, please,' I pointed to a seat.

'Thank you.' He sat and sucked in some air. 'I do like this garden, very much indeed.'

I blew a smoke ring just to see it rise up and away on a thermal coming from the nightspot's kitchen ovens.

'Yes. And thank you for the activity with young Blaze there. You didn't have to.'

'It's my job, I do have to. Besides he was being a total goblin's out-hole.'

The mild profanity made me chuckle. 'Mind if I ask how you come to be working door here? Doesn't seem to be the obvious occupation for an elf.'

He thought about this for a while before replying. 'Perhaps it's more of a calling than an occupation. Yes, a calling – I rather like that.'

'And what do I call you?' I asked, sending another smoke ring into the trade-marked Widergard velvet star-studded blackness.

'Whatever it pleases you to call me, Master Dwarf.'

I smiled before replying, 'The Elf with No Name. Certainly, has a certain ring to it.'

'Yes, I like that as well. The Elf with No Name – excellent!' He slapped the arms of his chair with pleasure. 'I'll get cards made up.'

'Never hurts to advertise. Or so I'm told.'

'Very true, but anonymity can be a friend too.' The elf cracked a smile that only hung around his face long enough to check out how the neighbourhood had changed.

'And now, do forgive me, I must get back to my duties.' He rose in that enviable elf fashion, made a small bow, and was gone without leaving even a hint of skin freshener.

I smiled to myself. An elf I liked that wasn't in a dress. I was getting far too mellow.

I finished my pipe and attended to the cleaning duties, knocking it out in an ashcup that was far too tasteful for such a mundane task. The band sounded like they had been given a shot of vital factors, so I went and had me a listen.

They were beginning to cook quite nicely in a style that mixed some gnome rhythms with more traditional elf phrasing. The floor was filling up with the younger scions of the Citadel's White and Wise, all out to parade their credentials. Blaze and Selicia Brightfire were noticeably absent. Bron had joined the band and was playing the elf horn one-handed with considerable expertise. Impressive, but then again, he wasn't going to play the double bass, was he? I wondered what the story was there.

The drive out to Milkwood went without incident. I was hoping that my burglary skills weren't going to be necessary as my breaking-and-entering apparel was still at the cleaners and I didn't have a spare. I was in luck. The nightlife wasn't restricted to Bron's this evening.

10

BIGELOW PICTURES

I parked the Dragonette up under some convenient low-growing branches and walked back to the road, scratching my head, and my chin, and then my head again for good measure. Unsure how to approach this I was saved from further deliberation by powerful headlights approaching along the quiet Milkwood Road. The coach pulled out and the driver wound down his window. 'You for Bigelow's?'

'Sure am,' I replied, with all the gusto I hoped a new entry into the world of smutty pictures would exhibit. 'A pal dropped me off, but we must be further away than I thought.'

'Just a couple of miles. Hop in, you new guys are always getting lost.'

In I hopped.

This, apparently, was the boys' coach. They liked to keep the sexes apart, presumably to discourage any misbehaviour that could affect a later performance. My fellow artists were getting lubricated in an amicable manner so I took my turn on the bottle as it was passed round. Nobody questioned my presence; names, when given, were obviously professional markers and 'Bunny' was treated with the ribbing and frankly filth-filled observations such a boast probably warranted. The mix was pretty much as in the glossies the Elf King had shown me, except

I was the only dwarf, a situation that suited me down to the ground. I really did not want to meet anybody I knew this particular evening. Unfortunately, none of the 'talent' was recognisable from Vericeema's smutties.

The coach passed through the Picture Production House gates with no questions asked. I hoped the rest of evening would be as straightforward. Of course, I was winging it wildly and just trusted to the powers that look after improvising dwarf detectives that I'd come out with my reputation and my virtue intact. I'd settle for one out of two.

We disembarked in fine spirits, but then the security tightened somewhat and two men, bulked up by more than early nights and healthy living, treated us to a body search. I had left my arsenal in the wagon and was currently armed with nothing more than my rapier wit and quick-fire repartee. Usually that's enough to get me out of most situations. I hoped it would do tonight.

We were herded into a small room with no windows and two doors: one door in and, opposite, one door out again. Did this make it nothing more than a short fat corridor? I didn't have much time to ponder on this.

We hadn't yet been introduced to our co-stars, which was rather disappointing. Even if the errant elfess didn't turn up, the short dark-haired girl might be able to give me a lead. I was hoping for a quick chat before vacating the party with the aforementioned virtue intact.

I soon found out the reason for our continued separation: a security guard told us it was time for our examinations. The women were to see Nurse Bitterbite and the boys Physic Hardcastle. I assumed this was the normal procedure, as the announcement did not appear to come as news to my co-stars, but I began to get an uncomfortable feeling – even more uncomfortable than the thought of having the family jewels examined for colour, clarity, cut and carat weight.

My worst fears were realised when Dollface came waltzing into the room to have a quiet word with security and then start taking names. I pulled my hat down low and hoped I wouldn't be recognised. I didn't think the same trick would work when I came before Physic Hardcastle, not that we had previously become that well acquainted, but he might still recognise my face. I was wondering whether I could sell the tale of 'Bunny' being down on his luck when Whitestuff came in.

The large albino took one look around, his dwarf detector went off and he pulled out a shooter. Suddenly making Bunny's excuses seemed a rather poor option, whereas a hasty exit was well favoured. I decided to take a chance on the new door and was rewarded with my first glimpse of the female talent, elf-free and lacking in a certain dark-haired young woman too. I didn't linger but ran past the startled women, through another door, straight into a startled Argebester. I came off best and carried on sprinting onto a huge recording stage of the type I had seen while visiting Elsie. This was being set up for this evening's performance, which was to include more than just stills. I'd lost my chance for immortality, it seems. Oh well.

Argebester cried out to his pigment-lite assistant, 'Drop the dwarf!'

This left no doubt as to their designs on my future welfare. The bullet whipping past my ear only reinforced this. I sought another way out and found it through a door that led to a storage area full of backdrops, lit only by a single red safety light above the door. No problems here for dwarf eyes at all, thank you.

Despite my haste, I noticed a familiar pastoral scene propped up against a wall. I was certainly in the right place, even if the connection to The New Tree Renewal Parlour was going to take some figuring. First things first. Number one problem: I needed to get out of here in one piece.

'Where's the lights? Somebody find me the lights!' shouted Argebester. 'I want him in shackles!' Physic Argebester didn't like me. I'd live.

A couple more shots rang out, thankfully way off target. I moved in behind cover of a stiffened canvas screen. It depicted an elfin grotto, all twee lights and limpid pools, but I couldn't afford to be fussy.

'Don't nobody shoot nothing 'till we get the lights on!' Whitestuff screamed in a voice that said the last bullets had not been far too close to him for comfort. 'Not unless they want me to rip 'em a ruby smile!'

It all went quiet until, with the 'clunk' of a large switch made for 'clunking', the room was flooded with bright white light from a single huge lantern globe located up where the air gets thinner.

'Got you now, Bunny! Let's see how we can make you hop.' Whitestuff seemed to have taken an unreasonable dislike to me too, considering I hadn't yet done him any harm. 'Yet', of course, being very much the proper appreciation of the timescale.

The globe lantern did negate my advantage somewhat and I wondered how I might render the light non-functional. Wishing seemed enough to do the trick, as it exploded into a thousand shards that rained down onto my would-be assailants accompanied by nearly as many curses. I'd have to remember that wishing still had a role in the modern world apparently.

My eyes made out the faintest trace of peripheral movement and a voice I recognised immediately whispered low but clear.

'This way please, Master Strongoak.' It was the Elf with No Name.

Working on the assumption that he hadn't come all this way with evil intent, I followed him. We were soon behind a much larger stack of screens.

'There is only the one door and they've left a guard there,' he said, pointing to a man-shaped shadow.

'So, we rush him?' I replied.

'Not when we don't know what's behind the door. I fancy the good physic might have more than bullets up his sleeve.'

I couldn't argue with that. Argebester's sorcerous appearance really did suggest unusual and unwanted aptitudes. And I wasn't thinking parlour tricks – when he cut a woman in half I'm guessing she stayed cut. I hadn't forgotten the head in need of a new home that I'd seen in the parlour.

'How then?' I said, loathe as I was to ever ask an elf for assistance, as he undoubtedly knew.

'I hope you have a head for heights,' he said. I could feel the width of his grin even in the darkness. Heights, as the wise old saying goes, have never been a problem for me; it's the landings I'm generally more concerned about.

It turned out that there was a very clever pulley system built into the ceiling of this cavernous space that allowed the back-drops to be lifted and then moved across the top of the one wall that did not reach the ceiling. On the other side of that wall there was another recording stage that also housed the doors through which the elf had entered.

The rope-climbing wasn't that hard, but I was out of practice.

The elf ascended with a grace that made me want to break his fingers – well, after we were out of here, maybe. When we reached a high walkway, and he pointed out the ladder we could have used, I wondered if I would bother waiting that long.

The walkway took us safely over into the next cavernous space, high over the heads of the grunts and runts we heard crashing below.

'So, just happened to be strolling by, were we?' I whispered to my companion.

'Bron is very particular about the guests he allows into his club. You could say this is a background check. And what a colourful life you must lead.'

'Do I pass the test then?'

'Of course. We wouldn't want the club getting dull, would we?'

We slipped down the ropes onto the set floor. I could see the outline of the large external doors from the slight leaks of waxing moonlight. It looked like we were home dry. I said as much. That's when the explosions went off. It looked like the dwarf should keep his mouth shut.

They weren't real explosives, of course, but stage explosives are just as loud and impressive as the real thing when you are standing on top of them. More bang, light and smoke than actual destructive power, however my ringing ears and blinded eyes were not consoled. I tried to look round and see how my companion had fared.

Banks of spotlights blasted the recording stage, but the Elf with No Name was nowhere to be seen. I hoped this did not mean the Elf with No Name was now the Elf with No Skin.

'Get the mud-hugger!' I heard Whitestuff shout, as he entered the set through another door. Which wasn't really very polite and, on top of the fact that they had just nearly blown me to bits, was making me feel distinctly unwelcome. I hope they didn't treat all their talent this way.

'Looks like he set off the security system!' Full marks for stating the obvious, grunt! Sadly, deduct maximum points for unnecessary bad-guy exposition.

My senses had still not recovered sufficiently for a competent counter-attack and so I did what I always recommend under such circumstances: I flailed. For effective flailing, you really need a 'flail enhancement device'. I groped around and came up with what felt like a reassuringly sturdy scaffolding pole. Not a moment too soon, I began to flail. I almost immediately encountered man-flesh. Between pole and man, well, it was no competition. The satisfying crack of bone and the accompanying shriek of pain convinced me that my hearing was returning. I now added some forward motion to my flail, and whirling the pole like a dwarf flailing a pole over his head, I made my way in what I hoped was a door-ward direction.

One more thud of yielding flesh suggested that my assailants were suffering losses, but it would only take one obstruction of my flailing implement to leave me in great trouble. Either that or they'd get some…

'Where's the shooters?' I heard Whitestuff crossly cry. 'I've had enough of this doorstep.'

Oh, dear! My goose already had a huge handful of herbs up his out-hole and was now being well larded up. An unexpected, but strictly temporary, ally saved me.

'No,' said Argebester, 'I want to ask this one some questions.'

I kept flailing. 'Never be afraid to flail' as the saying goes.

It was then that I heard a roaring noise that I couldn't place at first, incredibly loud in the enclosed space, even for my ringing ears. It sounded like some monster from the days of old, a demon roaring defiance maybe, a worm thundering at the injustice of the invention of cold steel, or maybe, just maybe —a steam cycle! I turned and saw such a masterpiece of piston-powered construction heading in my direction.

'Nicely, put the pole down before you take my head off!'

The elf had a steam cycle! And not just any steam cycle, a legendary Grassalax 650 'steamburster'. I could learn to hate him after all.

I lowered the pole just as he sped past, picking me up embarrassingly easily, and dumping me on his pillion. We then headed for the door, via where Argebester and his men were standing conveniently grouped – because the opportunity was too good to miss. They scattered like skittles, especially as I now had the scaffolding pole extended before us, resting on the steamburster's handle-holds, like a lance belonging to the armoured horse knights of old. I scored a direct hit on a large security guard who was ridiculously hard to miss, and he collapsed onto Argebester.

'Score one for the dwarf, Argebester!' I shouted and saw his sorcerer's face contort in anger as he fell.

The elf then scored higher for executing a turn that had both wheels sliding like spit off an ice giant's lower lip and knocking another guard on top of the physic in the process.

'This is not over, Bunny!' Argebester screamed in fury.

'Bunny?' the elf asked witheringly.

'Long story, another time perhaps,' I replied.

With a revving of the accelerator, the elf recovered momentum, and with Argebester's men regrouping and setting off in pursuit, we headed for the door. The mighty boiler of the Grassalax hissed below us, as angry as an unclean spirit caught in a wagon auto-wash. The fact that I was sitting on a pressurised bomb heading for what looked like a very solid set of wooden doors was doing nothing for my piece of mind. However, the blood was up and I would have had to admit, if anyone had thought to ask me at that moment, that I was rather enjoying myself.

Steambursters like the Grassalax are things of beauty. To mount a steam engine on two wheels, and thereby produce a road-eating form of transport with an exposed crankshaft rotating the rear wheel by means of an eccentric pivot, is a work of art. To produce the pressurised spirit burner necessary to produce the required steam is a work of genius. To ride the resulting monster is madness. That's why they are regularly and often fatally called steambursters. Yet in fleet seconds the door was before us.

'Hang on, and close your eyes,' the elf added, totally unnecessarily because there was no way we were going to be doing anything after we hit the woodwork, apart from bleeding copiously and maybe looking round for spare limbs. It was going to take some pretty impressive elf magic to get us through this timber obstacle.

Elf magic, or perhaps a steam-powered canon that can send a fragmentation shell from your steam-cycle at a speed suitable for converting two heavy doors into so much kindling without upsetting the forward momentum of your Grassalax 650.

'I added the canon myself,' the elf shouted back when we were clear of the falling debris. 'I think it works quite well.'

I certainly was in no position to criticise. The guard at the gate also had nothing to add as he threw himself into the shrubbery while we sped past. Any other pursuit was soon lost behind sucking on our steam and picking out our wheel rubber from their teeth. I directed the elf to where my Dragonette '57 was hidden and dismounted, grateful to still be in one piece.

'Lovely wagon,' the elf said, admiring the trim and bodywork on my '57 Dragonette as I reversed it from out of the over-hanging trees. 'Does she require much pumping?' he added conversationally, as if we had just been out for a pleasant weekend drive.

I shook my head. 'This was the first model with auto-prime, makes all the difference.'

The elf patted his Grassalax affectionately. 'That's the trouble with this lady. It's why I had to nip off and get her ticking over before I could effect our departure. Glad to see you managed to keep them busy. I should have mentioned the security system, very ingenious – Silent Watchers using higher registers. Even I wouldn't have realised straight away, if I hadn't spotted the bats going frantic outside as I spied out the land. Just at the limits of my hearing they are. Thankfully you can still tell a lot from the behaviour of animals, you know.'

'Yes,' I agreed, 'I never go anywhere without a canary or two – if I can avoid it.'

'Well,' said the elf, 'thanks for a splendid evening. Better get back to work, though!' He saluted elf-style.

'Looks like I owe you another one, elf.'

'Not at all! I mean, Master Strongoak, one really can't have anything untoward happen to a hat like yours! Good millinery is so hard to find these days.'

'Most certainly, as are fine manners and excellent timing. You are to be congratulated.'

He laughed at this, behaviour which I fancied he did not partake of too often. 'Yes, a rather splendid evening, all considered. Now I will just say "Exchelsia" to you.'

'A salutation I have never heard before.'

A faraway look came into the gaze of the Elf with No Name that was even more distant than the look that elves habitually have.

'No,' he said, 'you shouldn't have. It is something more than a salutation, not commonly bandied about by my people, but if you ever have the need, you might find it of assistance.'

'Exchelsia,' I repeated.

'Exchelsia,' he confirmed.

'Then thank you, Master Elf.'

'My pleasure, Master Dwarf.'

I tipped the hat in his direction as he accelerated off into the warm night. It hadn't so much as moved an inch on my head. The elf was right, great hat-making like this is sure hard to find. Humble elves are even thinner on the ground, but I had managed to find one.

11

THE WHITE COUNCIL

I drove down to The New Tree Beauty Parlour first thing next morning, but even that was too late. A likely looking young scout was busy banging a new sign into the immaculate lawns. Of the old sign there was no sign; the new one simply said 'Premises to Rent' and gave a Citadel number for the agent.

'You handling this?' I asked the scout, casually strolling across from my wagon.

'Oh yes, Master! Just on the market, this very morning. Very desirable premises and a remarkably good price as well,' he boasted, getting into his stride. 'Beautiful aspect and very peaceful, but still convenient for the Citadel with good road access.' Boy, he had all the talk down pat. Impressive for one so young. I hope it didn't addle his brain.

'Are you looking for premises then, Master?'

'I might be,' I replied. 'What happened to the previous tenants? No problems were there? I'd hate it if there were problems.'

'Oh no,' the scout bounced back, a little too speedily. 'They simply dis... their contract just ran out and we didn't renew.'

'Their business... nothing that could cause a stink was it, the real kind or the other kind? I wouldn't want creditors knocking on the door.'

'Nothing like that, Master! I can reassure you, we handle all utilities and the like. That means you simply have the one payment to make.'

Very efficient, but that also meant fewer leads on Physic Argebester. Axes and blood, I should have moved quicker!

'Sounds good, I'll have a look around,' I told the scout, every ounce the successful small businessman.

'You really need an appointment,' he started to say before noticing the look on my face. 'But in your case, as you're here.' He took the lead, asking me casually, 'What line of trade are you in, Master Dwarf, if you don't mind me asking?'

'Rolling pictures, the technical side … the processing, not the making,' I explained, noting his interest. 'We're looking for somewhere closer to the Hill. Milkwood's fine but the travelling is getting expensive, especially for the dailies.'

'Ah, yes I see,' he replied. I wasn't sure I did, but it sounded impressive.

The inside of the former New Tree Renewal Parlour was cleaner than an elf queen's lacies. While I had been busy shaking hands with the Dream Prince, they had been busy emptying the building of everything that could have been of interest, even the false wall for the hidden room. I had been too slow off the mark. Poor form, Nicely. I took a card from the scout on the way out, anyway. He went back to banging the sign in. I told him to be careful of those immaculate lawns; somebody had gone to a lot of trouble to maintain them.

Next, I tracked down Master Bigelow of Bigelow Pictures, or at least his two-handkerchief mouthpiece name of Goosefit. The address the Citadel Business Roster provided for Bigelow was not too far away, part of the same Industrial Zone in fact, which was food for thought. I continued my pose as a picture maker, but this time I promoted myself to a producer, keen to find premises for shooting my latest masterwork. I found out that indeed I could hire their recording stages, and equipment, and at very reasonable rates too. Night-time usage was a possibility too, but dates were less flexible as they had regular clients taking advantage of the marvellous opportunity that Bigelow Pictures afforded. Although one regular had that very morning just moved on…

I thanked him profusely and asked for details to be forwarded to a Box address I used for such purposes. I had a feeling that the mouthpiece was telling me the truth. He had just the right air of desperation as he outlined the wonderful possibilities Bigelow Pictures offered, and somebody called Goosefit surely lacked the imagination to lie.

A wind sprang up on the way back to the Hill. I wasn't sure if it was heralding a change in the weather or if it was just the breeze from the wings of all the birds flying their coops. There was one place that I knew where I was always guaranteed to find a whole parliament of owls in session.

I am not at all ashamed to say that I had never seen the White Council in action before. Although it is frequently held up as the epitome of democracy in action, we dwarfs have another take on that. The Temporary Committee, which has been pretty much running dwarf affairs since the last dwarf king decided he preferred fishing to ruling, has been remarkably successful, but we dwarfs are not a boastful race. That is, except where courage, sexual prowess, ferocity, craftsmanship, intellect and humility are concerned.

However, the seniority of the dwarfs' Temporary Committee aside, we have one other factor going in the favour of our administrative system: the Bellatine Bell. The Bellatine Bell must be rung, and then held, by any dwarf who wishes to address the representatives on the Temporary Committee. If you don't like what somebody is saying, or they have gone on a bit, all any dwarf has to do is walk up and take the bell from whoever is speaking – anyway they want to, bar murder.

Now this might seem like a recipe for total chaos, where the bell is always going to be held, and the floor dominated, by the strongest and fiercest. That would probably be the case, if it was not for the fact that along with the Bellatine Bell there comes the Bellatine Belter. This is a ceremonial artefact of great age and dignity, some two yards long and two spans around, beautifully carved from ironwood with intricate runes and designs featuring all the Dwarf Great Families. Its sole purpose is to strike anybody unwise enough to hang on to the Bellatine Bell for too long.

It is a typically dwarf answer to the problem of executive verbosity. It works very well. The White Council could do with a Bellatine Bell (and Belter). While waiting to speak to Councillor Truelight, I sat through nearly a full hour of some worthy alderman droning on about planning regulations in the gnome enclave known to everyone as the Little Hundred, but which the White Council for some reason loves to refer to as New Farthing. This talk is totally pointless because there is no planning in the Little Hundred, which I know is rather the point, but nothing the White Council can do is ever going to change that. You are not going to change the habits of the gnomes, not unless you give them their homelands back – and you'll see a dragon play hopscotch before that happens.

The White Council Hall is quite a space – lofty, venerable and inspiring – but after an hour of this drivel I felt that I knew every fixture and fitting and suitably noble statue, and could quite happily have taken an axe to all of them. However, Councillor Truelight had requested a catch-up via my messaging system and I needed to ask a few more questions myself.

I was disappointed not to have got the results I wanted from my little evening adventure. Although I had identified the Picture House where the smutties were taken, it hadn't found me the identity of who was behind the scam. The presence there of

Physic Argebester and Dollface only confused things further. Were they really only present to check the sexual health of the 'talent'? Or were they more deeply involved? What was their connection to the missing Daisy, and who was their poor disembodied client at the clinic? I had plenty of time to think about the possibilities, while the good alderman gave his views on all things gnome, which really were none of his beeswax. Far too many questions were flying around my head while the good alderman droned on and on.

Finally, the White and Wise stopped rattling and paused to pat each other on their backs and say what a good job they were doing, before running off to their mistresses, boyfriends and spouses, or maybe all three. I met Truelight in his de-robing chamber – everyone should have one. What, you haven't? Then where do you keep your ermine?

'I'm sorry to have kept you waiting, Master Strongoak.' He offered me a seat, but stood standing himself. 'I really had no idea that business was going to go on so long. We certainly hadn't planned for it.' He took off the long white fur-lined robes of office and hung them on a former.

'That's the problem with democracy,' I said, lowering myself into a seat that looked like it had been crafted from a single piece of wood. 'Folk never do what they're told, it seems.'

'Cynicism, Master Detective?'

'Observation, Councillor Truelight.'

He stood there, his livery collar hanging like an anchor chain round his neck, which in many ways it was. He looked a lot older today, or maybe it was just the lighting. 'So,' he continued, 'any news to ease my burdens, detective?'

'I found out where the photographs were taken – picture house out in Milkwood.'

This surprised his royal elfness. 'Are you sure? A picture house – a trifle excessive for a handful of glossies?'

'I think it's rather a larger operation than that, Councillor, and even murkier.'

'That is not the news I was hoping for. You know my sister Brightfire is involved in picture making?'

'I do, but this is a more makeshift venture I believe – fly-by-night in nature.'

'And can you find these people?'

'I paid a visit last night. They weren't welcoming, but I will continue to investigate. However, I believe the fly-by-nights have flown, as is their nature. To be blunt, I really think it's time you had a word with your sister Vericeema. There are certain things worrying me.'

The Elf King slipped on a casual jacket that still managed to look like robes on him. 'There are certain things worrying me too,' he said gravely, 'one of which is that I can no longer contact my sister. She, apparently, never went to the destination she had told us about. Our relatives didn't know a thing about the visit.'

This was not what I wanted to hear. 'And the White Finger?'

'Still no word.'

I thought for a moment. 'Does the name Physic Argebester mean anything to you, Councillor?'

He thought before answering and then shook his head. 'I'm afraid not. Is it important?'

'It could be.'

'My family is generally very healthy, I'm pleased to say.'

Elves do have it easy in so many ways. On top of their exceptionally long lives, they are also not subject to most of the common infectious diseases that affect the rest of us mortals. Of course, there is a trade-off, a really low birth rate and some nasty ailments of the type that come with normal old age in other races; I've heard that elfstones can be excruciatingly painful, but elfcanker is the most deadly affliction.

I knew there was no real reason for any connection to Physic Argebester, but I had more dots than Spot the Dog at the moment and nothing to join them up with and no idea what the picture might be.

'If you are really concerned, Councillor, you should consider going to the Guard – they have resources I can't match.'

'No, no,' the Councillor insisted, 'it's not come to that quite yet. She is a free agent after all, and I don't want those pictures to become common knowledge.'

'I understand, but I think I should make finding your sister a priority.'

The councillor nodded. 'I think you had better as well.'

'I'm already on it, with your permission, of course?'

'Whatever you need, Detective.'

I left the Councillor to his thinking and left the Council Hall too. The rest of the White and Wise were heading back to restart their deliberations. And who should I see marching along with them, full of pomp and himself? None other than Getgold Grounding, all dressed up in his robes and chains and the picture of dwarfish sobriety. Now here was a dwarf who could ponder and deliberate with the best of them, but he still stood on a box to hit a golf ball. I snuck behind a pillar and let them all go past, lest I be arrested for laughing in an official space. They went in and sat down, very earnest, while the deputy council leader read out the order of business. I wondered if a single thing they were about to say was going to make the slightest bit of difference to anybody, anywhere. I also wondered if Getgold was sitting on his box.

The King of Elfland's secretary, Mistress Wiery Ensanders, did not live in High Trees, at least not full-time. She had a small, undistinguished, one-storey cabin off the Great East Road in a new development that was called Hobson's Mill, on account of there once having been a mill there owned by a body called

Pooterbury. Nobody wanted to live in Pooterbury Mill and so Hobson was chosen for the community's name as it was considered reasonably inoffensive, while being at least plausibly authentic. Presumably the local inn was called The Welcome Inn for the same reason: sadly there was little sign of any welcome amongst the rows of identical houses, each of which had a well-tended small plot, front and back, and a winsome name like 'Rest Easy'.

Number 65, Bank Row, owned outright by Miss W. Ensanders according to my contact at the Land Registry, did not have a name lovingly etched into a pierce of driftwood with a hot poker. I wondered idly what she might have chosen; I was tempted by 'The Dragon's Lair'.

I parked the wagon down the road a while and walked slowly back. The houses were all reasonably neat and tidy, with as much character as pulped parchment. The street was quiet, which suggested everybody kept regular hours. I like that in a neighbourhood. It does make breaking and entering so much more straightforward. Not that I was employed on any such mission. Mistress Ensanders was simply on a few days' leave, and if I wanted to talk to her, this was the most likely place to try first.

I was very surprised, as I neared Number 65, to hear the sounds of a baby crying. I rang the bell and was answered by a rather harassed looking Ensanders, who was obviously expecting somebody else, judging by her spluttered: 'You? What do you want?'

'My apologies for calling unannounced, Mistress Ensanders,' I said, hat in hand – I couldn't find a horn number for you.'

'I do enough talking all day, Master Dwarf. I do not have a speech horn. I like some peace when I'm at home,' she replied, with all the warmth of an ice flow.

The baby's cries continued to bounce around the small house.

'If you need to see to the…' I pointed vaguely with my hat.

'No thank you,' she said primly. 'My niece will soon have him quietened.' And as if on cue, the complaining stopped. 'There,' said Mistress Ensanders, 'he was only hungry.'

'Your niece, you say?'

'Yes, Poppydee. A lovely girl, but…' Mistress Ensanders lowered her voice and leant forward conspiratorially, 'between you and me, she has a terrible choice in men. This brute beats her, could you believe? So she's staying with me for a while. No man makes up for whatever problems he has with his own masculinity by beating my niece. I won't stand for it!'

I could well believe that and she had my full sympathies. Scum that picked on their spouses ranked lower than roadside remains on my roster too.

I got out a business card. 'I'm sure you have the matter in hand, Mistress Ensanders, but if your niece's husband should…'

'Dallard,' she interjected. 'He's called Dallard. I always found the name very appropriate.'

'Well, if Dallard should continue to inconvenience you or your niece, it would be my pleasure to assist. No charge, of course.' I handed the card over and I would swear that a small tear gathered in the woman's eye. Probably my imagination or the result of a cold breeze, surely?

'That is remarkably civil of you, Detective Strongoak. I will take great care of the card. Now, how can I help you? Would you like to come in?' She opened the door properly.

'No, Mistress Ensanders – thank you. I can see you are busy. I just had a quick question about Vericeema. I understand you are close? I wondered if you knew where she might be?'

'Vericeema?' she said surprised. 'She's visiting her aunt, I believe, at her place in Greathaven, for the season. Why?'

'She didn't go. She seems to have left the Citadel without a forwarding address.'

'And the Councillor has no knowledge of her whereabouts?'

I shook my head. 'It is rather urgent. I am of course asking with the Councillor's full authorisation.'

'This is most strange.' I could see the older woman flicking through her mind's box file. 'Not like her at all! From Fire I would expect this kind of behaviour, but Very has always been a very good girl.'

'And you've heard nothing from her?'

'I had a picture card from her earlier in the year: lovely large ships with full sails, I do so like them! Of course, she didn't actually say she was in Greathaven, I just assumed it.' She continued rummaging in her mental files.

'But nothing more recently?'

Ensanders shook her head, before admitting defeat. 'I'm sorry, Master Strongoak.'

'No romantic interests that her brother might not know about? Nothing she confided? I wouldn't normally ask you to betray a trust, but it is important.'

'I have a list of some of her old friends somewhere. Perhaps that would help?'

'Thank you, Mistress Ensanders. It might well do.'

'I'll have a messenger drop it at your office, as soon as I get a chance.'

'Thank you. And please don't hesitate to call me if you hear anything important – from Vericeema or Dallard.'

We exchanged goodbyes and I made my way back to the Dragonette. All was quiet in Bank Row again. So, hard-as-nails Mistress Ensanders had a niece called Poppydee, and was a doting auntie to boot. Just goes to show you never can tell.

12

THE GOLDEN RING

Sitting back in my '57 Dragonette, with the ragtop down, Elsie and I watched the moon smiling down on the steely, still waters of the Bay. There wasn't even a breeze up there in Elfland, just marvellously sweet night-scented flowers queuing up to do cute things to your nose. We were parked up on the Tall Trees Lookout, which was located at the end of an immensely long and rather splendid avenue of silver rain trees. It seemed to take forever to drive there, but from the Lookout you could see over the entire built-up area that was the Greater Citadel, spread now before us like a brightly coloured fairyland, lit for our enjoyment.

'Men say there is a man in the moon, you know,' said Elsie. 'And the elves say it is an elf. How about the dwarfs?'

'Oh,' I answered, 'we say it's an elf too.'

'Really?' said Elsie, with some surprise.

'Yes. That way we can encourage the dwarf children to get some exercise by throwing rocks at it.'

This earned me a dig in the ribs that didn't stop the laughter of either my companion or myself.

'You still owe me your honest opinion of the show, Nicely.'

Ouch, now here I was on dangerous ground – again!

I had been looking forward to my quiet evening at the theatre watching Elsie perform in what I hoped would be a suitably entertaining evening of theatre. Perhaps a comedy of manners or even a rant against the tyrannies of whatever or whoever is being tyrannous this week. I didn't know, because Elsie had never mentioned it, that this was a one-woman show.

So, no pressure there then – for either of us! Admittedly she had the somewhat harder task, standing up in front of an audience of discerning theatre folk and playing a dozen different characters one after the other, of all ages and races too.

I wasn't at all sure what to expect when she came on, dressed as a poor mother wrapped in an old shawl and starting to complain about not having enough breakbread. Now I like breakbread as much the next dwarf, but the problems of obtaining breakbread and splitting it between too many children are not likely to keep me engrossed for long, I must admit. And then I, and the rest of the audience, realised that as she was sitting fretting about the unfairness of breakbread distribution amongst society, and which of her children she should feed, she was in fact eating all the breakbread! The realisation started as a ripple of titter, which then became a wave of giggle, and ended up as a spontaneous ovation as, mouth full of breakbread, she departed. Only to return two minutes later as a young woman cursing most eloquently and repeatedly about the husband who had the nerve to make her feel guilty about running off with another man. And there were ten more roles like it, elves, women, dwarfs – even a goblin – not all funny, not all sad, but all moving in some way. The final applause was justified on every level.

I didn't know much about actors and actresses, but from what I had heard, juggling a dragon's eggs under the watchful eye of the worried mother was probably easier than critiquing a performance.

'I loved it. I wanted more,' I said.

'Really, Nicely?'

'Hey, want me to swear it on my badge?'

'No, that's good enough,' said Elsie the half-elf, cuddling a little bit closer. 'It's been a lot of hard work. I hope it's worth it.'

When I said I wanted more, I meant it. I could have sat there for the rest of the night and half expected to. Most dwarf dramas tend to be what other races would call 'on the lengthy side'. After all, if you're paying good money to be entertained, you should get your money's worth, especially as most dwarfs do not really like to be entertained. They can always stay in and count their gold if they need proper entertainment.

'I don't know any dwarf stories. Tell me one,' Elsera asked.

So there, under a bright moon, with all the smells of Elfland to lull us, I told Elsie the half-elf all about The Golden Ring. The Golden Ring, the greatest of dwarf stories, the definitive saga. It is about three days long and features lots of mock fights and generally a few real ones as well. Dwarf actors have long ago perfected what they call the 'method', as in the phrase 'method in their madness'. To perform in The Golden Ring is every dwarf actor's second greatest dream – to not die during the performance generally being their primary concern.

'The Golden Ring is the story of a brave and noble dwarf prince called Albright Goldgleaming. One day he is having an innocent bath in the river when three elf maidens leap in to taunt him. Although they make fun of his lack of aptitude in the swimming department, he is unmoved because he knows that he has skills they can never match, as he modestly tells them. When pushed to explain what he means, and noticing the beautiful sunlight falling on the river, he says he can capture that light and wrap it in gold. The elves laugh at the noble dwarf and tell him that this would indeed be an amazing gift, but it could only be accomplished by someone who loves gold more than he loves anything else in Widergard.

'Albright laughs at this rebuke and says he will show them this is not the case, he is someone who loves beauty in all its forms. Returning to his splendid stone halls, Albright sets about his task, to make a ring that captures sunlight, unaware of the treachery being planned by the elves.

'High in a tree, the Lord of the Elves, Wolond, contemplated his magnificent castle being built for him nearby by the stone giants, who were copying an original dwarf design, of course. The Lord of the Elves lived in a tree because he was too idle to build his own house. However, he did appreciate the comfort and security that good solid walls can bring and this was a castle the like of which Widergard had never seen before. The lord was lazy, not stupid. The lord was also worried, because with typical elf arrogance and penny-pinching, he had promised his sister-in-law/niece – the admittedly beautiful Virea – in marriage to the stone giant king, as payment for the construction work.

'As the craftsman Prince Albright went studiously about his task, weaving sunlight into a gold ring of overwhelming beauty, the three elf maidens told their father/brother about his boast. Ah, thought the sneaky elf lord, that marvel should be enough to buy off the Stone King – I'll offer the Stone King this fabulous ring instead of Virea. I'm sure I can trick Albright out of it somehow; these dwarfs are so trusting.

'The Stone King does agree but takes the lord's sister-in-law, who was also the three elf maidens' elder half-sister – genealogy being kind of tricky amongst elves in those days – as hostage anyway, as he knew all about elves! And so the Elf Lord, carrying a Staff of Power, won in a bet with a wizard, sets off with his army to steal the gold ring. However, Albright's brother Mica catches wind of the Elf Lord's plan and hurries to give his beloved brother a magic helm, the Dwarfhelm, and the dwarf-hammer Balthung, the mightiest sword ever forged, that he had himself made to help protect the realm.

'Albright thanks his brother, whom he loves deeply, being a good dwarf, and pledges to save all the dwarfs from the treachery of the elves. When the Elf Lord arrives, all smiles and sly intentions, he asks to see the wonder the dwarf Albright has created. Instead of the gold ring, though, Albright shows him the magical Dwarfhelm, which is pretty impressive too. The elf is impressed, of course, but when Albright puts on the Dwarfhelm and changes himself into a huge worm, the Elf Lord is shocked and surprised and the entire host of elves falls before Albright, declaring that the magic of the dwarfs is indeed great. Albright is pleased with the effect, and so when the crafty Elf Lord asks if he can turn into something small, as well as huge, he is only too happy to show off his brother's skill. Albright then changes himself into a toad and he and the Dwarfhelm and the sword Balthung are then taken by the elves, and Albright, now back in his own skin, is knocked unconscious by Wolond's Staff of Power.

'The Elf Lord takes the golden ring from the stunned Albright's hand and is filled with lust for its beauty, which has indeed captured all the beauty of the sun itself. It happens. Poor Albright is shattered to see his life's work fall into such hands and he curses the ring, but the Elf Lord only laughs. However, the Elf Lord still needs to get his sister-in-law back, or his wife will be sorely annoyed, but he no longer wants to give up the ring. He has another idea. With their prince held at knifepoint, he tells the dwarfs to collect all their gold and precious jewels, and when the Stone King arrives he then offers him this trove in return for his sister-in-law. The Stone King, who, as I may have mentioned, was no fool either, knows this is another trick and says he will take the treasure if there is enough there to completely hide Virea. The dwarfs, including Albright, are made to pile their gold and jewels around the elf lady, but being kind-natured Albright leaves a small air hole for the poor elfess. The

Stone King notices this, and when the work of the dwarfs is done, he declares he can still see one of Virea's eyes and forces the Elf Lord to put the golden ring on the treasure pile as well. Outwitted, the Elf Lord throws the ring on the pile furiously, but just as the Stone King is about to take the ring, his own stone giant brother, Faf, makes a successful grab for the Dwarfhelm, and putting it on, changes into Fafener, the greatest dragon Widergard has ever seen.

'Driven wild by a dragon's gold lust and the curse of the ring, in a mighty battle the like of which Widergard has never seen before, and which takes up most of the production budget, Fafener kills his brother The Stone King with the sword Balthung, shattering it into shards, and drives everyone from the dwarf kingdom. The treacherous elves make their way to their new castle, while Albright and Mica and the shards of Balthung are driven into exile, and deep is the sorrow of the dwarfs.'

I paused for breath, a small emotional lump in my throat, and silence slipped into the front of the Dragonette like a beggar at a banquet.

'Yes, that would be quite a long drama,' said Elsie, finally.

'Oh, that's just Part One,' I had to admit.

'Perhaps Part Two can wait for a bit?' she said, stretching. 'I'm getting a kiss from the Dream Prince.'

'Sure,' I said, pulling down the ragtop as the air was getting just a slight chill in it, and putting on the voice of the man who always says this kind of thing, added: 'Stay tuned to hear the exciting conclusion of our story in our next episode.'

Elsie stifled a yawn. 'Did I detect just a little bit of anti-elf sentiment in the story?'

I scratched my stubble. 'You know, now you come to mention it, there could be a pixie's pinch. I'd never noticed it before! Wonder why that is?'

Elsie laughed. 'I might even anticipate that the elves' version of the events would vary from those you describe – maybe just a little?'

I feigned surprise. 'I can't imagine how – that pretty much gives all the facts.' I pumped up the steam and took off the hand-brake. 'Still, folk can surprise you! Just earlier today a woman I suspected of having all the warmth of the northern ice cap turns out to be a devoted aunt.'

'Who was that?'

'Oh, Mistress Ensanders.'

'Who did you say?'

'Secretary to his not-really-royal Highness Evermore Solitude Truelight. When I first met her, sub-zero disposition, then she goes all mushy over her niece's newborn.'

'Oh really? As you say, you never can tell. Anyway, thanks for the low-down on dwarf drama, Nicely – very educational.'

'Drama? Shoot, no!' I grinned, reversing back from the viewpoint. 'Didn't I say? The Golden Ring, it's a musical!'

Elsie laughed appreciatively at my joke. I like a woman who does that, shows they have a good sense of humour.

The exhausted girl slept most of the way back to the Citadel, her head on my broad shoulders, which was kind of nice in a field full of wild flowers and tweeting birds sort of way. I dropped her off at her lodgings and was rewarded with a sleepy kiss that promised a lot more later. Later I hoped would be the supper she invited me around for on her next day off. I drove back to my rooms, floating on more air than could safely be contained in the four tyres of my '57 Dragonette.

The supper date could not come round quick enough. It looked like it would be an exciting few days. Except it wasn't. First off, I had a positive message from Josh the photographer, who had found a sketcher to update Daisy's photograph. Encouraged, I tried to contact Getgold, but was told he was 'away', which was very strange as he had not been 'away' the day before. I didn't like the attitude of Master Grounding, but did not want to annoy him any further as he was still the client after all. Meanwhile my further enquiries about Bigelow's night-time tenants were getting me nowhere on horseback. I was very much of a mind to go talk with the relatives Vericeema was supposed to have been staying with, even if it meant an outing in the Dragonette to one of the distant Havens the elves favoured. Before that, I had another elf to speak with.

Selicia Brightfire Truelight was not an easy elf to track down. She was surrounded by assistants and advisors for a start, and they had their own assistants and advisors that had to be circumvented first before you could speak to the real assistants and advisors. It was like she was famous or something! A whole morning wasted. So in the end I did what I do best, and should have done in the first place: I cheated. I bought myself a very loud shirt in an interesting mixture of primary colours and some expensive sunshades and suddenly dwarfdom's newest and hottest rolling picture producer, 'Dally Diamond-mine', was in town. Here, especially to sign up major star 'Brightfire' for what had to be the Biggest Theatrical Event of the Age, the first all-colour production of 'The Golden Ring'. Then you should have seen the assistants and advisors shift.

Drinks were arranged for mid-afternoon at the sort of place where drinks are drunk mid-afternoon.

'Bron's? Of course Dally Diamondmine knew Bron's! He was never out of Bron's when he was in the Citadel! On the roof garden? Dally Diamondmine loves the roof garden, marvellous view.'

I know a dwarf, who knows a man, who knows another man who drives one of those wagons that take up far too much space on the road and make too much steam, but for some reason easily impress folk who are easily impressed by such things. For a handful of corn, the man who knows a man, who knows a dwarf that knows me, will put on a hat and drive you places where folk are supposed to turn up in wagons like that.

It was a nice afternoon at Bron's. The tinted-windowed wagon pulled up outside the marble staircase and the Elf with No Name skipped lightly down the flight to open the door.

I stepped out, exuding good-fellowship from every pore and pressed low-grade buckskin into his hand.

'Thanks, Bleach, buy the family a new treehouse!'

The elf blinked twice before replying, 'Has the Master Dwarf had an accident with his shirt?'

I looked down as if surprised. 'Well, I guess not.'

'Only it appears to be screaming, Master Dwarf.'

'Trends come and go but style lasts for ever, Bleach-baby!'

'That is certainly a shirt I will never forget, Master…?'

'Diamondmine, Dally Diamondmine. Here for drinks with Selicia Brightfire Truelight on the roof garden,' I said, stepping lively up the staircase.

'Oh yes, of course.' He followed me with a sad lack of enthusiasm. 'Highlight of the afternoon. Mind you,' he added, picking up the pace, 'it might just now have got a bit more interesting.'

The elf introduced me with an impressively straight face. 'Master Dally Diamondmine for Selicia Brightfire Truelight. Do let me know if there is anything else you require, please.' He withdrew with just a hint of a smile playing around his lips.

Looking at the laden drinks trolley, I couldn't think of anything else that I might require, apart from a new liver. Selicia was spread all over a day bed looking better than double cream on honey-bread. She stood up in a single motion that redefined gracefulness for a new generation and extended her arm and hand, more refined than the most elegant of swans.

'What a pleasure to meet you finally, Master Diamondmine. I have heard so many good things about you.'

'Hi Twinkle,' I said, taking off the sunshades. 'Missed me?'

'Bunny Bedwell!' She turned to the imagined help. 'Take away the good drink and bring out a flagon of common ale!'

'Hey Twinkle, don't be like that. I don't mind a drop of the good stuff.' I walked to the trolley and helped myself to something that looked sticky and expensive.

'Yes, because of course it isn't 'Bunny Bedwell', is it?' She sat down again, much more matter of factly. 'Or Dally Diamond-mine – it's Master Detective Nicely Strongoak.'

'BUZZ! The lady answers correctly. Now will she take the prize on offer or go for the treasure trove?'

'What can I do for you, Master Detective, apart from work on your script?' She took a long drink from her high glass like she needed it.

'Maybe I was just wondering whether that window was still open?' I said, sitting down next to her. 'Or maybe I was wondering exactly where your sister Vericeema is?'

'So it is about her,' she sighed. 'Isn't it always?'

'That didn't sound exactly sisterly, Twinkle. No ill-will, surely?'

'What, just because she is my brother's favourite?'

'Which would not encourage you to do something to, perhaps, muddy her name? Get your own back for Evermore's neglect of you?'

'No, of course not! Anyway, I didn't say he neglected me, and she is my sister after all.'

'Your half-sister.'

'We still shared a father; she is still the same blood.'

'But you don't know where she is?'

'No, why?' She sounded genuinely puzzled 'The last time I saw her was months ago and she was behaving strangely then. Moody, if you must know.'

'Moody?' I queried. 'That's an interesting thing to be. Define moody for me? Moody like unsettled, or moody like unsettling?'

'Look...' Selicia Brightfire put down her drink and stared me in the eye. 'I don't always see eye-to-eye with my sister. She is of a romantic nature, given to long walks along the beach at sunset and moonlit hikes in the old forests. The full elf-queen narrative. Myself, I am somewhat more pragmatic. This is the Modern Age and we have to get on with it. That whole doleful maiden business is out of date; virginal, pure and dutiful daughters have gone the way of the princes with the big shiny swords and excellent dentition. We all have a living to make, but if you're looking for Vericeema, she's probably trying to find a horse white enough for bareback riding or a pool she can stand winsomely in. Now, if there is nothing else, and you're not going to offer me a starring role in one of the most one-sided pieces of dwarf self-promotion ever put to parchment, I had better get on.'

I finished my drink, and put it down, still holding her eye. 'For what's it's worth, Twinkle, I believe you. Thanks for your time and the drink.' I turned to leave.

It was then that Blaze walked in, to 'accidentally' bump into the big-time dwarf producer who may just have a role in his next film for a tall dark-haired actor with more jaw than grey matter. He was about to go into his well-rehearsed spontaneous speech when he recognised me and his brow creased up in what was either pain or thought.

I turned back to Selicia Brightfire. 'Honestly, Twinkle, you can do better than that!'

'I know,' she said mournfully.

Blaze wanted to say something clever. I could see him trying. Sadly, it was not a time for anything hearty.

You sometimes reach a time where the board is set and the pieces are all moving and the game unfolds. At other times, the board has been used to light the fire, the pieces are still in the box, and probably a few of them are missing as well.

The next day I sat and contemplated in the office. I was trying to draw up a plan of campaign when the messenger arrived. The plan wasn't looking very good so far, lacking what a plan usually requires, to wit a strategy, tactics or a workable approach. The waste bin was full of previous versions of the plan that contained even less. The current rendition had three headings: priorities, procedures and predicted outcomes. I think I read about this approach in a popular self-improvement scroll I never got round to finishing properly. Each column was empty, as was my head. I promised myself to never ever consider self-improvement again. I'm not saying I didn't have room for it, just that I kind of liked me the way I was, which essentially was somebody who didn't read self-improvement scrolls or make plans on parchment with three columns drawn out on them.

The waste bin was full to overflowing, and actually over-flowed just as the messenger rang the waiting room bell. I invited him in. He was wearing a tabard. Not the sort of tabard that the young folk wear to the beach either, which feature witty slogans or have cute pictures drawn on them. The messenger was wearing the full-fellowship, with tassels, crests and intricate embroidery, which is still inferior to needlepoint in my book. He didn't quite have a silver tray, but he did carry a scroll with a seal I recognised: High Councillor Evermore Solitude Truelight. I broke it and read that High Councillor Evermore Solitude Truelight would no longer be requiring my services. The matter was now settled to his satisfaction and he thanked me for my efforts on his behalf and the scroll contained remuneration for the contracted amount with a bonus for my 'much appreciated discretion'.

The messenger asked if there was a reply. I wanted to give him a reply, but decided that my 'much appreciated discretion' was best exercised here. I gave the messenger a good tip, though, after all, my finances had just received a considerable boost and I had a much-anticipated date with a beautiful woman awaiting me. Yes, the world was good. And here I was ready to rip the head off a stone troll and make a rockery out of his innards. Matters were not settled to my satisfaction.

I closed the office up early, before I did it any damage. Trying not to let the world interfere with my love life too much, I visited a florist to see how much inflorescence one dwarf could carry at one time. The young man in the store, who assured me that quality counted more than quantity for ladies of quality, which was why they were ladies of quality in the first place, dissuaded me from this action.

I had a beezer teaser on ice in my rooms at the Armoury, ready for just this occasion. Then, shirt ironed, suit pressed, dragon-hide hat at just the right angle, I strolled over to Elsera's place. It wasn't too far, and it was a nice night for the time of year. I tried not to worry about work and herded the niggles into the niggle pen for the evening.

Elsera lived in a lovely part of the Citadel, an old gated, much sought-after, community called The Park that hadn't been touched by redevelopment. Of course, being sought-after, rents were ridiculously expensive, which is why she lived in a three-sided building. Actually, it had been built where two almost parallel roads converged, which meant it came to a point. Elsera lived in the top floor of the pointy bit. Cute, but it would take some getting used to, and given half a chance I would as well. At one time, the building had housed infantrymen, so it was quite reasonably known as The Barracks.

The communal front entrance to The Barracks was open, so I slipped in and made my way upstairs. Knocking on her door I felt ridiculously bashful, which is not a look that sits well on a dwarf. Fortunately she answered quickly and then I had other things to think about. Now I am a very modern dwarf, and equality between the sexes has been a taken amongst dwarf-kind for so long that I have to retune my mind to even consider any other option. But occasionally, just occasionally, you meet a woman and something about her just makes you want to go off and slay a dragon or two on her behalf. It's probably why there are so few dragons left now.

'Oh,' said Elsera, her face beaming in delight, 'Night and Day – how exquisite!'

'Ungh,' I said, or some similar other stupid noise of that ilk, forgetting I was even holding flowers, then vaguely thrusting them at the poor woman on the doorstep.

'These are the only flowers with two different perfumes, depending on the time of day you know? But you shouldn't have – these are unbelievably expensive!' She kissed me on my freshly shaved cheek, which appreciated it immensely and was willing to share.

'Ah yes, quality over quantity, I always say.'

'Of course, every time! Oh sorry, do come in, Nicely!' And in I came, my nose now treated to the smell of good home cooking as well.

'I hope you like hoggart,' Elsera said, looking for a vase for the flowers.

Do I like hoggart? Is the Dark King evil? Do wizards weave spells in the woods?

'Take your jacket and hat off,' she called through from the tiny pointed kitchen. I did as requested. Her rooms, though small in number and size, were decorated in an agreeably unfussy style. She had used a lot of reclaimed elements, from old halls and chambers, to create a fun but uncluttered space. Good lighting too.

'Will you fix the drinks, please, Nicely? I'm nearly there.'

The beezer teaser had warmed me during my stroll over, so I looked for some ice, but couldn't find it. I said as much.

'Curses,' said Elsera, coming out of the kitchen with the flowers beautifully arranged. 'I knew I'd forget something!'

'No matter,' I said, grabbing my jacket. 'I passed an all-night store on my way over. It won't take me a minute to fetch some ice.'

'Are you sure, Nicely? It would be shame to have warm bubbles.'

'No problem at all.' I gave her cheek a quick peck too.

'Hurry back.'

'You won't know I've been gone.'

I headed off, taking the stairs two at a time. I opened her front door, stepped out, and didn't see the Citadel again for over a year.

BOOK TWO

THE MINES OF ORIA

13

THE ARRIVAL

I woke up in a place called Pain. It's down the road from Helplessness and just a spit and cough away from Oblivion. Everybody has visited Pain, but I'd moved in and bought the homestead. It was dark and hot here and the drums inside my head were as loud as those thumping outside on the streets of Pain. I was having trouble hanging on to the floor; it wouldn't stop moving, so I let it go.

Sometime later, Widergard moved on its axis, continents shifted and I woke up again. The Spawn of the Dark King was forcing something down my throat that was technically a liquid but owed more to chemistry than brewing. I was then fed the skin off a goblin's shinbone. I asked for seconds, it was that good. Nobody had the decency to tuck me in, but fed and watered little Nicely rolled over and fell into something finally closer to sleep than a coma.

The third time I woke, a shaft of light penetrated the gloom, as surprising as a Wizard with a hard-on, and I got the distinct opinion that, just maybe, I was actually still alive.

There is an old joke that goes like this: what did the dwarfs invent first, the hammer or the nail? Answer: nails, because they could always bang them in with their heads – they are that hard. It happens to be true. It's the only reason I wasn't currently lying

157

in a cold dark tomb next to my departed forefathers, who all said I'd come to no good and would thus be as pleased as a dead dwarf can be.

My vague pleasure at realising that my head hadn't been split open, again, and I was actually still vital, was soon replaced by the gloom that accompanied my understanding of the predicament I was in. I was undoubtedly chained up in the hold of a filthy steamship, deprived of my liberty and a decent trouser press. And that's when the fever kicked in.

I went west for another eternity or two, which involved a certain amount of stumbling and retching accompanied later by the rumble of train on tracks. This episode stretched into something even longer than an eternity that had all the scholars in Widergard puzzling to give it a name. In the end, they called it a Strongoak. Good name, a Strongoak.

'Dwarf! Over here, dwarf!' The man shouting had forgotten this one simple fact. His yelling disrupted the swing of my pick. Don't you just hate it when that happens? Style is everything in the excavation trade.

I turned to see who was so anxious for my company. It was Overseer Scruple in his leather cap. He was not a pretty sight, even by lamplight. The flickering shadow only seemed to accentuate the missing half of his face. He had no right eye, no right ear, a gamey leg and no scruples, which is how he got his name. He also always carried a set of brass knucks that he called 'Uncle Knuckles', and had a habit of sniffing you up and down, as if to make up for his other sensory deficiencies. We did not see eye-to-eye, me and Overseer Scruple, not even the one eye that he had still working properly.

'Boss wants to see you.' He pointed at the lift and the goblin captain that waited in there for me, hardly liking to leave his precious lifeline to the surface.

I nodded, put my pick carefully down and approached the wrecked remnants of a man. 'Thanks for memorising all that, Overseer Scruple. Must have been a lot of work for you. I appreciate that.'

Scruple made a noise at the back of his throat, which in anybody else would have heralded a serious bout of vomiting.

I made my way to the lift. The goblin captain, Grimboil, a grunt of few words and fewer manners, slammed the trellis gates together, pressed a button and the engine kicked in. Gradually we were hauled up from the depths of the mine to my first taste of noonday sunlight in three moons.

I had arrived, still delirious, at the operational headquarters of the Oria Mercantile Mining Company, along with my fellow involuntaries, in a trackway cattle truck that had been deemed unsuitable for transporting livestock. This was judged to be a vast improvement on the hold of the big steamboat that had chugged its merry way from the Bayside wharf to whatever part of the blasted South Lands we now called home.

I was unconscious for most of the latter part of the journey too, dropping in and out of the delirium that accompanied the fever I had picked up in the stinking ship's hold. My health had not been of much concern to my shipmates, mostly because the food provided had at least been adequate. Otherwise, dwarf might well have been on the menu for a couple of the less fussy impressed workers, because that's what we were – very unim-pressed, impressed workers. All brought here to eke out our days grubbing in the earth for any rare gems or ore that still lined the tunnels and galleries of the old dwarf mines of Oria. 'Slaves' is another name for this predicament, and that suited us a lot better, but in the modern mining industry, as elsewhere, presentation is everything.

I was also lucky in that I had been left with most of my own clothes, dwarf apparel really only being suitable for fitting dwarfs. That included my leather jerkin. Although they had emptied my pockets, they had missed my 'pick-pocket's foil'. This is a pocket sewn into a jerkin's lining with a very hard-to-find entry slit under the armpit. As was my habit, I kept in the foil small items vital for any case I was working on, a certified document related to my name, age and history and a five hundred new crown note. This last one was, potentially at least, my way out of here. First, I had to concentrate on survival and learning the ropes, although I did have a head start on the rest of the slaves. This was fortunate, as the training was brief. We were given a pick, put into a tunnel and told to dig. Made you wonder why we dwarfs had ever thought it worth producing training courses that took years of study. This was certainly a time-saving approach to education, but not recommended for those going into anything involving brain surgery.

I remember one likely lad, about twice my height, muttering in the lift as we descended into the ground on our very first day. 'I've got a plan, they'll never hold me!' he said, as the rock closed in around us. They held him. They held us all. That poor sap's plan, like the plans of all the other poor saps, was soon forgotten thanks to some clever security measures. These measures were simple. They worked us for twelve hours every day, half a league underground, and then took us back to the surface and locked us into huts where we were fed before we fell exhausted into sleeps only occasionally punctuated by dreams of sunshine and fresh air. Then they woke us up and we did it all again.

There were occasional 'rest' days – not for our benefit, but most likely for machine maintenance or for the guards to sleep off their hangovers. However, you never knew when they were coming, so you couldn't make any plans. The windows were not barred on account of the fact that there were no windows. This is because there were two shifts – 'day' and 'night' – although you pretty much never knew which one you were on. The lack of windows ensured there were no cracks of illumination to disturb light sleepers. This was as considerate as they got.

The inadequate ventilation and nocturnal gaseous emissions of thirty males of various races, with different degrees of gut efficiency, meant that as soon as the door opened in the morning you were too busy grabbing at air to consider escaping before you were put underground again.

Tunnelling out from the huts? Forget it. The ground was hard; the guards were harder still. Known as 'captains', each had a shooter and a nasty braided whip called a 'Lugburg Lick'. They were, without exception, goblins. Now I know it is far too easy to be gruntist, and I have known plenty of good goblins. They are, after all, excellent with tools and engines, and I wouldn't leave my '57 Dragonette with anyone other than my local grease goblin, but when they are bad they are the scum of Widergard. And these were the scum that the other scum had thrown out of the Scum Guild for being just too disreputable. Their mothers had probably all run away from home at the first opportunity, and then taken vows of celibacy. The fathers, I'm guessing, were generally murdered before the captains all reached puberty, if they were lucky. If not, poor old Da probably had a far worse fate in store. Growing lads need protein.

Although it was hard to choose between such a collection of beauties, by general consensus the worst two captains were a wiry, greasy, runt called Wissal and a huge grunt bruiser with the very apt name of Wetfang. Wissal, all slicked hair and loud shirts, was an artist with his lick. He could take the top off your ear from ten feet and stripe your back a fingernail deep before you even knew what was happening. And he enjoyed it too.

Wetfang had a more direct approach to man, gnome and dwarf management: a 'slap' that left your ears ringing like you had just spent the day playing head-butts with an armoury wall. He didn't particularly enjoy doing it; he just didn't care either way.

I'd had a few run ins with Wissal and felt the lick, though thankfully both my ears were still intact. He seemed to be a little nervous around me, as if dwarfs were something of a novelty for him. One time, apparently, I was too slow getting on parade – the head count they carried out at the start and end of each shift. Wissal gave me some encouragement that I felt cut right through the thin kecks that counted as a uniform. When I didn't yell out, he gave me some more, which brought me up some. I was ready for the third one and didn't even flinch.

'Tough little ground-hugger, ain't you?' said Wissal, all snarky. 'Hard Master Dwarf, all the way from New Iron Town – well, in case you ain't noticed, you're a long ways from home, trip hazard!'

'Very good – "trip hazard", I like that. Did you think it up all by yourself?'

'What's it to you, hoof-licker?'

'Now, that was just trying too hard, Wissal.'

'Hey!' I continued before he could think of a comeback, 'do you know the maximum weight a standard spruce pit prop can support?'

'Now why would I want to know that?' He smiled. 'I don't need to know nothing like that!'

I smiled in what I hoped was a cheery fashion. 'Of course not. I just want you to remember that I do know the maximum weight a standard spruce pit prop can support. You might want to bear that in mind, when you're underground – you know, walking down a new galley. By yourself, maybe.'

Wissal didn't look too snarky at me after that. And from then, whenever he was supervising a shift he kept well away from me and any new tunnels I'd been near.

I hadn't had occasion to cross swords with Wetfang and I didn't want to. He was the number two in the mine and didn't offer second chances. One wrong move or word and you could be shovelling one-handed. Fortunately he didn't get under-ground much; none of the captains exactly rushed to. Who can blame them? It was ridiculously hot and the air quality wasn't what it should have been despite the steam-driven bellows. Most of the on-hand supervision fell to the overseers. These were ex-workers who had shown their skill for stinking on their fellows and were thus freed up from the hardest graft to ensure production didn't ever fall behind. For this they got better accommodation, a drinks ration and a daily taste of fresh air. Of course, they also had to be looking over their shoulders every two minutes for the occasional flying pick head that had 'acci-dentally' come loose; not my idea of 'advancement' at all. The men had rather jolly names for them all. There was Overseer 'Lucid' Pucid, who had a very bad speech impediment, Overseer 'Nimble' Kimble, who limped badly, and the six-foot-tall brick privy of a man, Overseer 'One-candle' Noncle, who really wasn't very bright at all. Oh yes, and Overseer Scruples: half man, half scar tissue.

The rest of us workers, well our job was clear: to take the rocks from the ground and to do it without giving any grief to the captains and especially not to the Boss. The Boss wanted a quiet life and so you didn't make any fuss, not if you wanted to live to fuss another day. They weren't really trying to kill us, though – the food at least was filling, if rather dull. The coffee, however, stank. It literally stank. I don't know what they made it with, but it reeked. Beans, if indeed beans had ever been involved in the process, were probably thrown into a large stew pot and allowed to cook for a day or too while the pot was kept topped up by goblins relieving themselves at will. Only then was something added that produced the same effect as coffee without any of the taste or pleasure. The men all called it Witches' Widdle. I called it a crime against coffee-drinking and to serve it should have been a punishable offence – if it wasn't for the fact that we were all being held against our wills anyway. Somebody was going to pay for that and pay double for making us drink the Witches' Widdle.

Mostly, though, like Wetfang, the captains just weren't that concerned whether we lived or died. Actually, that's not true. Dead workers would mean having to replace us, and that meant sending out the snatcher gangs to strong-arm the drunks in the lowest taverns of the Citadel or jump preoccupied dwarfs on their way to collect some ice for cocktails.

I had it relatively easy compared with my fellows. Being underground was second nature to me of course and I had spent my compulsory year in the mines of New Iron Town carrying out my Societal Service. This is designed to instil into young dwarfs a sense of nationhood and an awareness of their cultural identity. It is actually a form of cheap labour and a way for a young dwarf of either sex, full of hormones raging as only dwarf hormones can rage, to direct their energies in a useful direction and lose their virginity along the way. You also learnt how to wield a pick and follow a seam.

My fellow workers had been picked for their reasonable physiques, as well as their ability to get blind drunk and be carried away to a waiting ship. Some with ogre blood were just too big to ever be comfortable in the tunnels and they had it tough. There were some gnomes, who got drafted for all the really close-quarter work, plenty of men and just the one dwarf. There was even a troll who never made it past the main gallery and happily spent each day pushing full rock-filled wagons into the lifts as if they were just filled with spun-sugarloaf. It was nobody else's idea of a fun time, though. There wasn't even the compensation of a payslip waiting, or a bag of corn. 'Dig till you drop' was the order of the day and these mines had seen their fair share of digging and dropping.

The Dwarf Mines of Oria are old, old by anybody's measure. The word was that Oria was never prime dwarf living accommodation – too far south! These were therefore not the magnificent halls of Elder Dwarfdom or even typical of the functional cosiness of New Iron Town – here it was all about the rocks. This was deep-cast work and the dwarfs had simply been visitors to the south, exploiting where the deep mantle rocks had been pushed closer to the surface by geological processes, searching for that most elusive and valued of gems: dragon's eyes. These are the red diamonds that make every other gem look like so much cheap glass, almost magically bending candle or daylight into a breathtaking kaleidoscopic explosion of colour, changing from a vivid mulberry to a blazing sunset orange as they are rotated. And amazingly, unlike other fancy diamonds, their colour is not down to impurities. These are as pure as the most prized colourless diamond; some other chemical magic brings about the incredible transformation. Unless of course the legends are right and these are the buried eyes of long-departed fire-breathing worms looking down at us across the ages.

The Mines of Oria were abandoned by the dwarfs ages ago when the mineral wealth had been judged to be all but exhausted and extraction was proving too difficult and expensive. It had taken the development of the steam engine to make them viable again. As long as you didn't have to do anything too crazy, like paying the workers. Which is probably why the goblins ended up in residence here. Nobody can ever say that the goblins don't make good steam.

Lifts driven by two huge wheeled engines sent the workers down the mine and then brought the wagons of ore up. They did it all day and then they did it all night. These wagons were connected in trains and then coupled behind either of two further huge engines that pulled the wagons along a single track to sorting and smelting plants far, far away to the north. It wasn't just red diamonds that were found in the Mines of Oria. Lots of other minerals were present and even the gangue was probably finding a use in these more needy times.

It was all very simple, and well worked out, and really the chances of anybody ever escaping seemed practically zero. However, I, of course, had a plan.

As I reached the surface and walked out of the lift cage, the heat smashed down on me like a lava landslide. Still blinking my eyes rapidly after the darkness of the mine, I was escorted across the compacted compound parade ground by the captain. There wasn't much to the compound: the men's huts, the better accommodation and offices belonging to the 'management', their canteen and a train shed, which was probably never used because the trains never seemed to stop running. Interestingly the shed had an incredibly tall pole attached to it, with something like a platform at the top. An extra lookout post maybe, but looking for what? A high fence that wasn't half as discouraging as the desert beyond it surrounded everything in the compound.

We strolled across the compound to the Boss's main office building, trying not to bake in the scorching air. The captain opened the door to a small outer room where nine fat flies buzzed around a lazy ceiling fan that didn't manage to stir up enough dust worth commenting on.

'Wait,' said the captain, with an economy of words one of those modern poets that get talked about in the news scrolls would envy. 'Sit,' he added, to show the first epic wasn't a fluke. He left me and went into the office. I was alone and unguarded for the first time since I'd arrived here.

If I wanted to, I could probably have run off, vaulted the inadequately guarded fence, and got clean away into the surrounding wastes where, dying of thirst, I would probably have made a good meal for the circling buzzards within a day or two. I sat and waited. The flies were as glossy, bloated and nasty as a tax auditor's ambition – black riders on the wings of corruption.

The captain finally came out of the office, grunted, 'Stand,' and gestured me in, presumably having exhausted his vocabulary, to where I would have my interview with the Boss.

Almost everything about the Boss screamed 'goblin' – the huge head with enough rolls of fat to carpet an abattoir, the arms that could double as legs on many other races and eyes that might have been filched from a passing bullfrog. The only things that didn't quite fit were the teeth. They were small, neat, very white and very pointy. I would have suspected advanced dental work if I hadn't previously seen a similar set in the mouth of a Hill hoodlum who was classifiable as a man; he even had a certificate to prove it by all that's White and Wise. The lowlife was called Petal. This Boss, as I now found out, went by the name of Blossom, and they say wizards' fire never strikes twice in the same place, eh?

The Boss was at his ease, the room's large picture window wide open and a proper fan adding to the breeze. A large map of the area around the compound, with the approximate positions of the subterranean mine workings dotted in, dominated the main wall. My, but it was large. We dwarfs had been busy here, that was for sure.

The Boss sat behind a desk that quite rightly should have been found in a wizard's seminary. There were runes cut into it from every angle. This was a desk with a story. The rest of the furniture was just places to hold things or put things, except for a lonely looking birdcage which had no bird at home. The desk, however, was something else, an epic in oak.

'Sit yourself down, dwarf,' said the Boss. Sit, stand, sit – my, what a busy day I was having already.

'Buy you a drink?' he continued.

Now that was an invitation that wouldn't get left on the mantelpiece, so I sat down on the business side of the desk and relaxed a bit.

'C'mon dwarf, name your poison?'

'Anything colder than a Snow Queen's titta should hit the mark, thanks.'

Blossom the Boss got up with the grace you sometimes find in big men that are built to be that way. Two strides and he was at a cupboard door that opened to reveal a small kitchenette that, joy of all joys, had – along with a tidy stove – a genuine ice box. A blast of cold air announced the arrival of two infantry-men who had come visiting from the right part of Widergard.

Blossom flipped the caps and passed me a condensation-decorated soldier. I tried not to down it in one – some hope.

'Let's chase that with something sticky, just to be sociable.' He took two clean glasses from the kitchenette and introduced them to a spirit that had been keeping good company as well. He put one of them down on the desk in front of me.

I tried it for size and nodded appreciation before saying: 'One free drink gets a thank you. Two gets me suspicious. Three gets me wondering if I should be buying a wedding dress.'

Blossom sat down, laughing, and had a rock in his big seat while he sucked on his ale. 'Cute. The captains said you had yourself a lip, but you knew how to keep it buttoned too.'

'Stoic is my middle name,' I said, my eye inevitably drifting to the icebox. This was, of course, just a ploy to convince the Boss I could be easily bought, or so I pretended.

Another two soldiers arrived with their caps off and soon joined the dead men. I sat back and played with the small glass of toffee. 'That's laid a lot of dust, how about you give me the pitch now while I'm good and mellow.'

'I have it on good authority that you use to be a private peeper, dwarf.'

'Now, I wonder where you heard that?'

'No matter, dwarf. Enough that you had something of a rep for doing the job and playing it straight.'

'Uh huh – honourable is my middle name too.'

'That's a lot of names, peeper.'

'They just call me Happy at home.'

'I've got me a dead body, Happy.'

I put down my glass, carefully, before I spoke. 'Probably not your first, probably not your last.'

Blossom shrugged and the neck fat did a whole little dance all of its own invention. 'Sure, we lose some workers along the way, but this is different. This is one of the captains, and he's been deflated: had his balloon well and truly popped. I want you to find out who did it.'

I thought for a moment. 'Suppose I do, what's in it for me? Apart from the pleasure I always get seeing justice prevail, which is honourable, but it doesn't cool you down during the day or keep you warm at night.'

'Depends what you're after, dwarf. It won't be a ticket back to the Hill, though. An overseer's cap might be no problem.'

'Oh great, hate of my fellow prisoners and the suspicion of the other overseers – there's an offer that's easy to refuse.'

'You're back with the pick then – after an agreeable little holiday.'

'I'm getting a little weary of the practical mining engineering too. I could have taken that option in New Iron Town, without any of Oria's fringe benefits of course, but I would have coped somehow.'

'You name it then?' said the Boss, finishing his drink.

I gave it some more thought and then finally said, 'Show me the body first.'

'Easy enough.'

I got up and stretched. 'Just one question, before we go any further, Blossom.'

'What's that, dwarf?'

'You got kin in the Citadel?'

'Not that I know of. Why?'

'No reason, no reason at all.' I followed the goblin-man out of the office.

Blossom and the captain took me out to the captains' quarters, a big building that had the luxury of separate rooms for the crew. The room we were heading too apparently belonged to Captain Wissal. He still occupied it, in the sense of taking up space – not living there, though. He wasn't living anywhere no more.

'There's a surprise, him being so social and well liked,' I commented. 'Are you sure I didn't do it?'

'No,' said Blossom, showing me those pretty teeth again. 'There's so many screwy things about this drop I'm not sure about anything much.'

The captains' quarters had proper working fans and proper windows too. A captain I didn't recognise was standing watch outside Wissal's door, or what remained of it. Some heavy axe work had reduced it mostly to firewood. I raised an eyebrow.

'Crabb here went to raise Wissal when he didn't make his shift. He discovered the door locked and couldn't get a squeak from Wissal. He found Wetfang, my number two, who was shift chief – he's got a master key, but couldn't get no interest either on account of the key still being in the hole on the inside. It was his axe work. Found the body just like you'll find it.' He motioned me in.

'Where is Wetfang now?'

'Doing his job and keeping his mouth shut. I don't want this causing any more problems than it has to. There was gyp juice between Wissal and Wetfang,' he grunted.

'There was gyp juice between Wissal and Wetfang,' I grunted back. 'Well fancy that, them being so even tempered.' It looked like I was back in the detecting business.

14

AN OLD CAREER IN A NEW TOWN

I stepped carefully into the room, looking out for splinters. Wissal was never a pretty sight at the best of times. This was not his best of times; all his time had run out. He was lying on the bed, dressed in air and flies, a half-eaten plate of something very spicy by his side, still sprinkled with something green – not a common colour in the local diet. A whole stack of smutties, a fresh bottle and another with a big bite out of it testified to the fact that Wissal was having himself a little one-goblin sleaze party here. The half-dozen puncture wounds still oozing rubies from his chest had put an end to the fun. His dead eyes glistened as he stared at a stain on the ceiling.

'Nice,' I commented to Blossom as he followed me in, leaving Crabb outside with the other captain.

'Yeah, and we have such strict employment criteria too – makes you wonder what the personnel department are all about.'

I looked around the rest of the small room. There was a badly sprung chair, an open trunk with scraps of clothes that had all seen better days and a small cupboard that had what I could only presume were his personal effects: a curved cutting knife, brass knuckles and an open blade razor – all the keepsakes of home. I sniffed at the remains of Wissal's last meal; the air was still rank with the smell of spices and the taint of death. The main window was locked and barred from the inside with a small open glass awning at the top being the only ventilation.

'So,' I said looking round, 'it seems that sometime after he had his grub last night, one of the most hated of the captains gets himself well and truly pricked in his room, locked from the inside, with nobody seeing or hearing a thing?'

'That's about the size of it, dwarf.'

I sat on the chair, which was actually even more uncomfortable than it looked.

'Right, this isn't going to be sorted overnight. So I need myself a room where I can do some talking – to captains, overseers, even the workers if I need to, and I need me a room where I can do some thinking too.'

Blossom looked around and I quickly added: 'And not this room, thank you. This here is a crime scene and remains that way until I've pulled everything apart and put it back together again.'

Blossom was about to protest, but thought better of it. 'As long as you get me the full set of rings. I don't want the crew going bite-size on each other.' He looked at me almost apologetically. 'It happens!'

'I'll find out who dropped your captain,' I said. 'Solve the locked room mystery too.'

'And then what?'

'I won't take your overseer cap, that's for sure. Neither do I really want to be breaking my back digging dirt. But I might be able to do you and me a favour.'

Blossom looked interested. 'What's that, dwarf?'

'There's better than the ore in this mine that your boys are not finding, my nose tells me. I'll scout for you, do some sampling too. And if I don't deliver, I go back with my pick and join the rest of the boys. Dukes?'

'Dukes,' he agreed. 'But I want your word you won't try anything smart like attempting to escape while you're investigating.'

'My word?'

'You dwarfs are big on that sort of thing, I hear. Don't mean an elf's eyelash to me.'

'Ok, Boss – my word, while I'm investigating, no escaping. Now, if you could find me a quill and parchment, I need to make some notes.'

He nodded and then left, saying, 'I'll sort you out that room space too.'

'And find me something to cover this plank, will you?' I shouted after him. 'He's putting me right off my lunch as it is.'

I had another look at the disturbing sight of Wissal's corpse. Whatever had stung him had been thin and sharp – like a Sidel ice pick. I counted up the number of blows. Somebody had wanted Wissal very dead. He had gone so far west I was surprised he wasn't coming back round again. I walked over to his locker and helped myself to the unopened bottle I found there. After further investigation, I also found a full purse of pipeweed in his strides. It may not have been Wissal's lucky day, but it certainly was mine. I slid down the wall and sat on the floor, that being mostly blood-free. I filled a pipe and had me another drink, trying to figure out how long I could keep this particular ball in the air and me out of the mine. I mean, I already knew how Wissal must have been killed and who did it and I sure didn't give a fairy's fart as to the why. In the meantime, a few good nights' sleep in my own room would not do me any harm at all.

The room Blossom picked out for me was identical to the quarters of the late unlamented Wissal. The same locked window and vent, the same superfluous fireplace and the same furniture. No stinking body, though, for which I was very grateful. This would do me just fine for the moment, certainly while the master plan was being cultivated.

I had collected all the evidence I needed from Wissal's room and boxed it up while he went to the ice-room ahead of his final journey to join his ancestors. I carried out a more detailed examination of the body in the ice-room, not that I thought it would yield very much. I just wanted to spend a few hours in the chill. As I thought, nothing much to write home about. The wounds were even deeper than they first appeared and some of the blood was only now beginning to clot. Somebody with proper strength had inflicted these wounds. Either that, or a madman, or perhaps a mad, strong man, or a mad, strong goblin even. There were no signs of defence wounds on the hands, which was hardly surprising as Wissal had not defended himself.

I investigated the bottle I had liberated from Wissal, profoundly glad that he had spent his money on something other than smutties and the local gut-rot. Talking of which, I was obligated to at least take a peek. Putting it off, I first of all checked out the green leafy seasoning I had scraped from the condemned goblin's last meal. Because condemned he indeed was – no crime of passion this: Wissal's demise was the product of advanced planning and cold calculation.

I nibbled a tiny corner of the little flavouring, and recognising the bitter, pungent, but not unpleasant taste, immediately spat the rest into the hearth: sickleweed, just as I had suspected. Suitable for killing old ladies and putting large mutts and small goblins to sleep. In New Iron Town, we call it sleepswell.

Sleepswell is a very potent relaxant. You learn about it on Day One of the Citadel Guard's Poisons course. You get to taste it and, despite many warnings, some of the guards get a few hours more sleep thanks to it. I was very familiar with it because it grows in the lower foothills around New Iron Town, a long way away from here. It is commonly used by old-mine physics, who also swear by extended leech use, as it helps prevent the blood from clotting. Hard to imagine sleepswell ending up on Wissal's supper by mistake.

I sighed, took another drink, and opened the box containing the smutties. They were all depressingly familiar, but I guess imagination doesn't win any prizes at this end of the trade. I then realised there was actually something very familiar about a couple of them. The pretty little doll with the long dark hair – she was the same young woman who featured in the pictures with the King of Elfland's little sister Vericeema, looking even younger. Now that was scary. To find that connection here of all places.

Then I felt the whole of Widergard revolve around me as something else fell into place. Something very nasty and very worrying and with ramifications I couldn't even begin to think about at the moment. It was a moment of clarity the like of which I couldn't properly describe. The elves probably have a word for it, but then again the elves have a word for everything – except humility. And to think it had only taken a split skull and a jaunt half-way round the world for me to realise this. I really should do this more often when a case gets tricky. Yes, and I should take to wearing leisurewear in pastel colours too. I took the smutty and put it safely in my foil pocket along with the rest of the documents and the five hundred crown note.

Sleep did not come easily that night. I lay in my bed planning and scheming. Good plans and good schemes too, although they did all rather rely on me being out of here and in the Citadel. Through the vent I became aware of the smell of cooking meat – rather late for outdoor eating, I thought to myself. Not unappetising, though. I went to the window for a look-see. My stomach did a flip when I realised what was going on outside: on a speedily improvised bonfire, Wissal was on his final excursion to join his ancestors in whatever eternity they occupied when their time was up. I don't imagine they would let him in.

Around dawn, I went out for a smoke, enjoying the early morning cool. The nightshift was still at work and the guard was asleep in his tower. I strolled over to take a quick look at the Boss's steam wagon. It was a big old monster of a vehicle with thick tyres nearly as tall as I was. Not fast, but constructed to cover every sort of landscape imaginable. If my Dragonette '57 was a work of art, this was a brick. Although the cab could only hold two or three, the tarpaulin-covered back could probably accommodate another ten. I felt the engine, still warm – evidence of a late night in the flesh-pots of the imaginatively named Coast Port. These crazy goblins, eh?

15

INTERROGATION TIME

'I don't answer no questions from no ground-hugger!' growled the big scarred goblin captain sitting opposite me.

I pulled on my pipe, enjoying the luxury of a full purse of pipeweed, and sent a pretty fair smoke-ring heading skywards. 'Well, that's fine with me, Grazbul.' I looked down at the roster of names in front of me. 'In which case, I'll just tick this little box labelled "guilty" next to your name on this scroll and thank you for making my job much easier than I thought it would be and wish you all the best for the rest for your, understandably short, life.'

The goblin had a think and you could hear the little cogs clash through unaccustomed usage. 'I didn't say nothing about being guilty!'

'You don't have to, lodhead! It's what we call "admission of guilt by non-co-operation" – don't worry your head about the details. It just saves us getting hung up with all that "evidence" business and lets us get on with the much more entertaining hanging.'

'Look…' he began.

'No, you look here, slag for brains!' I jumped up and smashed my gaffer-club down on the table. 'I am trying to do you a favour here! You think your fellow captains are sleeping too well nights at the moment, knowing as how somebody seems to be able to wraith through doors and sting with impunity?' He thought about this; I could see the steam rise. 'No,' I continued, 'and they would like nothing so much as some poor sap to throw to the ghouls simply so they can catch up on the beauty sleep they sure are in need of.'

'I ain't gonna be no dog food for no one!'

'And I'm no dewbaby!'

'Got no beef with youse, anyway,' he muttered.

'Good, then answer the questions and we can all go and find ourselves something more productive to get on with – you can whip a few workers and I can whittle myself a new nose-peg.'

'Shoot then, ground-hugger.'

'You've done that one, big boy. Let's hurry on through this here list and then we can work on some new insults and see if we can't up your creativity homework score so teacher doesn't make you stay behind later.'

With nothing much of importance riding on matters, I was rather enjoying myself.

The room Blossom sorted out for the interviews had everything I needed – essentially one large solid table between me and the interviewee. I'd asked for an axe and been given a gaffer-club instead. The captains were being de-fanged personally by Blossom, so I felt reasonably secure in the room. My long-term health was more in doubt.

I took Grazbul through my roster of questions and was not at all interested to find that he personally had no beef with Wissal, had not been anywhere near Wissal's room on the night in question and did not even own a blade. Furthermore, he wrote home each week to his mother, gave regularly to charity and had once considered a life devoted to helping others before he decided he was, on balance, much better qualified for helping himself. Which made Grazbul just about as white as all his fellow captains. Even his bosom buddy, Gozpol, as unpleasant a piece of runty goblin flesh as ever drew breath and poisoned the landscape with his waste products, managed to master the common tongue long enough to put himself in the clear. Although his collection of grunts and throat clearance barely constituted speech, he still managed to insist on his charitable nature and desire to bring peace to all of Widergard. Yes, everybody certainly bore Wissal no ill-will.

Everybody but Wetfang that is. My interview with Wetfang proceeded very differently indeed. 'I hated the little runt. Made me want to hurl, just being in the same room. I've wiped better from the sole of my boot.'

'Come on, Wetfang, give it to me straight! You didn't like Wissal, did you?'

Wetfang had proper goblin teeth – each one fighting to be bigger than the last and each with its own personal drool collection. He moved his lips into something like a smile to give me a full view of his dental work before answering, 'Fond of your own shrill ain't you, short stuff?'

'I won prizes for speaking at school. They had great hopes of me becoming a famous government orator, but drink and drugs got in the way. I couldn't keep up with the rest of the politicians.'

'Be a shame if someone was to pop the pea from your whistle some night.' Wetfang's smile turned into a leer that would send other leers right back to leer school to take extra lessons.

'Like you did to Wissal?' I banged back. 'That sounded like a real gold ring confession to me, Wetfang.'

'He wasn't cut no ruby smile, I sawed him. Stung all over, not my style at all!' he insisted.

'What do you think he was stung with then?'

Wetfang shrugged. 'I don't know and I ain't getting paid to figure it out. Just ask your questions, tooth pick.'

'Take me through what happened the morning you found his body.'

Wetfang shrugged again and examined his nails before speaking. 'Like I told Blossom, Crabb came to find me when he couldn't raise Wissal. The little runt was far too keen on his weed and bottle, which was understandable – I don't think he saw any tit as a child. I'd had to shake him out before now, but this time he didn't want to be moved.' Wetfang had himself a chuckle at this.

'Ah, stop drawing me a map with moon ink, will you?' I shouted at the goblin.

'I'm giving it to you straight, toe warmer! He didn't move, on account of him being deflated, but you probably noticed that – on account of you being a real live detective.'

'And when you'd finished making matchwood out of his door?'

'I went in and saw the little runt, just like you saw him. Nasty little blisterskin, would have stuck him myself some time, but no way I could that night.'

'On account of the door being locked?'

'Well, stick a rose up my ass and call me an elf queen, you really are a detective then?'

'Ah, get out of my sight, Wetfang!'

Wetfang got up and stretched, joints popping like a shoot-out at a goblin's wedding. 'That's a genuine pleasure, dwarf. Hanging around your kind only makes me hungry.'

'Just don't leave town.'

He leant down and put hands the size of shovels onto the desk before speaking: 'And what could you do to stop me, white bait?'

Grinning his spittle-charged fang-fest, he turned and leisurely strode out of the room with that particularly confident goblin roll that makes you wonder whether they really will inherit Widergard one day.

Overall, though, I thought it had gone pretty well.

One of the perks of my new job was the chance to eat in the dining hall rather than to have my nutritious but barely edible slop thrown into a bowl in the confines of the sleeping quarters. The dining hall was a long room with a shuttered counter down one side, where we queued for what tasted like culinary gold after the normal pigswill. Whole vegetables, real bread and meat – what sort of meat was anybody's guess, but I'm thinking anything with four legs was 'game' in these parts, just hopefully nothing on two. One particularly chewy steak was said to come from a striped horse that lives even further south, but I have a feeling my top-knot was being pulled: horses don't wear night clothes. Not that I was overburdened with conversation at meal-times. I was treated with the suspicion usually reserved for law enforcement officers everywhere. We were allowed to eat in our rooms too, like Wissal had that fateful night, but these were looked over by the shift manager to make sure nobody was shown any favouritism. It's amazing how many fights can start over an extra steak slipped under the mashed roots.

On that first morning at breakfast, when the shutters went up with a bang and we all started shuffling forward, metal trays in hand, Overseer 'One-candle' Noncle queried whether I should get the same helpings as everybody else on account of me being a 'doorstop'. I didn't want to start trouble on my first day, but I needed to ensure my authority was recognised, otherwise the interviewing would be a non-starter. I wondered how to best address the problem and then realised I was overthinking the matter and flattened him with the tray. I'd love to say it left an Overseer Noncle-shaped impression in the metal, but it was too hard. Noncle did gain a remarkable flat section to one side of his head, though. He missed breakfast and lunch and supper too, and then Blossom fined him a day's pay for non-attendance. Fair result, I thought.

The next day in the company of the goblin captains was equally tedious, but interviewing the overseers subsequently was more fun than throwing brass rings at a bull's horn, while the bull is charging. They couldn't ignore me and neither could they mouth me off like the captains tried to. What they could do was seethe, and this they did with a proficiency that only long practice can bring.

Overseer 'Nimble' Kimble had a grudge against the world. His main complaint was that the boys from Oria had waylaid him a week after his wedding and not a week before. You might think he would have been grateful for at least having seven days with his sweetheart, but none of it. The reason he was out drinking that fateful night was that the extent of the terrible matrimonial mistake he had recently made was just beginning to dawn on him. The extent of his more recent error only becoming obvious the next day when he found himself lurching from wave to wave out of sight of land on the Good Ship 'Abandon Hope All Who Enter Here'. Now, if he was ever to make his way back to the hovel he called home, he was convinced his wife would have had him declared dead and sold all his belongings. I think this is probably true and I would wager a reasonable amount that it was the goodwife who had arranged for his sudden departure, so loathsome was the set of unpleasant habits that passed for his personality. It's what I would have done in her position, anyway.

'Listen here, Strongoak, you can't go talking to me like that! I'm an overseer I am. That's not right at all, it's not. Not right at all!'

'Well, here's the problem, Nimble...'

'Kimble, the name's Kimble!'

'Sorry. Here's the problem, Nimble Kimble. As I see it, Wissal had to get his smutties from somewhere, but none of the captains are putting their hand up for it. So I'm thinking it must have been one of the overseers.'

'Where would we get those sort of tasty treats, eh? Tell me that, Master Detective. 'Specially when we don't get down to Coast Port like the captains.'

Coast Port was the local port where the supply ships and the slave-labour pleasure boats docked. It wasn't deep enough for the ore boats, though, hence the need for the great cross-desert track way. The track ways from the different mines and quarries all joined together at the huge deep-water terminus to the north that was the shipping point for the whole of the mineral-rich South Lands continent: Coal Town.

Nimble Kimble had a point, not that I had any need to acknowledge it. Having figured out the ins and outs of the murder, what I was doing now was just for pure entertainment. And the entertainment was varied and interesting. Nobody came forward for the murder, but what else I learnt would have been a real eye-opener if my view of the good folk of Widergard wasn't already somewhat jaded. As it was, I had enough information regarding illegal and corrupt employee activities to point the

White Finger at half of the administration of the Oria Mining Company. The only reason that Blossom didn't act on these indiscretions I'm sure is that he was behind the other half, and had taken a percentage of the first fraction too.

So I nodded knowingly at everything said, made copious notes, walked around with what I hoped was an unfathomable expression and caught up with a lot of sleep, drinking and smoking. I also found myself a tasty little hand axe that I sharpened up until it could split an infinitive at fifty paces, which is to be properly feared.

I then spent some more time interviewing the mineworkers. This was a completely redundant business, of course, as there was nothing they could tell me, but I thought the lads could probably do with a day off and I managed to get a small beer quota out of Blossom in order to loosen their tongues. The sharper tools amongst them realised that they were on to what is technically known as a 'good thing' here, and considered the questions carefully and fully, cold ale in hand, before elaborating at some length on their answers. The born suspicious, not able to recognise a 'good thing' if it came along and tickled their fancies, and thinking it was all a conspiracy they couldn't fathom, had a lot more quality time to spend in the huts, sucking in the same old stale air.

I hadn't really had much chance to talk with my fellow workers since my nabbing. I wasn't the full pint on the ship or the track train and conversation wasn't exactly encouraged in the mine. That left a scant few minutes each day while eating or getting to sleep. Insomnia was not a big problem amongst the work crew.

As I suspected, most had a similar story involving one drink too many after a long working week, an offer from a woman so gorgeous they really thought their luck was in – it wasn't – or simply walking along, minding their own business in the wrong part of town. I hadn't been in the wrong part of town and I was pretty sure my luck was in no doubt until that point, which got me thinking. That got me thinking a lot, when I could find the time to do it.

I felt particularly sorry for the country boys, fresh from the fields and in the big city expecting the streets to be paved with gold. There was gold, but they had to dig for it and give it to somebody else. The gnomes had it hardest. Their small size meant that they were the 'seam breakers' – they did all the digging at the workface, where it was hardest and the most dangerous. They didn't complain, though, another thing I like about gnomes. For now, there wasn't much I could do to help them. For now, I was eating so high off the hog that if I didn't watch out all I'd have to eat was the crackling.

Sadly, all parties come to an end – even that of King Lupold the Great of Widergard, now more commonly known as Lupold the Last. His Citadel coronation bash went on for five years. It is said to have been responsible for the extinction of at least two species of water fowl, the emergence of a virulent strain of genital warts, the Citadel's greatest population bubble and the enthusiasm with which democracy was then welcomed in Greater Widergard.

I was out watching some overseers load on the coal for one of the great steam engines that pulled the ore carts on the train's week-long trek across the desert. A huge mountain of the black stuff was piled behind the train shed, but it still needed to be loaded onto the engine, which meant some proper work for the overseers. Today it was Scruple's turn. Good. I took another toke on my pipe and blew a ring, friendly like, in his direction. He didn't say hello back. Sometimes I wonder why I bother to be so polite.

The engine really was a handsome beast, dwarf-made, of course – dating back to the time before the goblin companies began making cheaper but aesthetically inferior copies for the mass market. It had a 4–8–4 wheel arrangement, that is two leading axles, four powered axles and two trailing axles, which dwarves favour because it is nicely symmetrical. Sadly, the original name had been long replaced and it was now known as the Slag Express, which tells you more than you need to know about goblin humour. Along with its twin, the Slag's Sister, it handled all the heavy trafficking, sharing the single track and passing each other mid-way on the week-long journey at the passing loop wittily named 'Slags' Crossing'.

'I wouldn't enjoy watching them work too much, Strongoak. There's already enough resentment amongst the boys regarding your advancement,' said Blossom, disturbing my review.

'Advancement?' I queried. 'Is that what this is?'

'You'll soon find out, unless you deliver some results pretty sharpish.'

'Strangely enough, I was on my way to see you.'

'What, to say you had it all figured?' he added rather too cynically.

'Yes,' I replied. 'The final piece has fallen into place.'

Blossom registered genuine surprise. 'That's not bad going, dwarf.'

'Well, I didn't get my detective's badge just because they had to tick the racial quota box that week,' I informed him.

'In that case, I'd better arrange a meeting of the Works' Committee and we can get on with nailing the sod's jolly bags to the dining hall door.'

Yes, Blossom, we'll let justice run its course.

Although the Mines of Oria were 'government of the Blossom, for the Blossom, by the Blossom', there was a pretence of democracy in that there existed a Works' Committee where major decisions were supposedly made. There was even an election every two years to elect Blossom to run the committee. It also presided over all important rule infringements, usually by nailing things to the dining hall door. Justice was swift and kind of messy in Oria.

The meeting was held in the dining hall (for ease of nailing) with all workers safely locked up and 'double bunked' in the sweltering heat of a South Lands' day. I was just glad I wasn't amongst them, for the time being.

All the captains and the overseers were there, although only the captains had a vote: a goblin's idea of democracy, got to love it. The mood was bullish, folk were restless, and in the meantime, the floor, as they say, was mine.

'Goblin captains, overseers, and our Boss, Blossom. It is a sorry duty I have to perform now, to put before you the details of this wicked deed performed in our little community and unmask the culprit. Because I do know the culprit!' I eyed them all in what I hoped was a suitably enigmatic way, designed to get the hardest goblin worried. I failed, but didn't let that deter me.

'At first sight, this looks like an impossible murder: a locked door, the corpse inside – our dearly departed colleague Wissal.' This got the laugh I knew it would – I was playing to the cheap seats after all.

'Who could possibly have entered Wissal's room overnight with the key still in the lock? Was it man, gnome, goblin or something else entirely – something fell?' This got the intakes of breath I knew it would do – superstitious lot, your goblin criminal.

'It was a dark night, but could any darkness hide so foul a deed?'

'We all hated him. Get on with it, doorstop!' shouted Wetfang, to larger laughs. Just what I needed, a popular heckler.

'Ah yes,' I said, taking this in my stride, 'Captain Wetfang, the goblin who found the deceased.'

'I did, and he was no prettier in death than in life. No, thinking about it, maybe he was! At least he wasn't making any noise now.' The best laugh yet for Wetfang. Tough audience.

'No,' I said. 'He wasn't making any noise, despite the banging on his door by his shift manager and yourself.'

'That's right,' said Wetfang, slightly unsure where this was going. 'The dead don't normally answer back. It's one of the things I like about them.'

'Yes!' I replied quickly, before the laughing could start again. 'The dead don't answer back – and neither do the drugged!'

'What are saying, doorstop?' said Wetfang, put out. 'What do you mean drugged?'

'By a massive dose of sleepswell put in his food.'

'I don't know about that!'

'No? Not when you were shift manager that evening and checked his tray?'

'Hey, I never…'

'Enough sleepswell to stop him answering the door in the morning, so you could break it down and enter by yourself…'

'That was in case of trouble inside… I don't like where this is going!' Wetfang was now up on his feet.

'So you could enter by yourself and stab the drugged Wissal repeatedly so that when further help eventually came to check, he was indeed dead!'

'No!' shouted Wetfang, thumping the table. 'The little grease-spot was dead when I got in there, I tell you. It wasn't me!'

'Well, Captain Wetfang – it couldn't have been anybody else, could it? You were the first one in there and you ventilated him!'

The goblin looked around, his eyes filled with panic. 'It wasn't me, I'm telling you! They're fitting me with a red cap! It's a fix!'

He went to run, but a group of Blossom's loyalist captains was positioned just as I'd instructed and soon had him pinned. He fought well, I'll give him that, protesting his innocence, and cursing me, Blossom and the entire mine management right up until the moment his throat was cut, which was about two minutes later.

As I said, justice was swift and kind of messy in Oria, but at least this time it wasn't down to me to clean things up.

16

NIGHTLIGHT

I cannot pretend it was fun to be back underground. Underground is fine, don't get me wrong. It's just that subterranean meanderings weren't exactly top of my list of things to be doing at this time of my life. At least my 'pick and shovel' days were behind me, for the moment. Blossom had been as good as his word and I was on scouting duties, which was all right with me. I soon repaid his trust by finding a rich vein of elf-tin, a mineral much in demand for many of the new industries that require lightweight, ductile, non-magnetic metals.

We were bosom buddies, oh yeah, and dragons are big on anonymous charity giving.

It wasn't the Boss or even the captains that were my major headache. I also still got on fine with most of the actual workers. My main problem was the overseers. They weren't sure where I fitted in the hierarchy and they didn't like the fact that I had achieved some seniority without ruining my credibility. Scruple was particularly unpleasant, so no change there.

Nuts to them, but I watched my back when I was underground. However, I did need to be underground for my escape plan to succeed. Strange as it may seem.

Makeshift detective work aside, it was taking me rather longer to find what I was after than I had anticipated. The large steam-driven bellows were partly to blame. They were so loud and did such a good job of pulling down air from the surface that they masked what I was searching for.

Then my fortune changed – luck found me, or rather I found luck, a full moon after Wetfang's reluctant wet resignation.

She was asleep on a small ledge in a side tunnel off the long-exhausted gallery where I was sitting eating a little light lunch. I was some distance from the gallery and had stopped to have my snap. I rested my torch, content to eat my victuals in the comfortable blackness, when I realised everything wasn't as black as it should be.

I sought out the side-tunnel and the faint, almost non-existent (to other than dwarf eyes) glow therein. Not more than half a dozen paces from the entrance was a shelf for lanterns and she lay there fast asleep, her glow fluttering along with her laboured breathing. A genuine, real, look-I'm-sober, wild pixie – and she was not in a good way. The way her internal glow was flickering reminded me uncomfortably of a candle about to go out.

'Come here, little nightlight,' I said, moving her gently to try to judge the extent of her injuries. She never even woke, simply made tiny groaning noises as she tossed in her stupor. One of her wings was broken, very badly, that much was obvious, and she was covered from top to bottom with scratches and bruises, but her limbs at least seemed intact. Injuries aside, she was just your average beautiful, two-hand-high, magical wild fairy.

I wetted a none-too-clean kerchief from my flask and very gently wiped the worst muck off her. It didn't achieve too much. I poured some of the water into the flask cap and tried to get her to drink. This she did gratefully, still without waking to anything like proper consciousness.

I filled up the flask cap again and she almost wrenched it from my fingers: 'Easy there, nightlight. Easy girl.' She finished the capful and the effort seemed to drain her of all energy and she passed out again. Although still obviously dazed, she was at least breathing more easily and her glow waxed and waned in a less worrying manner.

I took my padded cap off and manoeuvred her into it. This had to be more comfortable than solid rock. Within a few minutes she was asleep, a little more naturally. I stood and watched her, as entranced as a child seeing the first snow fall in his own back garden.

I didn't know much about the pix, but then again nobody really does. As the folks of Widergard get smarter, so the Wise and White, in their tall towers, have developed a lot of clever ideas about how we're all related and might even share a common ancestor: men, elves, dwarfs, goblins and gnomes. Yes, even tree friends, trolls and ogres. But then there are the pixies. Nobody knows where the pix fit in. They just don't seem to. It's that damn magic business, you see. Magic doesn't really exist – that's the story we tell. So there can't be anything magical about the pix, but as was once said, the pixies aren't magical: they are magic. Many of the old legends, especially those big on the exploits of elves and men, don't even mention them, a bit like the embarrassing family relative who doesn't get mentioned when the rich new neighbours come to visit.

Pixies are also increasingly rare. This is because pixies are supposed to bring good luck. And wild pixies are the luckiest. This has made pixies an endangered species. There are urban pixies, but they aren't so lucky, probably because they have bad manners and tend to run to fat what with all the junk food they put away. Still very good company, though, and you are best advised not to get on their wrong side.

Want to know how to tell the difference between a wild pixie and an urban pixie? Simple, wild pixies fly and don't wear clothes and, quite frankly, I was glad to get little Nightlight, as I had now named her, covered up.

I broke off a piece of breakbread and dipped it into some water. I couldn't interest her in it, though. I left it by her side in the cap, along with some of the dried fruit my new position had made me eligible for.

I sat and watched her for an hour or three. She didn't seem to be getting any better, but she didn't seem to be getting any worse either, which was some relief.

I hated to leave her there, but I didn't have any other option – not if I wanted to get myself, and her, out of Oria. Especially now, because finding the little pixie had told me the one thing I wanted to know. I was close to my goal. The pix do not, as a rule, live underground. This meant she must have got down here somehow and I think I knew the 'how' of it. It also meant I was probably totally wrong about the murder of the unlucky Wissal, and the execution of Wetfang. The last one I could live with.

I filled up the flask cap and wetted some more bread, leaving them close to the grounded pixie, then made my way back to the main gallery. The overseers were already looking for excuses to play head-butts. I didn't need to add lateness to their list of invented grievances.

Little Nightlight was miles away from the main dig and it was highly unlikely that she would be found by the next shift, but I still wasn't easy as we returned to the surface. This unease stayed with me through the night, and for the first time since being waylaid and shipped off to Oria, I found it hard to sleep.

I tossed uncomfortably on my hard pallet, memories mixing with imaginings in a most disturbing manner. When I finally got to sleep, I dreamt that I was on a steam train heading to the Citadel on tracks made of red diamonds. I kept looking at my timepiece, aware that I was late. I knew that Elsie, Vericeema and Nightlight would be pacing anxiously outside my rooms wondering where I was, but the more steam I piled on and the faster the train chugged, the further away the Citadel seemed to get. I had to tell the engineer to pile on yet more steam. By the time I made it to the engine house, I could see something terrible through the front window: the three women were tied to the tracks ahead of us. I shouted at the engineer to brake; he turned around and shrugged apologetically. It was Councillor Truelight and he had his hand on the throttle. I woke up in a sweat, shouting incomprehensibly.

I didn't disturb anybody else fortunately, as this is how most folk wake up in Oria.

Heading down on the lift after breakfast the next day, I tried not to appear too keen to get back to the mine, as that would cause more suspicion than a goblin captain coming round with a charity collection box. Finally, giving Overseer Scruple an itinerary for the day that he had absolutely no interest in listening to, I headed out, torch aloft.

She was just where I had left her, sleeping peacefully. The water and food were both gone, so I topped up the flask cap, wetted some more bread and broke off a piece of fruit. She still didn't wake, so I set off, hopefully to complete the search that had occupied most of my time since my brief spell as Oria's first and only private detective. I found it in minutes; maybe some of that pixie luck was rubbing off already.

The draught was persistent, though hardly noticeable unless you were looking for it. I was looking for it and I had found it: a dwarf chimney. Every mine had two, maybe three of them. These were last resort only, drilled when the mines were first dug. One straight chimney, too small for a man, too big for a gnome – just suitable for a dwarf to climb up out of. There was only the faintest, most distant glimmer of light visible, but that was enough. It was my way out, and I think it was probably the way that Nightlight had come in as well. Thinking about the little pixie made me suddenly concerned about her welfare. The chimney had been there a long time; it wasn't going anywhere now.

I moved quietly, not wishing to scare the injured sprite in case she was just waking up. Awake she was, chewing carefully and very precisely on her bread, while taking an occasional sip from the flask cap like a miniature elf queen at her table. I wasn't too sure about the protocol for greeting wild pixies, so I just crouched lower and smiled, holding the torch out front to show I was harmless. Of course, as I had been many months without a razor this may not have been as reassuring a move as I had hoped, having a grinning face full of hair pushed far too close; however, it seemed to do the trick. Or rather she took matters into her own hands and held out the flask cap, her little mouth open, making a high-pitched noise that was instantly recognisable as 'want' in any language. I guessed that seemed to establish our relationship, she wanted; I delivered. She may have been a pixie but I had a feeling she was a woman first, though I would say that as a certified trouser-wearer.

I gave her some more fruit, which was eagerly received too, and by a certain amount of dumb play we established that I was 'Nicely' and she was something too far out of my hearing range, and with too many vowel sounds to be repeatable. So Nightlight she remained.

I poured some more water out into my snap tin lid, put it on the ledge, and she attended to her toilet as best as she could, drying herself on a clean kerchief especially rinsed out for this purpose. I turned away while she was doing this, which evoked what could only be called a set of giggles. When it all then went quiet, I look backed, concerned. Nightlight was examining her busted wing, the smallest tears in the world running down her cheeks like tiny diamonds. How do you reassure a fairy in a gold mine with a busted wing that everything is going to be all right? You keep on with the pointing, generally upwards, improvise a pixie sling and a lot of climbing and eventually they get the message. When it was time for me to get back, she didn't seem too concerned. In fact, she was stifling large pixie yawns. I made sure she was comfortably tucked up in my cap and reluctantly said my goodbyes, leaving her with what I hoped was a reassuring smile that promised my speedy return.

I must admit to being more than a little relieved, as I walked back through the maze of tunnels, my ears and eyes continually alert to the possibility of bumping into other wandering miners. Preoccupied as I was, I almost missed the largest dragon's eye that I would ever have the pleasure of becoming acquainted with.

Do I believe in luck? Was my nurturing of the little pixie being rewarded in some fashion? I am tempted to say you make your own luck, but I didn't make a red diamond and place it in a mine in the blasted lands of the south. That was all down to millions of years of heat and pressure and a volcanic pipe that forced it way through the buckling landscape as the Sundered Lands departed and modern Widergard came into shape. So, exactly how many dwarfs, goblins and men had walked down these tunnels on the lookout for exactly this precious gem before I stumbled along and stubbed my boot on it? I don't know for sure. All I know is that life had now got both easier and more complicated.

One thing for sure was that I wouldn't be able to get the raw diamond past the overseer body search that took place at the end of every shift. No matter, I simply backtracked and left my find next to the sleeping Nightlight. She looked a lot better already; hopefully a few more days would make a whole world of difference. I didn't think I really had much more time than that. Of course, her wing wasn't going to fix itself, but there was nothing I could to do about that for the moment. As if to underline my worries, in the lift Scruple passed a message on to me: the Boss would like the pleasure of my company for drinks after supper.

I had no choice in the matter of course, but I felt rather unsettled. This was the first time in an age I had seen Blossom and certainly not since I had found Nightlight and worked out how the Boss had played me for a gull, and made me responsible for the execution of the goblin Captain Wetfang. I had no love for Wetfang but I did not like being played for a gull: that I can't swallow easily.

'Sit down, dwarf – oh you are. Not much difference really is there?' Blossom was on sparkling form, legs splayed behind his unnecessarily large desk.

'What can I do to help you now, Blossom? Want to take advantage of my two-for-the price-of-one deal on murder deductions this season and have me work out who attempted to wraith us all by serving up whatever it was that they tried to pass as meatloaf last night?' I looked around hopefully in case there was a cold ale lurking anywhere that needed saving, but I guess it wasn't that kind of social call.

'I've got a problem, dwarf.'

'I hear there's a place in Coast Port where they're not too fussy.'

Blossom got up and stretched, pushing against the ceiling. If he thought his height was going to intimidate me, he had forgotten a lot in the last few weeks.

'I don't need to pay for my fun, dwarf! No, my problem is you. The others are getting rather concerned about all the preferential treatment you have been receiving from the management.'

'By others, I'm guessing you mean the overseers?'

'Well, they've worked hard to get their little bonuses and they think it doesn't seem right you having got all the privileges so easily.'

'You struck the deal, Blossom.' I tipped back in my chair, looking up at the goblin-man. 'I didn't think you were the sort to go back on a deal?'

'I'm not!'

'Especially when it was your suggestion and I saved your out-hole a considerable amount of trouble.'

'I know that too.'

'Unless there's something else going on here, I think I deserve some gratitude.'

Blossom looked slightly peeved now. There was, of course, something else going on and I now knew what. 'My point is, dwarf, I need some more results from down the mine.'

'I can't find ore that's not there, Blossom.'

'In which case, you'll need to help out digging what we do have.'

'How about you give me some more rations and I won't have to keep going back to check in with the overseers? That way I can head out further, try some of the older workings. That's where they are most likely to have missed something.'

'Yes, sounds good! Do that, dwarf!'

'I will.'

'And no tricky stuff!'

'Blossom, I am in a hole, leagues underground. What am I going to do?'

'Yeah, nothing! I'm forgetting, nothing you can do is there?'

Wrong goblin-man. I'm going to climb out, that's what I'm going to do.

17

ESCAPE FROM ORIA

Little Nightlight was looking a whole lot better and if her 'twitters' were anything to go by she was full of beans too. The wing, sadly, would take more fixing than could be done in this part of the world. With a dragon's eye to now aid my escape, there was no reason to delay.

I left the lift and gave the overseers my normal cheery goodbye and headed off to where I still had the little pixie safely hidden. I hadn't gone far before I was aware of footsteps behind me like a misplaced echo. Marvellous, today of all days they decide to check up on me! Fortunately Overseer Scruple – I could tell by the constant sniffing – really had no idea about the whole trailing business. He must have believed he was being really quiet; he sounded like a whole marching band to my dwarf ears. Oh, Scruple it really wasn't your lucky day.

I didn't need a torch so I blew mine out. Scruple did need one of course. I saw him coming from a mile off.

'You're up to something, I know you are, you little doorstop: SNIFF, SNIFF. I'll put an end to you and your "special treatment". The only special treatment you'll be getting is from Uncle Knuckles!'

It was the longest sentence I'd ever heard from him, and the last for that day at least. I hit him with my pickaxe handle and he went to the place where poor unfortunates like him go when they close their eyes at night. I'd say a better place, but it probably wasn't much of an improvement given his complete lack of imagination. Maybe with more beer and a willing woman or two, or more likely an unwilling woman or two. I couldn't find it in me to terminate his miserable existence, but I judged I'd given him an eight-hour knock, and that would have to do.

Nightlight was pleased to see me, which is worth a fortune in a place like Oria. I had tried to explain my intentions the day before and only managed to convey the idea that 'something is happening'. As far as Nightlight was concerned, any action was now good action. Me too.

I quickly knotted the improvised sling I'd made from a clean pair of breeks. She wasn't over-keen, but she got the message and stepped in. With her little body safely protected, and the dragon's eye safely stashed, we made our way to the escape chimney.

I cleared the last of the accumulated debris away from the bottom of the shaft. Nightlight recognised the chimney, as well she might, having once been thrown down it. She made what I can only describe as a cross between a long drawn-out whistle and a moan, which easily translated as, 'What, you're really going to climb that?'

'Yes,' I told her, 'we both are.'

It wasn't the hardest thing I'd ever done in my life. I'm sure I must have had more trying tasks, but unless I did ever pick up my Dragonette and carry it to the mechanics or maybe exchange head-butts with a stone troll and have just completely forgotten, this was certainly the most tiring.

I'd found as much padding as possible for my shoulders, but they still took the brunt of the job. Fortunately I had my leather jerkin and once again it proved its worth. Slowly, slowly dwarf climbee chimney!

I couldn't afford to make any mistakes, but neither could I afford to hang around (ha). If I hadn't had the months of enforced work out in the mine, I wouldn't have made it. Of course, if I weren't stuck down a mine, I wouldn't have needed to escape in the first place. Swings and roundabouts, eh?

Nightlight was very quiet on the journey, just muttering quiet noises of what I took to be encouragement. I suppose it all brought back some unpleasant old memories to her. I was busy making some unpleasant new ones.

I stopped at what I judged to be half-way and had a long drink from my flask. It was hotter than a dragon's tonsils in the shaft. The chimney was doing its job, in that there was air being drawn up from the depths – it was just that the air in question did nothing to cool you down and everything to dry you out. I was looking forward to the nice cold ale I intended to remove from Blossom's icebox, whether he liked it or not.

The little patch of light was getting bigger and brighter and I was getting more confident, but also more tired, and that's when I slipped. Erosion of some description must have got to the wall and the surface behind me gave a little. That was enough to make my right hand miss its placing and then suddenly I was falling. Arms and legs shot out and a moment later I wasn't falling any more, but in that moment I'd aged about a hundred years and saw my life flash by in front of my eyes – just the bad bits, of which there were far too many. I decided that I had to increase the fun quotient in my life, if and when I got out of this hole.

Nightlight was still hanging on tightly to her sling, her head still buried under my jerkin. In the language of the Citadel news coverage, she was 'not available for comment'. I eased back and got my shoulders up against the wall, and after a couple of long, slow, deep breaths, got on with the climb.

Looking up, I was slightly discomfited to see that the patch of light was not appreciably brighter. As I inched ever closer, I could see why. There was a whole mess of scrub over the entrance. Not nice, soft, pleasant-smelling, mattress-making, plant growth of course, but the thorny acrid stuff that just loves living in a blasted wasteland like that surrounding the Oria Mine. Great, just what was required after a three-hour haul out from the underworld. In the end, the tough stems did at least afford me a grip, even if I had to shred my skin to reach them. Nightlight climbed out first, over my face – which was disconcerting – and she managed to clear some more of the debris away, so I could at least see what I was doing.

I rested for as long as I thought was reasonable, Nightlight now chattering away quite happily on the sandy soil besides me. I needed to get into Blossom's rooms before his afternoon kip. Not that I expected security to be too tight, what with half the men being locked in their rooms and the other half safely underground – well, apart from one revenge-seeking dwarf and a pixie similarly motivated.

Of course, I was some distance from the compound. Certainly further than I had hoped. Security was not just lax, it was also concerned with folk breaking out, not breaking in. I also happened to be covered in dust from the mine and so was rather wonderfully camouflaged. We crept slowly but surely towards the main gate. It wasn't much fun and I was slightly put out to find the gate unattended. I could have strolled in whistling

'The Dwarf King of Bigger Bottom' and nobody would have noticed. Just for variety, we now edged along towards the Boss's quarters.

As I suspected, the picture window opened easily. We slunk in, showing my versatility of slow movement, moving the tatty blind aside without a noise. Well, apart from a small hiss of hate escaping from Nightlight, like air from a perforated lung, when she realised where we were.

We found what we needed in the top drawer in that magnificent rune-worked desk, and I pocketed some spare ammunition as well. There were all sorts of tasty victuals in Blossom's icebox and I found a backpack large enough to pack them all. No point in escaping the mine only to scrimp on a few luxuries.

Nightlight accepted a few pieces of apple that must have cost a pretty penny to transport and we settled down out of sight in the shadows. We didn't have that long to wait.

Blossom came in, stinking of beer and goblin. A loud belch added something spicy to the stench. He made his way to the window to push the blind to one side.

'You don't need to touch that, Blossom, I can see just fine thanks; certainly fine enough to give you a new parting with one bullet from the desk shooter. Hands up, please, let's be traditional.'

Blossom raised his hands and turned to face me. 'So you made your move, eh, dwarf? I thought that little nudge would do the job. It was bugging me, the waiting.'

'Yeah, very smart. Except you seem to be the one facing the wrong end of the shooter.'

Blossom laughed, unpleasantly. 'Don't that seem to be the way? And how did you manage to do that?'

As if to help him out, I felt Nightlight move, a mini explosion of speed and spite. She half leapt, half flew, from my lap onto the desk and grabbed the paper knife, slashing it across Blossom's hand.

I'll give him this, he barely flinched, just slowly raised his hand to test the welling blood.

'Oh yes, the pix.'

'Yes, your unwitting accomplice.'

'And you fell for it.'

'I did.'

'I gulled you real good, dwarf. You swallowed the whole mess.' Blossom was looking very pleased with himself. Maybe he was forgetting the shooter. I waved it a bit to get his attention.

'She flew in through the vent, didn't she? Stole the key for you from the drugged Wissal in the dead of night. You let yourself in, pop the pea from his whistle, and let yourself out, locking the door behind you. Then you simply get her to put the key back. It's all dark so she never even knew.'

'And I got me rid of one far too ambitious number two, and a runt who was just too ugly too live. Oh yes, and you swallowed it all.'

'I did Blossom, although I should have been suspicious when I saw the birdcage.'

'Yeah, the little dustbug was always trying to escape. Thought they were supposed to be loyal when I caught her, and bring you luck. Never brought me much luck.'

'Your luck ran out the day I arrived, Blossom. After that it was just a matter of time.'

Blossom looked at his hand again, raising another, louder, hiss from Nightlight.

The boss gave her an equally venom-filled look. 'I thought she'd be done for – should have broken her little neck and not just her wings when I threw her down there. I guess that means you…'

'Climbed all the way up the chimney, Blossom.'

'That's a pretty mean feat, I'll give you that.'

'Well, I've been in training.'

'It's like you're not happy at your work, dwarf! You should have said something!'

I got up. 'Work's fine, Blossom, it's had its compensations.' I gave him a view of the dragon's eye and the loathing in his gaze now changed to anger.

'Dragon's eye!'

'It is too.'

'That should be mine! I'm the Boss, no one never found a dragon's eye!'

'Life eh? Ain't that just the way? Some of us finally get just what we deserve and some finally get just deserts. Fate, we could talk about that all day I'm sure. But now you have to help us get out of here.'

'There are guards, you know? You expecting to stroll through the gates, maybe?'

'No, first we're going to have a cold ale and then we're strolling through the gates.'

And that's what we did. Well, after I relieved him of all his ready cash, plus the gold I knew he had stashed away in the safe I had marked on my first trip here. Then, cold soldiers in hand, laughing away – just two happy folk on an afternoon stroll with their ales – we left the office.

The compound was completely empty and as silent as a ghoul's whistle. The big engine, the Slag's Sister, was all loaded up with ore. Ready to steam off, as soon as the driver sobered up, later that afternoon, for its week-long trek across the desert.

We only actually walked as far as the Boss's wagon of course; I wasn't heading back to the Citadel by foot.

'What now, dwarf?' the seething goblin-man asked.

'Now we get in the wagon and have ourselves a little ride.'

'How about the guard on the gate?'

'He seems to have gone off for a little snooze – like every other day.'

Blossom looked up and saw the truth of my words. 'I'll have his hide.'

'Well, I'll have to leave the management arrangements to you from now.' I gestured him towards the driver's door. 'See if you can do it without killing too many other staff, or workers for that matter. We're out of here, you see.'

And see he did and out we were.

The big old boiler was so hot it hardly needed any pumping to get up a good head of steam and we were out of there before you could say 'disgruntled goblin-man with a knife at his neck held by an even more disgruntled pixie'. Not particularly fast, but as unrelenting as a magician's marching band.

As soon as we were well away from the compound, we swapped seats and I took the wheel. Nightlight perched behind Blossom, the paper knife still at his throat. The road was just bumpy enough to raise a sweat on the goblin's brow as the sharp blade scraped across his skin with each new jolt.

Blossom was still trying to rain on our parade, though. 'You won't get far, dwarf. You know that!'

'Don't be a sore loser, Blossom,' I said, avoiding potholes. 'I won't have any trouble hiring a ship in Coast Port with the sort of collateral I'm offering. We'll be half-way to the Citadel before you even get back to the mine.'

'What do you mean, get back?'

'You don't think I'm taking you with us, Blossom? Your company isn't that great. And to be rather blunt, you stink in a way no amount of skin-freshener is ever going to hide.'

A couple more hours passed by in a silence only broken by the movement of the cogs in the goblin's head as he tried to figure out how to escape his predicament in one piece. But I had one hand on the wheel and the other on the shooter and Nightlight had two hands on the knife at his throat – no easy answer to that dilemma.

The rugged hills of Oria began to flatten out, which even hills will do given enough time and distance, and eventually I pulled up the wagon.

'Ding, ding! All passengers for Loser Town next station!' I turned to Blossom. 'Hey, this is your stop, goblin! 'Don't forget to take all personal belongings with you – oh no, you don't have anything do you? Apart from a really long walk ahead!'

The goblin spat something in his own tongue, which I guessed wasn't a cheery 'fare-you-well'.

'Look, Blossom, just be grateful I don't let Nightlight here give you some alternative aeration. You know I really think she would be up for that.'

Nightlight's nod indicated that although she hadn't yet mastered Common Speech, her understanding was coming on just fine.

Blossom eased himself out of the wagon and looked around.

'Only one way, Blossom, and that's back! We'll be sailing out of Coast Port long before you can catch us up there, so stop worrying.'

His shrug spoke volumes: he wasn't convinced we were going to make it clean away. And he might well have been right. I didn't know how frequently the ships left Coast Port or what sort of clout he had in the port. Maybe our chances would be slim, except we weren't going to Coast Port, of course. We drove on another hour or so, certainly well out of sight from the tall lookout in the compound, even with the strongest glasses. Finally we found the road I had spotted on Blossom's very helpful wall map. It meandered some way northwards and some way backwards, but that didn't matter. What mattered is that before it trickled out – pretty much in the middle of nowhere, for reasons not immediately apparent – it also ran alongside the Oria Mine Ore train track.

I checked the hour on my very nice new timepiece. The one I had liberated from Blossom's arm as I dropped him off in Loser Town. As far as I could tell, we were pretty much on schedule. The midday shipment should even now be winding its slow chugging way up and down the Oria Hills, ready for us to take advantage of this hardly speedy, but very reliable, means of escape. We had provisions and we had water, and to be honest the thought of four or five days being lulled to sleep by the clitter-clatter of steam engine on track was not worrying me in the least.

Nightlight gave one of those strange tinkly noises that I could now interpret as being a general sign of well-being.

Of course, it couldn't be that simple.

I know about contour lines; I'm a dwarf, after all. When young, we read maps like other children read the funny scrolls. Especially if there might be treasure involved. I know maps, I draw maps, and I know how important a contour line is. Unfortunately, whoever drew the map on Blossom's wall thought contour lines were for wussies and didn't think to add anything to illustrate the hundred-foot drop we now discovered separating road and track.

18

LAST TRAIN TO COAL TOWN

We had approached in good time. I could actually see the steam from the engine chugging its way along an incline some way to the south. It was only then that it became apparent that although the road was indeed going to continue to run right alongside the track for some distance before it petered out, it was going to do it some considerable distance away in the vertical direction.

'Ooops,' I said.

'Ooopee,' Nightlight added – close enough.

I got out of the car and had a look down. Yes, it did indeed go down and in a manner that really did cram those contour lines close together; no chance of descending here without the climb turning into a backbreaking fall, not without rope. I hadn't thought to look for rope. I'd hoped my climbing days were over for a while.

I had a squint under the tarpaulin – just in case somebody had left an unimaginably long coil of rope in the back. Or maybe a flying rug, the sort they are supposed to travel on in exotic climes. No such luck. The total load consisted of a pile of dirty old blankets, probably to make life a little more comfort-able for late-night revellers, a toolbox and a spare tyre. One of the large deep-treaded tyres that gave the wagon its off-road capabilities.

I looked at the tyre.

I looked at Nightlight.

She looked at the tyre.

She looked at me.

She shook her head.

I nodded mine.

It was a crazy idea, but I couldn't think of anything else. Even with the blanket padding in place I fitted, snugly admittedly, inside the tyre. Would this protect me from the pounding I'd take rolling down an incline I couldn't even climb down? Only one way to tell. I sure wasn't going back to Blossom's welcoming committee. Driving on and dying in this waterless waste wasn't too appealing either.

Trying to convince Nightlight, and myself, that I still was in possession of my faculties, I got our possessions together. Nightlight was noticeably upset that she couldn't just flutter down the slope on her gossamer wings. I was just hoping there was something to the pixie luck business. We needed all we could scrape together, or they would be scraping us off the tracks. Nightlight obviously thought I was mad. I probably was, but I suddenly needed to be back in the Citadel very badly. There was a new glossy picture folded carefully in my jerkin foil pocket, right next to the young Daisy's, that hopefully was part of the solution to a very worrying problem. I'd been distracted long enough.

We threw our water and food down the slope first. Only one of the water casks broke, which was good going, and the blanket-tied provisions all stayed together. Best of all, the beer seemed to be intact. Luck holding so far. I got inside the tyre, just as the engine whistle blasted from back down the track. It was going to be close.

This spurred Nightlight on. She could see how limited the options were. She tucked herself up as snugly as was possible inside my new coat, which had been Blossom's best jacket and smelt the least goblin. The hardest part was actually getting close enough to the escarpment edge to get the tyre rolling. After that it was, as they say, all downhill. And what a hill!

The tyre absorbed more impact than I imagined it would. Sadly, there were far bigger bumps than I could ever have imagined. We didn't roll, we bounced, and each bounce was enough to compress me down to gnome size. The result was one pounded and delirious dwarf crawling out of the tyre some way up the other side of the ravine.

Nightlight stepped out of her sling, brushed herself down and looked slightly bored.

I, unfortunately, didn't have time to die – the sensible option at this time. I needed to get the provisions together and find a place to hide away from the engine driver so we could jump on the rear guard carriage as it went past. It was called a guard carriage, but there was never a guard. Who wanted to sit by themselves on a week-long journey across a wasteland that was the blueprint for all other wastelands, where actual waste would have been welcomed to provide some interest and variation in a land which really was much grimmer than waste could ever be?

I decided that the best way to collect our vital provisions was to wander round in circles until I bumped into something that looked edible or drinkable. This was a task for which I was currently more than qualified. You could say that it was the only job opportunity presently open to me – apart from stumbling. I could do good stumbling too.

Still, what doesn't kill me makes me stronger, eh? As adages go, that one is up there with 'too many dwarfs spoil the brothel' for stupidity. What doesn't kill me probably leaves me in a critical condition on life support waiting for a greedy relative to flick the off switch. It's not so catchy, I admit, but not all of life can be put on a T-shirt.

Eventually my senses cleared and I did find the food and water and beer. And by judiciously partaking of the last on the list I was, in the nick of time, in a position to try the famous moving train boarding manoeuvre, as practised by gentlemen of the road ever since trains first steamed up.

Luckily the large sliding door down our side of the carriage was open and I easily hefted our goods into the rear wagon. Nightlight half jumped, half fluttered into the cool and inviting interior. She turned to urge me on. It wasn't too much of a leap. Normally, one run would have been enough, because normally I hadn't been rolled down a steep incline in a rubber tyre.

I ran with no problem, and gathering all my strength, fell flat on my face, as some part of the back of my right knee showed its contempt at being bounced like a ball in a game of pitch and toss.

Nightlight's worried chitter-chatter roused me as the train began to reach the top of the incline, ready to start speeding up as it coasted down onto the flatlands beyond. Now my running didn't look too impressive at all, at best not more than a fast limp. No way was I going to catch the train at this rate, let alone get on board. I changed to an irregular skip that was faster but wouldn't get me aboard either.

Nightlight urged me on with what just had to be pixie cursing, and then I noticed what appeared to be a set of steps on the back of the carriage. Steps leading up to a back door. With one supreme effort I went for it, jumped and found the foot of my good leg on the bottom rung of the ladder. The rest of me was unfortunately falling backward, until a small hand with surprising strength grabbed hold of nine months' growth of beard, and with the other arm hitched around the hand rail, Nightlight pulled for all she was worth.

It was touch and go, but pixie power and dwarf hair tensile strength eventually won the day. Somehow, I found myself sitting at the top of the metal steps staring backwards as the Hills of Oria gradually shrunk behind us. Battered, aching and exhausted, that seemed as good a place to sleep as any, so that's what I did.

I woke with a start some time just before dawn, Nightlight glowing softly in the crook of my arm as she slept. The first fingers of sun slipped through the gaps in the distant mountains and lit the blasted rocks, ready to bake more boulders into pebbledom. It was cool and there was something like a breeze. I sighed, like a greybeard reviewing lost loves of his youth. This had not been the leave I had wanted to take as I was wheeled into the accident ward all those months ago. As breaks go, it wasn't one! Still, I was finally free of the foetid bondage of the mines. Except I would never be free while there were still poor folk slaving away down there. That would have to be corrected. First things first. I carefully got up and carried the sleeping pixie through the thankfully unlocked door to curl up in the welcome shade of the guard's carriage.

The regular rhythm of the steam train was relaxing and reassuring and I soon fell into an even deeper sleep. When I woke, the sun was already beginning to nudge the western horizon. Nightlight was looking out of the carriage with a wistful expression on her face. It took me a moment to figure out why, but then I realised. The train that was taking us to freedom was also taking her away from her own land and people – never an easy thing for anybody, especially a pixie.

I took an apple from the backpack and went to sit next to her, my legs dangling in the open air. I cut her a slice and she chewed it quietly as we watched the sunset together. The magnificent display of reds and golds was a light show put on especially for the two of us. Right on the horizon I could see something, almost floating, like a huge balloon. I wondered about dragons and the likelihood of them surviving in this wasteland. Well, pixies did. In the end, I told myself to relax, which I did, with a sigh, as the sun dipped lower.

'Beautiful,' I said.

'Boo-ful,' she tinkled in her best pixie manner.

I looked at her with as serious an expression as I could manage without scaring the non-pants off her and tried to convey a difficult message with rudimentary signing. 'Nightlight, we have to go now – a long way from here. Across the big water. There we can get you fixed.' I pointed at her injured wing and gestured flying. She seemed to understand and smiled enthusiastically, if still unsure whether such a thing was indeed possible.

'Then,' I continued, 'I will bring you back here and you can fly home. Understand?'

She didn't at first. I guess she had been brought up to believe that all big people, if they ever found a pixie, would hang on to them forever. When I finally got her to understand, she was ecstatic, bouncing round the carriage like a mad thing. I opened one of the ales and she drank hers from the cap and together we watched the last of the sunset.

Coal Town was big and Coal Town was busy. As cities go, it had all the charm of dysentery. The last part of the journey through the crowded streets and houses seemed to take nearly as long as our trek across the desert. That had been, thankfully, uneventful if somewhat monotonous. Quite frankly I was happy to handle a little monotony. The highlight of the journey was at Slags' Crossing. Fortunately we were running a little late and the Slag Express was already waiting for us. All the goblin crews had to do was jump out and change the points so both trains could continue. Being goblins, there was the normal boasting and good-natured rivalry, which involved a reasonable amount of physical violence. This didn't leave much time for socialising between trains, just the sharing of a large flask of clear spirit, which I suspected was also used for cleaning the working parts of the train.

This was all good news, as I had been concerned that somebody would require something from the guard's carriage. The guard's carriage actually didn't contain much of interest – a simple table and a chair and a whole pile of straw (thankfully fresh) which served as a bed. A hole in the carriage floor served for ablutions. In the table drawer, there were a pencil stub, a few scraps of scroll parchment, a piece of board and some of those rubber bands you always find at the bottom of drawers everywhere, along with the key to the unknown lock. Oh, and a pack of playing cards. The cards turned out to be of the soft 'girlie' variety, which Nightlight found hilarious. Not at all put out by the procession of well-upholstered females of every race, I managed to teach her a few simple games, like 'Chase the Elf' and 'Ransom', although she did have a habit of collapsing into gales of pixie laughter whenever she drew a particularly hilarious card. Of the four suits, she found the Queen of the Dwarfs particularly hilarious and much pointing at me and tugs at my beard always followed her disclosure. The Queen of the Men was a little too obvious for my taste, while the Dark Queen was positively scary. I actually found the Queen of the Elves rather disconcerting as she reminded me of Elsie in a way I couldn't quite explain. This, I still insist, is how Nightlight managed to defeat me so many times.

With Slags' Crossing out of the way, I relaxed a little bit more, but my card play didn't improve. I also tried to teach Nightlight more common speech, but this proved harder than I'd expected. I've heard urban pixies speak it perfectly clearly, but with Nightlight it all came out as an engaging but largely indecipherable series of trills and whistles. At least her under-standing was coming on leaps and bounds, which would be important when we had to mix with folk after we reached the end of the track, which eventually we did. It took the best part of a day, though. I'm not sure if Coal Town was bigger than the Citadel, but it certainly spread nearly as far. Hour after hour of switching and sidings until the train finally came to what seemed to be a permanent halt.

We had half-closed the carriage door, to discourage nosy track personnel from looking in. Now was not the time to be discovered, not after all this trouble. However, I also wanted to disembark at a good spot, a place where we could quickly get lost in a crowd. Preferably without having to clamber over too many fences.

In the end, the decision was made for us. The train pulled up and we were checking the lie of the land, when we saw another smaller engine approach from other direction. I realised that we were about to experience some heavy shunting action. This probably indicated that the ore wagons were going to be decoupled and shunted off to one of the refineries I had spied further down the coast. What would happen to the guard carriage? I didn't intend to stay around and find out. We needed to be gone, so we went.

I still had my leather jerkin and Blossom's jacket doubling as a coat, so I didn't immediately shout 'slave labour'. I had also spent some time, with assistance from Nightlight, combing the snags out of my hair and beard. This allowed me to tie a few knots in both, which gave me an air if not exactly of wealth, then at least not the stink of desperation.

The shunter engine was moving round to the front of the ore train and rattles and jerks testified to a certain amount of decoupling going on. I hoisted Nightlight into her improvised sling and we slipped out of the back door of the guard carriage.

The hot afternoon was getting to the point where all any sane person of any value was beginning to think about was cold ale.

With my jerkin and Blossom's jacket, I felt rather over-dressed. Coal Town itself didn't feel much cooler than the desert, although an occasional salty breeze, slipping through the track buildings, spoke of the sea and a blessed relief from the heat. Coal Town also stank. I'm no stranger to industry and the forges of New Iron Town do not add anything to the mountain fragrance. This was different, not just enterprise, and fishing, but something else as well. The stench of desperation and the reek of naked ambition perhaps. I double-checked the safety of the dragon's eye in my belt pocket. This was not a place to become careless.

We strode down the tracks as if we belonged there. To complete my disguise, I had attached some of the parchment to the board with two of the rubber bands and placed the pencil stub behind one ear. That's the clincher. A man, dwarf or even a goblin with a pencil behind his ear has that unofficial seal of approval that says he must know what he is about.

So when someone cried out, 'Ho there!' I didn't turn with the air of somebody who has just been found out, but with the confidence of somebody who needs to get on and so this better be good. What's more, I made a note on my board. It worked.

'Sorry to disturb ye', but have you fire?' The accent was strange, but the pipe hanging out of his mouth told me all I needed to know. The track worker was carrying a long metal pole that I knew was used for 'sounding' track to hear for faults and cracks. A responsible job. I did indeed have fire, or rather Blossom had fire that I was taking care of for now and the foreseeable future. Handsome the lighter was too, spirit-filled, shaped like a small dragon, with a good chunk of flint that struck even in a strong wind. It seemed churlish not to oblige the man.

'Very tight,' he said, returning my lighter.

'Won it on a bet.'

'Oh aye?'

'Yes, he bet me he could knock me down and rob me, before I could floor him. He lost.'

This tickled the track sounder. 'Tha's Coal Town for you!'

'It's most places these days,' I added sagely.

'I guessed it so, I guessed it so.'

'Better get on,' I sighed. 'I hate late shifts. Already dying for an ale.'

'Know wha' you mean. Tha's good drinking down Castle's – tha's pop'lar with you dwarf folk, I'm told.'

I shrugged a shrug of the unconvinced. 'Between you and me, I had my fill of dwarfs back home. I'd rather spend my time with men – or at least women!'

This got me another big laugh and we parted the best of chums. Not once had he asked me what I was about, or for whom. The power of the pencil stub, that is.

I walked on and added a whistle to my knowledgeable gait and occasionally stopped to stare at a piston or two. A twitter from Nightlight told me she had just about had enough of this messing about. Me too. We were both saved from further agitation by a blast from a horn that seemed to mark the end of the working day for most folk trackside. I found a home for the piece of board, but being sentimental, hung on to the pencil. Then we walked out with the rest of the workers and we were finally in Coal Town.

Nightlight and I immediately headed deep into the city proper, and what a place it was. What it lacked in charm it made up for in nothing else at all. The architecture wasn't worthy of the name and the streets were laid out with no consideration for traffic or pedestrians. There was nothing as sensible as streettrains; there would not have been room for them anyway. Instead, small three-wheeled wagons were everywhere, delivering goods, picking up people and filling the air with steam and smoke. Fast and surprisingly manoeuvrable, with two large powered rear wheels and a smaller front wheel by which the vehicle was steered, the whole vehicle was driven by an ingenious chain drive. I soon learnt these were called 'steamers'. Careful to not be flattened by one while crossing the street, we plunged deeper into Coal Town. Here, tannery rubbed shoulders with nursery and granary. The well-off walked the same cobbled streets as the poor, the really poor and the folk who licked the walls next to restaurant vents for their supper. All the peoples of Widergard were represented and some that looked like they had dropped in for a visit from other places a lot further away. I spotted quite a few dwarfs but they all seemed to be my eastern kin, much darker-skinned than the northern tribes, and herders, not miners, by vocation. Relationships were not exactly strained between the two branches; we just didn't see a lot of each other, and when we did, we took chunks out of each other, in a friendly family way, of course.

It was the actually the elves of Coal Town that were the most disturbing. Now I have been known to criticise numbers of the blond pointy-eared Citadel fraternity, with notable exceptions, for a list of faults I could enjoy recounting at leisure, but these dark-haired fellows were of a very different metal. Like everybody else, I had heard the legends about Shadow Elves, the branch of elfdom that supposedly had spent too long looking into things that really didn't bear looking into and consequently had lost their sunny outlook along with their blond locks. I thought they were something of a myth, but now I wasn't sure. These elves walked like they owned the streets – not an uncommon elf attitude. The difference was that these elves looked like they were about to charge you rental for the pleasure of walking down said streets and you wouldn't be able to afford it – they weren't happy about this.

In fact, they weren't happy about anything. I hurried on by when I saw one walking towards me on a particularly quiet street and I heard Nightlight give a small whimper of relief as we passed him. She whimpered a little too soon.

'You are a long way from your northern hills, Master Dwarf?' said a quiet voice, as smooth as silk and as scary as a five-day hangover, seemingly inches from my ear.

I turned slowly, which seemed a good way of turning under the circumstances, and I was pleased to see that the elf wasn't in fact breathing down my collar. Nice trick, though.

'And you are a long way from your forests, Master Elf,' I replied evenly.

'Not all elves are wed to tree and leaf, Master Dwarf.'

'And neither do all dwarfs require the weight of an axe in their hands, or the close embrace of tunnel and shaft, Master Elf.'

The elf in question produced a dismissive noise that was partway between a laugh and a snort of derision. From this distance, I was able to get a better look at him and the result was even more disconcerting. He was tall, dark and brooding, his hair pulled back so tightly his eyebrows looked in danger of disappearing into his hair line. Undeniably elvish, with the obligatory perfectly sculptured cheekbones and pointy ears, but the dark hair was unusual. Not unheard of, but this black was so black it made his pale skin all the more translucent, like an image seen in passing in a street store window. If shadow elf he was, they were well named.

'Well, Master Dwarf, I am pleased to see one of your kin taking an interest in the wider world, not tied to the pursuit of wealth and property.'

'Whereas I am saddened to see that elves everywhere still have the most annoying habit of sticking their noses into matters that don't concern them,' is what I wanted to say, but for once, bearing in mind my precious cargo and lack of weapon, I simply said, 'Indeed.'

We both then went on our ways, but I kept looking over my shoulder until we were safely back on a main thoroughfare. For a very hot evening, it was very cold for a while there.

I had made a mental priority list on the train, which included finding accommodation, having a bath and shave and getting some quotes for a ship back to the Citadel. I added 'stay away from elves' to my roster. Top of my list still was 'coffee'. After what I had been forced to drink for the last months, this even trumped 'staying away from elves' and the need for ale, which I had at least managed to occasionally find.

A good coffee-lodge can be hard to identify from the street. The aroma is always a reasonably good indication, but that doesn't tell the whole story. The make of pressure system and how well it has been cared for is another good indicator, as are the folk in there drinking. Gigol's Coffee Cabin looked to be the business: nice shiny equipment, which I guessed to be dwarf-made, no-frills decoration and their own roaster turning in one corner, adding magic to the beans. And if you don't believe in magic beans, you are not a coffee drinker.

I went into Gigol's and ordered a four-shot, the choice of the genuine bean-head in need of a pick-me-up that would pick him up into the early hours. The price was reasonable too and the service from the old gnome behind the counter came with that blessed lack of inquisitiveness that is the mark of all large cities. I took my cup to a corner where we were comfortably inconspicuous, and drank my coffee like a new baby first finding the tit. Nightlight snuck out from the jacket and took a sip from the saucer. Judging from the sigh of pleasure, she approved.

Relaxed in a way I hadn't been for a long time, I looked around Gigol's little establishment. It certainly was no-frills, but it was clean and the furniture was built to last. The coffee cups were white and reassuringly heavy in the hand and did not exhibit any of the cracks or chips that can detract from the proper enjoyment of a good cup of coffee.

Gigol was rather like his establishment: a small but perfectly presented gnome, no frills but, if I am any judge, dependable and with a pleasingly bald head that had taken on the colour of one of his own perfectly roasted beans. He was busy wiping down the counters and, judging by the way the customers were paying their bills and saying their goodbyes, getting ready to close for the evening. It was then that I noticed the 'rooms to rent' sign tacked up next to the coffee machine. I finished my coffee, took the cup and saucer back to the counter and thanked the gnome behind it. 'Any chance of looking at one of those rooms, Master?'

'Do you mind living above a coffee-lodge?' he asked, his voice giving nothing away as to his origins.

'Depends how much extra I have to pay,' I bounced back at him and got a laugh by way of reward.

'Let's go have a look then. I'm just about closed up.' I was indeed the last customer, so he slipped the bolt across and turned around the 'closed' sign hanging on the door.

'I have a couple of sets available,' Gigol explained, as I followed him up the back staircase.

'Does either have a bath?' I asked.

'Just the one.'

'I'll take it!'

He chuckled again. 'Well, why don't you look and see what you think first?'

'Because I can't believe anybody who makes a cup of coffee as half-decent as you do would provide anything other than very pleasurable accommodation?'

'Ha! I think we could get on, Master Dwarf.'

We reached the rooms, which were at the top of the house. As I expected, there were no frills, but all was clean and tidy. Just what I needed and I said so.

'And for how long would you be wanting the rooms, Master Dwarf?'

That was a good question and I wasn't sure of the answer. 'How about I pay two weeks in advance and we go from there? Would that do?'

It would do very well indeed, and so we spat on it.

'And I won't be charging you any more for your little friend,' the gnome added.

'Ah!' I said. 'I wasn't as discreet as I thought then?'

'No, Master Dwarf. Not much gets past me.'

'I bet it doesn't. Come on out, Nightlight, and say hello to Master Gigol.'

Nightlight crept shyly out and extended a hand. Gigol's face broke into a wide smile as he bent down to take it. 'Isn't she a wonderful thing?' he said to Nightlight's delight. 'But what's happened to her?' Gogol was immediately concerned when he saw her poor wing.

'Something that somebody has paid for and will pay more for in the future, after we have taken care of the injury.'

Gigol shook his head sadly. 'I don't think you'll find that sort of skill in Coal Town.'

'No, I think we'll need to be looking further afield.'

'Right,' said Gigol, 'I think I've pried into your business far enough.'

'Not at all,' I assured him.

'But you would do right in keeping her well hidden. Pixies, sadly, fetch a lot of money in these parts. Wild ones especially so. Keep her hidden, keep her safe.'

I thanked Gigol and said I would pop the cash down later. He said there was no hurry. Anybody that would nurse an injured pixie was good folk on his scroll. I gave my name as Ironhead, which made me feel just a little guilty.

19

A NIGHT OUT

The bath was complete bliss. Fortunately it was not built for gnomes, and Gigol said there was unlimited hot water as well, all thanks to a clever water tank on the building's roof heated by the sun. There was a lot of this sort of thing in Coal Town, which despite its name was now becoming very much Sun Town.

Nightlight found the whole bath idea hilarious. I don't think she had ever seen so much water in one place and the prospect of actually immersing yourself totally in it was obviously a very un-pixielike concept. She watched, fascinated, as the scalding water bubbled and gurgled out of the tap, darting her hand into the flow and withdrawing it before any damage could be done. She wanted to watch as I bathed as well, but I put my foot down there and placed her firmly outside the door, locking it for good measure too. She may have been a pixie, but she was female as well – albeit on a much smaller scale than I was used to.

There was plenty of soapstone available, and boy did I need it. The water was soon the colour of the coffee they had served up in Oria, so I emptied the bath and filled it up again. I scrubbed the months of grime and filth off and removed a fair amount of the mine from my hair as well. It felt better than good; it felt like a rebirth. I lay in the bath for an age, listening to the mountains get raised and the continents crash into each other. Then after they had been eroded down to dust, I topped up the bath and did it all yet again. I decided to keep the beard for a while longer. From what I had seen of the other Coal Town dwarfs, clean-shaven was not the local look, and I didn't want to stand out more than I had to.

All too soon I had to return to Widergard from the Land of Soak, and I dried myself off with some towels with just the right degree of roughness. There was a mirror in the bathroom and I rubbed away the steam and had a look at what enforced labour had done for me. I had to admit it had been a workout and a half and there were now new muscles standing proud where the previous ones had merely posed. Good, as I was looking forward to further physical action and somebody was going to feel the difference. I was sure of that. First things first, though, Nicely my lad – we weren't home and dry yet. I needed to find us both a ship and that wasn't going to be cheap. I didn't want to work my passage, not with Nightlight to look after, and I didn't want to end up knocked on the head and thrown overboard either. That meant passenger rates and probably a couple of changes too. Despite its size, I'd never heard of Coal Town and I knew most of the destinations for the Citadel Bay's shipping lines. I had my five hundred crown note and what I had lifted from Blossom, but we needed to live in the meantime too. Of course, I had the dragon's eye, but I didn't fancy showing that around the town and I was more likely to get another nudge on the head than a good price. I needed some inside information, so now seemed to be as good a time as any to do a little snooping around and see what I could turn up.

Gigol, bless his little brown pate and his polished boots, had provided me with some clean kecks and overs. A previous tenant had done a runner and left them in lieu of payment. I offered to buy them but Gigol wouldn't hear of it. They weren't too bad a fit, although I had to roll up the bottoms in a way that Gaspar would not have approved of at all.

Looking in the mirror again, I almost looked like the dwarf of old – well, with two foot of beard. Of course, what was missing was a hat. I thought of the midnight-red beauty that Gaspar had made for me. If only I had worn it when I'd gone for the ice, I might not be in this mess now. It would have been enough to turn whatever instrument of malice it was that had been applied to almost take off my head. I'd given that some thought too. Any number of cudgels, clubs, batons, truncheons, coshes, night-sticks, or bludgeons might have been employed for the task. I was familiar with them all, but I had a feeling that my humbling could have been done by something a little different. I hoped not, but the feeling wouldn't go away. I also hoped Elsie had taken good care of that hat, as I was coming back for it, and her, real soon.

Nightlight gave me an appreciative round of applause as I left the bathroom, along with a 'Nice smell tinkle tinkle'. Her language was coming on. I did a small bow by way of thanks and essayed a spin to more applause. I then showed Nightlight to the bath I had run for her in the basin. She couldn't quite believe that all this water was for her benefit and I had to solemnly assure her it was. I also pointed out the soapstone, but this was no novelty. I next needed to explain that I was going out and I'd be taking the key. This was harder to do, especially when she was in a hurry to experience the novelty of the bath, but I eventually got my message over. Leaving Nightlight to play happily, I went out on the town.

Rule one of orienteering in a new town: always make sure you know where camp is. In this case I soon found out that Gigol's was on Rope Walk, a long street that I judged had once been the seat of much industrious rope-making: fancy that! As with a lot of industry, I judged rope-making had moved further down the coast because bigger boats demanded deeper drafts. This would make this Rope Walk easy to find – there weren't that many straight roads amongst the maze of streets of Coast Town.

A right labyrinth it was too. Coal Town was built round a natural harbour and that still handled a lot of the smaller traffic. This is why the train tracks converged there to begin with. However, as the harbour began to silt up and traffic increased, the refineries I'd spotted earlier were built, with their own piers, and the ore and coal were shunted along to them. Passenger ships departed from the harbour, but most were local and a few even still relied totally on the wind. The larger ocean-going steam vessels had their own quay in the area known as the 'Kidney', a dredged deep-water haven near the harbour wall.

I learnt all this from a particularly garrulous gnome called Ladello, who ran a fine stockroom filled with hats of every shape and form. I had been directed there by the equally friendly gnome who ran the pipeweed store from where I'd picked up a fine new pipe and enough leaf to keep me happy for many moons. The gnome was happy to see a dwarf who knew his leaf and wanted to stock up with it. Gnomes, I was quickly beginning to realise, were doing fine in Coal Town, particularly in the store-keeping and supplies lines.

Ladello was only too happy to chatter on and give me the low-down on Coal Town as I sorted through his selection of new and used headgear. Understandably there were a lot of hats designed for various jobs associated with shipping – not quite what I was after. Similarly, there were a lot of hard hats for mining and building; those I never wanted to see again. Neither did I want a hat a dwarf or man might only wear for a special occasion or meeting the parents of the goodwife-to-be. Not that the two are necessarily mutually exclusive.

The hat I finally chose I found right of the back of the store and it was not in my normal style. It looked a little forlorn and unloved, but this was the hat for this time and place, I realised, and at least according to the gnome merchant, it could have been made for me. It was as black as midnight in the mine and had a medium brim and a high crown with a crease, but no dents. It had an almost formal air that said here was a dwarf that you could do business with, and that meant business too. It was made of a hard-wearing local material and apparently called an 'Elf Tower' for reasons that nobody knew. I wasn't going to hold that against it. A good hat.

My next stop was a little more specialised, but again the gnome network worked to my advantage. I needed to get some clothes for Nightlight, not just for propriety's sake, but because we were heading to climes a little less clement, certainly for pixie flesh. The wheeze I had was to look for a doll and doll's clothes for my non-existent daughter 'back home'. She is called Silverseam by the way and is ten years old and likes dolls she can dress and undress and arrange in typical dwarf-girl activities, such as axe-throwing and open-cast mining. She has very dark brown eyes, almost black, which she gets from her mother Lustre's side of the family as they have dwarf royal blood. When I get into a part, I do not mess around.

Ladello pointed me to exactly the right place, which I would never have found myself if I had wandered for an age. I also picked up a useful knife and small axe for my son, who is called Grievance on account of his father's having unfinished business on his mind. I put everything in a tough leather backpack that Ladello had also found for me.

I then started on my way to the Kidney. This turned out to be further than I wanted to go at this time of night, and through streets it was probably not sensible to walk through at any time of day. At this time, I'd found myself in a district full of the sounds of drinking and dancing, and the smells of food and pipeweed. I remembered what the track sounder had said about the Castle, popular with my kin, and unsure what else to do, and partly against my better judgement, I set out to find it.

Apparently, according to the first man I stopped, it was quite nearby. I never got there though, as turning the next corner I was stopped in my tracks by a voice from the past I thought I'd never hear again. I was spellbound in an instant and I didn't need to read the chalked-up sign outside the inn to know that The River Woman was singing here to tonight.

The inn, The Dark Horse, an even darker building, but now alight with lamps and torches, was full to groaning – she hadn't lost her popular appeal. She hadn't lost her remarkable looks either; in fact, she looked even lovelier than the last time I'd seen her, more in control and at home in her own skin. Her song was different too. While not exactly a 'knees-up' or 'comic turn', it felt more hopeful and less tinged with melancholy. The months had been good to The River Woman since I'd last seen her. I hoped I wasn't going to bring her any more grief, but I needed to speak to her as she might well have the answers to questions I never thought I would get round to asking.

First of all, I needed to make sure that I was not going to fall foul of any of the new friends I supposed she had already made. This involved some heavy investment in some expensive wine of the sort that barkeeps like to see their customers buying. The things I do for my profession. After this, asking the management, a jolly barkeep called Dulse, darker than The Dark Horse itself, to see if The River Woman would care to share another bottle of the expensive wine with me was no problem at all. With my new hat and beard, I hoped she wasn't going to recognise me immediately and run off again. I seated myself away from the nearest lamp, with my back to the stage, just in case.

'I am pleased you enjoyed my singing,' she said by way of introduction.

'I always have,' I replied, turning as I spoke. Her face betrayed a degree of panic that made me regret any attempts of subterfuge.

'Steady there!' I said hurriedly. 'I'm not looking for you, and I'm not here on behalf of Lobsk. It's just one of those strange things that life throws at us sometimes.'

'Honestly?' she said nervously.

'On my heart and axe,' I said, which is just about as solemn an oath as you can get from a dwarf. 'Now, please sit down and have a drink with me. I haven't seen a familiar face in a very long time, and a pretty one in even longer. Besides, the barkeep is going to be cross with you if I don't buy a second bottle of the good stuff.'

The River Woman sat and she smiled for the first time, well, that I could remember seeing, anyway. It suited her in the same way those whiskers suit kittens and cherry blossom suits a spring wedding.

'The barkeep won't get cross with me, Master Strongoak,' she said sitting down. 'He knows why this place is full every night.'

I looked around and indeed the place was heaving, with folk of all varieties, and many of the habitual trouser-wearers were looking at me enviously. 'I'm not surprised. From what I've heard, you're singing even better and I wouldn't have thought that was a possibility to be honest.'

'Thank you. Let us say that a certain weight has been lifted from my shoulders, or at least I thought it had.'

I held my hands up again. 'As I said lady, if I had taken a different turn this evening our paths would never have crossed again. If you want the full Ten Scrolls, I'm willing to read them.'

'Try me,' she said, as the barkeep arrived with that second bottle and another glass. She poured herself a finger or two; I helped myself to a fist. It was the good stuff, worth every belt of corn.

I couldn't tell her everything, as I was still pretty sketchy on the details myself, but I told her what I was sure about. 'I went out one evening on an errand and woke up later in a gold mine with a six-week-old beard. Now, under other circumstances I'm willing to call that a really good night out, but in this case no alcohol was involved and so I'm feeling just a little grumpy.'

'I could see how that would put a body out,' she said carefully.

'Add to that the enforced labour and the year or so I have now missed from my life and it's payback time. First, though, I have to arrange myself some safe sea transportation.'

She looked at me. 'And this really has nothing to do with me and Lobsk?'

I thought about that for a short while. 'Well,' I said finally, 'it has certainly got nothing to do with you. Let's just say I would really like to have a long chat with Lobsk and another client of mine. As Lobsk is otherwise busy, I will be catching up with my erstwhile client as soon as I possibly can.'

She considered this. I topped up the drinks. Stick to what you're good at, Nicely.

'I came to find you, the day Lobsk was arrested,' I said, by way of an explanation or perhaps an apology.

She sipped at her drink. 'I wanted to be gone, to get out while I could.'

I raised a questioning eyebrow, she looked uncomfortable.

'You can tell me. It won't go any further,' I said, trying to draw her out.

'You are still a dwarf, with allegiances,' she said quietly.

'I was also a Citadel Guard, and now I'm a Master Detective, and those count a lot more to me than accidents of birth.' She still wasn't convinced.

'How about you tell me your name, for starters? I can't keep calling you River Woman, though it is a good name. It's got quality.'

She smiled properly for the first time. 'Thank you – it was my mother's stage name too. She called me Myril.'

'That's a good name too, Myril. Good health!' We toasted before I continued. 'And where is your mother now?'

Myril shook her head sadly. 'I don't know. I only found out that much through another singer I bumped into on the circuit. She said I looked just like her.'

'Did she have to give you up, Myril?'

She nodded her head sadly. 'Yes, it just wasn't possible… to be on the road with a young child. I needed schooling and a chance for a real home. She found a place…'

'Which was?'

'Harrowfeld Hall.'

'The Harrowfeld Hall Home for Troubled Children,' I said, feeling pieces of a puzzle that was much larger and more inter-connected than I had ever suspected begin to fall into place.

'Yes, have you heard of it?' She looked at me, weighing up what she should say.

'In passing, but surely you weren't troubled?'

'No, that was just the name. It existed to place children – mostly girls, like myself – supposedly to good loving families where they could find a fresh start.'

'Sounds admirable.'

'That's where Lobsk found me.'

'Who has not got a family.'

'No, it seems that it was also a way for some folk to find cheap domestic help.'

'Anything else?' I had to ask, hating myself.

Myril looked carefully at her drink. 'There were rumours, stories that got passed around between the girls who managed to keep in touch.'

'I see,' I said – seeing far too well and too much.

'Not that Lobsk ever touched me,' she said hurriedly. 'But as I got older… it was made clear that if I was… interested, he would be amenable.'

I realised that my hand was now clenched so tightly that I was in danger of breaking my glass. I tried to relax, while all I actually wanted to do was go and break down a few doors and kick a few heads around the streets of the Citadel.

I went to my foil pocket, being careful to take out the right picture.

'Do you know this girl, Myril?' I asked, passing across the image of the gap-toothed smiling child.

'Why yes,' she said, surprised. 'That's Daisy Cartersong, Solophie's girl, taken on the Gnada.'

It was my turn to be surprised. 'Are you sure?'

'Of course I am. I took the picture, on a lovely day out we all had.'

Wow, here was news from the Old Thrush indeed and I only had to travel half-way round Widergard to find it out.

'What are you doing with a picture of her?' Myril continued, concerned.

'Could you just tell me who Solophie Cartersong is please and how you know her?'

'She was in Harrowfeld Hall with me. She was older, but we got on well – she was like a big sister. We managed to keep in touch when she left.'

'Left to go where?'

'To that rich dwarf Getgold Grounding.'

'And this was when?'

'Let me think. I was four years old when I went to Harrowfeld and Solophie was eight. She went into Getgold's when she was about twelve as I recall.'

'And was this Getgold the sort of dwarf … you heard "rumours" about?'

'No,' said Myril, and then thought on it. 'Not that Solophie ever mentioned anything at least. He was always very good to her. I think she felt quite guilty about running off with her man Daff from the travelling show. And then when Daff turned out to be the wrong choice and she came back to the Citadel with young Daisy, I said why not go talk to Getgold to get your old job back, but she was against…Oh my!' Myril put her hand to her mouth in surprise.

'This Daff… ?'

'I never met him,' she admitted.

'No, I expected as much, somehow.'

'I saw a picture of him, though! Very tall with an amazing mane of black hair.'

I shrugged the non-committal shrug we get taught in Guard School when we don't want to disillusion helpful witnesses.

'But Daisy looks nothing like…' Myril's sentence trailed off, as if not finishing it would make it less true. It didn't.

'In this type of mixed "marriage" the children can look quite like their mothers, or so I've been told,' I added. 'Certainly when they're younger.'

'I never suspected a thing, poor Solophie!'

'No, I imagine she didn't want you to.'

'I was still at the Hall when she came back with little Daisy. I went to Lobsk's soon after and I couldn't see so much of her then, although we would meet up in secret – she always wanted to know how I was doing, whether I had… any problems with Lobsk.'

'How long ago was the picture taken, Myril?'

'Let me think,' she cast her mind back. 'Around five years ago I think. Daisy was ten. It was a birthday treat.'

'She looks a lot younger.'

'She was always small for her age.' Myril stopped abruptly, suddenly aware of what she had said. She shook her head with regret. 'Solophie always liked to dress her up in young clothes. Like she didn't want her to grow up. I can see why now. Oh, what a fool I was!'

'Don't beat yourself up, Myril. You were a child yourself, as was Solophie for that matter.'

'You still haven't said how you got hold of Daisy's picture.'

'First I have to tell you some sad news, Myril. I'm afraid Solophie is dead.'

'Oh no! That's terrible. I had no idea.' Her beautiful face collapsed in on itself, like a blooming rose moving backwards in time. 'What was it?'

'The Wilting Hurt,' I said simply. I couldn't say it was quick or painless because we both knew this wasn't the case.

'She told me she was moving away from the Citadel to the country somewhere,' Myril continued. 'She said there were too many distractions for young Daisy, who was turning out to be quite a handful. She promised to send me an address but never did.' A single tear escaped from Myril's prison of grief.

'And now, well, I'm afraid that Daisy is missing.'

'Then we must find her, Master Strongoak,' The River Woman said, determined. 'She was a lovely child, bright as a crown and clever as well. Very inquisitive too. We must make sure she is safe, for Solophie!'

'It seems Solophie had a final request for her old boss, to do that very thing.'

'But Getgold, surely he could have had no idea as to the girl's true parentage?'

'I'm guessing not, Myril. Otherwise I don't think he would have hired me to find her in the first place.'

'Oh, poor Daisy,' she sighed, shaking her head at the vagaries of that thing we call life.

I feared that 'poor Daisy' wasn't the half of it. I had a picture in my pocket to prove that, but couldn't bring myself to show Myril.

20

OLD FRIENDS

It was good to be out in the fresh air, not that there was very much fresh about Coal Town air. You couldn't exactly cut it with a knife, but you could probably strain it through an old sock. Actually, the air outside The Dark Horse tasted like it already had been. Still, it was all that was on offer, so I dragged it down gratefully and looked forward to the prospect of a long lung-cleansing sea voyage.

Myril, The River Woman, had offered me very good advice with regard to my planned return to the Citadel. As I suspected, it was best to do it in stages, which would actually be cheaper and arouse less suspicion. That last item was important because, apparently, Coal Town was run by a number of guilds, divided on race lines, and anybody doing something suspicious – for example, a strange dwarf going to the wrong shipmaster – was going to get tongues wagging. And, as Myril pointed out, I probably didn't want tongues wagging as that can always lead to batons swinging. We arranged to meet at the same time the next day and she promised to bring me news as regards berths and sailings.

I had done the right thing by not going to the Castle apparently. The Eastern Dwarfs that frequented it were the most closed guild of them all, and they were not known for their affability, even with other dwarfs. Bumping into The River Woman again might have been one of the best things to happen to me in a long time – Nightlight's store of luck rubbing off? One thing was for sure, Coal Town was not the best place for the two of us to be hanging around for long at the moment. I certainly didn't intend to.

I bought some fruit from a stallholder, a friendly gnome who didn't seem to be at all bothered by the nightshift. He picked out an interesting selection, which I'm sure would intrigue Nightlight. I bought another basket for Gigol, by way of a thank you for all his help. When I finally made it back to the Rope Walk, I found the two of them in his parlour laughing like mad things.

'Oh, Master Ironhead, she is a one!' said Gigol, through his tears of joy.

It took me a beat to remember my name, but I quickly caught up and then replied, 'I didn't know you spoke pixie?'

'Oh, I don't, but you don't need to with this one! Her impressions are so funny, you should hear her do you! It's as if you're in the room.'

'Oh, is it now?' I said, looking in Nightlight's direction. She at least had the good grace to look sheepish, which, considering she had probably never seen a sheep, was good going. I don't know what pixies ate out there in the desert, but she sure did like fruit. She fell upon the basket's contents as soon as I'd removed the cover and Gigol seemed genuinely pleased by his gift too. He offered to break open a bottle but I went for a cup of his wonderful coffee instead. We then spent an interesting hour talking coffee lore, by which time Nightlight, roundly full of prickleberries, was snoring lightly in a wrapping-paper-filled empty basket. I thanked Gigol profusely again and carried her up to bed in the same basket. She didn't stir.

I don't know if it was the unaccustomed intake of coffee, but I didn't sleep well. My dreams were full of a sense of foreboding. No bad omens or mysterious visions, just an all-pervasive feeling of dread. I think I would have preferred fanged daemons. Those I can cope with, as I hope my record shows; the hidden monsters of the mind are a far different and more dangerous adversary. However, the morning broke fair and there was something of a breeze from the sea, which diluted the air somewhat and made it breathable rather than just drinkable.

After we broke our fasts, Nightlight tried on the clothes selection I had purchased the day before. She found the whole idea hilarious, again, but she loved trying everything on, and I was pleased to see that quite a few things fitted her well. She then took everything off again and refused to wear a single stitch. I tried to explain to her the need for some sort of outerwear. It didn't go down well. The idea that the weather could ever get so cold that water falling from the sky became solid was obviously so ridiculous a notion that no sane folk could give it credence. Frankly, it was as stupid as the idea that there could be so much water that it could fill the whole of the horizon and be called the sea. And anyway, it only rained once a year, so what was the point in clothes?

In the end, I showed her the White Finger. If she didn't put the clothes on, I wouldn't show her around Coal Town. It worked, finally. Getting her unobtrusively out and about was even harder to accomplish. Gigol saved the day again, providing me with a sack wagon onto which I loaded a couple of empty rough-made crates, with Nightlight in the top one. This provided plenty of viewing and lots of air holes. Thus arranged, with me in appropriate delivery clothes, of which Gigol had plenty, we went on our tour.

If anybody has been following us, they might have wondered what sort of delivery we were making! However, in the early morning we were just one of many out on such a chore. I wanted Nightlight to see the sea, or the harbour at least, so it didn't come as too great a shock. I found a quiet spot near a stretch of coastline that could almost have qualified as a beach, if the sand had not been quite that shade of grey. I sat down and gratefully lit a pipe. I had some smoking to catch up on.

'So, Nightlight,' I said quietly, after the pipe was pulling satisfactorily, 'this here is the sea.'

There was no sound from Nightlight's crate, so I opened it carefully to check on her. She was pressed up against a crack, her mouth a perfect 'o' of amazement. She looked up at me and tinkled an 'oh' as well.

'And,' I added, pointing with my pipe stem, 'all of that can freeze and fall from the sky onto the ground, where it will lie for weeks, if not months.'

'Oh!' she tinkled again.

'Oh, indeed,' I said back to her and we didn't have any trouble after that about the clothes. We took the scenic way back. There was still a long time until the evening and we picked up some more fruit and a delicious refreshing drink made from local lemon fruits and bubbles.

This became our regular routine for the next few days. I even did a little real delivering for Gigol as he was a major importer of the magic bean and it gave me the opportunity to sniff around the docks. Nightlight and I both enjoyed the opportunity for a little downtime above ground without the wilful interference of goblin-kind. Not that there weren't plenty of the goblin folk in Coal Town, but, by and large, they seemed to get on with their own business. Nightlight and I got on well and we established a strange sort of friendship.

It was the Shadow Elves, if that is indeed what they were, that I found the most disturbing aspect of Coal Town life. Elves in the Citadel were just a fact of life and I could take them or leave them. Although many left me unimpressed, others like the Elf with No Name I had more time for. These other elves of Coal Town, I had to say, they worried me, and after a couple of days, after consultation with Gigol, I bought myself a shooter. It was a nice weapon, compact, but with real stopping power. The bullets were easy to obtain too and came in all the flavours you could want. I know you never have to reload an axe, but they aren't the weapons of choice for discouraging folk at a distance. Gigol was discretion itself; he didn't need a weathercock to know the way the wind blew. I had confided in him properly on our second night. It only seemed fair and I was fed up with being called 'Ironhead', which had not been my most inspired choice of aliases. He appreciated my candour and was sympathetic to our predicament, if not surprised to hear of it.

'The South Lands are strangers to the concept of law, Master Strongoak, which is why they remain so constantly colourful. Stories about these mines abound, but as long as the ore and gems keep a-coming, nobody is of much of a mind to do anything about them.'

I'd have to see about that.

Myril, The River Woman, had found me and Nightlight a good berth with Captain Broadman Carster aboard the *Standfirst Lady*, the very captain and ship who had delivered her safely to Coal Town and somebody else who had fallen under her spell. Passengers were something of a sideline for him – just enough cabins to allow him a mooring in the Kidney, but the ship was a solid steamer that would not be held up by the vagaries of the southern winds. Accommodation would not be luxurious, but Myril reassured me it would be a tremendous improvement on my previous voyage.

Everything was looking as if it was working out very well until, just short of a week later, Nightlight and I got back to Gigol's from our saunter and I had delivered Gigol' goods like an expert.

'Your coffee, Master Gigol,' I said, putting on what I hoped was my most agreeable, but still dignified, accent especially for his customers.

'Thank you, if you could put the crates in my store, Master Ironhead. I've a message for you to take back, if you'll wait please,' he continued, with just a trace of anxiety in his voice.

I took the coffee crates out as directed and we waited. I didn't have long. 'Master Strongoak,' Gigol said, bursting in, 'there are fell-folk looking for you, goblins and worse.'

I started in surprise. Nightlight, perched on a crate, immediately picked up on my alarm. How could they have located us so quickly? Even if Blossom had not fallen for my Coast Port ruse, it was still a full week's journey between the mine and here. We had passed the Slag Express at Slags' Crossing only slightly behind schedule. That still left them with another three and a half days' journey to the mine, and even if Blossom had set off immediately, that still meant a total time of over ten days was needed for the journey. How had he done it? I had permitted myself a week's grace, but I secretly hoped that Blossom wouldn't even bother with any pursuit. I had underestimated the goblin's greed and need for revenge – a bad mistake.

'They are offering a large reward, Master Strongoak, and many ears have been twitching, many eyes peering, and not a few mouths whispering,' Gigol continued.

'The stores I've used, they were all gnome-owned,' I said, thinking aloud. 'Will anyone mention anything?'

'Of course not, Nicely,' he said, slightly affronted. 'It was those very gnomes that warned me through our network. You have been named a gnome-friend. That means that all gnomes will assist you when they can.'

'Thank you a thousand times, and a thousand again, Gigol!' I said, relieved. 'You are a dwarf-friend too, or at least to this one. I'll never be able to repay you enough.' I started to think quickly.

'I had better see The River Woman and arrange to get on board the *Standfirst Lady* as soon as possible. We should be safe there away from prying eyes.'

'Nice'y worried?' Nightlight tinkled, her little face crinkled up with concern.

'Just a change of plans,' I said, as reassuring as I possibly could be. I checked the pocket watch I had liberated from Blossom.

'I don't think I should wait to see her at The Dark Horse this evening. She gave me a home address and I'll find her there. I'm not keen on going through the streets in daylight now, but neither do I relish being out after dark. If there are goblins looking for us, they're bound to have the docks covered, especially the Kidney.'

'I have a friend with a steamer,' Gigol said excitedly. 'I can arrange for him to take you to the docks this evening. Nobody will see you inside one of them and they certainly can't stop them all to search.'

'Good thinking, Gigol! Again, it seems we are in your debt.'

'Just get the small one safely away and whole again,' he replied.

'That's top of my list, Gigol. Along with staying alive myself.'

Myril's home address was unfortunately the other side of town, but by now I had a pretty good idea of the main routes and thoroughfares. I kept to the backways, though, which was just as well, as crossing the colourfully named Wet Willy Way I spotted a face I had hoped never to see again.

'Well, well! Scruple, the overseer,' I muttered to myself. 'They've let you out to come frighten the local children, have they?' I ducked down behind a parked steamer and watched him. He seemed to be engaged in stopping as many people as possible and questioning them in a way guaranteed to get him nothing but disappointment. Soon a number of the stallholders that can be found pitching their wares on every street and alleyway of Coal Town had had enough of him and convinced him of the need to move on. This he did with exceptional bad grace, earning him a direct hit with a rotten lemon fruit. He looked about to respond in kind, but just in time remembered where he was and sloped off again. He was not making himself popular, which gave me an idea.

I approached the fruit stall and bought myself a bag of the rather delicious and juicy clingstones that were in season.

'He looked a nasty piece of work,' I remarked casually to the holder, handing across some corn.

'Nasty isn't the spit as we say. Bad in looks and manner,' he replied, passing me my purchase. 'Said he was looking for a dwarf, from the far north,' he added thoughtfully.

'Can't say as how I've seen one in Coal Town ever! Very different from us Western Dwarfs, or our Eastern kin they are – most uncommon to look at, very short too. Mind you,' I took a bite thoughtfully from a clingstone, 'I have heard of a gang of rogues, goblin too, that go around only pretending to be looking for a dwarf.'

'Oh yes?' said the stallholder, his interest piqued. 'and what is their real intent?'

'Child-lifters, evil kidnappers! Steal children to work down their mines they do, and worse, I'm betting! Do you have children? Lock them up if you do.'

'I have three and each is the apple of my eye,' he said, concerned. Here, Ketch!' he shouted at the stallholder next to him, a butcher, who was taking a keen interest in our conversation. 'That fell type stopping people out in the street, has he been seen with goblin folk on his quest?'

Ketch stroked his chin. 'There have been strange goblin folk around asking a lot of questions, annoying good folk, too.'

'Then send the word out, we might have child-lifters at work.'

'No!'

'Sadly so and you know Grasper of the Goblin Guild, don't you?'

'I do – good customer of mine, very big on his offal.'

'Well, tell him there might be some of his kin in town that could be doing his folk a disservice.'

'Right, I will!' said Ketch. He took off his apron and gave his assistant his money purse. 'No time to be lost there!'

'And look out for a big goblin, said to be the leader. Ferocious he is, but with teeth like a man – very distinctive, they say,' I added.

'Thank you, Master Dwarf. You've done the town a great service.'

'I hope so,' I said. 'I really hope so.'

I hurried on to Myril's rooms, stopping only to buy some more sweetmeats and flowers and to let a few more civic-minded people know all about the gang of child-lifters in Coal Town. By the time I reached Myril's rooms, the stallholders were telling me about them! Nothing spreads faster than a juicy rumour, except news of an even juicier murder that is.

Myril's rooms were in a most pleasant backstreet. Boxes of plants – flowers and herbs – hung from every window, and they much improved the scent of the air. The houses had been freshly painted and, although tall, were not overhanging and so allowed plenty of light to filter through to the street. Myril's house had weatherboarding on the upper storeys, stained a pleasant shade of russet. Everything about it was perfect, except Myril wasn't there.

I chewed at a nail, a bad habit of mine I thought I had got out of. In the end, I threw it away, but the taste of iron still lingered. I needed a drink and I knew just the place to try first. I just hoped she'd had the same idea.

The Dark Horse was busy for the time of day, or at least I assumed so. I am not, habitually, an afternoon drinker. Midday imbibing, especially in conjunction with a five-course snack, is fine as there is plenty of time to stop; evening is ideal as you don't have to stop, not before bed beckons. Afternoon drinking is a wasteland full of good intentions and forgotten dreams and the stink of disappointment.

I was slightly surprised then, when the barkeep, Dulse, greeted me with a hearty, 'Afternoon Master, the usual is it?'

I had become quite friendly with Dulse, but certainly didn't have a 'usual'. Not slow to pick up on a cue though, I replied in the affirmative.

'Aye, usual please.'

'How's the wife and young 'un, Master? Didn't you say he was having problems with the croup?'

'That's right,' I replied in my best 'regular' tone, 'he is still coughing, but on the mend the goodwife reckons.'

'Oh good,' the barkeep said, passing me ale, before adding in a quiet voice, 'Don't go into the back. There's fell-folk drinking there, asking the wrong sort of questions!'

I listened hard and heard a loud braying of voices that sounded far too familiar from long days in the mines of Oria.

His eyes flicked upwards. 'She's in the meeting room, about to send out a messenger. You can use the door behind me.'

I caught the messenger on the stairs, telling him to keep the wage and saving his legs from a walk across town. I found Myril in the meeting room, pacing anxiously.

'Master Strongoak, thank goodness!' she said 'Have you heard about the strangers?'

'Heard and seen,' I said. 'They're from the mine alright.'

'I have contacted the *Standfirst Lady*. The Captain has agreed to set sail tonight. He has clearance.'

This was better news than I could have imagined. I sat down with some relief. 'I have no idea how they got here so soon,' I admitted. 'Not unless they flew!'

'It's possible,' Myril replied, quite seriously.

'What?!' I asked, startled.

'There are airships to the south, large balloons powered by engines that connect the most far-flung communities. Coast Port sounds like just the sort of place to be on such a circuit.'

I took my hat off and rubbed my head with a sigh. 'How am I supposed to make brilliant plans if I don't have all the facts?'

'Sorry, Master Strongoak, I didn't think to say.'

'I'm joking,' I said with a laugh. 'Please don't apologise, Myril. I'm not blaming you, just myself.' I rubbed my face this time, suddenly tired. 'I have heard of such things, of course, and thinking about it I believe I might have even seen one from the train. They don't fly around the Citadel because the winds are too strong in the north to steer.'

'I think that's why the airship station is some distance inland from Coal Town. The coastal breeze is too strong here as well. It's only in the south that the air is calm enough to allow them to navigate with the light engines they are forced to use.'

'So, they wouldn't be able to follow us when we are at sea, would they?' I asked, seeing a silver lining to this particular balloon-shaped cloud.

'Oh, no! And it's unlikely that they will be able to hire a ship or even get a berth easily to follow you.'

I had to speak about what was now worrying me. 'I think you should come with us, Myril. I'm concerned that they've found The Dark Horse. They are not good folk.'

It was The River Woman's turn to laugh. 'Please do not worry on my behalf, Master Strongoak. I have made a large number of friends here, in Coal Town, of all the guilds, even the goblins who, to my surprise, have an ear for a melody.'

I wasn't convinced about her safety or a goblin's musical appreciation, but didn't like to argue.

'We need to get you two safely on board the *Standfirst Lady*, and then I assure you they will not be bothering me.'

'Hopefully not when the whole town is convinced that they are child-lifters!' I told Myril of my rumour-mongering and she found that entertaining.

'I am worried that they will be at the docks too, Nicely.'

I then explained Gigol's idea of using a steamer. She approved. 'Yes, good thinking. There are guards on the dock gates. They will not take kindly to steamers being stopped and searched by a strange gang. Not when you have passes.' She brandished two passage passes for the *Standfirst Lady*, which I accepted with pleasure. I wasn't too keen about her wanting to accompany me back to Gigol's though, but she was determined and wouldn't be gainsaid.

'I am determined and won't be gainsaid,' she said, to drive home the point, putting on a hooded cloak that hid her golden hair. She pulled it around herself and you wouldn't have known if it was man or woman hidden inside, which was quite a trick.

I wasn't happy with this, but found it difficult to say 'no' to Myril. Besides, she knew the back way out of The Dark Horse. The River Woman also knew the back ways through Coal Town far better than I did, so we made it back to Gigol's Coffee Cabin in double-quick time. Night was beginning to fall by the time we walked onto the Rope Walk, just two dark shadows fading into the dusk. The cabin was closed and shuttered, with the one light burning downstairs. I could see Gigol's outline through the blind covering the entrance door, but something did not feel right here. Every sense I had worthy of the name was shrieking at me: 'Don't go in! Don't go in!' I went in.

'Gigol, everything alright here?' He was sitting on the customer's side of the counter, apparently deep in quiet conversation with an equally engrossed Nightlight, perched on the counter's edge.

'Gigol, Nightlight?' I walked towards them, looking around carefully, now really concerned and not a little spooked too. 'Hello?'

A voice I recognised spoke quietly in my ear. 'That will be quite far enough, I think, Master Dwarf.'

The shadow elf. I turned to find him, my hand instinctively reaching for my waist.

'No moving please, Master Dwarf, no moving at all,' he said, suddenly separating himself from the deeper shadows behind the counter.

I wanted to laugh at him; I wanted to spread his perfect nose all over those perfect cheekbones. I wanted to do a lot things, but I couldn't do a single one. I could not move a muscle. The voice, as smooth as silk, as dangerous as ogre's milk, was now the only thing I could hear; it had completely mastered me in two short sentences.

'Ill-prepared, Master Dwarf. I thought our paths might cross again, but I didn't realise it would be quite so profitable.' He patted me down, looking for weapons, but found nothing. 'You have made some powerful enemies, Master Dwarf. Powerful and very wealthy, I'm delighted to say.'

He relaxed back against the counter and pointed to my friends. 'They are well, in case you are concerned. It's just the same spell I have you under, which isn't really a spell as such. It is actually more like a trick, a clever trick you would probably say, an elf's trick. Dwarfs have low opinions of elf tricks, I know. They will be fine when I release them. At least, the gnome will be.'

The elf took a drink from the coffee cup still on the counter. 'I would hate Coal Town to lose somebody who can make coffee of this quality. The pixie sadly will have to go back with you to your employers.'

He put the coffee cup down, just as someone knocked urgently on the cabin door.

'Ah, talking of which, I think that may be them.' The shadow elf moved quietly to the door. He seemed to do everything quietly – talked quietly, walked quietly; I just wished he would die quietly. And if he didn't feel like it, I would be more than happy to help out. I couldn't see the entrance from my immobilised position but I could see the stockroom door opening very, very slowly.

'Do you have him?' spat a voice I recognised: Scruple!

'I have him, but I do not think you are the Seeker. You are the Seeker's dog.'

I just hoped that Scruple would be his customary obnoxious self and do something to annoy the shadow elf. Sadly, he seemed to have learnt some sense, for the moment at least.

'The Boss is at the docks to make sure our little ground-hugger and his pigsie cock-warmer don't try slipping out.'

'My, but you are an unpleasant fellow, aren't you? You'd better come in before the neighbour's children use you for target practice.'

'Ah! What is this? Filthy elf magic, I expect.'

'And not a civil tongue in his head.'

Scruple finally came into my view, which was not significantly improved by his leering face, and then proceeded to sniff me up and down in a fashion that only seemed to underline the elf's comment. 'What does it matter to you, elf, as long as I'm the man that can get you the corn?'

The elf joined Scruple in my sight, both now with their backs to the stockroom door. 'It's not about corn, you fool! The word was that your master could obtain for me a dragon's eye and I'll hold him to that promise. I need it for a very sensitive study I am carrying out, a very sensitive study indeed.'

'The boss will give you what you need, never fear.'

'I am not afraid,' said the elf, with what I hoped was a note of testiness.

Scruple wasn't paying attention, though. He was too busy giving me an extra special leer, for old time's sake. 'I'll teach you to try to drop me, doorstop! Me and the boys are going bitesize on you, oh yes we are! And we're going to make your rabbit's foot squeak as well; we are that! She'll squeak and squeak before she runs out of pixie dust!'

'Excellent!' said the elf, clapping his hands for attention. 'Well, now you're happily reacquainted, perhaps, eyesore, you could see your way to fetching your boss and getting me my diamond!'

Scruple turned to the elf and spoke. 'We take them to the docks.'

The elf was much put out. 'We do no such thing! I have found your dwarf and it is up to the Seeker to collect his prize. I am the Finder!'

'We have to take them to the docks!'

The elf sighed. 'Apart from anything else, the spell does not enable me to march them across town like so many puppets!'

'Then we knock them out and bundle them. Find ourselves a cart for him. I've brought Uncle Knuckles.' Scruples displayed his hand furniture, the much-feared Uncle Knuckles.

The elf turned to me, shaking his head in despair. 'I'd like you to know, this isn't personal. It's purely business, if I hadn't found you, somebody else would have.'

He had a point, but not one I was willing to concede. The stockroom door was now open enough – we needed something to happen before I was bound and senseless.

'Did you not hear me, dwarf? I asked if you understood that this was not personal?'

Without me even realising it, I was permitted to speak again. I cleared my throat, wondering what I could say to convince the elf of the folly of his position and the virtue of ours. Nothing came to mind. Then I remembered another perilous situation I had been in with another elf. An elf that I now realised had something of the character of the shadow elf looking questioningly in front of me now. There was only one thing I could say under the circumstances: 'Exchelsia.'

The shadow elf's face registered a degree of surprise that elfin faces are not designed to register. In other circumstances, I would have enjoyed it.

'What did you say?' he finally managed to spit out.

Scruple did not enjoy being left out of the conversation. 'What is all this out-hole grease? Let me get to work with Uncle Knuckles and then you can get your corn!'

The elf turned to Scruples with a furious look that seemed more at home on his face than surprise. 'Shut up, you pitiful excuse for dragon bait!' he snapped, his voice an equal mix of power, ferocity and anger: a fearsome cocktail. 'Do not move or speak unless I speak to you, and be very careful that I do not restrict your breathing too!' Scruple stopped in his tracks, one hand raised and a sneer now fixed on his face. It wasn't exactly an improvement, but it would do until I could find a box to put him in.

The elf recovered his composure. 'Now once again, please, Master Dwarf.'

'Exchelsia,' I said, as clearly as I possibly could. Not a time to mumble.

'You are aware of the import of what you say, I take it?'

I wanted to nod, but as this was still not possible, I added an 'I am'.

'Then that really does place the wolf amongst the gnomes, I must say.' He returned to his coffee and took a sip, but it didn't bring any pleasure. 'Cold,' he muttered, before eyeing me again. 'So, a friend to all elves, of day and shadow; somebody, somewhere, must have liked you.'

'I'm a likeable sort,' I replied.

'You must be, but you haven't done me any favours recently. What do I do?'

'It's simple, let us go.'

'Unfortunately, I have a contract with this fool's boss,' he indicated the unmoving Scruple, whose eyes showed the panic the rest of him couldn't.

'Did you spit on it?' I queried, trying to find a way out for the elf.

'Not exactly,' he admitted thoughtfully. 'When success cannot be guaranteed, a contract is not exactly possible... and no advance was made. It's more in the way of a reward.'

I was getting somewhere at last, so I applied some more gentle pressure. 'Plus, no way could the Boss fulfil his side of the bargain.'

'What's that?' said the elf, now really put out. 'He has no dragon's eye?'

'I heard as much from his lips, and as an elf you will know I tell the truth.' Which of course I was doing, telling the truth. What Blossom might do with the dragon's eye, which was currently nestled in amongst Nightlight's clothes in my backpack, if he got his spade-like hands on it, was anybody's guess. Passing it over to the elf was not something I would put the family shirt on, though.

'You do tell the truth. Be free,' said a small quiet elfin voice in my ear.

I collapsed forward, finally supporting myself on the counter. 'And my friends, please?' I managed to say.

The elf sighed, and looking at Gigol and Nightlight, muttered something under his breath. They both slumped forward gratefully released.

'If he so much as licks his lips, shoot him in the back, Myril,' I said loudly as soon as Gigol and Nightlight were moving again.

'Understood, Nicely,' said The River Woman, coming out of the stockroom, the shooter held high and steady.

'He needs to see you to pull his voice enchantment, I do believe. Aye, Master Elf?'

The elf nodded slowly.

'And while we are at it,' I continued, 'could I see your hands in the air for the sake of propriety, please?'

The shadow elf raised his hands.

'Not quite so ill-prepared, eh? A shake of the head will do now.'

The elf shook his head.

'Fine, now we've established that much. You can put the shooter down please, Myril.'

'But Nicely...' Myril said, her voice full of concern. Gigol and Nightlight looked similarly worried.

'Are you sure about this, Master Strongoak?' asked the gnome.

'Yes, there is nothing to be anxious about now. Is there, Master Elf?

The elf shook his head again.

'No elf can ignore the obligation that the utterance of a word as powerful as "Exchelsia" brings, can they?'

'No, Master Strongoak. They cannot, though I would be much obliged to be told who gave this to you.'

'Sorry, I can't. This elf had no name.'

'Ah, that would explain it,' the shadow elf said, as if he was now fully informed.

Myril walked carefully around the elf and handed me the shooter. The elf smiled at her with evident pleasure. 'The River Woman! How delightful. Another who can make magic with her voice. An unexpected pleasure. I have enjoyed your singing on many an evening. I'm so glad this has ended up without unpleasantness, although I am going to have to search far and wide to find myself a dragon's eye.'

I shrugged in what I hoped was an extremely non-committal manner.

'Oh well, I must be going and you, I do believe, have a ship to catch. Have a pleasant voyage.'

The shadow elf turned to leave, but Gigol called him back. 'Master Elf, you have forgotten something.'

'I have?' queried the elf.

'Half a crown for the coffee, if you please.'

The elf laughed, as unexpected as snow in July or a price tag on a magic ring. 'My apologies,' he said, placing a crown on the counter. 'Please keep the change.'

'What about him?' I said, pointing at Scruple.

'Yes, what about him?' said the shadow elf, and with that he walked out of Gigol's Coffee Cabin without looking back.

There was only room for two in the steamer, with the driver in the front perched over the third wheel. Myril now insisted on accompanying Nightlight and me to the docks, so I said a fond farewell to Gigol, pressing extra corn into his hand to assist with the removal of Scruple. Where to was really not my concern at the moment, not after what he'd said about Night-light. She had become very subdued following the shadow elf's enchantment, eyeing up Myril in a way that did not look entirely trusting. It occurred to me briefly that she had probably never seen a woman before, indeed probably had never seen a female of any race but her own. I wondered what she made of her, but now wasn't the time to ask. She slipped back in her sling and I put her safely inside the basket, which now doubled up as something very similar to a carry-cot. I had a feeling we might need all her luck before the night was out.

The steamer driver was one of Gigol's numerous nephews, a bright-eyed youth named Symbol. He was expert at his job, spinning the wagon round corners that were really too tight for such adventures, certainly not without toppling over. Yet, somehow, he managed. It would never beat a '57 Dragonette as a ride, but I was beginning to think that one of these might be the answer for getting quickly around the Citadel too.

As we approached the docks the road became particularly busy, which was something of a concern. A long row of steamers was stacked up at the dock gates, horns and bells blasting their impatience.

I checked my pocket watch, but Myril told me to relax. 'The tide does not turn until later. We have time a-plenty.'

'This doesn't look good, though,' I mentioned to Symbol, leaning forward. 'Should we take our chances on foot?'

He looked over his shoulder, his handsome boyish gnome face breaking into a huge grin. 'No need, Master! Just sit there and see.' And as we sat there and saw, almost magically a way opened up in front of us.

'It's what we call safety in numbers,' he laughed, his grin getting even larger. 'With such business on the road, the dock guards are not going to take kindly to any further delay called by your unwanted goblins. These are all good friends of mine!'

In Coal Town, it paid to be nice to the gnomes. Something they could maybe learn from in the Citadel. We passed through the dock gates with only a cursory wave of the passes. I spotted a couple of figures I recognised lurking by the gateposts, Grazbul and his runt mate Gozpol, two of Oria's finest. Neither of them paid much attention to the steamers, most of which, like ours, had their shades down. Nightlight released a hiss of displeasure from inside her basket when she saw them. This wasn't lost on Myril.

'Friends of yours, I take it?' she said.

'Oh yes, two of Blossom's captains, which rather points to the goblin chief being here or hereabouts.'

'Well, we're in the docks now and it's not far to the Kidney, so I think if he did have something in mind, he's probably left it a little late.'

'I hope so,' I said, not completely at ease. 'If I've learnt one thing, it's not to underestimate this goblin. Mean and vicious he may be, stupid he is not.' However, we made it through the docks and the extra gate that marked the entrance to the Kidney with no difficulty.

'There she is!' said Myril, pointing excitedly. 'The *Standfirst Lady*, I'd forgotten how much I liked her.' We pulled up close to the gangplank that still connected the ship to shore.

The object of her affections was definitely my kind of ship too. She wasn't going to win any prizes for beauty or for speed, but there was a solid quality to the *Standfirst Lady* that just shouted unsinkability. Three chimneys, painted bright red, sprang from her deck, like a welcoming committee of soldiers at attention. White lifeboats hung reassuringly from her sides, lots of them. Yes, definitely my kind of ship.

The dwarfs' antipathy towards water is often overplayed. After all, we wash in it, we cook vegetables in it, we even drink it when there is no ale is available. It just so happens that we also sink in it very well. There are denser substances in Widergard than dwarf bone, but they mostly are made in a forge. A proclivity for drowning would put anybody off sea travel.

Moored next to the *Standfirst Lady* was the sort of ship that only made me want to cling even tighter to solid earth. She had two hulls, when one is certainly sufficient for anybody, and a very large single sail, which does not at all address the whole point of sail redundancy. She was called *Sea Spume* and looked faster than a wizard's curse and as reliable as a goblin's promise. I know which ship I wanted my berth on.

A last few crates were being winched onto the *Standfirst Lady* by busy dockworkers. Everything looked properly industrious and as it should be. That worried me most of all.

'Let me out first, please,' I said to the gnome. 'Could you stay with Nightlight, please, Myril?'

The River Woman sighed. 'You are really worrying too much!'

'Please?'

'Oh, all right!'

I stepped out of the steamer, using its bulk to hide me from any prying eyes in the dock buildings. It all looked safe, nothing out of the ordinary, so why was I so worried?'

They came from the *Sea Spume*, swarming along the gang-plank and even up the nets on the side of the wharf. Not just Oria goblins, but local bruisers too. Shots were fired, but more for effect than intent to maim. Blossom was in the lead, waving a larger shooter and shouting at the top of his voice, 'No shooting! Don't kill the dwarf, he's mine! I'm gonna suck his bones! No shooting!'

I had no such reservations and took out my weapon, ducking down and taking aim. The dockworkers looked on, surprised by events and on the *Standfirst Lady* orders were given. Before anybody else could react, Myril took the initiative, stepping from the steamer, carry-cot hugged to her not inconsiderable breast. 'The child-lifters,' she shouted in her clear penetrating voice. 'They are after my baby! Stop them, they're all on board the *Sea Spume*. The poor children!'

The effect was remarkable. My rumour mongering had worked better than I could reasonably have hoped, and that, followed by Myril's impassioned, heart-felt declaration, sent everybody into action. Crates were dropped and wicked long gaff-hooks were picked up and wielded by righteous men who knew the sharp end from the other. Even some of the local goblins with Blossom glanced round looking for the miscreants, before realising it was actually them. They didn't look too happy about this. Expecting to only be faced with an uppity dwarf, a dock full of aggravated burly boatmen was worth better wages.

'Get the dwarf!' shouted Blossom in frustration. 'This is his doing, I just know it! Make him…' Whatever his gang were supposed to make me do, we were never to find out, as Blossom dived for cover, my bullet sadly passing harmlessly over his head.

The Oria gang was now heading back to the *Sea Spume*. Enterprising lads aboard the *Standfirst Lady* were relieving the ship of any surplus weight by throwing it from the prow in the direction of the flimsy twin-hulled vessel. One or two direct hits were not doing their woodwork any good at all.

'Yargh!' shouted Blossom, in anger, watching his crew hightail it. Enraged, his eyes swivelled, looking for me again. They didn't have far to look as I was now standing in front of him. I was the one with his fist raised. The fist that quickly reduced the distance between us further, introducing itself to the goblin-man's nose first of all. I don't think it was pleased to see us, that nose, not pleased to see the fist or me, the one putting all his mine-improved strength behind the fist. The nose had a little wander over the rest of the face.

'Yargh!' shouted Blossom, in pain this time. My, what a lot of usage he got out of such a simple sound. At which point Master Fist's friend, Master Other Fist, investigated how much air could be extracted from one goblin-man in a single 'whoosh' after connecting with his gut. Of course, Master Other Fist insists that he is really Master Fist and the other fist is Master Other Fist. I don't argue with them, as long as they are doing what is required and they were doing it very well indeed.

It was a great deal of air in that 'whoosh' and it told a story of too much spicy food and raw liquor. So Master Fist (or Master Other Fist, depending on your point of view) pushed the goblin-man away by connecting with his jaw.

'Yargh!' screamed Blossom, at a lower volume this time, because of the lack of air. Sadly, it was the last 'yargh' for the moment, as I had to take shelter behind some crates while a goblin looking very much like Grazbul sent lead in my direction. Fortunately, he was as bad with a shooter as he was with sentence construction. However, by this time the dock-workers, spurred on by Myril, were getting themselves organised and the Oria crew was in full retreat. Frustratingly, I was still pinned down.

'Dwarf!' shouted Blossom, leaking blood as he ran back down the gangplank to the *Sea Spume* chased by the angry dock-workers, 'it's not over, Strongoak!' But it was for him. That fancy sail proved highly flammable, as an improvised burning arrow from the *Standfirst Lady* was quick to show.

Nightlight laughed herself almost sick as the *Sea Spume's* captain was forced to have his men row away from the wharfside and attend to the fire at the same time. It did not look as if he was at all happy with the goblin that had presumably hired his vessel. The last I saw of Blossom, as the *Standfirst Lady* chugged its merry way out of port, he was standing on the quayside, ice on his nose, watching our ship disappear as the dock guard questioned him. I waved. He didn't wave back.

21

BACK HOME

The Citadel was cold. I'd forgotten what cold felt like. You think you remember what cold is, in the same way that in winter you think you can remember the heat of the sun. It's not the same as really feeling it, though; the reality of both can take your breath away. My breath was still there. I could see it as I breathed out, and this was only autumn.

I had been away for just over a year. A lot had happened, but the Citadel keeps to a different sort of calendar, where decades are ticked off like minutes and a year is hardly worth a mention. I was not the same dwarf that had been taken in that warmer hopeful spring; my beard was a lot longer, for a start.

The journey had been uneventful. Nightlight and I had left Myril on the wharfside with Symbol and friendly boatmen, who all seemed to be great lovers of her work and not at all in favour of visiting gangs of goblins from the south. I tried to reimburse Myril for her trouble but was met with a stony glance and just one promise that I was happy to make. 'Find Daisy.' That certainly was my intention.

The *Standfirst Lady* was comfortable and the company was good. Broadman Carster put us on to a trusted fellow captain at the next port, who put us onto his brother's boat. He recommended a good friend, whose brother-in-the-law had an excellent craft, and in that manner we had made it back to the place that for many a year now I had called home.

It was a misty evening as we steamed into the Bay, but the upper levels of the Citadel gleamed brightly above the haze. Nightlight was in awe.

'Home?' she asked, in her little singsong voice.

'Home,' I said.

'Oh!' she said.

Nightlight's mood had improved as soon as we left Myril behind. She was chirping and tinkling like her old self. If I hadn't known better, I would have said she'd been jealous. The Citadel sent her quiet again. The size of the Hill was staggering if you weren't even used to seeing a mountain, let alone one that was fully built upon.

I didn't advertise my return. There were folk who didn't need to know this news. I had work to get on with. I found us some rooms in the Wizards' Quarter. Fell-folk and bad people stayed away from this part of town as the security measures there were rumoured to involve cats – not a major problem unless a spell has changed you into a mouse first. I had heard good things about the owner, Slandon, and he seemed completely uninterested in me after he had met Nightlight. Good folk, like Gigol and Slandon, trust a body with a pixie. Bad folk get a hungry look in their eyes that Nightlight can spot a mile off.

I had a number of 'crisis stashes' secreted around the Citadel for exactly this sort of eventuality – well, not exactly this sort, as I had never actually predicted being sold into slavery. I needed to consider even more eventualities, it seemed. However, leaving Nightlight looking out of a slit between the curtains, I hurried out to collect what I could find. The first stash was still safely secreted under a water tank outside a Sixth-Level street-wagon stop. The second was in the name of Loamley at the Citadel's main station left luggage store. The final one was at the Eagles' Sports Field; luckily they did not have a match on. Now equipped with a useful amount of corn, spare identity papers for Master Detective Nicely, as well as others for mining engineer P.J. Loamley, I felt ready to do battle. At least I would, after getting some Citadel ale down my throat. That first night back, lulled by the noises of the city and making ready for the fray, I felt better than I had in a year. Nightlight wasn't so sure.

First off, I needed to see to Nightlight's injury. This was not something that could be cured overnight, I knew. It would take skilled healers and time. The healer Tollingburn, who had put me back together after the Spot the Dog escapade, was a good place to start. Fortunately they are sworn to an oath of confidentiality, and so I knew that news about the return of Reckless Strongoak would go no further. I was loath to leave Nightlight alone with strangers in a strange place. The answer was a gnome I knew well, Arito Cardinollo. Not only a scholar and good folk, he also shared his abode with a pixie. A very city pixie and, like most of that kind, wingless. He was gruff and did not have the best personal hygiene, but he had proven himself in battle and Wilmer was good folk.

They lived in the New Little Hundred – built after the last election's politically motivated fire – which was developing into an exciting new district for the Citadel, boasting many fine gnome eateries, music houses and pipeweed markets. It would never have the charm of the old place, but at least it had roads and sanitation and they were kept separate.

Wilmer was much taken by Nightlight. For her part, she wasn't sure what to make of the trench-coated, unshaven, city pixie. Although she undoubtedly enjoyed having one of her own kind around, she wasn't sure about being left there with him.

'Nicely go now?' she tinkled anxiously.

'Yes, but back soon.'

'Promising?'

'I am promising.'

Arito saw me out. 'A lot of people were very worried about you, Nicely,' he confided in his nice new entrance lobby, by the round oak door.

'Yes, sorry. I wasn't in the sort of place that you could write letters home from.'

'So I gather. Just remember, they are still there for you too – those friends.'

'Thanks, Arito, I appreciate it.' And I really did. 'I'll let them all know as soon as possible, but for now this has to stay between you, me and the Baldy Man.'

Arito nodded, and with a last goodbye to Nightlight, I went out into my busy city. Tollingburn was surprised to see me, very surprised; I'm putting it down to the beard. Once I was assured of confidentiality, I explained the situation. He was intrigued; it certainly was a first for him. Pixie surgery wasn't even a speciality in the Citadel, but he had been investigating some new bone replacement materials that might work. They were mostly being looked at for strength, without much consideration for weight. The challenge I had proposed intrigued him and he was even willing to make home-calls, especially after he saw the dragon's eye.

The dragon's eye was actually next on my list, and as mining engineer P.J. Loamley, I went to see about changing that into a more convenient form of currency. Now, as a former member of the Citadel Guard and a fully licensed Master Detective, I am, of course, a law-abiding member of the community and always pay my taxes. Paying your taxes is important, otherwise the streets don't get cleaned, the rubbish isn't collected and the children don't get taught not to spit on the cobblestones. It's just that my expenses tend to be a little different from most people's and I was going to have enough trouble as it was, trying to explain how I had managed to live for a year without any income. There isn't a box for 'slave' that you can tick on the tax forms, and this sort of thing worries them in the tax office. Certainly the sale of a fabulously expensive gem would exercise their creative tax assessment skills as well, and so it was that it was P.J. Loamley who became a very wealthy dwarf.

I couldn't go to the strictly illegal purveyors of such gemstones, because they would assume it was stolen and the price on offer would be adjusted accordingly. The completely reputable were off-limits, too, because of their requirements for extensive records. Fortunately there is the Third Way. This is the Hill name for an essentially suspect route for the movement of goods of indeterminate origin.

The process goes something like this. The bearded dwarf, obviously well travelled and not one to be messed with, approaches the gem buyer, another dwarf, of course. The buyer admires the gem and his jaw drops a little as he calculates its worth and hence his percentage. He licks his suddenly dry lips and considers the new bedroom furniture his wife has been after and the shoes the children require. He casually asks the bearded dwarf if he has provenance for this gem, which of course won't fetch the gold he would undoubtedly like as the market for this type of gem is currently suppressed. The bearded dwarf replies that there is no provenance, because he found the gem himself. This is of some concern to the gem buyer, as he would need to see a certificate of discovery from the place of unearthing, as well as the appropriate import certificate for the Citadel, of course. Oh dear, says the bearded dwarf, that is difficult because the place of unearthing did not have certificates of discovery, just large goblins with shooters who would be much inclined to take the discovery and drop the discoverer down a hole in the ground.

It is the gem buyer's turn to look disconcerted, because he is a completely legitimate trader who completely abides by the law. Of course, says the bearded dwarf, he completely understands and only wishes to abide by the law himself. He thanks the gem buyer profusely and is about to go on his way when the gem-buyer says, 'One moment please, there may be a Third Way.'

The Third Way requires you to supply a copious amount of documentation, far, far too much documentation, just not necessarily the right documentation. Origins, prices and identities are hidden under a mountain of paperwork of Iron Hills proportions designed to confuse and perplex and to ultimately defeat any interested parties. When questioned, the buyer can then always shrug and say, 'It all seemed legitimate to me.'

And P.J. Loamley had exactly the right sort of documentation required, and lots of it. And so P.J. Loamley left the gem buyers a very wealthy dwarf, and the gem buyer's wife got the new bedroom furniture and his children got new shoes and maybe there was even a little put aside for himself as well. That's how the Third Way works.

Now I only had one thing left to do, the most important thing.

I knocked on the door to Elsera's rooms as it was getting dark, after first checking for any snoopers. She was dressed casually, as if she had just been cleaning or doing other chores. She looked at me, expressionless, for what seemed an eternity, before saying, 'So, where is the ice?'

I had it behind my back.

A little while later she said, 'The beard has to go!'

A good while after that, laughing, she said, 'All right, the beard can stay for a while.'

A very long time later, with the wine I had bought a lifetime ago almost finished, we lay in bed together, the waxing moon shining brightly through the gap at the edge of the blind. I had just given her the broadest outline of my misadventures.

'I don't think I want to know any more now, Nicely. It's almost all too much to take in. I can't make sense of it. I was so worried. There was no trace of you at all. Now you're back and my head's in a whirl.'

'I know what you mean,' I admitted.

'Talk to me about something else instead.' She snuggled up closer. 'Tell me the rest of the story of The Golden Ring.'

So, with her soft head resting on my chest, that is exactly what I did.

'You may remember that we left the noble dwarf lord Albright Goldgleaming and his mistreated people exiled from their homelands, thanks to the treachery of the elves and the murderous nature of the stone giants. Great was Albright's peril in those days and sorely were his people tested, but they came through all the trials put before them by adversity because their hearts were good and true. And, like all dwarfs, being fair-minded and industrious as well, they were never without employment. So after many years they found themselves in the land of the Hammerlings, who were as close unto dwarfs as goblins are to men (and don't let anybody tell you anything different about goblins). Albright was by then at the height of his powers, and with natural dwarf good looks, almost inevitably the Hammerling princess Gemima fell deeply in love with him. He returned the passion and so they were wed and the two folk joined as one. And because their union was true, she soon fell pregnant, with what everyone was convinced would be a son and future king of both Dwarfs and Hammerlings.

'Life for the treacherous Elf Lord, however, had not been all that he had anticipated or longed for, because there is some justice in the world. In fact, an elf sorceress Erdra predicted that the end of the elves was near, and so Wolond, the Elf Lord, sent his three elf-maiden sisters/daughters out into Widergard to bring all his people back to protect the castle realm he now called Halla. Wolond knew that the golden ring and the Dwarf-helm might save him, but they were still guarded by Fafener, the greatest of dragons. Through his machinations, though, he hoped to find an innocent hero to do the dragon-slaying job for him. When Wolond hears that Albright is to be a father, fear freezes the Elf Lord's blood, for this is the event that was prophesied to herald the end of the elves as part of the curse Albright put on the ring. Wolond therefore plots afresh.

'Albright's brother, Mica, since the loss of the golden ring and the Dwarfhelm, has laboured long and hard to try to forge a weapon as mighty as the Dwarfhelm or as beautiful as the golden ring, and hence help his noble brother regain their realm. Being so preoccupied, he has never married, but instead the kindly dwarf lord has adopted a young ward, a parentless young dwarf called Viction, who, Mica has foreseen, will one day be a great hero. Mica has tried to re-forge the sword Balthung that was shattered on the stone giant's skin, but he cannot. His fear for his people's well-being has weakened him and he knows that only one without fear can remake the sword. And swords like this are not purchased from the 6–12 store.

'One day, as Mica labours, a wanderer approaches – actually it is the Elf Lord Wolond, using his powers of enchantment to sneakily disguise himself. The Elf Lord inveigles Mica into a battle of wits, but the clever dwarf soon beats Wolond in the rhyme game. When the Elf Lord then tries to cheat Mica at hangman, he realises who it must be and calls Viction for assistance. Fearing that this young dwarf is Albright's son – elves really have trouble keeping track of time – the Elf Lord flees.

'Mica tells Albright of the Elf Lord's visit and, now worried for his wife and son-to-be like a good husband and father, Albright sets out for Fafener's cave to reclaim his ring and Mica's

Dwarfhelm. In his forge, Mica hears of his brother's departure, and terribly afraid for him, rushes to assist. He has not gone far before he is joined by Viction, who unbeknownst to Mica, and being without fear himself, has re-forged the sword Balthung.

'Albright has now reached the dragon's cave, but before he can do battle, Wolond, disguised as a wanderer again, approaches him. Albright sees through his disguise, shaming him and saying he should battle Fafener with his Staff of Power. Wolond will not do this in case his staff is broken, and after a short fight that ends in a stalemate, the Elf Lord sneaks off. Albright, tired by the fight, rests before he takes on Fafener. Unfortunately, the excited Viction blows his horn to reassure Albright that reinforcements are on the way, but wakes an enraged Fafener, who falls upon Albright. Dwarf and dragon are locked in mortal combat and each injures the other sorely. Albright swoons while Fafener goes back to his treasure cave to lick his wounds.

'Mica and Viction arrive, and crying, Mica applies his skill to save his brother. Determined to see an end to this conflict, Viction enters the cave of Fafener. The dragon, seeing the lone boy approaching, laughs, pulling himself up to a tremendous height, shouting: 'Look at me and quake, child. Do you not fear me?'

'It is now Viction's turn to laugh and he tells the dragon, "I fear nothing!" And with one blow from Balthung, he cleaves Fafener's giant head from his body.

'Wolond has been lurking nearby, and now disguised as Mica, congratulates the boy, asking him for the golden ring from the treasure. Being obedient, he hands it over, only to be struck by the treacherous elf's Staff of Power. The elf runs off delighted.

'When Viction recovers, the head of Fafener, now once again in stone giant form, says with his last breath how he was been cheated by Wolond, disguised as Mica. Taking the Dwarfhelm, Viction rushes out, only to find Mica waiting. Thinking him to be Wolond, Viction slays his dwarf master, only realising his error when he cannot find the golden ring.

'Distraught, Viction cannot forgive himself and goes into exile, while Albright, his life saved by his poor brother Mica, deeply saddened, can now at last regain their kingdom from the dead dragon's thrall. He is joined by his wife Gemima who gives birth to a son they call Hagen, and although he always misses the beauty of his golden ring, he has the beauty of his family to console him. Wolond, meanwhile, can only wait in his castle, brooding over the stolen ring, but waiting for the judgement that he knows Albright's son will visit upon him.

'Not so many songs in this part,' I added by way of explanation.

'And all of this, just because Wolond's three daughters laughed at a dwarf while he was having a quick wash. Remind me not to giggle at you in your bathers!'

'We're sensitive creatures, we dwarves, easily bruised,' I said in my defence. 'And they were Wolond's sisters, or was it his daughters? Argh, elf relationships were a lot trickier in those days, you know?'

I had a sudden thought and sat bolt upright as the full import of what I'd just said sunk in.

'Nicely, are you alright?' said Elsera, concerned.

'I may be. I may be very all right.' I jumped out of the bed and grabbed my kecks.

'Nicely! What are you doing?'

'I am sorry, I really, really am sorry, but a lot of things might just have fallen into place.' I leant over and kissed her quickly, but like I meant it. 'Are you busy tomorrow?'

'No, but what's this about?'

'It's about elves, that's what it's all about. It so often is,' I half cursed. I tugged on my boots and put on my jerkin and jacket. 'I'll pick you up at around Midwatch. Dress like a demure recently married woman, if it's not stretching things too far.'

'I can do demure,' she said fluttering her lashes. 'Oh Master Dwarf, you are so very masterful!'

'That's good.' I kissed her again, because the last one had been so much fun. 'Don't worry, this time nobody is taking me away anywhere.'

The Hat was waiting for me on Elsera's hat stand. I picked it up on my way out, but it wasn't time to put it back on. Not yet.

22

SOLUTIONS

The office looked like it always had done, like it would do all the time I was in residence anyway; even the dust hadn't changed. The glossy scrolls in the waiting room were out of date, but they always had been. An eclectic mix, they didn't reflect my reading habits, but rather the interests of the folk who had left them there while waiting on the presence of the detective whose name was above the door. Some heavy financial tomes sat happily amongst ephemeral works on fashion, good housekeeping and hair – a surprising number concerned with follicular management in fact, which maybe says something about my clients, I'm not sure. Oh, the copies of *Modern Axe* are mine, but I've no idea where *Divination Today* came from, which definitely tells you something about my precognitive powers.

Peat, the office porter, had collected all my post and separated it into piles for me. He had also left a message pinned to the dartboard: 'We're worried – call!' Underneath in smaller letters he had added, 'I've watered the plants. The elf rose flowered!' Peat was good folk.

I looked through the important pile and one missive in particular caught my eye. The writing was simple, almost childish, and I felt something like a chill as I broke the seal. The letter was short, the penmanship even more elementary. I read it slowly.

274

Good Master Strongoak,

I have been told that you are looking for me. I would like to ask you to stop. I am well and very happy as you can see from the picture I have included. She has a wonderful Daddy (he is taking the picture). I know I have done some stupid things and I upset my mother and I am sorry. I am so very sorry I did not know about the Wilting Hurt. I miss her very much.

I have now made the clean break the elf lady told me to make with the money she gave me. I know that Daff has been looking for me too. If you can find him in the White Horse Travelling Show, could you tell him to stop worrying too, please? I'm sorry he was not my dad, but that wasn't his fault. Sometimes I think none of this is anybody's fault. Sometimes like mother's Wilting Hurt things just happen.

But as I sit here now, I have to say that I think life is good.

The letter was signed Daisy 'Cartersong'. The picture enclosed showed a happy mother with a smiling girl on her lap. The young child was the spit of her mother, right down to the gap-toothed smile and the slightly crooked nose. The mother, of course, no longer had the crooked nose or the gap-toothed smile, but she still was a sweetheart, even more so with her hair piled up dwarf-fashion.

In amongst the rest of the post there was a letter from Josh. Included in it was the sketcher's impression of how Daisy would look now. He got it pretty right, but he didn't know about the nose job or the teeth straightening either. In with the pictures there was a note from Josh, something I'd never seen before. It said, 'Call me, you little squeak of out-hole grease. You expect me to pay for these?' Underneath he'd added, 'Look just call!'

The office chair welcomed me back with a satisfied creak as I sat down. I looked at the picture again and couldn't help but smile: yes, just occasionally life is good. But not for poor Daff, and somebody would have to pay for that.

I looked out of the window and sat and thought until I saw the first signs of dawn creep over the Hill. Then I kicked myself into action.

I was parked up outside Mistress Ensanders's place on Bank Row before the morning really had its boots on. The wagon was hired as it wasn't yet time for Daddy to see his Dragonette. That was fine as I didn't want either the wagon or me to be recognised. Unfortunately, the hired wagon also needed to shout 'wealth', so it wasn't exactly unobtrusive, or cheap for that matter.

The house was quiet, no young children crying here, but I soon saw a light and detected signs of movement. As I suspected, Mistress Ensanders was an early riser. After a short while, she came out and pumped up her wagon and then went back indoors. Another short while, probably to eat something with more fibre than a throw rug, and she comes back out and heads off.

Mistress Ensanders did not immediately drive to Tall Trees. Instead, she went some distance out of her way, heading north of the city to cross the Evermore at the Troll's End Bridge. From there she followed the river north and east again. She stuck to the smaller roads that mostly served the remaining light industry that hadn't upped and moved down to the larger estates near the Bay. In between the manufactories there were surprisingly attractive old-fashioned residences of some note, quite large halls whose grounds had been sold off for profitable commercial usage. Some of these halls still had lodges, homely oases now cast adrift in the trading seas. Mistress Ensanders pulled up outside one such lodge, complete with the sturdy gates that once led to something grander, but now protecting a much more humble home. The gates opened in front of her, which was impressive, and slowly closed behind. I parked out of sight and approached the lodge by foot using the ample cover.

I settled down to wait. I didn't mind waiting. I'd done waiting and it was a lot better than mining. When the gates opened again, Mistress Ensanders was out in a hurry, presumably to miss the morning rush and still make it across town to Tall Trees in time for his Elfness. I slipped in through the gates before they closed behind me with a satisfying click.

There didn't seem to be any additional security, but I still trod carefully – no point in not getting the practice in when you can, which reminded me, I had neglected my shooting recently as well. I really wanted to find somebody to help me out with that.

The lodge has all the right features in all the right places to make it what I believe is generally called a 'very desirable residence', that's if it hadn't been quite so out of the way. 'Out of the way' I was guessing was the most desirable characteristic about it for the current owner. I heard a voice, female, singing from out the back, so I headed in that direction. It was a nice voice, not a great voice, not a River Woman, or even an Elsie, but very pleasant in the elfin way. I didn't recognise the tune and I didn't know the words, but it made me feel a little sad, nostalgic for a time I never knew. The elves have a word for that too. It's a lovely word, very poetic, but I still think they should add 'humility' to the dictionary instead.

A child laughed in the way that they do, simply for the joy of laughing – a light female child's voice. The owner of the laugh came running round the side of the lodge and took one look at me and stopped laughing. She was new to the running business, and new to dwarfs too, if I was any judge. I put my fingers to my lips and went 'shhh'. She thought this was silly and ran off again. I followed her to where she now sat perched on her mother's lap.

'She has her father's eyes,' I said to the seated woman.

'Do you think so?' she replied.

'For the rest, she takes after you, I'm glad to say.' And she did, a small toddling, blonde-haired, very pointy-eared version of her mother, all summer sunshine and forget-me-nots.

'Sorry to call without an appointment, Lady Vericeema. I understand they are very much the thing these days, but you have proven rather hard to track down.'

'That was the idea, Master Strongoak. It is Master Strongoak, isn't it?' she replied, offering me the free seat on the small outside paved area that I took to be recently vacated by the secretary Ensanders.

'It is. Nicely Strongoak, at your service.'

'My brother said you were "off the case", as I believe they say.'

'Did he?' I had to ask. 'Or did he say I was "off the map" perhaps, or "out of the picture"?'

She thought a moment. 'No, definitely "off the case". Such a colourful expression.' She laughed and her daughter laughed with her.

'You're a full elf, aren't you? I didn't realise.'

'Oh yes. Evermore and I may not share the same mother, but my mother was an elf too. His aunt in fact.'

'Yes, I had forgotten how complicated elfin relationships can be until recently,' I admitted. 'Very complicated.'

'Do you think we are terrible creatures, Master Dwarf?' She fixed me with that thousand yards stare that they have. The one that can tell the colour of your undergarments through your chain mail.

'I'm no arbiter, My Lady.'

'That doesn't answer my question, Master Dwarf. You see, when you live as long as elves do, families become complicated; relationships change, develop and grow in unexpected ways.'

'Then why didn't you tell your brother, when you fell pregnant? Why keep it a secret from him?'

'Because I was cross with him!' Suddenly Vericeema wasn't all sunshine and forget-me-nots. There was more than a trace of that quality which someone at some time once described as being as "dark and terrible as the toothache", or words to that effect.

'I was furious, in fact!' she continued. 'Being pregnant was certainly not in my plans for that year and the care of an infant was not my top priority!' Her look softened, though, as she smiled at her child.

'Do you have children, Master Strongoak?'

'Not so you'd notice, Lady.'

'It really does change everything, just like they say, but you never really believe – not until it happens to you.'

'So you never went to any relatives, where your condition might be commented upon. Ensanders helped you out and you became her "niece"?'

'Yes, that's right. Ensy is a treasure.'

'Because she has known you since you were young?'

Vericeema laughed again. 'Since she was young, Master Dwarf! You forget whom you are speaking with.'

'Of course, my apologies.'

'But after Silemisi was born, my mood softened.' She lovingly hugged her daughter and spoke in low tones. 'Look, Silemisi, this is Master Strongoak and he is a dwarf. Say hello to Master Strongoak.'

She pointed Silemisi in my direction and Silemisi waved shyly. I waved back, because that's what you do, and never trust a man, dwarf, elf or wizard that doesn't.

'And you thought she should know her father?' I continued.

'Of course.'

'And so he took me off the case?'

'It wasn't necessary. After all, I was safe.'

'But why the smutties?' I needed to know. 'Were you so angry you wanted to blacken the family name? Get back at him?'

'I didn't send them, Master Detective! I think my condition at the time would hardly have warranted the taking of such pictures.'

'So the little sister did it after all?' I said, partly to myself.

'I think that is something you will have to take up with her.'

'I will.'

'As for us, my daughter and I are quite happy here. We will not be going to Tall Trees until Evermore's current run as Council Leader has finished. Tongues will wag at some point, but preferably not for a while.'

'Of course.'

'Now, if that is enough, I will bid you farewell, Master Dwarf. We will all count on your discretion now.'

'Just one last question, if I may, please. Your ring, the birthday ring, what happened to it? You're not wearing it now I see.'

The elfess looked down at her hand, as if seeing it for the first time. 'No, when I fell pregnant my hands quickly began to swell. I took it off and left it in my room in Tall Trees. Strange, I haven't thought about it for ages. Is it important?'

'It could be, my lady. It could be. Now, I had better be going.'

'Wave good bye to the nice dwarf, Silemisi.' The little girl, all serious again, waved. I waved back. It's what you do.

I left mother and child playing happily in the weak autumn sun, not a care in the world. How could they have? I'd collected the full set.

I just missed Tollingburn at Arito's, but it had all gone well. Nightlight liked the burly healer and was buoyed up by his optimism. Arrangements had been made for the surgery and Wilmer had volunteered to keep Nightlight company – just try to stop him!

I'd borrowed a change of clothing from the office locker and added a few items I keep for the express purposes of personality creation. In the relative privacy of Arito's study, after a minute or three, I looked every inch the successful dwarf, Sustenance Goldstream, who had made the appointment the day before to visit the Harrowfeld Hall Home for Troubled Children. Nightlight, naturally, thought I looked hilarious.

'Nice'y big fat old dwarf now?' she tinkled.

'Nice'y always looks like big fat old dwarf,' added Wilmer, unhelpfully. 'Now he's just got a beard.'

I picked up Elsie bang on time. She took one look at me sitting in the wagon with my knotted beard, large gold watch chain and diamond stock pin and asked, 'What, is it the driver's day off?'

'I fired him,' I replied, in no mood for further criticism.

'Why?' she asked, getting in on the passenger side.

'Because he asked too many questions.'

I filled her in on the part she had to play as I drove. She was the young wife of the wildly talented and filthy rich dwarf trader, Sustenance Goldstream, in need of the little bundle of joy that nature had not seen fit to deliver. We understood that Harrowfeld Hall might be able to help us. Elsie asked if I was paying Guild rates. I told her there might be a little something in it for her later if she was lucky. She said that there'd better be.

The drive took longer than I'd allowed for and I hated being late. Fortunately, Sustenance Goldstream couldn't give a pixie's fart, so I took my foot off the steam and we enjoyed the ride. When we finally rolled up, we didn't even have to ring: the gates parted in a most agreeable fashion.

The Hall was exactly the sort of pile of rocks the name promised and it was panelled in enough rare wood to have sent a conservationist a-weeping. A flunky showed us to some very comfortable chairs in a very agreeable room. I spent my time harrumphing in rich dwarf trader style, while Elsie wrung a handkerchief in a convincing fashion. On the wall of the room was a beautifully engraved plaque to thank the Hall's benefactors and staff. Under the patrons I found the names of G. Grounding and L. Wideswing, as I'd expected. There was another name I did not expect to see there: C. Lief. This, though, was as nothing to the names I saw on the staff roster.

Head of Hall, Deselia Stormcock, was not as I had anticipated: all dried out and a bit crusty round the edges. She was a battle-axe, beautifully put together, highly polished, and as sharp as the day she was forged. Beautifully turned out too. I had to keep reminding myself I was here on business. Fortunately, the occasional jab from Elsie kept me on track.

'What you are asking is slightly unusual,' Deselia Stormcock said, after the pleasantries were over. 'Our remit really is to help older children, ones from troubled homes.'

'But it does happen? There are babies as well? Gold is no object, whatever my goodwife desires.'

Deselia Stormcock coloured slightly. 'I assure you, Master, gold has nothing to do with anything. It's the children's best interests that we have in mind.'

'Please excuse my husband, Mistress Stormcock,' Elsie said, in her best long-practised husband-apologising manner. 'Like many of the dwarf brotherhood, Sustenance is known for speaking his mind, sometimes without the appropriate consideration for custom.' She gave me such a look of total devotion that I felt obliged to respond for Sustenance's behaviour too.

'Yes, my goodwife speaks truly, Mistress Stormcock. I sometimes forget that dwarf ways are not the ways of every folk.' I wanted to add a 'more is the pity', but decided to shut up for the moment.

'Like yourself, Mistress Stormcock,' Elsera continued, wringing her handkerchief most effectively, 'we are only interested in providing a needy child with a loving home. I understand that there are young girls, on their own, who find it hard to cope with motherhood. We simply wish to help provide a loving home for that child.'

'Then I'm sure we can help you,' Deselia said.

'And your medical staff here, are they any good? The children are healthy?' I said, keeping the Sustenance role ticking over.

'The very best, brilliantly qualified, young and enthusiastic.'

'This would be the Argebester fellow?'

Deselia's eye twitched involuntarily. 'No actually, Physic Argebester retired recently. For his health. He will be missed but he was close to retirement, as was his nurse. It has allowed us to find excellent replacements. Why, did you know Physic Argebester?' The question was phrased quite naturally, but there was something else going on behind those sparkly eyes of hers.

'Me?' I replied, as if affronted, 'certainly not! Haven't been to a healer since I don't know when! Healthy as an ox. Just read it on your board next door. Need to get your board updated!'

'Yes,' she nodded, 'there have been a few changes recently. All for the better, I'm glad to say. I myself have only been here for just over a year.'

Ah, now I understood. Yes, it seemed that the changes had been for the better.

We had the full tour from Stormcock's assistant. The Hall did look very well maintained and the children seemed happy and healthy. The healer was very young and not at all sorcerous. His nurse appeared competent and unlikely to have any deviant sexual interests. All seemed well at Harrowfeld Hall. I left them my messenger service's number, which is totally anonymous, and Mistress Stormcock promised to be in touch. Elsie dropped some gold in a box they had for such purposes. Nice touch – attention to detail makes a great actress.

'Well, do I get the job?' Elsie asked, when we were safely out of the Hall gates.

'The part is yours! The donation was a nice touch.'

'Glad you think so. I'll be billing you for it. Now, are you going to tell me what that was all about?'

'I promise I will.'

'Good!'

'But could you wait until I have everything in place? Otherwise you might think my much-heralded detective powers are not all I make them out to be.'

'I suppose so, but I will hold you to that.'

'I swear it on my badge and axe.'

'That will have to do. Now home please, driver, I need to collect my wages!'

I put my foot down. I hate to be a late payer.

23

PAYBACK

I got back to the Armoury eventually at around Midwatch, when good folk are sound asleep and bad folk are hard at work. All was unnaturally quiet and my rooms were now just occupied by ghosts and memories. I would do something about them later, but for the moment I had other priorities. I fetched some sharp scissors from the kitchen drawer and found my razor, which I stropped up good and proper. Then we retired together to the bathroom. The beard took a lot of cutting and the face that the shave revealed looked strange, like it belonged to somebody I had known in another life. I just hoped I would grow into it again.

I reintroduced myself to my wardrobe. My, how my suits had missed me. A few of them would need some work from tailor Gaspar Halftoken to accommodate the extra muscle I now carried, but a double-breasted insulated buttock freezer did the required job. I picked up the Hat; it was time. Less than one hour later and Nicely Strongoak was back in town, dragon-hide hat dipped strategically below one eye. I had stoked up the '57 Dragonette and filled the boiler before going upstairs. She started first time. I could tell she'd missed me too.

The entrance to Bron's looked pretty much the same, as did the Elf with No Name, taking the air at the top of the marble staircase and looking out across the Citadel.

'Master Strongoak,' he called down, 'how pleasant to see you. I was beginning to wonder if our humble establishment was not to your liking.'

'Not at all,' I replied, climbing the staircase. 'I have been… away.'

'A furlough perhaps?'

'No, not a furlough.'

'Ah?' he replied, leaving the question hanging in the air.

'To a part of the world I believe you might know.'

'Perhaps, I have travelled extensively,' he said, by way of explanation.

'Perhaps even familiar to your kin as well.'

'They too… get around.'

I joined him on the same step and admired the same view. 'A fine night,' I said, eventually.

'Yes, cold and crisp,' he replied. 'They say it will be a hard winter and we might even see some proper snow.'

'Is that your prediction?' I asked.

'Oh no, the weather experts playing with their seaweed and pinecones, I expect.'

'Only I have it on good authority, by which I mean myself, that you may be imbued with some of that famous elf farsight.'

'And why would you think that, Master Dwarf?'

'Because I think you foresaw trouble in store for me and gave me something that would assist me with that trouble.'

The elf laughed good-naturedly. 'Trouble follows you like a hungry wolf follows a wounded ice-deer, Master Dwarf! I do not need any second sight to know that!'

'Perhaps,' I replied with a shrug, buttoning up my jacket against the chill, 'but I'd like to pay the debt nonetheless.'

'It is not necessary.'

'Still, by way of thanks I wondered if I can interest you in helping me out with a task fate has put before me, not strictly legal, but morally to be applauded.'

The elf clapped his hands in delight. 'My most splendid dwarf, why didn't you say so? It has been a dull old year without you around.'

Getgold Grounding's house was big, but not technically a separate town. It was in Cliff Tops, which is as ultra-exclusive as you can get unless your ears are pointy and your cheekbones can cut cheese. The men and women who live in Cliff Tops think that they are better than other men and women because their ancestors, by and large, made their gold doing things to people that were legal then, but aren't now. How this makes them better and not just luckier is anybody's guess. Getgold was one of the few dwarfs to be allowed into these hallowed grounds. I bet he was made up about that.

Getgold's house had plenty of those new Silent Watchers, the ones that the Elf with No Name had to strain to hear. He strained, he heard them, and we avoided them. The two-legged security should have been dropped from the eponymous Cliff Tops, so useless were they. And as for the four-legged security, they decided it was a good idea if we went in unmolested after a quiet word with my elfin accomplice.

In the hallway, there was a set of golf clubs ready for Getgold's morning round. I thought for a moment: was this a job for a wood or iron? I chose an iron. It wasn't easy to find Getgold's room as it was possible to mistake it for a ballroom. Similarly, why anybody his size required a bed that size either doesn't bear thinking about, so I didn't. I was just glad that he was alone tonight.

I walked softly to where he was sleeping, his face lit by the open fire that had been stoked against the autumn chill. He was not an advertisement for dwarf manhood. He was wearing a silk night-robe that would have looked better on somebody a quarter his age, a third his weight and with breasts. His hair was tucked into a soft nightcap, designed to keep his crowning glory pristine, and his beard was in curlers – oh my.

I woke him with a gentle tap from the golf club. He was not pleased to see me.

'You!' he spluttered finally.

'Me,' I replied.

'I am not in the habit of talking to employees in my bed-room,' he said, pulling his blankets up higher. His eyes darted involuntarily to his right, which I now knew was the place he kept his panic button.

'Before we go any further, we should clarify matters a little, Getgold. Your guards, not worthy of the name, are safely and tightly trussed up in their watch-room and all lines to outside have been cut. Your personal assistant is now assisting my assistant by opening all manner of strongboxes and files and…' I stopped him from interrupting with one raised hand. '… and I am not your employee, and never was, as I've had to point out before.'

I had a little practice swing with the club, just limbering up.

'Now, as regards our contract, that has been invalidated by the small print that says "clients to not beat up on the detective!"' I brought the club down with a thud on the bed next to him. It made a very satisfactory noise. I was pleased to see Getgold nearly jump right out of his silky nightie.

'Was this the one, Getgold?' I said tersely. 'Was this the iron you used to stove my head half in? Or is a wood better for such tasks, eh? What number's best for taking out a dwarf?'

Getgold pulled his blankets up even higher, for all the good that would do. 'I'm sure I don't know what you mean!'

'Oh, come off it, Getgold. Only another dwarf would know how hard you can hit a dwarf without splitting his skull in two. Unless that was the intention?' I looked him in the eye for clarification. 'No, I don't think so, not when you can turn a profit on the operation as well. It's what made the Getgolds rich, after all.'

'Preposterous,' he said, back in splutter mode.

'I don't think so, Getgold. I really don't think so. Now,' I said, and squared up the iron again, 'this is what's going to happen. It's your turn to leave the Citadel, but you're not coming back. You have suddenly been struck by the need to reconnect with your dwarfish roots, way, way up north. There you will seek to declutter your life in line with your newfound lust for the simple life and you shall give away your fortune to a number of children's charities that I will outline for you.'

He actually had the gall to laugh. 'And why should I do that? For some unprovable accusation about what I did to a goose-guard of low reputation?'

'No, Getgold, for what you did to an underage girl and the help you gave to others of your ilk to find similar girls from the Harrowfeld Hall Home for Troubled Children.'

He went a very satisfying shade of grey that did not match his silky night-togs at all.

'I found Daisy, you see, Getgold. And she knows everything,' I fibbed a little.

The dwarf in the bed went even paler.

I swung the club a few more times. 'Plus, as a patron on the board of the aforementioned home, you aided and abetted the activities of one Physic Argebester and his nurse to procure young girls for the vice trade, offering them so-called "renewal treatments" such as nose straightening and teeth readjustment as an incentive.'

'That was all Argebester's idea,' he stammered.

'And a nice little earner it was. Until you found out that the daughter you didn't even know you had sired had got herself involved in it.'

Tears now began to fall down the dwarf's face. I wanted to wipe them away with the golf club, but held myself back.

'I didn't know, I honestly didn't know. I thought the show-man Daff was her father,' he insisted. 'He came looking for his daughter once.'

'That much I believe, Getgold. Otherwise I wouldn't have been hired, but you rather liked having the Citadel's only dwarf detective at your beck and call, didn't you? Showed just how important you were.'

He nodded.

'Say it!' I spat at him.

'I did, I'm sorry. I did.'

'That's why you boasted to Councillor Truelight about me, about my "discretion". In the Council Hall, was it? While you were robing up?'

'Yes, it was. But what of it?'

'Never you mind, Getgold. Just as long as you're clear about what you need to do.'

Getgold had recovered some of his spark. 'Look, Master Strongoak, we are both dwarfs, men of business, I'm sure there must be another way we can solve this little misunderstanding.'

'Are you?' I asked him. 'Really sure?'

I turned to the elf hidden in the shadows. 'How about you? Do you think there is another way?'

'Oh yes,' said the Elf with No Name in a voice that had me quaking in my boots, 'we kill him now and I roast his entrails over this fire.' He stepped forward and the fire in the grate shot upwards, making his face a nightmare mask of flames and shadow.

Getgold cried out in terror.

'I would introduce you,' I told Getgold, 'but he doesn't have a name. I think you'll know him again, though, won't you?'

Getgold simpered a response.

'And you'll know him, won't you?' I asked the elf.

'I could find him now even if he tried to hide across the sea, or in the Frozen Lands or in the deepest mountain. Nowhere would he be safe from my revenge,' the Elf with No Name said.

'I'll take that as a "yes" then, thank you.' I turned to the quaking Getgold. 'Well, that seems pretty conclusive, Getgold. I judge we have a deal!' Getgold nodded, terrified, but I also had him sign the confession I'd written out earlier.

We left through the main door. So much easier than messing about running across lawns.

'Yes,' said the elf as we walked down the drive, the dawn breaking around us, 'a very fine night.' He hummed a merry tune as he walked. 'I should tell you,' he continued, 'after our last little adventure I made a few enquiries of my own.'

'Oh yes?' I said.

'The character you called Argebester, who I judged to be in charge – a very unpleasant countenance.'

'No argument here. Vice wasn't his only trade.'

'I adjudged that he might have sorcerous leanings.'

'Yes, I feared as much too. A skin-changer at least, and perhaps not too fussy about how he changed the skin.'

'And worse.'

'Worse? How much worse?' I asked, almost not wanting to know.

'Necromancy.'

'That's worse.'

'There are ways that you can tell, if you have the training. When a practitioner of the Black Arts has been tampering with such things.'

'Signs like a severed head?'

The elf stopped to look at me. 'Exactly. And how did you find that?'

'There are ways, if you have the training.'

We walked on and the elf continued his story. 'Necromancy is not just about communicating with the dead. It can be about putting off death too. Robbing life from one person, to give to another.'

'And making a tidy profit if you do it retail. Putting an extra spring in the step of those that can afford it in a renewal parlour, and making out it's monkey glands.'

'Even harnessing sexual energies too.'

'Hence the vice trade then. That's one all-round bad body.'

'It is, Nicely. Why, did you think they'd all gone away? All the Dark Kings and the sorcerers?'

'Not really – evil doesn't always come swathed in dark robes and carrying eldritch weapons. Sometimes it wears a white coat and has nice premises.'

'Well put, Master Dwarf.'

'And what of Argebester then, Master Elf?'

'He, and his woman – I'm afraid they flew the coop. Very speedily.'

'I saw as much. I didn't have time to look further, before I was distracted.'

'The word is out on him now. Do not worry, he will not escape punishment. Widergard is not as big as it used to be.'

'Good,' I said, and took a breath. 'You know, I think it will be a fine autumn day too. I love the colour of the leaves at this time of year. Nothing like that sort of colour down south, Master Elf.'

'Indeed not. You know, life is much more interesting with you around, Master Strongoak.'

'Never a dull moment, Master Elf.'

I grabbed a couple of hours' sleep in the office, after a quick catch-up with Peat. Apparently, some of the more notable figures of my acquaintance had opened a book on the odds of me returning in one piece. Peat was delighted to see me. He had me at fourteen months and five to one. I had just made him quite a windfall. Words would be had with anybody who bet I wouldn't be making it back.

Candy Lief's store was quiet and dark and there was a closed sign on the door. No enticing smells wafted out from the manufactory and no children laughed or played. I went round the back to the delivery entrance and found the gate ajar. I went in.

Candy was sitting at his empty bench staring into space, despite the early hour. Where once fizzballs, rocettes, and magic mushrooms had been made, there was now only the slightly sour smell of lost dreams.

'Candy?' I said quietly, trying not to scare him. He turned to me and I could see he had been crying.

'Nicely, my deario!' He wiped his eyes. 'How splendid to see you. I'd heard you were missing. I am so very glad you are all right! Oh yes.'

He got off his stool and walked awkwardly across to give me a hug. I could see and feel he had lost weight. A sweetmeat maker shouldn't lose weight; it's against the natural order.

'What's happened, Candy? Your store...?'

'She left me, Nicely. My Cassada ran off with my own nephew, can you believe it? Oh deario. The one I was training up to inherit everything! They took my recipes and went off, disappeared like the morning dew.'

'Oh Candy, I am sorry.' I gave the distraught man a hug back.

'I can't find it in myself to make anything, Nicely. Love was my secret ingredient, you see, and now my love is gone and everything that was sweet is ruined. All is lost.'

I hated to do it, but I needed to ask him a question. 'Candy, I'm sorry to ask this now, but did you ever have anything to do with Harrowfeld Hall, the children's home?'

'Harrowfeld Hall? No, why? That was one of Cassada's good works, she was a patron there you know. Many a child that she found on the street, looking in at the sweets, she would find a place for them there. It's the sort of folk she was.'

The poor man broke down again. How could I tell him exactly the sort of folk his wife really was? Part of a network that existed within our own Citadel whereby the children who should have been cherished fell into the hands of sick and evil folk of every race and background. Then to end up as what? In the vice trade or worse, if the Guard figures about missing children were to be believed. However you looked at it, it was grim. As grim as the stories of old, where at least you knew who the fell-folk were.

I had to leave Candy, but I promised to come back soon and help him get things started again, because that's what you do as well.

I drove us out to the Tall Trees Lookout. Elsie wanted to take a picnic, but I said we should eat on the way back if we were hungry. The weak late autumn morning sunshine had managed to burn off the morning haze and it left the Citadel looking deceptively tranquil. It was only skin-deep, though; I'd always known that.

Scholars tend to argue about why the dwarfs made such a success out of living in the cold barren lands of the north. One theory is that a long hard cold spell kills off all the bugs and parasites that would otherwise spread and infect the locals causing illness and disease. It's a trade-off: stay north and it's a harder life, or go south and it could easily be a shorter one. Looking down at the Citadel, I thought the whole place could do with a long, hard cold spell to knock back some of the vileness and corruption growing there.

So in that cheery frame of mind, as promised, I told Elsie all about the two strangely interconnected cases. How Getgold Grounding had hired me to find Daisy, the missing daughter he never even knew he had sired. About The River Woman, who was a friend of Daisy's mother from their days at the Harrowfeld Hall Home for Troubled Children and who narrowly escaped a similar fate to Daisy's mother at the hands of the lustful Lobsk.

How rebellious Daisy, growing up too quickly, fell into the clutches of the home's perverted physic, and in return for renewal treat-ment, took to posing dressed in air, before, thanks to the largess of an unknown elf lady, she managed to get away and start a new life. Unfortunately, when the man who thought he was Daisy's father turned up looking for her, he asked in the wrong places and ended up on Physic Argebester's dissection table. Fodder for his necromantic 'healing' sorcery.

Meanwhile, the King of Elfland sleeps with his younger sister, a not exactly unknown event in immortal circles apparently, even today. He thinks he is about to be shown the White Finger when he receives smutty photographs, supposedly of this younger sister, not knowing she is pregnant and thus not the lady in the pictures. He, of course, doesn't know the other dark-haired young woman in the photograph is Daisy Cartersong, and, worried, he contacts the same dwarf detective that Getgold has hired and recommended. All fine until things begin to fall apart and the dwarf gets too close to the dirty linen, when it's good-night Nicely and off to the slave mines with you.

'That is a story and a half, Nicely,' Elsie said eventually.

'And probably only the tip of a dirty iceberg, I'm afraid,' I said, looking sourly over the Citadel, 'especially if the Guard's fears about missing children are true.'

'Oh my! That's terrible.'

'It is. We should all be ashamed of ourselves.'

'But who was the elf in the smutties that were sent to Evermore?' asked Elsera, apparently perplexed.

'His little sister, of course.'

Elsera laughed. 'Good luck in getting Selicia Brightfire to admit to that! She'll deny everything!'

'Not Selicia Brightfire,' I said. 'His other sister – you, Elsie.'

She went quiet, words for once failing her. Finally, she said, 'How long?'

'Have I known? For certain? Only just now, but maybe part of me always knew. After all, you told me yourself that you were half elf. Your sisters…'

'They are not my sisters!' Elsie almost spat. 'Only Evermore and I share a parent, a mother. My mother may have been married to their father but that doesn't make us kin! My father was a woodsman, just a woodsman.' Real tears, not the actor's kind, started rolling down her cheeks. 'You don't know what it's like, when you're young, Nicely.' She looked at me imploringly. 'The Elf Lord can go around having his dalliances, even with mortals like Selicia's mother, and the children get all the advantages, the glamour, the long life. When it's your mother who is the elf, it's looked down on, the fling with the mortal – not the done thing – especially not to get pregnant! That's a slur on elf manhood, that is!'

'Why the pictures, Elsie?'

'I knew about Vericeema and Evermore, all their carrying on. And I knew when she fell pregnant too. I heard her being sick and I knew where she kept her birthday ring when she took it off. The rest was easy. I am a good actress and I have to do my own make-up too. I got the skin tones and the birthmark. The wig was easy, plenty of those in the picture business.'

'That's still not a why.'

'I wanted to kick out, I suppose. I was angry! Vericeema the perfect elf princess! I wanted everybody to see her as she was. And I knew Selicia would eventually get the blame and she deserved it too. She never so much as talked to me on set, never even acknowledged my presence, let alone helped me out or gave me a hand. Evermore deserved it too!'

'Because he'd never looked at you. This wonderful Elf Lord brother never paid you the attention you wanted? The attention he paid Vericeema?'

'No! Not that, not ever!'

'Really?'

'Oh… maybe, Nicely! I'm not sure, but it's in the past now. Everything's different, isn't it?' She looked at me imploringly.

'You never went through with it, the full exposure, because of Daisy?'

Elsie nodded. 'The poor child, that's what made it real. It made me realise the fell-folk I was dealing with and how it was those like Daisy who were really suffering.'

'So you found the gold to get her away. That was well done.'

Elsie brightened somewhat. 'I know I did a stupid thing, but I made up for it, didn't I?'

'The thing is, Elsie, the thing I couldn't understand is why Getgold acted when he did. Why I was taken, coming out of your rooms.'

Panic filled her eyes. 'That wasn't me, Nicely. I would never do anything to hurt you.'

'No, but it was you who told Evermore about Ensanders's niece, wasn't it? It had to be, because you were the only person I mentioned it to, and you knew she didn't have a niece. You knew who it had to be that Ensanders was protecting.'

Elsie looked down at her lap, her hair falling over her face.

'And that got the King of the Elves thinking. He began to put two and two together. Just how long Vericeema had been away and what this meant. The last thing now that he wanted was a troublesome dwarf snooping around, especially when it was obvious that I wasn't going to be bought off. And I think he had a word with his dwarf colleague on the council, the one who had recommended this detective, and the scales fell from his eyes too and they realised they needed to do something about this meddling dwarf.'

'I didn't know, Nicely. Honestly, I didn't know what they'd do,' she said, between sobs.

'But you knew you shouldn't tell him, didn't you? You knew that.'

She didn't answer me. She didn't have to. We both knew the answer.

I offered to drive her back to the Citadel, but she said she would stay at her brother's, in the King of Elfland's sylvan castle in the sky.

Elsie picked up her coat from the bucket seat. She seemed about to say something, but changed her mind. I watched her walk away down that long, straight, tree-lined avenue, but never caught the moment she finally disappeared, like how you never see the last leaf of autumn fall.

She never looked back.

EPILOGUE

There was a sea mist. A strange affair, the like of which I'd never seen before, warm and almost uncanny. I spoke to the captain and he told me that there was a strange current that flowed all the way up from the Frozen Lands, following the coastline, and when it hit the warm waters of the Southern Sea, it sometimes caused these dense fogs. Frequently it brought other things too.

The Frozen Lands are isolated, haunted, places where nothing should be able to live. But if half the stories are to be believed, things do live there. Monsters, perhaps, ice dragons waking up only once a century when they smell warm blood, huge snow trolls that fish for mighty-tusked walrocks through holes in the ice, and huge flightless thunder birds that can break a man in two with just one kick and then peck their bones clean with a razor-sharp bill. They even say you can find an entire race of humble elves there, but that's surely just too unbelievable.

Sometimes these things are picked up in the current and sailors talk of seeing them rise out of the mist, bloated corpses of unwitting mariners stranded on flows of ice. All silent reminders that there is more to this land called Widergard than we might care to remember in this age of steam and rationality.

I shivered, although the mist was strangely warm – not long now. Nightlight flew forward excitedly to join me.

'Home, Nice'y, home!' she tinkled in her singsong voice.

Her wing had healed fabulously. It would never be as good as it was originally, of course, but the little pixie could fly with no problems now. She had quickly made up for lost time, exploring parts of the Citadel that I knew nothing about and making many 'interesting' new friends that quite perplexed her benefactor and landlord. I blamed Wilmer and he seemed extraordinarily proud of himself.

The physic had used a new material that he called synthetic dragon bone, remarkably light but incredibly strong. The operation had taken a fair chunk out of the earnings from the sale of my gem. Most of the profit had gone on the hire of the boat about me. The boat and the fifty good soldiers now relaxing in the hold below. All properly contracted and well aware of the task ahead – no point in taking slaves to free slaves, because that was our appointed task. I'd chosen men mostly, with a few trusted dwarf captains that I knew were less than impressed with my treatment and the management style of the Mines of Oria. 'Ginger' Oliver Groundstroke was there because one whiff of a scrap and he won't be gainsaid.

'Home, Nice'y, I smell home!'

'Yes, won't be long, Nightlight,' I reassured her.

'Smell it, need to go!' The small thing was very agitated, worse than I'd ever seen her.

'I'm sure Coast Port isn't far now, Nightlight. Just be patient, we have to go slowly with all this mist.'

She stared ahead, looking really hard. 'Must go,' she said, and she was gone. Disappearing into the mist faster than a politician's promise after election day.

I was rather taken aback. She had been my companion for so long now, I couldn't believe she had flown away so abruptly. However, I soon had other things to think about.

'Message from the captain, Sir,' said the ship's boy. 'Lights have been spotted, you might want to get steam up and raise your men.' I most certainly did.

The ship had approached Coast Port with full sail. We didn't want to let anybody in Coast Port know of the approach of a strange vessel, especially if any of the mine captains were enjoying a quiet night out of drunken debauchery. We had also brought our own wagons, small, fast but tough, and easy to steam up, just like steamers. They would be unloaded and ready to go in less time than it takes a troll to find his out-hole and scratch it.

The night-ride across the desert was fast and furious, with boilers at maximum pressure and pistons pounding like possessed things. We'd been in and out of Coast Port before they knew what was happening. Surprise was on our side and we made the most of it. At present, a small well-armed team was rounding up any locals who might be less than impressed by our arrival.

All was going well, and that's when we saw the airship. It looked like it was hanging motionless in the sky, just a dark shape occasionally outlined by the full moon that we had chosen for our arrival. In fact, the airship was really travelling, much faster than we were, which didn't feel possible, but was none the less true for that. This was not good. We did not want to get into a siege situation, not with half the men underground and us poorly provisioned.

I cursed proficiently in five languages, but the airship didn't slow down. Modern technology, eh? No respect for traditional hexing. The airship was already descending, presumably to tie up at the pole I mistook as a lookout post. I did some more cursing and this time it seemed to work. The airship was still descending but it was doing it far too quickly and totally in the wrong direction. This was no landing; this was a very elegant and exquisite crash.

Blossom and his captains never knew what hit them. Hung-over and marvellously unprepared, there was only token resistance; one fatality amongst the captains and a handful of injuries to my men, none serious. Blossom himself was more indignant than angry. Handcuffed and shackled, he watched as we released the sleeping slaves.

'For them, you came back for this rabble? You have a dragon's eye. You could do anything.'

'Had a dragon's eye,' I corrected. 'I spent it all to come free this "rabble", Blossom.'

'Why?' he asked, unbelieving. 'Just tell me why?'

I shook my head. 'You'd never understand, Blossom. That's why I am what I am and that's why you and your men are going back to the Citadel to face trial. And I imagine they will not just throw away the key, they'll melt it down too.'

He was a broken goblin-man. His basic conviction in the badness of all folk had been destroyed.

There was worse for him to come. Descending from the sky, in a stunning display of iridescence and fairy dust, came a whole squadron of pixies, with Nightlight in the lead. Each one carried a long sharp cactus needle like a small sword.

I laughed loudly, as did my soldiers. 'It was you, Nightlight, you took down the airship! Well done, well done all!'

'I sawed it, Nice'y,' she tinkled, 'but I not have the words for flying thing. Easier to find my people and do something! Meet family!'

So while we waited for the other shift to come up from underground, I met the family. Of course, Nightlight was a princess – no she wasn't – as far as I could work out her parents were both dew collectors, which is a pretty good thing to be in the desert. Nightlight was looking forward to getting back to her job as well.

'I'll miss you, Nightlight,' I admitted as she perched on my shoulder while the last of the men and prisoners were loaded onto the wagons.

'I miss you too, Nice'y, but I belong here.'

'Yes,' I said, watching the sunrise on another beautiful but blazing desert day. 'I do believe you do.'

'Like you belong in Citadel, Nice'y,' she tinkled. 'Helping all the good folk.'

'You could be right there too, Nightlight.'

And with that she fluttered up into the air and, to my surprise, planted a kiss straight on my lips.

'Well, thank you, Nightlight!'

'A kiss from pixie, very lucky! Just you wait and see Nice'y – very lucky!' And with that she flew up high into the sky, waving as she went, and then was gone.

A kiss from a pixie, yes that has to be lucky, doesn't it?

GLOSSARY

baldy man – a bogie figure said to scare dwarf children

beezer – nose

beezer teaser – sparkling wine suitable for tickling the nose (beezer) with bubbles

corn – gold/money

dewbaby – an easy touch

dressed in air – naked

drop – a murder

bleach (noun) – an elf – rude

bleach-baby – an elf of poor pedigree – even ruder

buckskin – paper money, a poor substitute for gold

draw a map with moon ink – to explain, but not very clearly

filth-fellowship – police department dealing with pornography and vice

fit with a red cap – to incriminate somebody. It refers to the legend of a goblin who supposedly dyed his headgear in human blood, which was rather a give-away.

going bite-size – goblin fighting, usually involving teeth

grease goblin – a goblin mechanic, almost always a runt

ground-hugger – rudely, a gnome, also more rudely a dwarf (see also 'trip hazard')

grunt – a large goblin, not normally too bright (see also 'runt')

insulation – a paper money thank you, pre-emptive bribe

lighten (verb) – to chop something off somebody – usually with an axe, particularly a beheading

low-grade buckskin – low denomination paper money

mist (verb) – to shoot somebody dead so they end up as a wraith

mole peddler – a photographer of naked women (any race)

pop the pea from your whistle – cut a throat (see also 'ruby smile')

rub someone's wand – to wind them up

runt – a small clever breed of goblin

sharp's comforter – an axe, usually the first axe a dwarf child is given

a soldier – a bottle of drink that is 'killed' when finished

sting (verb) – to stab someone

swinging the axe – having a good time in female company

thumb font – identification print

toshery – rubbish, now usually shortened to 'tosh'

trip hazard – a gnome, bad name for a dwarf too

a two-handkerchief type – weakling, the sort to take not one but two handkerchiefs on an adventure

wormback – a very strong spirit said to produce an effect like riding on the back of a worm (dragon)

wraith (verb) – to kill somebody